Beautifully
BROKEN LIFE

THE
SUTTER LAKE
SERIES

CATHERINE
COWLES

MW00468614

BEAUTIFULLY BROKEN LIFE

Copyright © 2019 by Catherine Cowles and The PageSmith LLC. All rights reserved.

No part of this book may be reproduced in any form or by any electronic or mechanical means, including information storage and retrieval systems, without written permission from the author, except for the use of brief quotations in a book review.

This is a work of fiction. Names, characters, places, and incidents are either the products of the author's imagination or are used fictitiously. Any resemblance to actual persons, living or dead, businesses, companies, events, or locales is entirely coincidental.

Editor: Susan Barnes
Copy Editor: Chelle Olson
Proofreading: Julie Deaton
Paperback Formatting: Stacey Blake, Champagne Book Design
Cover Design: Hang Le

Dedication

For all the women who have fought this battle. And for the sisters who helped them do so.

And, as always, for my dad. I carry you with me on every step of this journey. Eternally grateful to be your daughter.

Prologue

Valerie

MY HEART BEAT SO FAST, IT FELT AS THOUGH IT WERE rattling my ribs, straining to get free. I eyed James from the backseat as he navigated through DC traffic. My driver, but also my warden. I wasn't sure he even knew it, but he was just the same.

James turned off the main thoroughfare and onto a quaint side street full of high-end shops and art galleries. I tried to steady my ragged breathing. He pulled to a stop in front of a salon. My port in the storm, the one place he or my fiancé wouldn't follow.

I gripped my purse tighter, knuckles bleaching white. "I'll be a few hours." I was impressed my voice didn't shake.

James nodded. "I know the drill, ma'am. I'll be keeping an eye out from here."

I wanted to laugh, but it would have come out in a disgusted tone. What was James keeping an eye out for exactly? Terrorists? Viking marauders? Certainly not the one person I actually needed protection from.

Garrett had introduced James innocently enough. All the fiancées and wives of the partners at Garrett's law firm had drivers. He didn't want me to have to navigate the craziness of Washington DC traffic. I'd thought it was sweet at the time. But then again, I had thought a lot of things were sweet once upon a time, things that I now realized were stones used to build my prison.

Then James had become driver *and* bodyguard. "I'm involved with some very powerful people, Valerie," Garrett had said. "Someone could try to hurt you to get to me. I just want you to be safe."

I rubbed a tender spot on my arm. Apparently, Garrett was the only one who was allowed to hurt me.

I straightened my spine. Those days were over. "See you in a few hours," I called over my shoulder as I hopped down from the SUV. My ribs cried out at the motion, but I kept my face perfectly blank.

I'd become a master at masks over the past few years. No one knew what lurked beneath my surface. The pain that wracked my body and my heart. But, most importantly, no one—save a single soul—knew the plotting and planning I'd been doing for months. It was the only way this might work.

I pushed open the door to the salon and scanned the busy space. I spotted Gena in the back corner. She'd switched her normal station at the front of the salon with another stylist for today.

I strode forward, weaving around people to get to my only friend in the world. A nervous smile pulled at her lips as she wrapped me in a hug. I stiffened. Gena immediately pulled back. "Shit. How bad?"

It had only taken a couple of visits to Gena's salon for her to begin to put the pieces together about my relationship. She hadn't pushed, though. Then, one day after she'd caught sight of the bruises around my neck that I'd attempted to hide with a scarf, she'd leaned down and whispered in my ear, "You don't deserve this. No one does. When you're ready to talk, I'm here." My story had spilled out in small bursts over the following months. And Gena and her salon had become my only port in the storm that was my life.

I shook myself from the memory and attempted a smile that came out as more of a grimace. "Not bad." And compared to other times, it wasn't. I had been careless. Gotten distracted as I was going over the plan in my mind and hadn't heard my phone ring at first. I had three rings to answer, but two was really best. Anything over three, and I would pay for it. And when Garrett had gotten home last night, I had.

Gena's lips pressed together into a firm line. "We are going to get you out of this."

I gripped her hand. "I know. Thank you so much."

"Anything for you, girl. Now, let's give you a new look."

An hour and a half later, I fingered the ends of my new bob. Gone were my long, golden locks, and in their place was a shoulder-length brunette 'do. I examined my reflection in the mirror. I looked different, I just wished I could do something about my eyes.

I'd always loved my eyes. They were the same as my mother's. One of the few things I had of hers since she'd died in childbirth. But their almost violet hue made them too unique.

Gena squeezed my shoulder. "I got you contacts. They'll only last two weeks, but it's long enough for you to get wherever you end up going, and then it won't matter as much."

I felt a flash of pain at having to hide what little I had left of my mother, but I knew it was necessary. "You've thought of everything."

Gena squeezed my shoulder again. "*We've* thought of everything. He's not going to find you this time."

I'd tried to run once before, but I'd made the mistake of taking off with no real plans and using my credit card at a hotel. Garrett had found me in less than twenty-four hours, and his reaction had ensured I didn't even consider running again for over a year.

I let out a long, slow breath. I was smarter now. Stronger. I had planned for every possibility. I rose from the chair. "Let's do this."

Gena led me back to a large bathroom where she handed me a paper bag. "Your contacts and a different outfit."

I peeked into the bag, and a smile pulled at my lips. Jeans, a t-shirt, and a hoodie. How long had it been since I'd worn something so casually comfortable? I honestly couldn't remember. College, maybe? I fought the urge to rip off the pencil skirt and cardigan I was wearing.

Gena cleared her throat. "First, we have to take pictures."

I froze. It was a vital step, I knew it. Something we'd started doing a couple of months ago. An insurance policy. Because if Garrett did come after me, I'd need all the firepower possible in my arsenal.

"Okay." I hated how weak my voice sounded. Despised that my hands shook as I unbuttoned my sweater and unzipped my skirt. Shame, thick and bitter, washed over me as the click and whir of a Polaroid camera sounded. I wanted to be stronger, to not allow the actions of someone else to make me feel this way, but I couldn't stop the cascade of emotions.

I bit my lip to keep the tears at bay as Gena circled me, photographing the bruises that littered my arms and torso. She'd take two sets. One for me, and one for herself to put in a safety deposit box in her name. We were covering all our bases.

"I'm done." Gena's voice cracked on the second word. "I'm so sorry, V. He's a fucking bastard." She lifted my chin with a single finger. "None of this is your fault. You hear me? There is nothing you could've ever done to deserve this, okay?"

I nodded, the ball of emotion in my throat keeping me from speaking. I threw my arms around her, ignoring the protests of my ribs. "Thank you. I don't know what I would do without you."

I didn't. Gena was the only person I had in this world. All I had was a dead mother, the grandparents who'd disowned her—and me by affiliation—and a big question mark for a father. Without Gena, I would be totally and completely alone. Tears spilled over my bottom lids.

Gena sniffled in my ear. "I'm going to miss you like crazy. But don't contact me for any reason. Promise me."

This was the hardest part of it all. Knowing that for this to work, we could have zero communication. Garrett had no idea that we were even friends, but he would scour the lives of every person I had regular contact with. We couldn't take the chance.

"I know." I pulled back. "Maybe we'll luck out, and he'll get hit by a car crossing the street."

Gena snorted. "That's too kind a death for him."

"He'll lose interest in me eventually. Then, I can get in touch."

Gena looked skeptical but nodded. I made quick work of pulling on the jeans, tee, and hoodie. When I slipped my feet into the pair of Converse sneakers, I wanted to sigh with pleasure. Never again would I wear shoes that pinched my toes simply because a man wanted me to.

Gena handed me a new purse. "There are four bus tickets and three train tickets in here. Don't tell me which one you think you'll use. I also gave you my ID. Use it until you get where you're going and then burn it. I'm sure Garrett will search for my name since this is the last place you'll have been seen."

I nodded and licked my lips.

Gena pressed on. "There's a small suitcase with the basics in my trunk. Don't put the contacts in until after you've gone to the pawnshop."

Gena was right. If Garrett somehow managed to track my engagement ring, I didn't want some pawnshop employee telling him I had brown hair and brown eyes. Garrett needed to think I was running in the same clueless fashion I had before. But I wasn't. I was smarter now, and I was going to win my freedom.

I fingered the ends of my newly cut strands. "Do you have something I could use to cover my hair?"

"Shit. I didn't even think about that. Hold on." Gena dug through her bag. "Here." She handed me a beanie. "This should do the trick."

"Perfect." I glanced at my watch and swallowed hard. "I better go."

Gena cleared her throat. "Be safe and be happy."

"I will." I pulled the beanie over my head and tucked my hair inside the woven cap.

Gena led the way out of the bathroom and down a narrow hall to the salon's back door. The door opened to a miniscule parking lot with five cars. We headed towards Gena's Ford Explorer. She handed me the keys. "There are sunglasses in the console. Wear them until you make it past Hulk out front."

I threw my arms around her one more time. "I love you, G."

"Love you more." Her voice sounded choked. "Now, get out of here. Quick."

There was a burning in my chest as I let her go. I was about to be totally and completely alone. *But alone is better than dead.*

I climbed into the SUV and turned over the engine. It had been so long since I'd driven, I hoped I didn't get into an accident. Carefully, I backed out of the parking space and headed for the driveway, taking only a moment to glance at Gena in the rearview mirror. She stood with her hands in her pockets, brows furrowed, nibbling on her bottom lip.

I forced myself to look away. I could do this. I held my

breath as I reached the end of the drive. The dark SUV that housed James sat, unmoving. I pulled into traffic, and my heart rattled again as I passed the vehicle. My eyes darted from the street in front of me to the SUV in my rearview mirror. It didn't follow. Step one had been a success.

I let out the breath I'd been holding and headed for a sketchy part of town.

I sat in the front seat of the Explorer, counting my cash. The pawnshop owner had raked me over the coals. He had smelled my desperation from a mile away and had only given me a fraction of a fair price for my massive diamond engagement ring and Rolex watch. There had been nothing I could do about it. I was running out of time, and I had to take what I could get.

I stuck the money into my purse and pulled out the array of ticket options Gena had purchased for me. I flipped through them. All big cities. New York. New Orleans. Minneapolis. My fingers stilled on a bus ticket to Portland, Oregon. It had to be a sign. I hoped against hope that it was. Maybe my mother was looking after me and guiding my steps from above.

Even if she weren't, and this was just some random coincidence, it didn't matter. I was on my way, and now I had a destination. Come hell or high water, I was getting my life back.

CHAPTER
One

Tessa

TWO YEARS LATER

SUNLIGHT WARMED MY FACE AS I STRETCHED, FREEING MY arms from the confines of the covers. I kept sleeping better and better. It had taken me months to get used to the unfamiliar noises of the country. Every cricket chirping or creak of my older apartment had me reaching for my bag to run. But I'd slowly become accustomed to the rhythms of Sutter Lake, Oregon. The sounds became comforting, the faces familiar. I'd relaxed.

I was still cautious. Careful. Always on alert to a degree. But I was no longer in a constant state of panic that Garrett would be around the next corner. I pushed to a seated position. *Time to start the day.* My routine was always the same.

Setting coffee to brew as I brushed my teeth and got dressed. Check the wooden boards I'd placed in the windows to prevent them from being opened from the outside. Move the cans filled with coins from in front of my apartment door to beside it. Double-check that my go-bag had all the essentials to make a run for it if needed. That bag was never more than five feet from me at any time. My security measures were low-tech, but they gave me that little extra reassurance that I would be fine no matter what.

I pulled my hair back into a braid. I'd let it grow out from the short bob Gena had given me but kept the darker brown color just in case. My heart panged at the memory of my friend. We'd had no contact, just as promised, but I longed for the intimacy of a friendship where you knew everything about each other.

I simply couldn't afford that now. My chest tightened. Gena had already lost so much because she'd helped me. I wouldn't put someone else through that just because I was lonely.

Moving the cans to the side of the entryway, I grabbed my bag and pulled open the door. Stepping into the hall, I listened for any unfamiliar sounds. All I heard was the hum of the walk-in fridge in the tea shop below and the rustling of the wind through the leaves outside. Pulling the door closed slowly, I carefully slipped a small piece of paper into the jamb next to the hinges. When I got home, if the paper was on the floor, it meant that someone had been in my apartment, and it was time to run again.

I closed my eyes against the painful idea. I loved Sutter Lake. The people were kind. The scenery was beautiful. It was home. And I would do anything I could to stay here.

I hurried down the steps and out the back door, being careful to double-check locks on my way out. The sun reflected off the beater of a car I'd bought off Craigslist for $1000 and never registered in my name. I'd had to steal registration stickers off vehicles that didn't seem to be in use. I'd left silent apologies in my wake, and cash for the fee in the people's mailboxes.

There had been no way around it. I needed a car, especially in a tiny town in the middle of nowhere. It was one more weapon for my arsenal in the battle to keep my freedom. It was also how I got to the first of my two jobs. The job I *loved*.

My car bumped over the dirt road as I pulled through the gate of Cole Ranch. My boss, Jensen Cole, and her entire extended family lived on the massive property. But she had her own corner of land for a very special project. Something I helped out with in exchange for my studio apartment above Jensen's tea shop.

As I crested the hill, I caught a glimpse of the herd below. The sight of them still took my breath away. Almost twenty mustangs. A group of mares with an assortment of different markings. The first time Jensen had brought me here, something about these beautiful creatures had called out to my soul.

They had been born in the wild, on state land about an hour and a half from here. But for one reason or another, they had been removed from their family bands. I felt their pain of being thrust out of their homes and their relief at finding a new safe place to rest.

I pulled my car to a stop in front of a small barn that housed feed and other supplies for the horses. Pushing open my door, I inhaled deeply, the now-familiar smells of horses, hay, and the pine trees in the distance filling my lungs. It was the scent of comfort. Peace.

A whinny sounded from the fence line. I grinned. "Hey there, Phoenix," I called, making my way towards the gorgeous mare. Her dark bay coat glistened in the sun as she threw her head back with a snort as if to say, "Hurry up, would you?"

I picked up my pace. Reaching the pasture, I extended a hand to scratch between Phoenix's ears, but that wasn't good enough for the mare. This morning, she wanted a cuddle. I let out a soft laugh as she lifted her head so that it rested on my shoulder, her breath tickling the back of my neck.

"Good morning to you, too." I ran my hands down her smooth neck until I reached her chest. My fingertips gently caressed a raised scar on her left shoulder. My blood still boiled that she had been hurt. Most likely taken down by a careless hunter who hadn't waited long enough to see that he was shooting at a horse instead of the game he was after. She was lucky to be alive.

A Forest Service law enforcement officer had stumbled across Phoenix and saved her life. But it had taken months for her to let anyone close, and I was honored that she had chosen that person to be me. Maybe she sensed a kindred spirit in me, knew that I, too, wore battle scars. The why didn't matter, all that mattered was that she had given me a truly precious gift: trust and love.

I gave the mare's cheek a kiss and released my hold. Phoenix let out a whinny of protest. "I gotta get you breakfast, sweet girl."

I made quick work of spreading out hay for the horses to munch on and checking water supplies. Once that was done, I settled on a large rock at the edge of the pasture. I dug into my bag for one of the few luxuries I allowed myself. My hand found the sketchpad and the tin of pencils.

Flipping open the notebook, I surveyed the view in front of me. The horses happily munching away on a hillside that rolled up and down in beautiful waves before it met a forest of towering pines. There was so much beauty. A bird dipped and rolled in the air. So much life.

I touched my pencil to the thick, white paper. I heard the same voice I always did when I started. *"It's a cute hobby, Val, but you're not talented enough for art school."* I pushed the voice from my mind. It didn't matter whether I had skill or not, I loved drawing. Slowly, I lost myself in the rhythm of the graphite scratching against the page, the creation of an entire world.

A tug on my jeans' leg brought me out of my trance. "Phee," I chided, using the mare's nickname as she tried to decide whether she liked the taste of denim. I dropped my sketchpad back into my bag and leaned forward to scratch her between the ears. "Was I not paying enough attention to you?" Phoenix let out a huff, and I couldn't hold in my laugh.

"Okay, we'll get in your scratches before I have to leave." I took a quick look at my watch. I'd need to hurry to make it back in time to shower before my shift at The Tea Kettle. But I couldn't force myself to leave quite yet.

Balancing a tray of scones that smelled heavenly, I made my way from the kitchen to the main room of the tea shop.

Jensen turned at the sound of my footsteps, her glossy, dark hair swinging. She was breathtakingly beautiful and didn't even try, though the shadows under her eyes told me that she still wasn't sleeping. "Perfect timing, there are only two left in the case. This new recipe of yours is officially a hit."

My lips tipped up. At least my years of cooking for Garrett had given me a useful skill. And I liked baking, especially when the recipients were grateful instead of criticizing. "I'm glad. I'll just stick these in the case and then get started on a batch of cookies for the afternoon rush."

Jensen grasped my shoulder in a squeeze, and I did my best not to flinch. I was semi-successful, but she immediately dropped her hand. "What did I ever do without you? Promise me you'll never leave me."

I gave a forced smile. "Never."

The bell above the front door sounded, and I fought a groan. Bridgette Henry. She was beautiful for sure, but in a way that made her look like a Stepford wife or a plastic Barbie doll. She was one of those girls who had been mean and catty in high school and never grew out of it. I hurried to empty my tray of baked goods faster.

"Hello, Bridgette," Jensen called in a tone of forced politeness. "What can I get for you today? Tessa just pulled some scones out of the oven, they're her brand new recipe."

Bridgette wrinkled up her nose at me as if she smelled something bad. "What kind?"

I cleared my throat and stood up straight. "They're spinach and feta with a hint of garlic."

Her lip curled. "I'll just take my usual chai latte, Jensen."

"Sure," Jensen answered through slightly gritted teeth. "I'll get that right out to you."

Bridgette nodded in response and left her three dollars on the counter before heading to one of the tables at the front of the shop. She didn't leave a tip. Shocker.

Jensen snorted. "You'd think almost getting killed would make someone a little nicer."

My jaw fell open. Bridgette had almost been kidnapped by a serial killer a few months ago. A madman who had ended up being Jensen's boyfriend at the time. Jensen thankfully hadn't been hurt, but she still carried scars from not realizing the truth about the man she'd fallen for. Jensen never talked about him or what had happened. Ever. My mouth opened and closed as I searched for words.

Jensen waved a hand in front of her face. "Oh, come on, the entire town thinks it. She almost got herself murdered because of her bitchy ways, and she doesn't even think about changing her tune?"

I reached a hand out to grasp Jensen's forearm. "J—"

She cut me off before I could continue, stepping out of my grasp. "I don't want to talk about him." Her hands shook as she placed the money in the register, a look of pain flashing across her face.

I twisted the strings of my apron around my finger. I was worried about her. Jensen's view of the world seemed to have shifted since her ordeal. I knew she was hurting, but I wasn't sure how I could help.

I shuffled my feet as I searched for the right words. "I won't force you to talk about anything you don't want to." Lord knew I carried my share of secrets Jensen knew nothing about. "But I just want you to know that I'm here if you ever change your mind."

Jensen jerked her head in a stiff nod. And I knew that was as good as I was going to get.

CHAPTER
Two

Liam

NOTES OF MY ABSENTMINDED STRUMMING FILLED THE air as I tilted my face towards the sun, soaking up its rays. It felt heavenly. Inhaling deeply, my lungs filled with the scent of pine trees instead of the smog of Los Angeles. It was such a welcome change of pace.

I let my eyes open, taking in the view in front of me. A creek flowed below my deck, making its way through a field where a couple of horses grazed. The pasture rolled right into an expanse of forest that seemed to go on forever. It was perfect.

No award shows forcing me to wear a tux. No schmoozing with record execs. No paparazzi dogging my every move. Here, I was free.

My fingers continued shaping chords, but no inspiration struck. I fought the urge to send my guitar sailing over the railing. I might have found freedom in Sutter Lake, but I sure as shit hadn't reclaimed my ability to make music.

Footsteps sounded on the stairs leading up to the back deck. A head of blonde hair appeared. When her feet landed on the top step, her hands went to her hips, and her eyes narrowed. "You've been avoiding me."

I bit back a grin. I was so fucking glad to see that my friend had her fire back. "Hey there, Taylor."

"Don't you try to pull your good-ol'-boy charm on me."

I snickered. "All right. Pull up a chair."

Taylor stomped over to the rocker next to mine. "Why are you avoiding me?" I glanced over, and my gut clenched at the uncertainty that flashed in her eyes. "Are you mad at me?"

My eyes widened. "Why the hell would I be mad at you?"

She twisted the ring on her right hand, staring down at it as if it held all the answers. "Because of everything that happened."

I took in Taylor's face as she studied her hands. The uncertainty shifted to something that looked a whole lot like guilt. "Taylor," I prodded gently. "Why would anything that happened make me mad at *you*?"

Her eyes remained fixed on her ring. "I almost got you killed."

My chest tightened at the reminder of that day. Not because I'd been hurt, I didn't give a fuck about that. But because Taylor had been taken. Held for hours by a maniac and still bore scars from her time with him.

I swallowed against the rage in my throat and set my guitar down so it leaned against the railing. I grabbed Taylor's hand, finally bringing her gaze to mine. "Taylor. None of that was your fault. If anything, I should be apologizing to you for not hearing him come in."

She shook her head vigorously. "No. That's ridiculous."

I squeezed her hand. "Okay, then I think we can both agree that the only person to blame is dead and gone."

Taylor swallowed hard, but she nodded. "If you're not mad at me, then why the hell have you been making up excuses not to see me? What's going on?"

I was officially an ass. I had made one of my best friends in the world worry just because I wanted to avoid questions about why I'd left LA.

Taylor studied my face.

I dropped her hand and leaned back in my rocker, staring out at the horizon. "I've got a bad case of writer's block. The studio is on my case about finishing my next record, and I think I have all of two songs done. I just needed to get away. I was hoping the beautiful sights of middle-of-nowhere Oregon would give me a little inspiration."

"I'm sorry, Li. Has being up here helped at all?"

I shot a glare at the guitar leaning against the rail. "Not so much with the music, but at least I don't feel like I'm going crazy cooped up in the city anymore."

"I thought you loved your place in LA."

I tipped the rocker back and forth, not meeting Taylor's gaze. "I do. Or I did." I blew out a breath. "I don't know. I just hit this point where I was so sick of the scene there."

I could feel Taylor's eyes boring into me, evaluating my words. She let out a soft, humming sound. "Why do I get the feeling that's not the whole story?"

This was the problem with good friends. They knew when you were bullshitting them.

I toyed with the guitar pick still in my hand. "Something happened in LA."

"Okay…" She drew out the word as if it would encourage me to keep talking.

"There was this fan…" I wanted to continue, but a mixture of guilt and frustration seemed to hold my tongue captive.

"Li, you know you can tell me anything, right?"

I nodded but still said nothing.

"This is a judgement-free zone. You're talking to the girl who drunkenly spilled her guts to you over shots of vodka because I couldn't handle falling in love with Walker."

A small smile pulled at my mouth at the reminder of Taylor bursting into tears at the thought of falling in love. It had all worked out in the end. I wasn't so sure my story would have such a happy ending.

Gripping the arms of the chair, I forced myself to start

speaking. "I meet fans pretty much every day. Meet and greets before concerts, while I'm eating at a restaurant… Hell, I've had people run up to my car when I'm stopped at a traffic light."

Taylor stayed silent, letting me spill at whatever pace I needed to. "It's impossible for me to remember them all. To sign every slip of paper. Respond to every letter."

My throat began to burn. "There was a young woman. I'd apparently met her at a meet and greet, but I honestly don't remember her. I guess she got a little fixated on me, obsessed kinda. She wrote me a bunch of letters at the label. They sent her an autographed photo, but obviously couldn't respond to every note she sent."

I inhaled deeply, trying to focus on the smell of the pines instead of the roiling in my stomach. "She started leaving crazy comments on my social media and blog, but I swear I didn't see them."

I met Taylor's eyes, pleading for her to understand that I was telling the truth. "I found out later, she said if she didn't hear back from me, she was going to kill herself."

"Oh, Liam, no."

"I was playing a concert in St. Louis. Some radio station gig. I went out with a few guys after the show but wasn't really feeling it, so I headed back to my hotel." My vision blurred as I lost myself in the memory. "When I got to my room, I found her passed out on my bed. She'd slit her wrists."

Taylor sucked in an audible breath.

"There was blood everywhere. Never seen so much in my life. I called 9-1-1 and, thankfully, they got there in time, but they almost didn't. Fuck, Taylor. What if I had stayed out just thirty minutes later?" I would never forget the feel of limp wrists in my hands as I'd tried to slow the bleeding.

"No one knows what happened yet, but it's only a matter of time." I tilted my head back to search the sky. "The media is going to crucify me. The fact that I was there when it happened? They'll twist it into something it's not and rake me over the coals. And to be honest, I'm just not sure I want to be a part of that world anymore. I love music, but I hate everything that comes with it."

Fame was this insidious double-edged sword. It made you feel powerful, special, your words being sung back to you by thousands of voices, people telling you your message got them through their darkest days. But everything could turn on a dime. Suddenly, you were a selfish asshole because you didn't stop for a photo. Every piece of your life was up for dissection on entertainment news shows. And now there were potentially deadly ramifications.

I fisted the guitar pick, the edge of the plastic digging into my palm. "I don't want to be the reason someone thinks about taking their life. I don't want that kind of responsibility."

Taylor reached out a hand to grasp my forearm. "This is not your fault." I wanted to believe her, but I wasn't quite sure where the responsibility lay. "It's not. She's sick, Liam. If it wasn't you, it would have been someone else."

"But maybe that someone else would have taken five minutes to write her back personally."

Taylor squeezed my arm. "But that would have only been good enough for a day. Then, she would have wanted another letter and another. She would have wanted phone calls and then in-person meetings. It would have been more and more. Surely, you see that?"

I let out a sigh. "I don't know what I see. All I do know is that I need a break."

Taylor released my arm. "Well, you've come to the right place."

I gave her a small grin. I was staying at a guest cabin on Taylor's boyfriend's ranch—well, his *family's* property. "I think you're right."

She pushed to her feet. "I'm always right." I scoffed, but she kept right on talking. "What we need now are baked goods. Treats make everything better and more manageable." My grin widened. "We'll eat and sort all this out."

Taylor knew the promise of food was my kryptonite. "Let's go."

My steps faltered as I realized where Taylor was leading me. "I don't even like tea."

Taylor slipped her arm through mine. "Come on, you big baby. You won't lose your man card just because you ventured inside a tea shop." I huffed. "They have the best scones you've ever tasted."

Scones were girlie food. Taylor pressed on. "Even a ham and cheddar one." My eyes lifted as my stomach rumbled. Taylor let out a chuckle. "You're so easily won over. I could get you to do anything with the right food as incentive."

I ruffled her hair. "What? I'm a growing boy."

I pulled open the door, letting Taylor pass in front of me. As we walked in, a wave of delicious smells filled my senses. Maybe Taylor hadn't steered me wrong.

"Hey, kids. What brings you in?" Jensen, Walker's sister, stood behind the counter.

Taylor strode forward. "We come in search of treats."

Jensen stepped back to eye the bakery case. "Well, you have perfect timing. Tessa just restocked our supplies."

Taylor rubbed her hands together with child-like glee, and I couldn't hold in my laugh. She elbowed me in the gut. "Like you're any better."

She had a point. I took in all the offerings, mentally planning at least three choices. A throat clearing had my attention drifting away from my upcoming meal. My gaze met a tall blonde done up to the nines. Her stilettos and pencil skirt didn't seem to fit in a town that was all jeans and boots. "Hey, Liam."

I forced a smile. "Hey…" Had I met this girl? I searched my brain for a name but came up with nothing.

She extended a perfectly manicured hand. "I'm Bridgette."

"Nice to meet you." I wasn't sure what else to say. She didn't have the true-fan vibe, but I couldn't quite get a bead on her.

Bridgette gave me a sultry smile, and the picture got clearer. "I just wanted to introduce myself and offer to show you around. I know all the best restaurants and shops in the area for people with discerning tastes like ourselves."

A snorted laugh sounded from behind me that I knew was Taylor.

Bridgette's eyes narrowed over my shoulder. "Taylor," she clipped.

"Nice to see you, Bridgette."

Bridgette huffed and turned her gaze back to me. "So, about that tour…"

I fought the grimace that wanted to surface. "You know, I'm pretty busy these days."

Bridgette stepped in close enough that our bodies were almost touching. "I'm sure I could make it worth your while to take a little break from whatever you're working on."

This time, both Taylor and Jensen laughed. At least Jensen attempted to disguise hers with a cough. Bridgette straightened and glared at the two women.

I took that as my cue to make a hasty escape. I pulled out my wallet and handed Taylor my credit card. "Here, get us a bunch of stuff, I'm going to find a restroom."

Bridgette's jaw fell open as if no one had ever rejected her *tour* around town. I might have been rude, but I just didn't have patience for people like her at the moment. I side-stepped her shocked form and headed towards a hall that led away from the shop's main room.

I didn't need a bathroom, but I sure as hell needed out of there. I glanced back to see Bridgette and Taylor in a heated conversation. At first, I felt guilty about leaving Taylor to deal with the girl, but then I saw the smirk on her face. She'd be fine.

I rounded the corner and slammed into someone. *Shit.* My hands instinctively went out to steady the person I had just body checked. My fingers encircled slim arms. "I'm so sorry—"

My words cut off because the woman shrank away from me with such ferocity, I felt like a monster. I gentled my tone. "I'm so sorry, ma'am. I wasn't looking where I was going. Are you okay? I didn't hurt you, did I?"

Her hand shook as she brushed dark brown hair away from her face. "I-I'm fine."

I froze. She was gorgeous, there was no denying it, but what had me hypnotized were her eyes. They were a color I'd never seen before, something that hovered on the border between gray and purple. I shook myself from the stupor. "I'm glad you're okay." I slowly extended a hand. "I'm Liam."

She studied my hand for a brief moment before accepting the shake. "Tessa." She held my palm for only the moment it took for her to say her two-syllable name.

I felt the loss of heat as soon as she moved away. "Can I get you a tea or something to apologize?"

Tessa's throat bobbed as she swallowed. "No, thank you. I really need to get back to work."

"Okay—" Again, my words were cut off, this time by her retreating form. I shook my head, trying to clear it from the odd encounter.

I peeked back around the corner to see if my admirer from earlier was still there and breathed a sigh of relief.

"The wicked witch is gone, you can come out now." Taylor's voice sounded from a table in the corner.

I made my way towards her. "She was, uh, interesting?" It

came out as a question.

Taylor let out a laugh. "She's the worst. But, hopefully, now that she knows you're friends with me, she'll leave you alone." I arched a questioning eyebrow. "Long story, but I'm not her favorite person. Hopefully, you'll be less desirable to her simply by association."

I broke off a corner of some kind of baked good. "See? Your friendship does have perks." I popped the piece into my mouth. It was some berry concoction of pastry nirvana.

"Good, right?"

"Amazing." I turned back to eye the hallway. "I accidentally ran into someone back there."

Taylor eyed me. "Okay…"

"I think she works here." Violet eyes flashed in my mind.

"Oh, Tessa probably."

I broke off another piece of berry goodness. "What's her story?"

Taylor's eyes narrowed ever so slightly. "What do you mean?"

I shrugged. "Just wanted to know more about her, I guess." Something was tickling the back of my mind. The hint of a lyric. Something. I tried to grasp it, but it disappeared like a wisp of smoke. I refocused on Taylor.

"I don't know her super well, but she's incredibly kind." A soft look overtook Taylor's face. "She was really good to me when I worked here. She lives in the apartment upstairs." I sensed there was more to the story. I didn't push. But, damn, those bewitching eyes.

CHAPTER
Three

Tessa

THE PANIC STILL HAD A HOLD OF MY CHEST, TIGHTENING its grip millimeter by millimeter. I ducked into the kitchen and moved to the main room, tapping Jensen on the shoulder. "I'm going to take my break." My voice came out slightly strangled, but there was nothing I could do about it.

Jensen's smile fell as she studied me. "Are you all right?"

I nodded, licking my suddenly dry lips. "Fine."

Jensen's gaze continued to prod, but her voice relented. "Take all the time you need."

"Thanks." I turned on my heel and walked as quickly as possible to the back door. Pushing it open, I felt the slightest bit of relief. The cool, early spring air was just what I needed. Leaning back against the outside of the building, I closed my eyes and inhaled deeply, trying to keep my breaths slow and steady.

It didn't seem to help like it usually did. My heart still beat in an erratic rhythm, and my breathing didn't seem to want to obey.

My back slammed into the hallway wall with a force that stole the air from my lungs. Hot breath, stale with the smell of whiskey, filled my senses.

"You were flirting with him. Just admit it." Garrett's hand tightened around my neck with a force that I knew would leave bruises.

Things were bad. So very bad if he would risk marking me in a place someone might see. My mind raced, trying to think of anything I could say that might placate him. "I—wasn't." *It was a battle to get each word out of my compressed throat.*

Garrett shook me like a rag doll, knocking my head back against the wall with such ferocity, stars danced in my vision. "Liar. You're a whore, just like your mother—"

The pain of my nails digging into my palms brought me out of the memory. My breaths continued to come in rapid succession. *Name five things you can see, Tessa. Just five things.* I searched around me. My lips formed silent words. *Grass. Fence. Dumpster. Stone. Car.*

I let out a slow breath. *Name five things you can smell. Tea. Cinnamon. Chocolate. Pine trees. Trash.*

I inhaled slowly. *Name five things you can touch. Jeans. Wall. Air. Steps. Grass.*

My awareness gradually came back to my body. That's what it felt like in these moments, that my mind hovered above my physical self, unable to reconnect. I sank to the ground, tears streaming down my cheeks. As I wiped them away, I saw that I had broken the skin on my hands. *Shit.* I'd have to cover that up as best I could.

My cheeks heated at the thought of what a basket case I must have seemed to Liam. Of all the people for me to make a fool of myself in front of, it just had to be him. A guy whose face often stared back at me from the magazine rack and whose voice often drifted over the speakers in the tea shop.

I groaned, letting my head fall to my knees. I'd thought I was getting better. When I first fled DC, I'd had panic attacks every single day. Occasionally, they were so bad, I almost passed out.

When I finally got to Sutter Lake, I'd gone to the public library and started researching. I obviously didn't have health insurance I could use and couldn't afford a therapist, but I'd found a surprising number of helpful tools online. Breathing exercises, plans for when an attack did come on, even meditations I could do.

Slowly, the panic had receded. But the thing that helped most of all was not being in situations that triggered me. That meant I was never—and I mean, ever—alone with a man. If I wasn't alone with a male, I couldn't feel intimidated or threatened. I wasn't reminded of *him*.

I knew it meant I was avoiding a fair portion of life, but I couldn't figure out another way to keep the attacks at bay. At least, not yet. A faint meow pulled me out of my depressing train of thought. A tiny orange head peeked out from under the dumpster.

"Hey there, little one."

The tiny kitten studied me but didn't venture out any farther.

"What are you doing out here by yourself? Where's your mama?" The kitten looked too small to be on its own.

The furry creature ventured two tentative steps out from its hiding spot.

"That's it. Come on. I won't hurt you." I slowly extended my hand. The kitten froze. "It's okay," I encouraged.

With careful, tiny steps, the orange, tiger-striped feline made its way towards me, sniffing the air as it came.

I held my breath as it reached my fingertips. Another sniff. Another step. It nuzzled my hand. "Aren't you the most precious thing." I scratched behind its ears. "We need to get you some milk or something to eat. I don't even know what to feed kittens as young as you are."

I had officially lost it. Talking to kittens in the back alley of my place of work, the remnants of tears on my face, and dried blood on my hands. I was a freaking mess.

A car door slammed a few shops down. The kitten bolted. I jumped to my feet, trying to track it with my eyes, but I lost sight of the tiny furball two shops down. *Shit. Shit. Shit.* That little baby should not be on its own. My shoulders drooped. I needed to get back to work. But first, I'd leave out a little milk just in case my new friend came back.

CHAPTER
Four

Liam

I SAT THE GUITAR DOWN WITH AN AGGRAVATED THUD. THE instrument didn't deserve my rough treatment, but I was frustrated as hell. It was as if the harder I pushed for lyrics to come, the more stubborn they became.

I leaned back against the couch, rubbing my temples. I couldn't create like this. Well, create anything halfway decent anyway. Expectations of fans and pressure from the label were a surefire way to quash any creative mojo.

I blew out a long breath and let my hands fall to my sides. I stared up at the ceiling, letting my mind wander. It drifted to a place it had many times over the past few days. An image of Tessa shrinking away from my touch filled my mind, her gorgeous eyes flashing.

A melody began to tickle the recesses of my brain. I closed my eyes, trying to catch it. It was there, a whisper of something. I hummed, trying to find that progression of notes. I couldn't quite capture it.

My phone buzzed on the coffee table, nixing any possibility of harnessing the fleeting wisp of a song. I cursed and roughly grabbed for the object that had interrupted the first inkling of music I'd had in months.

"Hello." My voice was not welcoming.

"This is Detective Ruiz with the LAPD. Am I speaking with

Liam Fairchild?"

My spine straightened. "You got him. How can I help you?"

"You're a tough man to track down."

That was exactly as I'd intended it, but I didn't share that with the cop. "Sorry about that. I can't exactly have a listed number."

"I get it. We were just concerned when we couldn't find you at your place of residence, and your record label couldn't tell us where you were."

I toyed with the guitar pick that had been lying next to me on the couch. "Why would you be concerned?"

The detective cleared his throat. "I'm the Los Angeles police detective handling your stalking case."

My fiddling ceased. I'd known the St. Louis police were going to inform the LAPD of what had happened, but I had no idea that it had progressed past that. "Oh. I don't know that this should really be a stalking case."

"Sir, Ms. Speakman's actions definitely qualify as cyber-stalking." I could hear the shuffling of papers in the background. "I just got off the phone with her doctor at the facility where she was being treated."

My stomach dropped. "Is she all right?" Thoughts of further self-harm filled my head.

"She's been released."

"So she's better?"

The detective sighed. "She's been on an extended mandatory hold…" He let the words trail off.

"Okay…" I let my own trail off, unsure where the detective was headed with his statements.

"It's difficult for medical professionals to secure an extended mandatory stay for patients that want to go home. They must prove the patient is a threat to themselves or others at the current point in time. Ms. Speakman claims she's better."

A wave of nausea rolled over me at the reminder of the young woman trying to end her life because I hadn't acknowledged her. Guilt pricked at my chest, followed quickly by a burst of frustration. Surely, this was too high a price to pay for simply wanting to make music and share it with people who would value it.

The detective pushed on. "Her psychiatrist asked for Ms. Speakman's hold to be extended, but the request was denied."

I started twirling the pick between my fingers again. "What does that mean?"

"It means that she's gone home, but her doctors are concerned."

I didn't fill the silence that hung on the line. I had no idea what to say. The woman was a danger to herself, and her mind had twisted in a way where I played a role in that. A role that I wanted no part of.

Ruiz cleared his throat again. "The psychiatrist is concerned about how intensely Ms. Speakman is fixated on you. He's worried that while no overt threats have been made, she may still try to harm you."

My jaw fell open just slightly. "Hurt me?"

"Yes, sir."

I stood and began pacing. "But she's only ever threatened to hurt herself." *And succeeded*, I thought.

"The doctor is concerned that the signs are there. Do you have security with you?"

I wanted to let out a laugh at the idea of towing a security team behind me in Sutter Lake. "I don't. But it's not necessary where I am. You saw how hard it was to even locate my phone number, and you're law enforcement."

"I think this is a situation where the extra precaution might be worth it."

I slid open the door to the back deck, cool air washing over me. I leaned against the railing. "I'm telling you, no one is going to find me where I'm at."

I thought of how respectful the townspeople had been. Sure,

some had asked for photos or an autograph, but nothing had shown up online. I was sure a big part of that had to do with Taylor's boyfriend, Walker, being the deputy chief of police. I knew he'd put out a quiet but strong word that I'd come here for some peace and quiet, and that if the press descended, I'd be forced to leave.

My little respite from the real world had remained intact, and I was incredibly grateful.

Detective Ruiz's voice brought me back to the moment. "I can't force you, but please save this number. It's my cell. You can reach me anytime. I'll keep you updated if anything changes."

"Thank you. I really appreciate you calling and keeping an eye on things. I just hope she gets help."

More shuffling of papers sounded over the line. "I do, too. I'll be in touch." And with that, the line went dead.

I stared out at the sun hanging low in the sky. My shoulders felt as though they carried a thousand pounds—the weight of responsibility. There was nothing I could do. I couldn't seem to give my label the record it wanted, and I couldn't give this young woman whatever it was she needed.

I was drowning in unmet expectations. I needed a change of scenery. Maybe I'd go into town and grab some food. Explore. Get my mind off the shitstorm that was my life at the moment. I strode back inside and grabbed my keys.

I parked my SUV at the edge of town, wanting the opportunity to walk, explore, and find a distraction for my brain that was currently obsessing over the things that I could do nothing about. The mountain air was crisp as the sun started to set, and the wind rustled the aspen leaves overhead. A few people milled about on the street, but not many. The town was closing up for the day. Maybe this hadn't been the right place to find a distraction. I should've called Taylor, invited myself over to her and Walker's house. They would've obliged without a second thought.

My steps faltered as I passed the closed Tea Kettle, my eyes catching on a bent head of dark hair. Tessa sat at one of the tables on the front porch, hunched over what looked like a pad of paper, furiously scribbling. My mind ran through scenarios. Was she a writer? A musician like me? One unencumbered by writer's block?

Before I could think better of it, my feet carried me closer. Each step up the path brought the picture into clearer focus. Her pale fingers held a dark piece of something and were smudged black from gripping it. The stick of dark material skated across the page in bursts of speed alternated with moments of stillness. In those moments of pause, her brow would furrow before she attacked the page again.

I paused in my progression to study Tessa's face. I grinned as I saw a smudge of black across her cheek, and found myself wanting to reach out to wipe it away. I frowned, remembering her reaction to my touch the last go-around.

I took another step forward, clearing my throat. Tessa jumped in her seat, gripping the drawing implement in her hand so tightly, it broke in two. "I'm sorry—" I started. "I didn't mean to startle you." I cursed under my breath. "I'm making a hell of a first impression, knocking into you and then startling you when you're clearly in the zone."

Tessa visibly swallowed. "It's okay, I just didn't hear you." Her eyes traveled the expanse of the street, and her body, strung tight, seemed to relax a fraction when she spotted a couple walking down the sidewalk.

"I guess those ninja skills I've been working on have a downside."

A small smile tipped the corners of her lips up, but it seemed forced. She said nothing.

I grappled to fill the silence. "I was just walking to find some dinner and saw you sitting here. I wanted to apologize for the other day. I don't make a habit of crashing into beautiful women if I can avoid it."

The words *beautiful women* made the small smile and the ease of her muscles disappear. She stood, gathering up her tools. "It's really fine. No big deal." Her words were cool. While the language was casual, the tone was forced formality.

I couldn't explain why, but I didn't want her to leave. "So, what are you working on?"

Tessa's eyes narrowed and searched my face as if looking for ulterior motives. "Nothing." She opened a tin and placed the broken piece of what looked like charcoal inside.

I was running out of time. "Didn't look like nothing."

She shoved the tin and her notebook into a bag. "Just messing around." She slung the bag over her shoulder. "I really need to be going. Have a good night." She turned and headed inside, locking the door behind her.

Why did "have a good night" feel like she actually meant, "stay the hell away?"

CHAPTER
Five

Tessa

"**S**HIT." I COULDN'T HELP THE UTTERED CURSE AS THE cookie hit the floor. I had been fumbling and bumbling all morning, my run-in with Liam last night playing over and over in my head. I wasn't used to attention, especially of the male variety.

In fact, I did everything I could think of to avoid it. I wore no makeup. I bought clothes that were a size too big so nothing clung to my curves. I avoided eye contact at all costs. But there Liam had come, literally slamming into my life.

I picked the ruined cookie off the floor and tossed it into the trash. I was making a big deal out of nothing. Liam was simply a nice guy. He felt bad for knocking into me. And I'm sure my over-the-top reaction to the encounter had made him feel even worse. Guilt churned in my gut. I hadn't made him feel any better with my response last night.

Shit. But there was something about Liam. He seemed to study me in a way that saw too much and connected dots I didn't want anyone to connect.

I pushed down worries of someone discovering my past. Not just the fear of someone knowing who I was, but the fear of the shame that would come with it. Shame for putting up with how Garrett had treated me for so long. Shame for not trying to get out while I still could. Shame for wanting nothing more than for him to love me—for *anyone* to love me.

I leaned back against the counter, hot tears pricking at my eyes. I wasn't that naïve, desperate girl anymore. I was strong. I had fought back in the only way I could. I'd run. I was making my way on my own. I wasn't Valerie anymore. I was Tessa.

Tessa. My mother's middle name. I had hoped that by claiming it as my own, I would also claim some of her strength. Even though she'd barely turned twenty, she had stood up to her conservative parents, refusing to abort me or give me up for adoption. They'd cut all ties with her and, in turn, with me. Not even after she'd died in childbirth did they reconsider. So, into the foster system I'd gone.

I closed my eyes and took a deep breath, trying to summon some of that strength I knew had to run through my veins, a gift she'd given me, even if she wasn't here to see it. I let out the air and opened my eyes again. I felt calmer, more centered.

I returned to the task in front of me. Slowly and carefully, I transferred the remaining sugar cookies from the baking sheet to the cooling rack. No more mishaps.

Jensen's voice rang out as she moved towards the kitchen. "Hey, Tessa. Can you man the register for a few while I meet with this supplier?"

I tightened my grip on the spatula in my hand. Manning the register was not one of my favorite parts of the job. Jensen knew this. I never said anything, but within a few months of me working here, she'd offered for my duties to be focused in the kitchen. I remembered the wave of relief I'd felt when she asked if I'd prefer that. I'd gotten better, though. The fear of Garrett walking through the doors lessened with each day.

Jensen gave my arm a gentle squeeze. "I'm not going anywhere. I'll be right there." She pointed to the table that sat just to the side of the front door and in full view of the register.

I licked my lips. "No problem." It wasn't a total lie. And Jensen had been beyond accommodating with my neuroses.

She gave my arm another gentle squeeze. "Thanks, you're the best."

I wiped my hands on a towel and followed her out into the main room. Jensen took a seat across from a middle-aged gentleman with a computer and got to work discussing orders. The place was fairly quiet. We had passed the pre-work rush and were now in the mid-morning lull. A young mother sat at one table, sipping her tea while cooing at the baby in a car seat resting on the chair next to her. A guy who looked to be college-aged was bent over a textbook, highlighting furiously.

A small smile pulled at my lips. I loved this town. This shop. This life I was building. It was quiet, peaceful. Mine.

My gaze caught on two figures in the window. It took me a second to recognize Taylor and Walker. He had her wrapped in his arms, his lips pressed to her forehead. When Walker pulled back, Taylor stretched up on her tiptoes and brushed her mouth against his. Walker looked down at her with nothing less than devotion filling his expression.

A sharp pang pierced my chest. How long had it been since someone had held me? Touched me with love and affection that wasn't followed by a fist? A foreign longing swept through me, fierce and strong. Keeping the world at arm's length had meant I'd escaped any possibility of a fist, but I was missing out on the chance for comfort and connection, too.

Lonely is better than dead. I repeated the mantra over and over in my head as I squeezed my eyes closed.

The bell over the door sounded, and my eyes flew open to see Taylor walking in. "Hey," I greeted, my voice just slightly rough.

She waved at Jensen but kept walking towards me. "Hey, girl. How are you?"

The smile on Taylor's face was one of true happiness. I loved seeing the light that now shone in her eyes. Eyes that used to be so dull with grief were now so freaking bright. That phantom pressure in my chest flared.

I shook my head, coming back to the present moment. "I'm good. How about you?"

"I'm doing great. Just got word that I got my teaching accreditation in Oregon. I'll be able to start teaching in the fall. Now, I just need to find a job."

"That's great news. I'm sure the Sutter Lake schools will be happy to have you."

Taylor let out a light laugh. "Let's hope so because I'm so ready to get back to it."

"They will." I glanced at the bakery case. "So, what'll it be today?"

Taylor's gaze traveled to the case. "Oooooh, yay, you have more of those spinach and feta scones. I'll take one of those and a lemongrass tea, please."

I pulled a scone from the case and set it on a plate. "I'll get that tea right up."

Taylor handed me a ten-dollar bill. "Thank you. Just put the change in the tip jar."

I shook my head. It was way too big of a tip, but I knew arguing with her would do me no good. I made quick work of brewing her tea, bringing the cup and a small pitcher of milk to her table.

Taylor beamed up at me. "Thank you."

"Of course."

The bell over the door sounded again. This time, my gaze landed on a large man. I fought the urge to step back. Swallowing, I rounded the counter, my gaze never leaving the customer.

I wiped my hands down my jeans as the man studied the café. His eyes traveled over the different patrons, the bakery case, and the menu above my head before finally landing on me. His smile was wide. "How can anyone decide what to order when everything looks so good?"

I forced myself to return his grin. "I can recommend something if you tell me what you typically like."

The man rubbed his stomach. "Well, I'm not much of a tea drinker, but I heard you have some of the best baked goods in town."

A sense of pride washed through me. "I think they're pretty tasty. The marionberry muffins are a favorite. Or, if you're looking for something savory, the ham and cheddar scone."

He studied my face. "Do you make these yourself?"

I toyed with the strings of my apron. "I do."

"Well, I'll just have to take one of each then."

I nodded. "Would you like them for here or to go?"

"I'll eat here, thanks. No point in taking them back to my hotel room when this place is so welcoming." I nodded again, grabbing a plate for the items. The man continued. "I'm Al Burke, here from Portland."

I gripped the plate I was holding a little tighter and studied him. He was dressed in tourist get-up. A fly-fishing vest, outdoor-type pants, and boots. But everything about the outfit seemed...wrong. The items were too new and didn't match the aura the man was giving off. He could be having a mid-life crisis and trying something new, but I had learned the hard way to listen to that little voice in the back of my mind that urged me to be cautious. "Well, I hope you're enjoying your stay."

Al chuckled. "I am, I am. And what's your name, little lady?"

This was one of the other reasons I didn't like working the register. People could come up and ask you anything, and they would consider you rude if you didn't answer.

I hit a few keys on the register. "Tessa. That'll be six dollars and fifty cents."

Al removed his wallet and handed me a ten-dollar bill. "Nice to meet you, Tessa. You grow up around here?"

My spine straightened as I gripped the drawer of the register. "No." I didn't meet his eyes as I pulled his change from the drawer.

He chuckled again. It grated against my ears. "Not much of a talker, are you?"

I handed him his three dollars and fifty cents. "I guess not."

Al opened his mouth to say something else but stopped when an arm encircled my shoulders.

"I can take it from here. Why don't you head on back to the kitchen?"

I wanted to sag in Jensen's hold. Instead, I simply said, "Okay," and forced myself to take one more look at the guy. To study his face so that if I ever saw it again, I would know that something was amiss. Al met my studied gaze with one of his own. A look that made a shiver go down my spine.

I broke the stare first, turning to retreat to the safety of the kitchen. I rounded the corner to the fridge and rested my head against the cool metal. *Polite tourist or one of Garrett's lackeys?*

The question circled on an endless loop in my brain. I hated that I felt like I couldn't trust my own perception of things. Couldn't tell if I was being paranoid or cautious. I ran through the exchange in my head. I compared it with conversations I heard Jensen have every day at the counter. Not one thing the man had said was something I hadn't heard before.

My shoulders slumped. I guess paranoia it was. I fought the urge to pound my forehead against the fridge. I didn't want to be like this. I just didn't know how to find a balance that would allow me to keep my guard up but also let others in.

Safe and lonely is better than dead, I reminded myself. But for the first time, it hit me how truly depressing my life's motto was.

CHAPTER
Six

Liam

I TIGHTENED MY GRIP ON THE ITEMS IN MY HAND, IGNORING the voice in my head telling me I was an idiot. I was simply trying to make amends. And, yes, maybe it was partly because the two times I'd encountered Tessa were the only moments in recent memory I'd had even the faintest flicker of the musical muse that used to flow so freely. I was desperate to have it back. And Tessa…she was a song in the making.

I readjusted my ballcap as I strode up the walkway to The Tea Kettle. Hopefully, she was working. Pushing open the door, I inhaled deeply and almost moaned. My stomach growled.

Jensen looked up from the counter at the sound of the bell. "Back so soon? Our baked goods must have made you a convert."

I patted my stomach. "I couldn't stay away." I scanned the small café. There were a couple of older gentlemen playing cards in the corner and a woman with a small child on the opposite side of the space. I could most likely go unnoticed here for a little while at least. "Do you mind if I hang out here and work for a bit? The silence at the cabin was getting to be a little much."

"As long as you make a purchase or two, you can stay as long as you'd like. Though I should warn you, we get an influx of teenage girls around three-thirty."

"Thanks for the heads-up." I'd get gone by then. I moved towards the bakery case. "And I don't think I'll have any problem with the purchases." I tapped the fingers of my free hand against the glass case. "Let's start out with a ham and cheddar scone, a marionberry muffin, and one of those peanut butter cookies."

Jensen let out a choked laugh. "Start out with?"

I shrugged. "I'm sure I'll be hungry again in another hour or so."

Jensen continued to chuckle as she pulled the items from the case. "You're my new favorite customer. Can I get you any tea to go with that?"

I grimaced. "How about a bottle of water?"

Jensen set the plate of baked goods on the counter. "Don't knock it till you try it."

"Maybe another time," I hedged, pulling my wallet from my pocket.

"I'll hold you to that." She punched a few keys on the register. "That'll be $12.50."

My gaze caught on movement in the back kitchen. A figure with a dark brown braid down her back reached up on her tip-toes to grab something off a shelf. Tessa was all long, lean lines, and she was focused in her practiced rhythm, a dance around the space that she knew by heart.

A throat cleared, and my gaze jumped back to Jensen. "Sorry, what'd you say?"

Her eyes narrowed slightly on me, the look somewhere in between curiosity and a warning. "That'll be $12.50."

I pulled out a twenty. "Keep the change."

"Thanks."

Taking the plate and bottle of water, I surveyed my table options. I opted for one that gave me a line of sight into the kitchen but not the one that was directly in front of it—not overly obvious. I set everything down on the weathered wooden surface. I pushed my snacks to one side and the water to the other, making room for my worn and battered notebook.

This thing had been through battles with me, including being thrown against a wall or two lately. It housed songs from more than two albums and dozens of tunes that hadn't made the cut. As well as some random thoughts that might turn into lyrics, single lines that needed to find a home, and some really crappy doodles.

I opened to a blank page. The emptiness of it seemed to mock me. I ignored the insult and glanced towards the kitchen. Tessa was removing what looked like cookies from a baking sheet and placing them on a cooling rack. *What is her story?*

I glanced down at the tin of drawing charcoal I'd made a special trip into the nearest city to get. Tessa snapping the piece she'd held in her hand flashed in my mind. I'd scared her. That kind of thing happened. Anyone could be startled under the right circumstances. But something told me there was more at play here.

I let my mind drift as I watched her move about the kitchen. Words flew through my brain. Just single pieces of text at first, and then slightly longer strings. I jotted everything down, not allowing myself to judge it, just letting the words fly. When I looked up again, my muse was offering Jensen a plate.

Jensen studied the assortment of baked goods. "Why don't you let Liam and the bridge club play taste-testers?" she asked, inclining her head towards me and the older gentlemen sitting behind me.

Tessa stiffened at the request, her gaze flicking to me and then back to Jensen. "Sure."

Clearly, I had fucked up with this girl. I really hoped I could make things right, and not just because she seemed to be my last hope of reclaiming my musical muse. I gave Tessa my best I-really-am-a-nice-guy-even-though-I've-scared-the-shit-out-of-you-twice smile, or what I thought that smile should look like.

Tessa made her way towards me and extended the plate. "I'm trying a few new cookie recipes. Would you like to try them and tell me what you like best?"

I flipped my notebook closed. "There's not one job I'd be more excited about or better qualified for." A hint of a smile ghosted Tessa's lips. Progress. "Tell me what we've got here."

She pointed to bite-sized pieces of cookie as she spoke. "Hot chocolate, potato chip chocolate chip, maple glazed apple crisp, and key lime."

My brows rose as she made her way down the list. "Impressive. I can get behind just about anything on that list except for the potato chip one. Potato chips are for sandwiches, not sweets."

Tessa let out a soft laugh. It was just the tease of a sound, but I longed to hear the full thing. "You'll have to agree to try them all if you want to be a taste-tester. I can't have an uninformed voter."

"Fair enough. I guess I can suffer through one potato chip cookie if the future of The Tea Kettle's menu rests in my hands."

Tessa pressed her lips together, stifling another laugh. I hated that motion, I was so desperate to hear the sound. "You're so very selfless."

"That's me." I reached out, opting for the apple crisp first. Heaven in food form. I slowly made my way around the plate, careful to take my time with each bite. I saved the potato chip cookie for last, grimacing as I lifted it to my mouth. I chewed slowly. My eyes flared.

The smallest grin appeared on Tessa's lips. "Good, right?"

"That's amazing. I need like a dozen of those."

Tessa tucked a strand of hair behind her ear. "It's the combination of salty and sweet. It always makes for the best concoctions in my opinion."

"You are clearly the expert. I beg ignorance. Please, make these every day."

"I'll see what I can do."

Tessa began to turn towards the table behind me, but I held up a hand in a gesture that asked her to wait. "I have something for you." Her forehead wrinkled. "An apology for making you break your drawing pencil the other night and crashing into you that first day."

Tessa's shoulders tensed. "You don't need to apologize."

"I do. It'll make me feel better." I handed her the tin of drawing charcoal. "For you."

She stared down at the tin, her eyes blinking rapidly. "This brand is the best," she whispered, almost to herself. A rapid-fire flash of emotions crossed her face, changing from one to the next faster than I could follow, as if she were at war with herself. She swallowed hard. "Thank you. This was very kind of you."

"No problem—" Before I could finish my sentence, she'd turned and strode away. I watched as she chatted with the men playing bridge. The longer they talked, the more her muscles seemed to ease. She joked and teased, making the guys' eyes light up.

Tessa asked one about what the doctor had said about his blood pressure at his last appointment, and another about whether his granddaughter had liked the doll he'd gotten her for the girl's birthday. There was genuine kindness and caring in Tessa, but I noticed that she artfully dodged all questions directed at her that were any more specific than how she was doing.

What was her story? And what was it about me that put her on edge? I flipped my notebook back open and tried to find the answer there, but it seemed those wisps of music had floated away when Tessa left.

CHAPTER
Seven

Tessa

I SLIPPED MY KEY INTO THE SLOT ON THE CAR DOOR, TURNING it until the lock popped down. The vehicle was so old that the remote no longer worked, but the relic got me where I needed to go, and that was all I needed.

I took a moment to survey the town around me. Pine Ridge was about the same size as Sutter Lake, maybe a little larger, and about an hour away. It was one of six towns I used to do my research. I didn't have a computer of my own, and I didn't want any library staff members wondering what I was doing there so often if I always went to the same one.

I adjusted the brim of my hat so that it mostly concealed my eyes and headed towards the library. I ducked my head as I entered, avoiding the video camera at the front doors. Not being caught on film *anywhere* was one of my cardinal rules. The good thing about small towns was that security measures like cameras were few and far between.

I moved through stacks of books until I found the computer lab. All that was required was signing in. I scrawled a random name and took the station most removed from the people already seated, and one that still gave me a view of the door.

Placing my bag on the seat next to me, I pulled out a slip of paper with a list of names. It had taken me a year of careful searches to come up with the list. A year of building fake social media profiles and sending messages, pretending to be someone I wasn't, just hoping I'd find the person I was looking for.

When Garrett and I had been at the beginning of our relationship, he'd talked more openly. He'd spoken of an ex, someone he'd said had almost ruined his life with lies. After going through what I had with him, I had a feeling this ex had nearly taken him down with the truth. I had to find her.

I wasn't exactly sure what I would do when I did, what the best approach would be. Was an email or call more appropriate when asking if someone's ex-boyfriend had beaten them, too? I rolled my shoulders back. If I could find this woman, and if she would stand with me, the police would have to believe us.

My stomach pitched. Garrett was such a good manipulator. Would he be able to convince the police that we were both crazy?

I gripped the edge of the computer desk. I had to try. Because what would my life be like if I didn't? Would I hide forever? Be afraid to let anyone in. The image of Walker gazing down at Taylor with pure adoration flashed in my mind. I rubbed my sternum, trying to relieve the spasm there. Maybe one day I'd have that.

It seemed impossible, like my own personal Everest. I'd have to scale so many things to get there. I took a deep breath. There was only one way to climb a mountain: one step at a time.

I tapped a letter on the keyboard, bringing the screen to life, and signed into one of my many fake social media accounts. There was a message waiting. One with a name. I scrawled *Bethany Lewis* on my piece of paper. I scanned the list of names. Eight in total. The girl I was looking for had to be one of them. It was time to start researching.

The hours flew by as I searched old yearbooks and public online photo albums. People didn't realize how much of their lives they left out for the world to see. How much information a complete stranger could gather with just a few keystrokes. The whole thing made me feel like a creeper.

I stood for a moment, stretching, trying to relieve some of the tension that had settled between my shoulder blades. I checked my watch. One more hour. I could afford one more hour before I needed to head back to Sutter Lake.

Easing back into the desk chair, I typed a new name into the search engine. Too many of the wrong hits. I typed in the name and a location this time. Virginia. Where Garrett and all the majority of these women had gone to college.

A slew of news articles filled the screen. My heart began to beat erratically as I clicked on one. *College Sophomore Missing Since Tuesday* the headline read. I double-checked dates and names. This was the right Bethany Lewis. One of the eight girls Garrett had dated before me. A girl he'd never told me had gone missing.

I clicked back to the search page, my eyes scanning the screen to see if she had ever been found. Another headline jumped out. *Bethany Lewis Presumed Dead*. My stomach roiled as I read each line of the article. *Garrett Abrams, Lewis's ex-boyfriend, has been cleared in her disappearance. Abrams had been a prime suspect after a report of domestic abuse to the campus police came to light. But, just recently, two fraternity brothers came forward to corroborate Abrams' alibi.*

My nails bit into the palms of my hands as I fisted them. Garrett had killed her. I knew it in my bones. He always had his bases covered. He'd grown up in a privileged family and had connections that had bought him protection from the moment he breathed his first breath. That had only grown as he'd gotten older. The right prep schools, colleges, fraternities, social clubs, and finally a job with one of the most prestigious law firms in DC. One that was notorious for fixing seemingly unfixable problems for the rich and powerful.

Tears of frustration pricked at the corners of my eyes. The girlfriend had been my one hope. The person I knew had been brave enough to speak up before. I had thought there would be safety in us coming forward together now. But Garrett had silenced her in the most permanent way. My gaze fell on a photo of Bethany's parents. They held a sign, begging for any information on their daughter's disappearance.

The poster had a large photo of Bethany. I shuddered. We looked incredibly similar. Or we *used* to. She was fair like me, had a white-blonde tone to her hair similar to what mine used to be like, and her eyes were light—not violet like mine, but a light blue. I shivered.

My head pounded as if a vise were encircling it and growing tighter by the second. I needed to get out of here. Needed fresh air. Time to process all of this. I hit print on five of the articles and stood, stuffing my paper and pen back into my bag. I grabbed the printouts as the machine spat them out and tossed the change owed for the printing into the dish next to the machine.

I hurried through the stacks, to the entryway, ducking my head again as I exited the building. Sunlight. Fresh air. I was safe. Garrett couldn't hurt me here. I sucked in air and tipped my head back, pulling off my hat so I could soak in the rays of the sun, uncaring if the people walking by thought I was weird.

"Tessa?"

My body stiffened, and my head jerked in the direction of the raspy tone. Liam. My mind whirled. "What are you doing here?"

He gestured to a building across the street. "I had some legal paperwork to sign."

My eyes narrowed as my palms began to sweat. "Why didn't you have it sent to Sutter Lake?"

Liam rubbed a hand over his stubbled jaw. "I'm trying to keep a low profile, and I don't really want my label to know where I am. I had to get the paperwork notarized, and I didn't want them to be able to track me through that."

I studied his face, searching for a lie. All I saw was the truth.

Tears of frustration wanted to surface again. I hated the paranoia that seemed to rule my life. Hated that my mind jumped to the worst possible assumptions of people.

Liam had been nothing but kind to me. I thought of the way-too-expensive drawing charcoal he'd bought for me. No one but he had even picked up on the fact that I drew.

Liam stepped closer. "What about you?" His eyes traveled to the library behind me. "Picking up a book?"

I drew the pile of articles I was holding to my chest, but the movement was too quick. A few sheets of paper fluttered to the ground. I let out a curse and crouched to pick them up.

Liam's hand shot out to grab one the wind had caught. He studied the paper, his brow furrowing. "A missing person's case?"

I snatched the article from his hand. "It's nothing. I really need to be going." I met his eyes briefly, forcing myself not to immediately bolt for the parking lot like I wanted to. That would only be more suspicious. "Good luck with your paperwork."

"Thanks—"

Liam sounded like he was going to continue, but I cut him off with a wave. "See you around," I mumbled and turned towards where my car was parked, making myself walk at a normal rate.

The last thing in the world I needed was for Liam to try and figure out why I was looking into Bethany Lewis's disappearance. Hopefully, he would just think I was weird. Socially awkward. My shoulders sagged. I was exhausted from being on alert all the time, from always worrying that someone would discover my past.

One day. It was a promise to myself. One day, I wouldn't be forced to have my defenses up at all times. One day, I could let people in. One day, I would know what it was like to be truly free. Not just free of Garrett's abuse, but free of the burden of constantly looking over my shoulder. One day couldn't get here fast enough.

CHAPTER
Eight

Liam

"WHO WOULD'VE THOUGHT? HOLLYWOOD HERE knows how to ride." Laughter tinged Tuck's voice. Tuck was Walker's best friend, and I guess, now a friend of mine. One who currently gave me a whole lot of shit.

I turned to Walker, inclining my head towards Tuck. "Who would've thought? A small-town Forest Service cop who knows how to string two sentences together."

Walker burst out laughing. Luckily, none of our horses were skittish, or the loud sound might've sent them running. Tuck stuck out his bottom lip, giving it an exaggerated tremble. "Now that's not very nice."

I snickered but gave no apology. Tuck grinned. Walker kept right on laughing. "You know, he has a point. I wouldn't have thought you actually knew how to handle a horse."

Sitting in the saddle with the land stretched out all around me felt as natural as breathing. It felt like coming home. "I grew up in a small town in Georgia. My grandfather used to take me out on his ranch all the time. Taught me to ride, fish, shoot. All the things a little boy loves."

Surprise shone in both Walker's and Tuck's eyes. I fought my own laughter then. Instead, opting for a smirk and a shake of my head. Just because I'd lived in LA for more than a decade didn't mean I wasn't a country boy at heart.

Walker nudged his mount up so that he was riding next to me. "Well, you're welcome to use the horses anytime you'd like."

I knew that was his official nod of approval. We'd gotten off to a bit of a rocky start when he thought I'd hooked up with Taylor, but we'd found our way. He had my utmost respect, but it was nice to know that I had his in return. "Thanks. I might just take you up on that."

Tuck came up on Walker's other side so that we were now riding three astride across one of the Cole family's many fields. Tuck's face had taken on a more somber look. "How's Little J doing?"

I knew the nickname belonged to Walker's sister, Jensen. I also knew that she'd been through the wringer lately. Walker's jaw hardened. "I'm not really sure. She refuses to talk about it. She goes through all the motions of normal life and is the best mom there could be for Noah, but I know she's hurting."

Tuck's hands tightened on his own reins. "I wish I could resurrect that fucker just so I could kill him personally."

"He'd deserve it." Walker stared out at the horizon. He hesitated before beginning to speak again. "I'm worried she won't let anyone in after this."

I'd picked up bits and pieces of conversations that I'd been on the periphery of like this one, and things Taylor had told me. Jensen had gotten pregnant in college. Her boyfriend at the time had ended things with her and run for the hills. Between that and this latest episode with her psycho ex, it was no wonder the girl had trust issues.

"I'll go by the guest house, see if she and Noah need anything. Or, if I can take the little man off her hands for an afternoon, maybe she can do something for herself for once." Tuck's voice was strung tight.

Walker swatted a fly away from his horse. "That'd be great.

Between working at the Kettle and taking care of Noah, she hasn't had much time for herself."

Tuck grunted in agreement.

The mention of the tea shop had violet eyes flashing in my mind for what felt like the millionth time. I shifted in my saddle. Silence filled the air. Nothing but the sound of hooves on soft ground could be heard. My curiosity proved too much. "There's a girl that works in your sister's shop. What's her story?" I tried to sound casual, but the look Walker threw me told me that I hadn't quite pulled it off.

He rubbed a hand over his stubbled jaw. "I'm not real sure, to be honest." He sent me a sidelong glance. "But she's one you want to be careful with."

It didn't take a genius to catch the warning in his tone. I sat up just a little straighter. "I'm just curious."

Tuck let out a snort of disbelief. "Curious about how gorgeous she is."

There was a burning in my gut at his words. It felt a whole lot like jealousy. "I had a little run-in with her at the shop and then again when they were closed. She just…" My words trailed off, unsure of what it was I was trying to express.

Walker nodded as if he understood exactly. "She's jumpy. Don't take offense. It took a year for her to not leave the room anytime I came in."

Thoughts flew through my mind as to what might have made her that way. None of the options were good. I tightened my grip on the saddle horn.

Walker pushed on. "My guess is she's been hurt, or she's running from something. Maybe both."

I thought of our encounter in front of the library, the article about that missing woman. Sharing that with Walker felt like it would be a betrayal somehow. "Jensen hasn't gotten the story? Tessa's worked there a long time, hasn't she?" The women I knew wouldn't rest until they'd unearthed every story their friend had to tell, especially if they thought something might be hurting their friend.

Walker shook his head. "You start asking her questions about her life before she got to Sutter Lake, Tessa will lock down tight. You won't get a thing out of her, and she'll start avoiding you like the plague."

I let out a quiet groan. She was already avoiding me. Normally, if a woman didn't seem interested, I moved the hell on—plenty of fish in the sea and all that. But there was something about Tessa, a fragile strength that made me want to know more about her.

A low chuckle sounded to my right. I turned to see Tuck wearing a shit-eating grin. "I love this. Hollywood comes to Sutter Lake and can't get the girl he's interested in to give him the time of day."

If Tuck had been within arm's reach, I would've elbowed him in the gut. Walker acted for me, smacking him upside the head. "You know, Tuck, some people want quality over quantity."

Tuck snickered. "You're just jealous because Taylor's got you locked down tight. Might as well be a married man. Me, I've got all the freedom in the world. And let me tell you, boys, variety is the spice of life."

I'd had variety. Plenty of it. When I was young and dumb, and my music was just taking off, I'd indulged in that scene—the groupies and the random women at bars. The models and actresses. But what no one tells you is that it gets lonely really quick. Women want in your bed for two reasons: to have a story to tell their friends, or in hopes of snagging their meal ticket.

I'd grown out of that phase before I hit twenty-two. I didn't date often, but when I did, it was someone I trusted. Trusted not to take a selfie with my naked ass while I was passed out, asleep.

Walker's voice interrupted my thoughts. "One day, Tuck, someone is going to come along and knock you on your ass.

You're going to be so taken by her, and she's not gonna put up with any of your shit." He let out a chuckle. "And I can't wait to watch."

Tuck's face lost the easy grin he usually sported, and his jaw tightened. "Don't hold your breath."

"Whatever you say." Walker turned to me. "We're having a big family dinner tonight at the ranch house. Why don't you come? My parents would love to have you."

Walker's whole family lived on the ranch, including his parents and his spitfire of a grandmother. They were a tight-knit clan that reminded me of my own family back in Georgia. I could use a dose of that. "I never turn down the offer of a free meal."

"Smart man. Come on over around six."

I adjusted my ballcap. "I'll be there."

Tuck urged his mount forward from where he had fallen behind. "And what about me? Aren't I an honorary member of the Cole clan?"

Walker shook his head. "You're the drunk uncle everyone is embarrassed they're related to." I couldn't help the snicker that escaped me.

Tuck grinned at Walker. "You're just mad your mom and grandma like me better than they like you."

Walker turned his gaze heavenward as if pleading for help and then shot a look my way. "Maybe you can help me keep this hooligan in check tonight."

I chuckled. "I'll do my best, but I think that might be a job for more than two of us."

"Damn straight," Tuck agreed.

A mischievous smile spread across Walker's face. "I think a certain tea shop employee might be there, too."

My body went on alert at the thought of having a real shot at talking to Tessa. One where she wouldn't just hightail it out of my presence immediately. At least, I hoped.

CHAPTER
Nine

Tessa

I LEANED AGAINST MY CAR DOOR TO SHUT IT. ADJUSTING THE large purse on my shoulder, I looked up at the gorgeous Cole family ranch house. It was everything I'd dreamt of as a little girl. A home full of warmth, love, and family. The house practically glowed with it.

A peal of laughter sounded from behind the closed door, and I knew that either Walker or Tuck was chasing Noah with the threat of tickles. Just like I knew Jensen would be pouring glasses of wine for all the ladies while they gathered in the kitchen to gossip and catch up as Walker's mother, Sarah, finished cooking.

But here I stood, on the outside looking in. Just like always.

It wasn't that the extended Cole family didn't make me feel welcome. They went out of their way to let me know they thought of me as family. Guilt churned in my belly. What would they say if they knew that Tessa wasn't even my real name? I could count the truths they knew about me on one hand.

These were good, kind people. They didn't deserve to be lied to. *The lies keep them safe. They keep* me *safe.* It was true. If the Coles or the rest of them knew my name and where I was from, what I had endured, the little haven of safety I'd created could all come crashing down around me.

"Are you heading in?"

I jumped at the sound of Liam's voice coming from my right.

He held up a hand and gave a sheepish smile. "I'm forever sneaking up on you. Sorry about that."

I swallowed against my suddenly dry throat. Liam looked incredibly handsome in dark-wash jeans that hugged his hips, and a button-down that brought out the green in his hazel eyes. His light brown hair was just a little shaggy on top, perfectly mussed in that way so many guys spent hours in front of the mirror perfecting. But you just knew that, for Liam, it was effortless. The look was complemented by the scruff covering his jaw.

It hit me like a ton of bricks—I was checking him out. I was looking at a man with interest instead of fear. A coyote howled in the distance, the sound jarring me from my thoughts. The darkening sky seemed to close in around us.

I was alone with a man. My breathing picked up speed. Anything could happen. My chest constricted as my gaze darted from Liam to the house and back again.

Liam must have seen the fear invade my expression because he took two large steps back. He moved slowly, the way I had around Phoenix at first. The tightness in my chest eased.

"I just had to finish up a phone call with my record label before I headed inside." A little bit of color rose in his cheeks. "I guess I didn't need to say it was with my record label. That probably sounded like I was bragging. I didn't mean it that way. I just—"

A small laugh escaped me at the image of this badass rock star so flustered at the idea that I might think him a showoff. I covered the sound with my hand.

Liam's eyes shot to mine and held.

I let my hand drop. "I didn't think you were bragging."

"I'm glad." He shuffled his feet. "Do you think we could start over? I feel like I've made a really horrible first impression with you, and our friends are basically family, so I think we're going to be seeing a lot of each other."

I pressed my lips together, reminding myself that there was a house full of people twenty feet away. People who had never hurt me. In fact, they'd all helped me in one way or another. "I'd like that." I forced myself to take a step forward. "I'm sorry I overreacted that first day. It had just been a long morning." It wasn't a total lie.

Liam studied my face. I fought the urge to squirm. His gaze was curious, calculating in a way that wasn't malicious, as if he were trying to put together a puzzle but wasn't sure he had the right pieces.

I cleared my throat, attempting to break his assessment of me. "We should head inside."

Liam nodded. "Yeah." He extended an arm. "After you."

I was careful to keep my distance, never venturing within arm's length until we were both standing at the front door and there was no other option. Liam reached up to knock, but the door swung open before he could.

Walker stood there, grinning and shaking his head. "Come on in. No knocking required. You know that, Tessa."

I gave a small nod, holding my breath as I scooted in between him and Liam. Two large men. *Just breathe.* I almost ran smack into Walker's grandmother, Irma.

"Well, well," she began, taking my hand and giving it a gentle pat. "Who do we have here?" Her eyes widened a fraction as her gaze moved from me to Liam and back again. "I like this. My psychic senses are tingling."

"Grandma…" Walker warned.

Irma just shook her head as though disappointed in him. "You would think you'd have a little more faith in my abilities after I predicted your and Taylor's match." She gestured to Liam and me with her head. "And you can't tell me these two wouldn't make beautiful babies."

I felt my cheeks heat and looked anywhere but at Liam.

Walker groaned, letting his head tip back as though praying for patience.

"Now, Mom, you're embarrassing Tessa," Sarah chided her mother-in-law as she entered the foyer and took my arm.

Irma gave a good-natured harrumph. "Always trying to spoil my fun."

Sarah shook her head. "Trying to keep you from making trouble is more like it." She bent her head close to mine. "Sorry about that. Let's hang up your purse and get you something to drink."

Sarah lifted the bag from my shoulder and hung it on the coat rack littered with objects. I fought the urge to take it back, cling to it like the lifeline it was. Sarah ushered me towards the living room and kitchen.

Irma followed closely on our heels. "I hope Jensen has my glass poured."

Sarah eyed Irma. "Only one, Mom."

"Buzzkill," Irma called over her shoulder as she bustled past us into the kitchen.

Sarah chuckled. "You'd think it'd be my grandson giving me gray hair, but it's her."

"She's a character."

Sarah placed a hand on my shoulder as we reached the kitchen where Taylor and Jensen were seated on stools, sipping wine. "Can I get you a glass?"

"I'd just love some water, but I can get it." I never drank. Didn't indulge in anything that could impair my judgement or slow my reaction time.

"Nonsense. I'll get it. You have a seat with the girls." Sarah went to work taking a glass from the cupboard, and I rounded the counter to pull up a stool.

Taylor shot me a warm smile as I sat. "Hey, Tessa. How are you?"

I slipped onto the empty barstool. "I'm good, how are you guys?"

Taylor took a sip of her wine. "Just drowning in teaching applications, but otherwise good."

Jensen reached for the wine bottle. "All good here." She refilled her own glass and then topped off Irma's.

Irma grinned at her. "You always were my favorite."

Jensen snorted. "Make sure you tell Walker that."

"Oh, I will. He was just doubting my abilities."

Jensen's brows pulled together. "What abilities?"

"My psychic abilities, of course."

Jensen choked on her sip of wine. "You're not psychic, Grandma."

Irma straightened her shoulders. "Well, of course, I am. I predicted your mother and father. Taylor and Walker. I even told you all our little league team was going to win that championship."

Jensen shook her head. "That's called recognizing chemistry and good odds."

Irma huffed, raising her chin in the air. "Don't you want to hear what my latest prediction is?"

Taylor raised her glass in Irma's direction. "I do. You know I'm a believer."

Irma gave Taylor a pleased smile that turned mischievous. "Why, thank you, honey pie." Irma's gaze turned in my direction, and I knew my face was the shade of a tomato. "It's about Miss Tessa here and that handsome piece of man meat in the living room." My face got hotter.

Taylor leaned in closer. "Which one?"

Jensen's spine straightened as her eyes found the gathering of men in the living space on the other side of the kitchen. Walker, Tuck, and Liam were talking with Walker's father, Andrew, while Noah zoomed around bodies with his toy airplane. It was certainly a gathering of attractive men.

Irma cackled at Taylor's question. "That musician friend of yours. I can see it now, lots and lots of babies."

Taylor shot a questioning look in my direction. I quickly shook my head. "There's nothing going on with me and Liam."

"Maybe not now, but there will be." Irma's words came out in a sing-song tone.

Irma could have her suspicions all she wanted, but I knew the truth. There would *never* be anything between Liam and me.

Sarah bustled around the counter, placing a glass of water in front of me and grabbing Irma's wine glass from her hand. "I think you've had enough of this for right now."

Irma followed Sarah and her wine, complaining as she went.

Jensen scooted closer. "Sorry about that. She means well, but we've all indulged her crazy stories a little too much."

Taylor said nothing, but her gaze traveled from me to Liam, a thoughtful look on her face.

After a raucous and delicious dinner, our group had fractured. Walker, Taylor, and Andrew were cleaning the kitchen, while Sarah and Irma chatted animatedly over coffee and dessert. My eyes drifted into the living room and caught on Jensen and Tuck. Jensen was shaking her head, a perturbed look on her face.

I was ready to make my excuses and head home, but first, I needed my bag. I eyed it in the foyer. Making my way towards it, my steps faltered at the sound of encouraging words.

"That's it. Your fingers are in the right spot. Now, strum." Liam's voice drifted out from the downstairs study.

Something that resembled a chord sounded next. "Wow. I did it." Noah's tone was full of wonder.

"That was great. You'll be playing songs in no time."

I crept closer, needing a visual of this moment. Reaching the side of the study, I peeked in through the door that was just slightly ajar.

Noah handed Liam back the guitar. "Now, you play something. I want to see how you do it."

"All right, little man." Liam positioned the worn guitar on his knee. He seemed to search for what to play. His long fingers curved around the neck of the guitar. The first notes filled the air. They seemed to float effortlessly from one to the next, weaving together to create something breathtakingly beautiful.

The first softly sung words of James Taylor's *Fire and Rain* had shivers shooting down my spine. Liam's voice. God, his voice. It was perfectly imperfect, with a rasp to it that felt like sandpaper lightly scraping against my skin. But the tone...that was rich and deep and full of emotion.

Liam's eyes were closed as he sang, as though the lyrics were searing his soul. Then his lids lifted. His gaze landed right on me. I knew I should look away, but I couldn't. His focus and the magic he wove with his music held me captive.

He continued to sing—right to me. I don't think I even blinked. As the last notes of the song sounded, Noah leapt up from his seat, clapping wildly and breaking the spell.

I immediately stepped back, out of sight and out of range of the powerful weapon the room held. I shook my head, forcing a small laugh and swiping the hair out of my face. No wonder the man had sold millions of records and who knew how many concert tickets. He was lethal with a guitar in his hands.

I turned to grab my bag and came face-to-face with Sarah. She seemed to have been studying me the same way I'd been watching Liam. She gave me a soft smile. "There are times when you remind me so much of a friend I had growing up."

I froze. Sarah shook her head, a wistful look on her face. "It's your mannerisms. They are so similar to hers. And the eyes. She had those same gorgeous violet eyes." Sarah studied my face. "But she had blonde hair."

"What was her name?" My words came out as a croak.

Sarah's soft smile grew. "Anne." I stopped breathing. "She didn't grow up in Sutter Lake, but her grandparents used to live here, and she spent the summers with them. When they passed away, she stopped coming. Eventually, we lost touch."

Sarah seemed to lose herself in a memory. "I hate that. She was a sister of my heart. I wonder if I could find her now." She tapped a finger to her lips and then seemed to come back to herself. "Sorry about that. Lost in memories."

"That's okay." My voice still wasn't totally normal. "I'm glad I remind you of someone you loved." It took everything I had to hold myself back from asking five million questions. To see if Sarah had any photos. To ask her to recount every memory she had of Anne in as much detail as possible. Because Anne was my mother.

CHAPTER
Ten

Liam

THE SECOND TESSA DISAPPEARED FROM THE DOORWAY, I stood. I didn't want to lose the moment, the spark that had flamed as she watched me play.

A small hand tugged on my larger one. "That was AWESOME!" Noah shouted the last word, and I couldn't help the grin that overtook my face. "I think maybe I don't want to be a fighter pilot anymore. I think I might want to be a rock star."

I stifled my chuckle with a cough. "I think either would be pretty awesome."

Noah's face took on a thoughtful look. "I wonder if I could do both."

I ruffled his hair. "If anyone could, it would be you."

He looked up at me with wide eyes. "You think so?"

"I do."

Noah's gaze went to his shoes as he started to fidget. "Do, uh, do you think maybe you could teach me? You know, some of the guitar stuff? It's okay if you're too busy."

My chest warmed. "I'd love to teach you some stuff. We just have to ask your mom first."

His head snapped up, eyes shooting to mine. "Let's go ask her right now."

Before I could respond, Noah started tugging me out of the room. He almost ran smack into Sarah and Tessa. "Guess what,

Grandma? Liam's gonna teach me how to play the guitar. I'm gonna be a rock star!" He shot his little fist up into the air on the last word, and I bit my lip to keep from laughing.

Sarah smiled indulgently at her grandson and then looked at me. "Is that so?"

I took a step forward. "If it's all right with Jensen." I couldn't help that my eyes seemed to seek out Tessa. When they found her, my body seemed to go on alert. Her face was full of wonder, but... *Are those tears in her eyes?*

Tessa ducked her head and slid her purse over her shoulder. "I better get going. Thank you so much for having me, Sarah."

Sarah pulled her in for a hug, an action that seemed to cause Tessa to stiffen the slightest bit before relaxing. "You know you're welcome anytime. I wish you'd come over more."

Tessa gave her a small smile as she pulled back. I wondered what she'd look like if a real one of those ever touched her lips. I had a feeling the effect would be devastating. "I'll see you soon." She leaned down. "Bye, Noah."

Noah released my hand and threw his arms around her legs. "Bye, Tessa."

Tessa's gaze met mine, her cheeks pinking just a bit. So fucking cute. "It was nice to, um, see you again."

I shot her my best grin. "You, too, sweetheart." I'm not sure why the *sweetheart* slipped out, it just did. I was caught up in trying to show her just how charming I could be, but it was apparently the wrong thing to say.

Tessa's face went white. I stepped forward a half-step, but she shrank back. "I-I need to go. Bye, Sarah." And with that, she spun on her heel and was gone.

I stared at the door for a good thirty seconds before a throat clearing grabbed my attention. "You certainly have a way with the ladies."

"Walker," Sarah chided her son. She gave him a light slap on the stomach with the back of her hand as she passed, leading Noah into the living room.

Walker just chuckled. "Come on." He motioned to the door, and we headed outside.

"I don't know how, or why, but I keep screwing things up." We walked out onto the porch and were about to head for the rockers when I saw that Tessa's car was still parked. My eyes zeroed in on her form hunched over the steering wheel, her shoulders shaking. *What the hell?*

I didn't think, I just strode down the steps and towards her vehicle. I circled around the front and knocked on the driver's side window. She jumped. *Fuck. When would I learn that this girl required movements the speed of molasses?* I slowly opened the door.

"What's wrong?" The words came out way harsher than I had intended. I tried to gentle my tone. "What's going on?"

Tessa furiously wiped at her face. "It's nothing."

I crouched down next to the side of the car so that I was below her eye level. "It's obviously something."

She sniffled, trying to get the tears leaking from her eyes under control. "It's stupid, I don't even know why I'm crying. It's not a big deal." Her rambling would have been adorable if I weren't worried as hell. "My car," she finally got out, "it won't start."

My shoulders sagged with relief. Car problems I could deal with. I stood, extending a hand to Tessa. "Come on, let me give it a try."

She hesitated a moment before taking my hand and letting me help her out of the car. "Thank you." I hated how weak her voice sounded, how embarrassed she seemed.

I gave Tessa's hand a light squeeze and then released it. "It's no problem." I lowered myself into the sedan that looked like it was on its last legs. The seat creaked and groaned as I shifted it back. My blood began to heat, and I tightened my grip on the steering wheel. Tessa shouldn't be driving this car. No one should.

I turned the key in the ignition. Nothing. I tried again. A grinding sound came from the engine. *Shit.* I pulled out the key. Bending down, I tugged the release for the hood. Smoke billowed out. *Double shit.*

I could just buy her a new car, something that would keep her safe. It would be so easy. My hands flexed on the wheel. From the bit I'd come to discover about Tessa, I knew she'd never allow someone to do that. She'd barely accepted some drawing pencils.

What the hell? It wasn't like I regularly considered buying random women new cars, but there was just something about this girl.

I shoved the runaway train of thoughts from my mind and pushed up and out of the vehicle. "Let me see if I can figure out what's going on."

Tessa nodded, worrying her bottom lip between her teeth.

Walker strode across the front yard. "Car trouble?"

I waved a hand over the engine, attempting to clear the smoke. "Yup."

Walker let out a low whistle as he took in the situation. "That doesn't look good."

I gave a small shake of my head, hoping he'd get the message. Tessa did not need any extra worry at the moment.

Walker pulled out his phone. "One of my buddies is a mechanic. Owns the shop in town. I can have him come and take a look. Maybe tow it to his shop."

Tessa took a step forward. "Don't."

Walker's brows pulled together. "Why not? He's great with cars."

Tessa's cheeks reddened as she looked from Walker to the porch that was now full of people. "I really can't afford that right now." Tears began to fill her eyes again, and I had to fight the urge to sock Walker in the gut.

Jensen reached our group just as Tessa finished speaking. "I can front you the money, Tessa. Don't worry about it. You can just pay me back a little at a time, whenever you can."

The blush on Tessa's cheeks deepened as she stared down at her feet. I could see warring emotions battling on her face. I wasn't sure if she was worried that she wouldn't be able to pay Jensen back, or if it was something else that held her back from taking Jensen's offer. But I couldn't handle the emotion that seemed to dominate Tessa's expression. Shame.

I took a step closer to her. "Look, I used to work on cars with my grandfather. I still do it for fun now and then. Why don't you let me fix it for you? Then you'd just have to pay for parts." I was already planning to lie my ass off about how much those parts cost.

Tessa's gorgeous eyes met mine. "I can't ask you to do that."

I gave her my best genuine smile and shrugged my shoulders. "I don't have a lot to do around here right now. You'd honestly be doing me a favor. I could use a project."

Tessa studied me carefully as if searching for some hint of an ulterior motive. She pressed her lips together and gave her head a small shake as if to clear something from her mind. "Thank you."

"It's no big thing, really."

Her gaze broke away from mine as she looked out across the fields surrounding the Coles' ranch house. "It is to me."

Walker cleared his throat. "Well, that's settled."

Tessa's head jerked in Jensen's direction. "What about the horses? I won't have a way to get here in the morning."

Jensen waved a hand. "It's no big deal. I can switch your shift to the afternoons and give you a ride out here after work."

Tessa's battle with her pride was evident on her face. "If you're sure."

"I'm sure. Now, why don't I drive you back into town?"

Tessa nodded. "Thank you."

I bit back the words that wanted to escape my throat, that I could take her. I knew I'd pressed my luck about as far as it could go for one day. I was going to fix her car. I had a reason to be in touch. An excuse to see her. I had my in.

As Tessa followed Jensen to her SUV, she turned. Her dark hair blowing in the wind against the backdrop of the rolling hills was a breathtaking picture. Her gaze caught and held on mine. "Thank you again, Liam."

That gaze packed a punch. "Anytime."

She gave a small nod and went to hop into Jensen's vehicle.

I had what was probably a dopey smile on my face when a hard thump landed across my upper back. Walker. "Good man." I watched as the girls pulled out and headed down the gravel lane. I ignored Walker, but he pressed on. "You're not going to tell her how much this all costs, are you?"

"No way in hell." I met Walker's stare. "Whatever happened to her…it was bad." I didn't have the full picture, but I knew the kind of fear Tessa battled, the walls she had built. Nothing good was at the root of those things.

Walker's face darkened. "I know. I just wish she'd open up to someone."

I looked back to where Jensen's SUV was disappearing, leaving nothing but dust in its wake.

Not unlike the girl the vehicle carried.

CHAPTER
Eleven

Tessa

EARLY MORNING SUN FILTERED IN THROUGH THE WINDOW as my fingers ran over the worn edge of the postcard. I knew I should stop. If I kept rubbing circles on it, the paper would eventually disintegrate. But I couldn't resist its pull. I wanted to touch the card my mother had once held in her hands.

I dusted my finger over the lettering that formed *Sutter Lake*. This postcard was one of four items I owned that had belonged to my mother. The only four things that tied me to my origins. When I had looked at the various tickets Gena had purchased for me, destinations where I might begin my path to starting over, Oregon had tugged at my heartstrings.

I never knew why my mother had a postcard from the small Oregon town. I had no one to ask those kinds of questions. But last night, I had been given a piece of my own history. My great-grandparents had lived here. I wondered if there was a way to find out what their names were, where their house had been.

That's the thing about not having something, it only makes you want it that much more. A dull thud reverberated in my chest at the thought of family. Home. Roots. A place to belong. It all seemed like an impossibility. I was courting danger from just how involved I'd gotten with the people of Sutter Lake.

Danger for me. And for them. Gena's face flashed in my mind, and guilt swamped me. Six months after I'd fled DC, there had been a fire at her salon. She'd been inside. Gena had almost died that day. I'd tried to follow the story as much as I could from afar. The fire inspector had found evidence of arson, along with a note spray-painted on a wall. *Mind your own business.*

There was only one person it could've been. Garrett had stolen Gena's business, her livelihood, her sense of safety, and almost her life. I couldn't put anyone else at risk. But there was still a part of me that wanted to push for more. Home. Family. Roots.

One day. It was a promise. A vow. One day, I would be able to reach for those things. But after my discovery about Bethany, I no longer thought it would be because Garrett would lose interest in me.

I used to think that he would eventually grow bored. Once every couple of months, I would dedicate my research time to looking through Garrett's social media, local DC papers and news reports, anything I could think of.

He was always looking. Every few months, there was a new plea for information. A higher reward offered. I would study his face on the screen and fight a shiver. Garrett was always the picture of grief, a prominent man devastated by the loss of his fiancée.

I didn't kid myself. He didn't long for my presence. He was livid at his *property* being stolen. And now I knew, without a shadow of a doubt, that if he found me, he would kill me.

I blinked against the dryness in my eyes from staring off into space. My gaze refocused on the postcard. I had made it out. Made it to Sutter Lake. I was building a life. So, it wasn't as full or carefree as I would have liked just yet. It would be one day. One day, I would be totally free.

I gently placed the postcard back in the notebook that protected it. I carefully put the sketchbook back into my bag, checking to make sure my cash, taser, and other essentials were still in place. Not having access to a car had put me on edge. I didn't want to think about what would happen if I had to make a quick getaway in the next few days. But I just couldn't afford to take the advance Jensen had offered me. I needed the money I earned at this job to buy myself information.

I'd poured over the articles I'd printed out at the library, but there was nothing in them that I could use. What I needed was an investigator. Someone who could get police files. Someone who could interview people who had known Bethany and Garrett at the time. I nibbled on my bottom lip. *But how will I know if I can trust them?*

I knew Garrett had to have bought people off in the past. What if he found out that someone was looking into him? What if he paid the investigator more than I ever could to find out where I was? My stomach roiled. Garrett couldn't find me. The thought of having to leave Sutter Lake had my chest constricting.

I pushed up from the edge of my bed, slinging my bag over my shoulder. I wouldn't have to run. Everything was fine. I was safe. I would just keep hunting myself, as much as I could. Save my money. Maybe, eventually, I could find someone I trusted to help me take the next steps, whatever those might be. Grabbing my keys, I pulled open the door to my apartment, making sure to slip my small piece of paper into the jamb.

Heading downstairs, I hung my bag on the coat rack in the kitchen and turned on all the lights. I never listened to music before Jensen arrived and the Kettle opened for the day. I wanted to be able to hear every little sound—just in case.

I moved around the room in comfortably familiar patterns, prepping ingredients for my first recipes of the day. The work was almost a meditation, a way to calm my body and slow my mind. But this morning, my mind kept drifting to a certain hazel-eyed someone. His kindness to Noah. To me. The way his voice had hit me right in the chest when he sang.

I shook my head. *Stupid, stupid, stupid.* If there was one person on this Earth who I couldn't get involved with, it was Liam Fairchild. His face was recognized everywhere he went. People asked for autographs, snapped pictures. All it would take was one photo in the wrong place.

My hands grew damp at the thought. Garrett would absolutely lose his mind. I couldn't imagine anything that would make him more furious than me getting involved with someone who might have more influence than he did.

I shook my head. I was being ridiculous. Liam had no interest in me. He was just a nice guy. That was all. A nice guy, helping out his friend's friend. That was it. I was blowing this all out of proportion.

A key sounded in the lock at the back door. I stilled until I heard Jensen's familiar tone. "I'm here, and I'm in desperate need of caffeine."

I let out a light laugh. "One green tea coming up." I set to work heating some water and readying the tea leaves.

Jensen kissed my cheek as she walked through the kitchen. "You are a goddess."

I snorted. "You're certainly easy to please this morning."

She stowed her bag under the register in the front and then headed back in my direction. "Noah was in a mood this morning. Cranky about everything. I didn't have the right cereal. I packed his lunch in the wrong lunch box. It was never-ending."

"Sorry, J." I studied her face. The circles under her eyes were darker. I bit my tongue against the urge to ask her if she was sleeping. I'd promised not to press. "Is there anything I can do to help? I can watch him for you if you need a night off."

Jensen shook her head. "You sound like Tuck."

My eyebrows rose. "Tuck offered to babysit?"

She let out an aggravated noise from the back of her throat. "He basically told me that I looked like shit and that I should let him watch Noah so I could get a good night's sleep."

I made a humming sound as I poured her tea. Tuck's delivery may have been lacking in finesse, but I didn't disagree with him. "Here you go." I handed her the mug.

"Thanks." Jensen took a sip. "So, how are you doing? Feeling any better?"

I could feel the familiar blush creeping up my cheeks, my overreaction at my car trouble still fresh in my mind. "I'm sorry I was such an emo mess last night. It had just been a long day." More like a long couple of years. I pretty much always felt like I was one thing away from a meltdown of epic proportions.

Jensen set her mug down on the counter. "You never have to apologize for something like that. We all have bad days, and car trouble is the freaking worst."

I pressed my lips together. "Well, thank you again for giving me a ride. And for switching around my schedule at the ranch."

"You'd do the same for me."

I nodded. I would do anything for Jensen. She had taken a chance on me when I had nothing to give her but a promise that I could bake.

She cleared her throat. "So…" She let the word dangle. "Liam seemed pretty keen on helping you out." A mischievous grin spread across her face.

I groaned. "He was just being nice."

Jensen chuckled. "Nice is offering you a ride. Offering to fix your car himself with rock star hands that are probably insured for millions of dollars? That's something else entirely."

I could feel the blood drain from my face. "I didn't even think about his hands."

Jensen stood, reaching over to still my suddenly staccato movements. "I was just giving you a hard time. You heard him. He does this for fun. He knows what he's doing."

I really hoped he did. I did not need a ruined billion-dollar career on my conscience. Jensen gave my arm a squeeze. "It's fine. I just liked the attention he was paying you. Maybe Irma isn't too far off in her predictions this time."

I pressed my lips together and shook my head. "Nothing's going to happen there."

"Well, why the frick not? He definitely seemed interested to me. And, as my grandma said, he's one handsome piece of man meat."

I returned my attention to the scone dough in front of me. "Because I don't want it to." The words tasted sour on my tongue. It might be a lie, but I wished it were the truth.

I straightened from my crouch behind the bakery case, sliding the door closed now that the shelves were freshly restocked.

"Hello again, Tessa."

I lifted my gaze at the greeting. It was the man from the other day. Al. The one with lots of questions. I gritted my teeth but nodded quickly. "Hello."

He eyed the bakery display. "What looks good today?"

I looked to Jensen for an assist, but she was busy helping another customer. "The huckleberry muffins are good."

Al grinned. "That sounds great. I'll take one of those for here, please."

I grabbed a muffin with the tongs lying at the back of the case and put the pastry on one of our mismatched china plates. "Here you go." I handed him the plate. "Jensen will ring you up." I turned to head back to the kitchen, but Al's voice stopped me.

"Can I ask you for some local recommendations?"

I slowly turned back around. *Don't be rude. Don't be rude.* "Sure."

He gave me a grin that seemed just a bit fake. "What's the best spot for some dinner grub?"

I toyed with the ties on my apron. "The saloon down the street has the best burgers in the county. Or there's a Mexican restaurant two blocks over with great *queso*."

Al rubbed his stomach. "A burger sounds like just what the doctor ordered. Is that your favorite restaurant?"

My eyes narrowed just a bit. "I have lots of favorites."

He let out a low chuckle. "I guess you can't pick just one being a fellow small business employee."

I shrugged. "I better get back to work."

"Oh, of course. Thanks again for the muffin and restaurant recommendation."

"You're welcome." I turned again and was almost to the kitchen when a different voice called my name. *What now?*

When I pivoted, I came face-to-face with the man I'd sworn off a few hours earlier. My heart rate picked up speed. Liam stood to the side of the counter, motioning me over. He wore dark jeans and a plaid flannel with the sleeves rolled up on his muscular forearms. His hair looked just a touch darker than usual, as though it were still damp from a shower. The moss green in his eyes seemed to twinkle.

I glanced around the café. No one seemed to be paying us much attention. I let out a breath of relief and stepped towards Liam. "Hi."

He grinned. This smile was nothing like the false one Al had worn. It was full of life. Genuine. "I'm just about to go pick up some parts for your car but thought I'd drop by and grab a snack first."

My eyebrows lifted. "You've already started working on it?"

"Been hard at work all morning. I actually don't think the repairs are going to be too bad. I think the smoke just made it look worse than it was."

My shoulders relaxed, releasing the tension I hadn't realized they'd been carrying since the night before. "That is a huge relief.

Thank you so much for doing this."

A hint of pink touched the apples of Liam's cheeks. "No problem. Like I said, you're really doing me a favor by giving me a bit of purpose."

I wasn't so sure about that. "Well, thank you anyway."

Liam flipped his cell phone between his fingers in intricate patterns that would have had my phone crashing to the floor and shattering into a thousand pieces. "Listen, I was wondering… would you want to grab dinner with me tonight?"

The muscles that had relaxed tightened again. "I'm sorry, I can't." I hated the words the minute they left my mouth.

Liam's brow furrowed. "How about another night?"

I fisted the edge of my apron. "I, um, don't date." It was the most truthful statement I could come up with.

Liam's eyes searched mine. His look was warm and compassionate, yet searching for something. "All right. Well, you let me know if that ever changes. I should have your car ready for you in a few days."

I let out a breath I hadn't realized I'd been holding. I'd been preparing myself for anger, or at the very least, frustration. I shuddered at what Garrett would have done if I ever told him no. Guilt flooded me. Liam was not Garrett. I had to stop assuming the worst. I could be cautious and prepared without thinking that every man in the world was a Garrett in the making.

"Okay." The word came out on a whisper. "Thank you for asking me." I couldn't hold his stare as I said it, opting for the riveting view of the floor instead.

"Nothing ventured, nothing gained, right?"

I looked back up, the warmth in Liam's eyes holding me captive. "Right."

He knocked on the edge of the counter. "I'll see you in a few days."

"Okay." I watched as he walked out, realizing that he didn't get his snack. I started to follow when my gaze caught on a figure across the street, one in a ballcap. My breathing and heart seemed to stop. He was staring right through the windows of the shop. *No, no, no.* I blinked my eyes a few times as my hands fisted. *Garrett?* Similar build, but I couldn't see his face. My breathing started again but came in rapid pants.

The figure turned and waved to a woman heading towards him. I stilled my trembling hands against my legs. Not Garrett. Just a tourist in a baseball cap. I needed to get a grip.

CHAPTER
Twelve

Liam

THE BELL SOUNDED AS I PUSHED OPEN THE DOOR TO The Tea Kettle. Jensen and Tessa looked up from the sheet of paper they were studying on the counter. Jensen grinned. "Back for more?"

Seeing that the café was mostly empty, I pulled off my ballcap. "I'm hoping those chocolate potato chip cookies made it onto the menu." My gaze met Tessa's. There was a little hint of pink on her cheeks. So fucking adorable. "And I wanted to update Tessa about her car."

Jensen looked from me to Tessa, and her grin widened. "Well, you'll be happy to know the chocolate potato chip cookies were a hit. I think you're making those next, right, Tessa?"

Tessa wrapped and unwrapped the string of her apron around her finger. "They should be ready in about an hour if you're going to stick around."

"I was going to hang out and work for a bit, this place has some good creative mojo." More like Tessa had some good creative mojo, but I didn't think admitting that would work in my favor. And I needed all the help I could get. I tightened my grip on the battered notebook in my hand. I'd gotten an email from my label that morning, asking when I thought I'd be ready to get back in the studio. Since all I had was the flicker of one song, I wasn't thinking anytime soon. *Fuck.* I needed the music to start flowing again.

Jensen broke my downward spiral of thoughts. "You're welcome to work here."

"Thanks." I looked back at Tessa. "I also wanted to let you know that they had to order a few parts for your car, so it's going to take a bit longer than I thought." A flash of worry filled Tessa's expression before she covered it. "I could take you to get a rental car if that would help."

Tessa shook her head. "No, I'll be fine. Thanks again for doing this for me."

"It's no problem. Like I said, you're giving me something to do." Something other than slamming my head against a wall, trying to write.

Tessa studied me, a bit of curiosity tinging her gaze. "Aren't you working on your music?"

"I'm trying to." I wasn't quite ready to admit what a total failure I'd been on that front lately. "But it helps to have something else to work on when I'm writing, especially a project using my hands. But even just a change of scenery can help."

Tessa nodded. "Well, good luck with it. I better get that dough made."

She made her way back to the kitchen, and I was left alone with Jensen. She smirked at me. "Why do I have a feeling it's not our baked goods bringing you back to our fine establishment?"

I felt heat creep up my neck. "Are you doubting the quality of your baked goods?"

Jensen scoffed. "I know lust when I see it, Hollywood. Just tread carefully, okay?"

"Is there a particular reason I should be careful?" I had no plans to be reckless with Tessa, but I wanted to see if Jensen would give me any clues about Tessa's past.

Jensen's eyes narrowed on me. "If you have to ask that question, you shouldn't be sniffing around in the first place."

I held up my hands in a placating gesture. "Fair enough." I met Jensen's gaze, letting her see nothing but honesty in mine. "I'm being as careful as I can." The set of Jensen's shoulders eased a bit. "Now, how about loading me up with some music-writing fuel?"

"That I can do."

I scribbled furiously, scratching out a handful of words and replacing them with new finds. I was getting there. Closer, anyway. I just needed one more line in this verse—

The chair across from me scraped against the floor as it was pulled back. The bottle blonde from my first visit to the Kettle eased onto the seat. I tried to keep the scowl from my lips. I really didn't want to be interrupted, not when I was making progress on a song for the first time in months.

The blonde...what was her name? Bambi? Barbara? No, Bridgette. Bridgette leaned over the table, giving me a perfect view of the breasts she was pressing together. "Hey, Liam."

"Hey." That's all I gave her. If she'd been a true fan, I would've been more polite. But I knew her type, you gave them an inch, and they took a mile.

She twisted a strand of hair around her finger. "Are you settling in okay?"

"Yup."

"You know..."—Bridgette leaned over even farther, and I worried her boobs would spill right out of her top—"my father owns a lot of rental properties in the area. Places that have more of the amenities you're used to. He'd be happy to let you stay at one for free—"

I held up a hand to stop her. "I'm happy where I'm at. Thanks for the offer, though."

A flicker of frustration flashed in Bridgette's eyes. "Just let me know if you change your mind. So…" She reached across the table, picking up my pen. "Working on new music? Can I hear some?"

My back teeth ground together. Some people had no boundaries. It was like because they saw you in magazines or heard your voice on the radio, they thought they could ask you anything. It was rare that I revealed what I was working on with the people I trusted most in my life, I sure as hell wasn't going to share with a random chick I barely even knew.

Just as I was about to tell her as much, Tessa appeared from the kitchen holding a tray of cookies. Her hair was piled on the top of her head, but some wisps had escaped the bun and framed her heart-shaped face. Her eyes seemed to glow as she laughed at something Jensen said to her.

A hand grasped my forearm that was resting on the table. "Liam—"

Bridgette's voice was grating on my ears compared to the purity of Tessa's laugh. It also brought Tessa's attention to our table, and her eyes zeroed in on Bridgette's hand on my arm. *Shit.* I pulled out of Bridgette's grasp. "Are those the chocolate potato chip ones?"

Tessa straightened her shoulders. "Yep. They'll be in the case if you want one." And with that, she made a hasty retreat to the kitchen. *Double shit.*

Bridgette let out a laugh. "God, she's so weird. Even the stuff she bakes is weird." Her words were purposefully loud, carrying into the kitchen.

I stood from my chair. "You're a real bitch, you know that?"

CHAPTER
Thirteen

Tessa

I PUSHED THROUGH THE BACK DOOR AND INTO THE LATE-morning sunlight. I needed air. Remnants of the jolt of jealousy I'd felt when I saw Bridgette touching Liam still simmered in my veins. I had no right to be jealous. Liam had asked me to dinner, I'd said no. Of course, he would investigate other options. Though I didn't know what it said about his intelligence that he would consider Bridgette as one of those options.

I kicked a rock across the small parking lot and into the alley. I had wanted to say yes to his offer of dinner. That surprised me most of all. I had wanted to say yes. I was so tired of Garrett and my fears holding me back, but I couldn't see a way around them or a path through them.

The sound of the back door closing had me spinning around. Liam stood there, looking handsome and oh so pissed. "Are you okay?"

I wiped my hands on my apron. "I'm fine, just taking my break."

Irritation flickered in his eyes. "Don't lie to me. That girl is a bitch and a half, and you shouldn't have to deal with anyone treating you that way."

My brows rose. It wasn't that Bridgette's words didn't sting, I'd just gotten used to them. "I don't care what she thinks of me." It was true. But I did care if it colored Liam's perception.

"Good, because she's lower than a snake's belly in a wagon rut."

The expression and the complete sincerity with which Liam said it startled a laugh out of me. "Lower than a snake's belly in a wagon rut?"

Liam chuckled, running a hand through his hair. "When I get pissed, my Southern comes out."

"Clearly. I appreciate you being pissed on my behalf, but it's really not necessary."

Liam took a step closer to me, the green in his eyes seeming to glow in the sunlight. My belly flipped. He stopped just a foot away from me. "I can't stand people like her. She reminds me of everything I wanted to get away from in LA."

"What do you mean?" I realized I wasn't sure why Liam was in Sutter Lake.

He looked out across the field on the other side of the back alley. "Fake, judgemental people. Folks who are so eager to tear others down."

My body tensed at the thought of what it must be like to be surrounded by people like that all the time. You'd never feel like you could let your guard down.

Liam looked back at me. "It gets so old, people wanting a piece of you without caring at all who they're actually getting a piece of."

Our gazes locked. I knew a little something about that. It was different but the same, the way Garrett had taken pieces of me, not caring at all who I actually was or who I wanted to be.

Liam's eyes widened as a car's engine sounded behind me. I started to turn, to look and see what it was, but before I could, Liam yanked me forward with such force it startled a scream out of me. Air rushed by at my back. Out of the corner of my eye, I saw a dark SUV fly by.

"Fuck! What the hell was that guy thinking?" Liam pushed me away from the hard body I'd slammed into when he pulled me against him. His gaze traveled over my face, scanning up and down the length of me. "Are you all right?"

My entire body began to tremble. What had just happened? Careless driver, or something more? Could Garrett have found me?

"Tessa? Are you okay?"

My vision went a bit blurry, and I couldn't seem to get the words out.

Liam kept a hold of one of my hands and ushered me towards the back door. "Come on. Let's get you inside and get you something to drink."

I nodded numbly.

Liam navigated me towards the kitchen, sitting me on a stool while he searched for a glass and filled it with water. He pushed it into my hands. "Here, drink some of this."

Jensen peeked her head in. "What's going on?"

Liam scowled. "Some asshole just tore through the back alley in his SUV. He nearly ran Tessa over."

"Seriously? Are you okay, Tessa?" She crossed to me, rubbing a hand up and down my back.

I swallowed, straightening on the stool. "I'm fine. Just scared me for a minute there."

Jensen's hands went to her hips. "Of course, it did. It has to be one of those dipshit high school boys. There's a few of them that think it's hilarious to play speed racer in areas you're only supposed to go twenty miles an hour."

Liam's scowl deepened. "You should tell Walker what happened so he can keep an eye out."

Jensen turned in his direction. "Did you get a license plate? If you did, Walker can arrest them and scare the shit out of them for good measure."

"I didn't get a good look. It all happened so fast, and I was worried about getting Tessa out of the way." Liam studied me carefully. "Are you sure you're okay?"

I forced what felt like a wobbly smile. "I'm fine, really." *It was just immature boys.*

CHAPTER
Fourteen

Liam

ANOTHER EVENING WITH NO PLANS. HERE I WAS, wandering the streets of Sutter Lake, finding myself pulled towards The Tea Kettle. Tessa had already said no to dinner, and the pain in her eyes when I'd asked meant that I wouldn't be repeating that question anytime soon.

What was it about Tessa? I couldn't put my finger on it. Maybe it was the mystery surrounding her. All the unanswered questions. Maybe it was because I had written my first lyrics in months when I was around her. Maybe it was just that she pulled back instead of leaning forward. I had gotten so used to people clamoring for my attention, it was weirdly nice that Tessa seemed to have no need for it.

I rounded the corner that brought the Kettle into view—closed up tight for the night, no one sitting on the porch. Disappointment flooded me. I'd gotten my hopes up for a few traded words. A glimpse of those hypnotizing eyes.

My gaze caught on a figure bent over near the side of the building. A long, brown braid hung down the figure's back. My heart picked up speed, just a little, as did my stride. This time, I remembered her jumpiness and called out while I was still more than ten feet away. "Hey, Tessa."

Her head snapped in my direction, her braid swinging around. My footsteps stuttered when I caught sight of her face.

It was white as a sheet, her expression stricken. "Liam. Can you help me? I don't know what to do. I think his leg might be broken. I don't have a car to take him to a vet, and my phone just died. Who would do this to a little defenseless thing like him?" Her words ran together like one long, run-on sentence.

"Hold on, what's going—?" My words halted when I saw the tiny orange ball of fur in her hands. *Shit.*

Tessa held up the kitten for my inspection. "His leg and his back. Look."

The poor creature's fur was matted with blood. A long gash ran along its back, and one of the kitten's legs looked bent at an angle that wasn't natural. "Okay. We need to get him to a vet. Is there one in town?"

Tessa glanced at her watch, cradling the kitten carefully in her other hand. "Not one that's open now. There's an emergency vet the next town over, but I don't have my car."

"I've got my SUV around the corner, we can take that." I started to walk, but Tessa didn't follow. Her gaze went from me to the kitten to the building behind us, her brows pinched together as if following me would cause her physical pain. My stomach dropped. Someone had hurt her badly. I wanted to rip whoever it was limb from limb. This woman's trust was nonexistent.

I pulled out my phone. "Do you want me to call Jensen instead? It might take her a bit to get here, but I'll wait with you until she does."

Tessa looked down at the kitten in her arms and then straightened her spine. "No. There's not enough time. Just let me grab my bag."

"Okay." Why did her acquiescence to just riding in the car with me feel like I'd just won the lottery?

Tessa walked quickly but carefully up the porch and grabbed her purse. "Can you pull up Caldwell Mill Animal Clinic on your phone so you know where we're heading?"

I punched in the name on my screen, bringing up a map. "Let's go."

We hurried down the street and back towards my Escalade. I went straight to the passenger-side door, beeping the locks and pulling it open. Tessa did a good job of disguising her hesitation, her stride stalling only briefly before she forced herself forward and up into the vehicle. That hesitation, I realized, was pure fear. The knowledge burned my gut.

I did my best to hide the rage that was now scorching my veins. I slowly, and with as little force as possible, closed the door behind her. Jogging, I rounded the car and got in, bringing the engine to life. "How's he doing?" I asked with a quick glance in Tessa's direction.

Her face was filled with worry as she stared down at the kitten. "I'm not sure." The poor guy was wrapped in Tessa's flannel shirt. I took in the fact that she was wearing only a tank top and that the temperature outside was in the forties.

I reached into my backseat with one hand while my other remained on the wheel. I felt around for the sweatshirt I'd tossed back there the other day before my run. "Here you go. You must be cold."

Our fingers brushed as I handed her the bundle, her smooth skin sending shivers up my arm with just that barest touch.

"Thank you," she said, her voice soft. "I'll put it on when we get out of the car."

She didn't want to jostle the creature in her arms. I turned up the heat. The navigation on my phone called out directions and declared that we'd arrive in twelve minutes. I shifted in my seat. "Have you seen him around before?"

Tessa stroked a tiny part of the cat's fur that seemed unmarred. He let out a small meow. "Only once. I've been putting out milk, and he's been drinking that, but he hasn't wanted anyone to get too close, I don't think."

Sounded familiar. "The vet will be able to fix him up."

She nibbled on her bottom lip. "I hope so."

The minutes seemed to drag on and fly by at the same time. When I pulled up to the small animal hospital, Tessa was out of the SUV before I even had the thing turned off. I hurried after her, catching up by the time she reached the door. I pushed it open and held it for her.

Tessa rushed to the front desk. "I found this kitten, and he's hurt pretty bad. Can you help?"

The older woman stood and rounded the counter. "Oh, no, that poor baby. I'll take him back to the doctor right now."

Tessa hesitated for only half a second before placing the kitten in the other woman's arms. "Thank you."

"Of course, honey. Just have a seat, and someone will be out to talk to you when we know what's what." The woman turned and quickly headed to the back of the clinic.

Tessa turned, hands fisting around the sweatshirt I'd given her. "He's so tiny." A shudder wracked her body.

"Why don't you put that on," I suggested, pointing to the item in her hands. "You're cold." It was silly to focus on that when I knew she was so worried about her little friend. But this was something I could fix. Something in my control when so much else was out of it.

She nodded and slipped the cotton material over her head. There was a weird tightening in my chest when I saw her wearing my clothes. There seemed to be a rightness about it. I was officially losing it.

I shook my head and gestured towards the chairs in the waiting room. "Let's sit. Are you hungry? Can I get you anything?" Fuck, I sounded like a worried mother.

Tessa picked a chair in the empty waiting room and sat. "I'm fine."

I glanced at the other empty chairs. *Is it weird if I sit next to her? Weirder if I don't?* I went for it, lowering myself into the chair on her left.

Silence filled the room, the only sound the ticking of the second hand on a wall clock. I flipped my phone between my fingers, spinning it in circles.

"How do you do that and not drop it?" Tessa's voice almost made me drop the phone. It was the first real question she'd ever asked me, the first conversation she'd initiated, even if it was because we were in forced proximity.

I chuckled. "I've been doing it forever. Guitar picks, drumsticks, phones. Whatever's around. My hands like to stay busy. Hell, I'm pretty sure my mom put me in music lessons to keep me from destroying items in her house."

"It worked, apparently."

I glanced in Tessa's direction. Her cheeks were rosy against her creamy, white complexion. Peaches and cream, that's what she was. I cleared my throat. "It did. I became obsessed. It was rare I was ever more than arm's length from my guitar."

She nodded, studying me with a thoughtful expression. "You really love it, don't you? Making music."

My mind flashed back to her watching me play for Noah. "I love most of it."

A tiny furrow appeared in Tessa's brow. "What do you mean?"

I continued twirling the phone between my fingers as I tried to think of a way to explain how I felt about it all. "The thing I love most is the creation. A concept can come to me in a million different ways. It's never exactly the same. Sometimes, it's a melody running through the back of my mind. Sometimes, it's a lyric that jumps up out of nowhere. Sometimes, it's a feeling that I'm doing my best to capture." It had been so long since I'd felt the pleasure of creating like that. My label's restrictions and requirements pressed down and stifled any creative joy I might have had.

A wistful smile took over Tessa's face. "That sounds magical."

"It is."

She tucked a strand of hair behind her ear. "What don't you like?"

That pressure clamped down on my shoulders, but I forced a chuckle. "What don't I like? I don't like the kind of box my label is forcing me into. I don't like the paparazzi hounding my every move, and the media making up ludicrous stories. I don't like that whole world."

I'd never actually said any of that out loud before. I'd always been aware that it would make me sound like a pompous ass, ungrateful for everything I had been given. I met Tessa's gaze, afraid of the disgust I might see there.

There was only understanding and empathy. "You probably feel like every move you make will be scrutinized. Always afraid you'll make a mistake, and there will be hell to pay."

My eyes widened just a bit. Tessa got it. "That's it at the core."

Her gaze drifted away. "That's no way to live."

"No, it's not." I leaned back in my chair. "But it's been nice here. People pretty much leave me alone." Well, other than that Bridgette chick, but I was sure she'd gotten the message now. "The fans that do come up to me don't post photos. No one even knows I'm in Oregon. It's a miracle."

Tessa played with the strings on my hoodie. "I'm glad you've gotten that here. Sutter Lake is a pretty special place."

I watched the flickering light from above play over her face. God, she was gorgeous. "It is pretty special."

Footsteps squeaked against the linoleum floor, and both Tessa and I got to our feet. An older gentleman wearing scrubs and a medical jacket rounded the corner. "Hello there, I'm Dr. Maroney."

I reached out to shake his hand while Tessa just nodded. "What can you tell us?" I asked.

Dr. Maroney's face grew somber. "I'm afraid the little guy has been through the wringer. I think he might have been hit by a bike or even clipped by a car. I've stitched up the wound on his back, but I'm afraid the break on his leg is going to require surgery."

I peeked at Tessa. Tears filled her eyes, but she did her best to hold them back as she fisted the material of my sweatshirt so hard her knuckles turned white. I met the vet's gaze. "Do whatever you need to."

Dr. Maroney laced his fingers in front of him. "I have to warn you, surgeries like this are risky and can be expensive. I can have Dolores ring up an estimate for you—"

I cut him off. "That's not necessary. Just do whatever you can to fix him up. Cost isn't an issue."

The vet's brows rose ever so slightly. "All right. We'll do the surgery first thing tomorrow. Let's just have you fill out some paperwork first."

Tessa and I settled back into chairs as I filled out forms with my contact and billing information. A delicate hand brushed my arm. The touch was light, barely contact at all, but heat flared where her skin met mine.

"Thank you for doing this."

I swallowed against the dryness in my throat. "Of course. We need to get that tiny guy fit to fight another day."

A small smile pulled at her lips. "It's really kind of you."

Heat crept up the back of my neck. "It's nothing."

Tessa's hand squeezed my arm for a brief second and then released it. "It's everything to him."

Leaning forward, I punched the dial on my SUV's stereo, music from an oldies station drifting from the speakers, a remedy to the silence that had been filling the vehicle. I relaxed back in my seat.

My gaze flitted over to Tessa. Her fingers twisted and untwisted the strings of my hoodie into and out of intricate knots as she stared out the window. The passing scenery was dark now, the trees casting ominous shadows on the road.

I cleared my throat. "Why don't you put your number in my phone." I slid the device out of the cupholder and held it in her direction. She stared at it for a good five count. I pressed on. "That way, I can text you when I hear from the vet tomorrow."

Tessa lifted the phone from my fingers. "Oh, right. Of course." Those same delicate fingers that had made my arm flare with heat tapped on the screen. "It's in there." She dropped the cell back into the cupholder.

The notes of Creedence Clearwater Revival's *Have You Ever Seen the Rain* were the only sound now. The song ebbed and flowed. When the final lyrics ran out, Tessa shifted in her seat. "Do you think he'll be okay?"

I couldn't help the small grin that came to my lips. Tessa was a total tender heart. "I think he's a fighter."

She nodded, looking back out the window. "You're right. He's strong. He was so tiny, but somehow, he's made it on his own this long."

I wondered how long Tessa had been on her own. The question escaped me before I could think better of it. "How long have you lived in Sutter Lake?"

Tessa stiffened in her seat. "Why?"

I shrugged a shoulder, doing my best to sound casual. "Just curious. I know you didn't grow up with the Cole family, so I assumed you moved here at some point."

She licked her perfect bow lips, the action making me sit up a little straighter. "About two years."

I wanted to know more. I wanted to know everything. "Where did you move from?" Even if she didn't answer, her reaction might tell me something.

Tessa wiped her hands on her jeans. "The east coast."

"Where back there?"

A touch of heat flared in her eyes. "You're really nosy, you know that?"

I had to bite the inside of my cheek to keep from laughing. "Okay...why don't you ask me something then?" Maybe if I turned the tables, I could get her to relax.

Tessa crossed her arms and stared out the window. "There isn't anything I want to know."

I drummed my fingers on the steering wheel. "Look, I know you have no interest in going out with me, but that doesn't mean we can't be friends, right?" She sent me a dubious look. "I only know a handful of people here. Taylor's all wrapped up in Walker, young love and all that. I could use some more friends."

Tessa let out a sigh. "I can't be a very good friend." Her words were soft, almost ashamed.

My tapping fingers stilled. "Why do you think that?"

"I *know* that. Because I can't talk to you about my past, and if you push me, I'll bite your head off like I did a few seconds ago. How can you be friends with someone who won't let you know them?"

Tessa's words broke my fucking heart. If this were truly how she felt she had to live her life, she must be incredibly lonely. A muscle in my cheek ticked. "Okay, no past. I can work with that."

Tessa's eyes widened a fraction. "You can work with that?"

"I can." I sent her a smile. "As long as you're good with telling me your favorite foods, I feel fairly confident we can build a friendship around that."

A surprised laugh erupted from Tessa. The sound was everything music should be. I knew in that moment I'd work my ass off to capture it in a song and make my inspiration repeat the noise as much as possible.

She leaned back in her seat. "Taylor mentioned you're easily motivated with food."

I let out a sound of affront. "What a little traitor that one is."

Tessa's smile widened, and I felt as if someone elbowed me in the gut. Jesus, that was lethal. "Good thing I know my way around the kitchen, then. I can always get you to do my bidding." She seemed almost surprised that the words had come out of her mouth, shocked that she would actually joke with me.

I didn't want the moment to end. "I'm perfectly fine with you bribing me with baked goods for any and all bidding."

Tessa began twisting the strings of my hoodie again, but the smile didn't fall from her face.

I pulled into the drive of my rented cabin to find Walker leaning against the door of his truck. I swung in next to him and hopped out, doing my best to hide what I was sure was a dopey grin on my face. Tessa had agreed to friendship. It might as well have been the keys to the fucking kingdom.

"Where have you been hiding? I was just about to give up on you," Walker called as he pushed off his rig.

I rounded my SUV. "Did we have plans?"

Walker reached into the bed of his truck, retrieving a pile of Tupperware. "Nope. But my mom was worried you might be starving to death over here, so she sent me over with a world of leftovers."

I rubbed my hands together with glee. "Come to Papa." Whatever it was smelled delicious.

He handed me the stack of goodies. "So, what have you been up to?"

I took the pile and motioned for him to follow me inside. "I ran into Tessa."

Walker's brows rose. "And how'd that go?"

I unlocked the front door and pushed it open, moving inside.

"Well, she found a kitten she'd been taking care of beat to hell. He was hit by something. We're not sure what. So, I took her and him to the emergency vet."

"That girl has a soft center." Walker scrubbed a hand over his jaw. "I'm honestly surprised she got in a car with you alone. She's never ridden with me, Tuck, or my dad. No man I know of."

Something about that filled my heart with pride. Tessa had been desperate, sure, but she'd given me that little bit of trust anyway. "I'm hoping she'll start to let me in a little more now, but I'm not sure. Any ideas?"

Walker tapped a finger against his lips. "Horses."

"Horses?"

Walker grinned. "Yup, she's real close to those wild horses of Jensen's. I bet if you invite her to do something involving horses, she might just say yes."

Horses it was.

CHAPTER
Fifteen

Tessa

I HUMMED AS I FLITTED AROUND THE KITCHEN, PUTTING the finishing touches on some cupcakes. My good mood had made its way to the confections in front of me, each cupcake decorated in an artful array of colors. I sprinkled pink sugar crystals on one, my mind drifting to the various texts I'd received over the past few days.

The first let me know that my sweet little kitten friend had made it through surgery with flying colors. The vet wanted to keep him at the clinic for about a week, but he was optimistic that the little guy would make a complete recovery.

Then the inquisition started. Usually, questions made me clam up and run for the hills, but Liam kept his promise. Nothing about my past. And true to his word, the questions mostly revolved around food.

Liam: *What's your favorite kind of cookie?*

Me: *What?*

Liam: *These are the important questions that are vital to our friendship. Favorite kind of cookie?*

Me: *Uh, gingersnap.*

Liam: *Interesting.*

Liam: *Hamburgers or hot dogs?*

Me: *Trick question. Cheeseburger.*

I laughed softly at the reminder. The easier the questions that came, the more my guard lowered, and the more I was charmed by Liam's unexpected and gentle humor.

A knock sounded on the doorway to the kitchen. I spun, the bag of icing I held in my hands erupting as I did. The frosting landed right smack in the middle of Liam Fairchild's chest. My hand flew to my mouth.

He looked down at his icing-covered shirt and then up at me. "Well, to be fair, I was going to ask for a cupcake."

Taylor, who had been standing behind him, dissolved into laughter. "His need to get to the food finally gets the best of him."

"Shut it." Liam turned, swiping some of the frosting with his finger and attempting to wipe it on Taylor's face.

Taylor dashed out of his reach and ducked behind me. "Save me, Tessa!"

I couldn't help the giggle that rose. Reaching behind me, I grabbed my mixing spoon. "Now, Liam, that's no way to treat a lady."

Liam pressed forward, frosting-covered finger extended. "That's no lady. That's a traitor."

Taylor peeked out from behind me. "Liam Fairchild, you wipe that frosting on me, and I'll tell Sarah not to give you any more leftovers."

Liam's hand and jaw dropped. "You wouldn't."

Taylor grinned. "I would."

"You don't fight fair."

Taylor released her hold on me, victorious. "I fight to win."

"Here." I handed Liam a towel. "Sorry about that." My cheeks heated.

Liam took the cloth from my hand, our fingers brushing for a brief second, sending a tingle up my arm. "No big thing. If I had to be mortally wounded, death by frosting would be a good way to go."

I ducked my head. "So, what are you guys doing here?" I

looked at Taylor, but she pointed at Liam.

"I'm here to tell you we're going horseback riding today. When you get off at two."

I set the empty bag of frosting down on the counter. "I don't know."

Taylor squeezed my shoulder. "I promise you, he's harmless. Well, as long as you don't come between him and his next meal, he's harmless."

I wanted to laugh, but all I could think about was how Garrett had seemed harmless at first, too. I'd thought he was kind and charming. How wrong I'd been. I squeezed my eyes closed. *Not every man is Garrett.*

Liam cleared his throat. "I invited Noah to go with us, too. I hope that's okay."

My eyes opened to Liam's hesitant face. There was uncertainty there that said he was worried he might have overstepped. I let out the breath I had been holding. A ride would be okay. Especially if Noah was along. "I guess I could go for an hour or so."

The smile that lit Liam's face hit me right in the ovaries. He couldn't just unleash that thing on the unsuspecting public. It was way too dangerous. "Awesome. I'll come back to get you in a couple hours."

"You don't need to pick me up. I'll just take—" I was about to say, "take my car," but my car was currently being put back together by the man who stood in front of me.

Liam grinned. The tilt of his lips was more mischievous than anything, but the effect was no less devastating to my nerve endings. "Like I said, I'll pick you up in a couple hours."

My stomach churned, my body battling against the protections I'd had in place for so long. I reminded myself that I had ridden with Liam the other night. But that was an emergency, an override of my rules and boundaries to save the life of a tiny, defenseless kitten. If I rode with Liam today, I'd be putting myself at risk for no other reason than I wanted to experience an afternoon of adventure with him.

It was playing with fire. Liam could hurt me. I didn't think he would, but you could never be one hundred percent sure of these things. *I* could hurt Liam. Not me exactly, but if Garrett ever found out, my selfish proximity to Liam could cost him everything.

I closed my eyes against the swarm of guilt, but I couldn't deny one simple fact: I wanted to go.

I opened my eyes, meeting Liam's familiar gaze, the same one that said he was still examining all my pieces and getting closer and closer to figuring out where they went. "I'll be ready."

Liam's shoulders sagged the slightest bit as his muscles relaxed. "Great. I'll see you then."

Taylor said nothing but squeezed my arm and gave me an encouraging smile. Then, they were gone.

My stomach was in a million knots. Sweat trickled down my back. This was a bad idea. What had I been thinking, agreeing to this?

The state of my nerves had been made worse by the fact that I'd spent my break on Jensen's laptop, devouring more articles about Bethany. I'd come across a small blurb in the campus newspaper about her reporting Garrett for domestic abuse. It sounded like no one had believed her.

God, did I know how that felt. To have the one person you trusted above all others betray that trust in the worst possible way, and then have no one believe it had happened. It was brutal. So, what in the world was I doing opening myself up to someone else, risking them betraying me like that? Some little voice inside told me that Liam would never do that, but maybe I was a total idiot for listening to that voice.

I paced back and forth in the small space for employee parking at the back of the Kettle. I'd texted Liam earlier to tell him to pick me up here. The last thing I needed was people seeing me getting into his car.

I tightened my grip on my bag as the familiar black SUV with its tinted windows pulled up. Liam shut off the engine and hopped out. I stayed put. Not even how handsome he looked in jeans, boots, and a ballcap could distract me from the sheer terror flowing through my veins.

Liam came to a stop in front of me. The smile he'd been wearing slowly slipped from his face as he took in my expression. "Tessa. We don't have to do this. We can wait. There's no rush. Or, I can call Taylor and see if she and Walker can come with us. We'll make it a big group thing."

My heart wanted to break at his kindness, his understanding, the way he never pushed too much. He seemed to be a master of gentle pressure. Enough to encourage me out of my comfort zone, but not so much that I felt bullied. "I'm scared."

It was his kindness that let me utter that one truth. Liam crouched just a bit so that he no longer towered over me. "What can I do to make you feel safe?"

I wanted to throw myself into Liam's arms and tell him everything, beg him to stand between me and anything Garrett could throw at me. But that wasn't fair to Liam. And how was running to another man for help going to change anything for me in the long run? I needed to stand on my own two feet. *I* needed to be in control. "Can I drive?"

Liam straightened, surprise creasing his features. "You want to drive my car?"

I nodded.

He rubbed a hand over his jaw. "That will make you feel safer?"

I nodded again.

Our eyes locked as he seemed to try and understand why I'd make such a request. *Who would put up with all my weird requirements and tics for more than a few days? Hell, more like a few minutes.*

Liam tossed me his keys. "She's all yours."

My brows rose. "Really?"

Liam's gaze met mine, a sincerity in them that nearly cracked my heart in two. "Whatever you need. Okay?"

"Okay." The word came out as a whisper.

Liam clapped his hands together. "Let's hit the road. There's an eight-year-old boy back at the ranch who's driving his grandma crazy asking when it's time for his horseback ride."

A small smile curved my mouth. "Can't keep Noah waiting."

"No, we can't."

Liam and I got into his SUV. I had to adjust the seat and mirrors to fit my much shorter height, but in a minute or two, we were off.

Liam tapped his finger in a staccato beat on the armrest. "So. Cake or pie?"

I burst out laughing. It was just the question I needed. "Cake. Definitely."

He made a humming sound at the back of his throat. "What's your favorite kind?"

I pulled onto the main road out of town. "I'm kind of a purist when it comes to cake. Vanilla butter cake with vanilla buttercream icing."

Liam's brows inched up. "I thought every girl loved chocolate more than anything."

Paved roads turned to gravel. "Not this girl. I mean, I like chocolate, but vanilla cake is my favorite." I stole a quick glance at the passenger seat. "What about you?"

Liam grinned. "Pie. Chocolate cream or pecan."

I made a mental note to include those in baking plans for the shop in the coming weeks. "Both solid choices."

He grunted. "I know my desserts."

"I'm sure you do." I turned off the road, punching in the code that would open the gate to the Cole Ranch. "Have you ridden before?" It had just dawned on me that Liam might have no idea what he was doing when it came to horses.

"My grandfather had me riding before I could walk."

"Really?" Surprise laced my tone.

"Really. I grew up in a small town in Georgia. He had a ranch there, and I spent a lot of time with him." Liam's drumming had stopped, and his voice had taken on a wistful quality.

"He doesn't have the ranch anymore?" I knew it was unfair of me to ask questions about Liam's past when I wouldn't answer any about my own, but I was so hungry to know more about this man.

"He passed away years ago. My parents didn't have time to run a ranch with their jobs, and my career was just getting going, so we sold it."

I could hear sadness and regret in his words. "I'm sorry."

Liam shook his head as if clearing the cobwebs of reminiscence. "I'll always have the memories. And it just makes the times I get to spend on land like this"—he gestured to the rolling pastures surrounding us—"that much more special."

I liked the way Liam looked at life. It wasn't overly Pollyanna, but it always put things in perspective. "That's a good way to think about it."

Liam sent me a grin. "Glad you think so."

I pulled the SUV into an empty spot in front of the ranch house. Before the vehicle was even turned off, Noah dashed out the front door and bounded down the steps. "I'm ready! I'm ready!"

I couldn't help but laugh, a smile stretching my cheeks tight.

"I think someone's excited for our ride."

Liam chuckled. "I'd say so."

We hopped down from the SUV, and Noah's arms immediately encircled me. I didn't get hugged often. The adults in my life had quickly caught on to the vibes I sent out about not going overboard in that area. The only people who even touched me were Sarah and Jensen. But Noah held nothing back. And I soaked up his easy affection.

The boy's little head tipped back. "I'm going to ride Stargazer."

I brushed the hair back from his face. "I think that's a great pick. What about me? Who am I going to ride?"

Noah's arms squeezed me tighter. "You're going to ride Lightning, and Liam's going to ride Bob."

Liam chuckled. "I'm riding a horse named Bob?"

Noah nodded vigorously. "Yup. I named him after Sponge Bob because he's got a yellow coat."

I pressed my lips together to keep from laughing.

Liam readjusted the hat on his head. "Bob, it is. Lead the way, little man."

Noah took off for the barn at a run, but Liam fell into step with me. He leaned in closer, whispering in my ear, "How come you get Lightning, and I'm stuck with Bob?"

Liam's breath on my neck sent tingles down my spine. "You could always ask to switch, but you know that would break Noah's heart."

Liam's gaze locked with mine. "We can't have that." He let out a sigh. "Me and Bob, best pals."

A soft smile stretched my lips at how sweet Liam was with Noah. "Just be grateful Noah didn't put you on one of the mules."

Liam shook his head. "Thank God for that." He pointed to the bag on my shoulder. "Don't you want to leave that in my SUV?"

I stiffened. My bag went with me everywhere, even on a horseback ride. "No."

Liam's forehead wrinkled. "Okay..."

I turned away, heading for where Noah was talking to one of the stable hands. I stopped where Lightning was tethered, giving his muzzle a gentle rub. "Hey, boy. You want to go for a ride?" Lightning huffed as if to say, "Of course."

I made quick work of checking the tack and fixing my bag behind the saddle. By the time I was finished, Noah was already up on Stargazer, and Liam was getting ready to mount. He looked at me. "You ready?"

My stomach clenched. "Ready."

I led Lightning to the mounting block and swung up onto his back. I reached back with one hand to make sure my bag was still in place. *You're going to be fine.*

Noah bounced in the saddle. "Let's go!"

Liam grinned. "You're in charge, little man."

Sheer joy and pride filled Noah's face. "I know the best ride."

Liam adjusted his hold on the reins. "I can't wait to see where you take us."

Noah urged his horse forward, leading us through an open gate and into one of the rolling pastures, this one free of other horses and cattle. Liam found his way next to me. "Grilled cheese, or PB and J?"

The tension in my shoulders melted a bit. "Like that's even a serious question. Grilled cheese all the way."

Liam clutched his chest. "That's it, ladies and gentlemen, I'm done for. A woman who appreciates the fine cuisine of grilled cheese as much as I do."

We rode for at least an hour before turning around and heading back. Noah chattered about school, the animals on the ranch, and his first guitar lesson with Liam. Liam and I could barely get a word in. It was perfect—the peacefulness that comes with innocent voices, beautiful landscapes, and time communing with horses.

Part of me had worried that once Liam got me semi-alone, he'd push. Ask me questions I couldn't answer. Demand to know more about my past. But he didn't. I didn't have to answer one question that made me uncomfortable. And not just because Noah was a little chatterbox.

Liam didn't push. He kept things light. The questions he asked Noah and me centered around favorite flavors of ice cream and who would win a fight between Thor and Captain America. It was easy being with him and Noah, my soul relishing in the human connection I'd had so little of these past few years.

I wanted more. And that terrified me.

We came to a stop outside the barn, each of us slowly dismounting and leading our horses inside the outbuilding. I tethered Lightning and began the process of removing his tack so I could give him a nice rub-down. I carried the saddle to the tack room, placing it on a peg that read, *Lightning*. When I turned, I almost crashed right into Liam.

"Sorry," I muttered.

Liam chuckled. It was low and husky and made my stomach flip. "We have to stop doing that." I nodded, taking a step back as he swung his own saddle up onto a peg. "So, did you have fun?"

I licked my lips. "It was great. Thank you for inviting me."

Liam reached out, moving slowly, and swept his thumb across my cheek. "You have a little dirt." His thumb lingered, his hand almost cupping my face.

My heart thundered in my chest. When was the last time someone had touched me this tenderly? I honestly couldn't remember. My breathing hitched.

A loud thump had us jumping apart. Noah's voice sounded from outside. "Oops. Can one of you help me with my saddle?"

Liam shoved his hands into his pockets. "Can't leave the little man alone to deal with his tack."

I shook my head, unable to speak as my heart still rattled in my ribcage.

Liam motioned towards the stalls. "I'll just go help him with that."

I nodded, clearing my throat, hoping that would somehow help my current mute status. "Yeah." It came out on a croak, but at least I'd spoken the word.

I needed some air. I made sure Lightning had water and then headed outside. The sun, low in the sky, gave the fields a beautiful, golden glow. I closed my eyes and angled my face towards the sun beams, breathing deeply. How could a simple touch undo me? Liam Fairchild must have magic in those fingertips.

The wind shifted, and my eyes popped open. There was an itchy sensation between my shoulder blades. I spun around, expecting to find Liam, but there was no one.

Unease swept over me as my eyes traveled around the Cole family ranch. Two men were filling a truck with hay. Sarah and Jensen sat on the front porch of the ranch house. Another ranch hand led a horse out to pasture. Irma motioned for Noah to follow her inside.

No one was looking in my direction, but I could feel eyes on me, boring into me. Goosebumps peppered my skin as my head whipped around, trying to find the source of the discomfort. A hand brushed my arm, and I jumped.

"Hey, hey. What's wrong?" Liam's concerned expression filled my line of sight.

What if someone *was* watching right now? Garrett? Or one of his minions? A paparazzi angling for a shot of Liam? Hell, even a ranch hand with a camera who wanted to make a few extra bucks by selling a photograph to some gossip magazine.

My breaths came in quick pants. How could I have been so stupid? Taken such an unnecessary risk? I shook off Liam's hand. "I have to go."

His brows pulled together. "Okay, I'll take you home. Just give me a minute to get the horses settled."

I shook my head. "I have to go now. I'll get Jensen to take me home." I took off towards the barn to grab my bag. "I'm sorry," I called over my shoulder. A completely baffled look filled Liam's expression, along with a touch of hurt. My chest burned, and I forced myself to look away.

I snagged my bag and headed for the front porch. Jensen and Sarah were coming down the front steps when I reached them. "I'm sorry to be a bother, but could one of you drive me home?"

They shared a worried glance, but it was Sarah who spoke. "Of course, honey. Let me just grab my keys."

"Thank you." She headed back up the steps, pulling the door open and unhooking a keychain from the key rack in the entryway.

"Is everything okay?" Jensen asked, voice soft.

I nodded, wrapping my arms around myself. "I'm fine. I just need to get back." I'm sure the Cole family thought I was a lunatic by now. Today would just add to their pile of evidence.

Sarah inclined her head towards an SUV on the side of the house. "Come on."

I followed her to the vehicle in a daze, getting in and fastening my seatbelt on autopilot. We were silent on the drive. I stared out the window, letting my mind go unfocused, trying not to think about anything. Before I knew it, Sarah had pulled up at the back of the Kettle.

I reached for the door handle. "Thank you." I couldn't even look at Sarah.

"Anytime, honey. Whatever you need, just ask. I'm always here."

Her kind words broke me. Tears streamed down my face as I slipped from the car without another word. My keys shook as I tried to unlock the door. It took three attempts before I got them into the lock.

I hurried to flip the latch behind me when I got inside. Running up the stairs, I unlocked my apartment door, my hand even shakier now as sobs wracked my body. I slammed the door closed behind me, flipping the deadbolt and hooking the chain.

Then I let myself dissolve, crumpling to the floor. The carpet at the end of my bed softened my landing, but it still jarred my spine when my knees hit the floor. I pulled the thick duvet from the bed. I needed its comfort, its protection from reality.

My cheeks grew hotter, and my sobs heavier as I thought about how crazy I'd just acted, my paranoia of being discovered wreaking havoc with my logical brain. No one in Sutter Lake had sold Liam out to the media, and he'd been here for months. Garrett hadn't found me, and I'd been here for two years.

I squeezed my eyes closed against the wave of embarrassment that encroached. None of it mattered now. No one would put up with this level of crazy. I wanted so badly to be normal, to go on a ride, or hell, even a date without panic destroying every tendril of enjoyment.

But I was damaged goods. I'd probably never be free of the hold my paranoia had on me. Normal would never be within my reach.

CHAPTER
Sixteen

Liam

ISTARED OFF AFTER THE SUV AS IT DISAPPEARED DOWN THE dirt and gravel road, dust kicking up in its wake. Particles that filtered through the air, slowly dispersing long after the vehicle was gone. *What the hell just happened?*

Guilt flooded my gut. Did Tessa freak out because I touched her cheek? I was trying like hell to move slowly. Not to make any sudden movements, literally or figuratively. But something about Tessa made my brain cells short-circuit.

God, her skin had been so soft. I swear I could still feel it against my hand. And when had that ever happened? Never, that's when.

A throat cleared behind me. I turned to see Jensen. She studied me in a way that said if I'd stepped out of line, she'd squash me like a bug. "What happened?"

I swiped the hat off my head in a frustrated pull. "The hell if I know. We were fine. I went to help Noah with his saddle, and when I came out here, Tessa looked as if she'd seen a ghost. She couldn't get away from me fast enough." And didn't that just cut deep? I fisted my ballcap.

Jensen's eyes narrowed ever so slightly. "Are you sure that's all that happened?"

I toed the dirt with my boot. "I might have touched her cheek."

The narrowing of Jensen's eyes turned into a confused squint. "You touched her cheek?"

I ran a hand through my hair as I turned to face the pasture in front of us. "She had some dirt on her cheek, and I brushed it off. She didn't jump or anything. But I'm wondering if that freaked her out." The desire to punch the wooden fence in front of me was strong. How the hell could I get through to Tessa if I didn't know what things would trigger her and make her run?

I spun back to face Jensen. "Do you know what happened to her?" Walker had said Jensen didn't know anything, but I wasn't so sure. And I needed all the help and insight I could get.

Sympathy filled Jensen's expression. "No." I just stared harder. "Not for sure. All I know is someone hurt her. I'm guessing it was a man because she shies away from them."

Rage pulsed through my veins at the thought of someone touching Tessa in a way intended to hurt. I fisted my hands tighter, my hat crumpling.

"You're gonna need to keep that anger in check if you want a chance with Tessa. She sees any hint of that, she'll be gone so fast your head will spin."

I released my death grip on the hat. "I know."

Jensen blew out a long breath. "I'm honestly surprised Tessa's let you in as much as she has. Walker has been trying for almost two years to get her to open up. Hoping she'll start to trust him and tell him what happened so he can help."

A quick flare of jealousy spiked. I tamped it down. Walker was just trying to help. And he was also so far gone for Taylor, it wasn't even funny. I knew he didn't see Tessa in that way. But still, I wanted to be the one Tessa let through those walls. The one she trusted with her story.

Jensen gripped my shoulder. "Walker hasn't even gotten her to be in a room alone with him, not even at one of our family dinners when she knows the rest of us are nearby. Obviously, some part of her wants to trust you."

I scrubbed a hand over my jaw. "I want to help her. I just don't know how. What should I do? Or not do. I feel like I'm walking through a minefield with no map, just praying I won't hit a trip wire."

"You do better with her than you think. Taylor told me how you navigated getting her out here today. Challenging her comfort zone but not pushing too far."

I pulled my slightly mangled hat back on. "I don't know about that. Look where we ended up, Tessa freaked and running. Maybe I did push too far." I hated that I might be the cause of the pain Tessa felt. Fucking despised it. It was a reminder that I'd been the cause of pain for another innocent young woman. That someone had almost ended her life because of my actions or non-actions twisted my stomach into knots.

Jensen took a step closer. "Those freak-outs are going to happen. You need to decide here and now if you can handle them or not." Jensen's eyes bored into mine. "Because if you can't, you need to leave her be. I won't have her start to lean on you, and then have you disappear. Tessa deserves better than that."

My spine stiffened, irritation bristling my skin. "I know you don't know me that well, but I'm not that kind of guy." My grandfather had taught me better. My father. Hell, my mom would tan my hide if she ever knew I pulled something like that on a girl as fragile as Tessa. But Tessa wasn't just fragile. She was also strong as hell.

Tessa had come through whatever had happened to her, and now she and she alone made sure that she was safe. I could admire that. I just wanted to help her carry some of her burdens. And I certainly didn't want to cause another freak-out like I had just now. I needed more information, insight into what her triggers might be. I just wasn't sure how to get it.

Jensen smacked me on the back. "I'm glad to hear that. I'm

rooting for you. I really am. If anyone deserves a happy ending, it's her."

My gaze traveled over Jensen's face, thinking about everything I knew she'd been through herself. Tessa wasn't the only one who deserved some happiness in her life. I thought better of saying as much, knowing it wouldn't be received well. "So, any suggestions?"

A grin tipped Jensen's mouth. "Slow and steady, my friend. Give her a day or so to get her head straight, but no longer than that. The more time you give her, the more she'll shore up those walls to keep everyone out."

There was no way in hell I was going to let Tessa do that. She might not recognize it, but there was a whole slew of people on her team now, and I planned on being the fucking team captain.

CHAPTER
Seventeen

Tessa

PHOENIX NUZZLED MY SIDE AS I SKETCHED. I KNEW SHE sensed my frayed nerves. I still wasn't quite recovered from my paranoia-fueled meltdown from yesterday. But time with the horses helped. Phee's comfort helped. Sketching helped.

I glanced down at my notepad. Angled cheekbones and piercing eyes stared back at me. God, he was beautiful. So very beautiful, but never to be mine. A famous musician couldn't be with someone who jumped at every shadow, and he wouldn't want someone who could barely keep from flinching when she was touched. Not when he could have anyone.

I ripped out the page and stuffed it into my bag. Phoenix huffed as though indignant about me destroying the image. I reached up and scratched between her ears. "It's for the best."

The sound of crunching gravel had me turning my head to make sure it was Jensen. Her SUV pulled to a stop next to the fence line, and she hopped out, long hair blowing in the breeze. "You finished getting them all fed?"

I shoved my sketchbook into my bag. "All done. You ready to go?" Jensen had kept to her word and was driving me to and from the ranch. My car was still in Liam's hands, and now I had no idea if I'd ever get it back. I certainly wasn't going to call him to ask.

Jensen ducked between two rails in the fence. "Let's hang with the herd for a bit. Unless you're in a hurry to get back?"

I shook my head. I could use some extra time with them today.

Jensen climbed up onto the boulder I was sitting on, settling next to me. She pulled a carrot out of her fleece's pocket and extended it to Phoenix. The mare sniffed the object and then hesitantly took it from Jensen's palm. "She's still unsure around me."

I patted Phoenix's neck as she chomped down on the treat. "She'll get there. Just give her time."

Jensen took in the grazing horses. "I'll give her all the time in the world."

We sat in silence for a long while, watching the horses against the backdrop of the sun lowering in the sky. A wave of gratitude swept over me. I might not be able to have Liam, but I had so much: this beautiful place, these amazing creatures, a friend who would sit with me and simply be. That could be enough.

Jensen bumped my shoulder with her own. "So..." She let the word dangle, and my body tensed. "Want to tell me what happened yesterday?"

I fidgeted with the strings on my hoodie. "Not particularly."

Jensen let out a chuckle. "Why don't you tell me anyway?"

I snuck a peek at Jensen. This was the first time she'd ever pushed when I dodged a question. Heat filled my chest, a yearning to tell her everything. I was so tired of carrying this weight alone, of acting like a freak and having everyone in my life wonder why.

My heart rate sped up, and my hands began to tingle. *Could I tell her?* The last thing I wanted was to put Jensen at risk. And she would be if Garrett found out that she knew the details of what had happened. Knew she had helped me. He would do everything in his power to ruin her, hurt her. Gena's face flashed in my mind. But maybe I could tell Jensen just enough. Broad strokes, not fine details of who I'd been involved with. Maybe then, I wouldn't feel so damn alone.

Pain rippled through me, exhaustion hot on its heels. I needed to let someone in.

I took a deep breath. "I was in an abusive relationship." It felt weird to say the words out loud. I never had before. It had taken months after running away from DC to finally name what I had been through. But there was a power in the naming. A power in declaring the treatment I endured as wrong. Evil. Twisted.

There was a stigma around the word *victim*. Something that said you were powerless or had given up. I was a victim, but I was also a fighter. I had clawed my way to freedom. And I would let nothing and no one put that freedom at risk—not even my own heart.

I jolted when a hand took mine. Jensen. She said nothing, simply held my hand, giving me the silent support to continue.

My body shuddered slightly. "We met when I was in college. He was finishing up law school. I'd never had what he gave me. The idea of belonging to someone when I'd grown up with no one. Foster families that had too many kids. School classrooms that were overcrowded. I never felt like anyone truly saw me."

I rubbed the fingertips of my free hand over the rough surface of the rock, letting it ground me. "He noticed me. It felt like this miracle, a precious gift I would do anything to keep hold of. But really, it was a drug. I was forever chasing the high of the first few months while running away from the lows. It didn't matter that my body was crushed by the addiction, that my soul was slowly dying. I *needed* that next fix. That one hit of feeling like the most important thing to someone."

I fought against the shame that wanted to overtake me, the degradation of the truth. That I had made the choice to stay for so long. I swallowed it down. "I always thought of myself as a strong person. A strong woman. That I would never put up with that kind of treatment. I worked hard. Stayed focused. Graduated high school with honors and a full ride to a good state school."

The girl I used to be, so proud and self-assured filled my mind. "It happened slowly and in a flash at the same time. I didn't realize he was changing me at first. Subtle suggestions about what to wear, who I was hanging out with. Asking me to cancel plans with my friends because he *needed* me."

Images flew through my brain, so many memories of times where I should've seen the signs. "I'd never been needed like that before. So, of course, I agreed. He helped me with school work, paid for things he knew I couldn't afford, wrote me long, romantic letters. I thought it was love. It was really a narcissist's master manipulation."

I fisted the side of my sweatshirt. "The first time he hit me, I left. He showed up at my dorm room hours later, sobbing. Begging to be let in. He would never forgive himself for hurting me. He'd live the rest of his days trying to make it up to me."

I let out a harsh breath. "I took him back." A lethal mixture of shame, guilt, and self-hatred swirled in my belly. "It was the biggest mistake I've ever made. It started a vicious cycle. I was the greatest thing in the world for a few days, and then I was lower than the dirt on the bottom of his shoe."

My voice began to shake as I pressed on. "His paranoia grew. The beatings got worse. When I graduated, he proposed. I said yes, hoping like a fool that it would change things, give us both a sense of security."

Jensen gripped my hand a little tighter as if sensing that I needed it. I held on. "He didn't want me to get a job. He needed me at home to take care of him. He got me a driver. I was never out of the line of sight of someone who reported back to him."

Rage pumped through my veins. "I tried to leave once. To go

to the police. He found out within the hour. He had them convinced that I was mentally unstable by the end of the day, and he'd found me by the next."

Jensen gasped. I couldn't look at her, afraid of what I might see. "I planned more carefully the next time, pretended he had finally broken me, that I was finally this automaton who would obey his every command, never thinking for myself. He believed it."

I was silent for a minute, trying to slow my rapidly cycling thoughts. Jensen squeezed my hand. "How did you get out?"

A small smile tipped my lips. "An angel in the form of a hairstylist. She helped me escape." Emotion clogged my throat. "I'll never be able to repay her for that."

A tremor rippled through me as I forced myself to look at Jensen. Would she think I was weak? Stupid? Would she pity me? When I met her gaze, I sucked in a breath. Rage burned in her eyes. "I want to kill him."

Of all the things she might have said, that wasn't what I had expected. But with my fierce defender, Jensen, I should have. She was always protecting creatures great and small who had less power than others. Look at the field in front of us, full of horses that had nowhere good to go, beings that needed a safe place to call home. She would destroy anyone who tried to harm them, so I shouldn't have been shocked that she wanted to do the same for me.

And I couldn't forget that Jensen also knew what it meant to discover that the man you loved was a monster. I squeezed her hand, a small smile curving my mouth. "I appreciate the sentiment, but I'd rather you not be sent to jail for the rest of your life."

She looked me dead in the eyes. "They'd have to find the body first."

Laughter bubbled out of me. I couldn't help it. And it just

kept building until tears streamed down my face and my stomach ached. It was the exact release I needed.

Jensen pulled me into a hug as my laughter subsided. "Thank you for telling me. I'm so sorry you had to endure that. You are so fucking strong."

The tears that leaked out of my eyes were now a different kind—a mixture of gratitude and emotional release. "Thank you."

We held onto each other, not moving or speaking until Phoenix tried to nuzzle in between us. We both laughed as the mare broke us apart. I pressed my face against the mare's furry cheek. "Everything's okay. Promise." Phee leaned into me.

Jensen studied me as I stroked Phoenix's face and neck. "Your name isn't really Tessa, is it?"

I stiffened. I'd told my story, but I couldn't ever give away my secrets. "No." Jensen raised her brows at me. "I can't tell you what it is. It would put you at risk."

Jensen's eyes widened. "What do you mean?"

I let the feel of Phoenix's coat beneath my fingers soothe my nerves. "My ex is really well connected." Understatement of the century. "If he thought you were helping me, knew my history, he'd do everything in his power to destroy you."

Jensen looked skeptical, so I pushed on. "He's done it before. That hairstylist I told you helped me? Six months after I left, her salon was set on fire with her inside. Thankfully, she escaped with only smoke inhalation, but she could've died. All because she helped me."

Jensen straightened. "You need to go to Walker. Tell him everything. Get a restraining order. You have resources now who will believe you."

I pushed off the boulder, needing to move. "I can't." I swiveled to pin Jensen with a stare. "And you can't either. Promise me." Panic raced through me.

Jensen rose, holding out a hand in a placating gesture. "I won't. I promise. I'd never betray your trust like that." My heart rate began to slow a bit. "But tell me why not."

My hands fisted at my sides. "To file a restraining order, you need to report where you live. That means *he* would know where I live. If he knows where to find me, I'm as good as dead."

CHAPTER
Eighteen

Liam

MY FINGERS SHIFTED ALONG THE NECK OF THE GUITAR, and my other hand absently strummed. I was caught in that half-conscious state of chasing a melody, a series of notes that had been stuck in my head since I first met Tessa. I couldn't quite find the exact arrangement, the perfect fit, the music that would put into words the riot of emotions that had taken up residency in my chest.

My ribcage squeezed. I wanted to go to Tessa now. The desire to see her and make sure she was okay was so strong, I'd headed to my car twice in the last two hours. I'd talked myself out of leaving both times, reminding myself of what Jensen had said: give her time to recover from whatever had happened yesterday, then let her know I wasn't going anywhere.

I focused back on my guitar, fingers flying over the strings. Closer. I was nearing the right combination of chords. So close. My phone buzzed on the porch rail, and I cursed. I should've kept the damn thing on silent, but I wanted to have it on just in case Tessa called.

I glanced at the screen and scowled. Definitely not Tessa. I answered with a gruff, "Hello."

"Liam, it's Dan. How are you?" The falsely bright voice belonged to an exec at my record label. He was pretty much the last person I wanted to talk to at this moment, but I knew if I ignored the call, my phone would just keep ringing.

I leaned my guitar against the porch railing. "Hey."

"How are things?" It sounded like an innocuous question, but I knew it was anything but.

"Fine." I'd learned that keeping my answers as short and non-committal as possible was the best way to deal with anyone at the label.

"Any new music brewing?"

My hand tightened around the phone. The music that was beginning to come together on the edges of my mind was personal. Private. I didn't want any of these greedy soul-suckers anywhere near it. "Nope."

Dan exhaled a ragged breath. "That's unfortunate. Listen, I think we have a solution. It's genius, really."

I flipped my guitar pick over and over between my fingers. "And what's that?"

"I know you're a huge fan of Richard Malstrom's work." The exaggerated cheeriness in Dan's tone had me on alert.

"Yes..." Richard Malstrom was an incredible producer. He had more Grammys than he could probably count, and I would kill to work with him.

"I spoke with him this morning. He has a few songwriters that have tracks we think would be a good fit for you. Why don't you head back to LA, and we can get you in the studio and recording?"

I squeezed the back of my neck, the guitar pick digging into my flesh. I loved collaborating with other musicians. The back and forth dance of spurring on each other's creative process was a high unlike any other, but this wasn't collaboration. I had zero desire to record a song I'd had no part in creating. "No."

"Liam, be reasonable. Your record is due in two months, and you have almost nothing. This is the solution that makes the most sense."

I stood, beginning to pace. "This isn't how I work, and you know it. Look, I've given you guys four multi-platinum albums. You know my work is good if you don't rush it."

Dan's voice lost all levity. "We've already extended the deadline once. If you don't deliver, you'll be in breach of contract." That was the thing about these people, they shifted on a dime. You were their best friend one second, and their sworn enemy the next.

My blood began to heat. "I tell you what, *Dan*. I'm going to get my lawyer and accountant on the phone. I'll make sure you have the album advance back by the end of business tomorrow. We can just call this one a loss and realize we never should've been working together in the first place."

Silence. A throat clearing. "That's not necessary. If you need a little more time, we can work with that. We know true artistry can't be rushed."

Exactly what I thought. It all came down to money. Money and power. My label wanted the claim to my music. It wouldn't do if I left them and went to another label. How would that make them *look*? After all, appearances were everything.

I ran a hand through my hair. "I appreciate that, Dan."

"Of course. Now there's something else I need to talk to you about."

"What?" My mind was already on the call I was going to make to my lawyer after this. I'd let Dan think I'd been placated, but I wanted out of this contract. I was done. I'd still make music, but I wanted to do it on my own schedule, without anyone trying to control my art.

"It appears we might have another issue with your stalker."

A sour taste filled my mouth. "What do you mean?"

Dan cleared his throat again. "We had some comments on your blog and social media accounts that our security experts believe are Ms. Speakman. There is no definitive proof, but the posts are of a threatening nature. We think it's best if you return to the city and have your security detail with you at all times."

I blew out a harsh breath. I lived with threats on my social media accounts every day. It was part of the gig. People wanted to see you rise, others wanted to see you fall. This was nothing new. And it pissed me the fuck off that my label was using a mentally unstable girl as an excuse to call me back to LA. "No."

"Liam…"

I gripped the railing of the deck. "I said, no."

"Well, at least tell us where you are so we can send your security detail there."

More like so they could leak it to the press and capitalize on a spike in record sales. "I said no. I'm perfectly safe where I am. If you can't find me, then whoever is making these *threats* won't be able to either."

Silence. More shuffling of papers. "You're a pain in the ass to deal with, you know that?"

I chuckled, but it had a feral quality to it. "Right back at you. Look, I need to go work on some music so that you can have that album you've got such a hard-on for."

"Fine." The word was said through what sounded like gritted teeth. "Let me know when you need me to block out some studio time."

Like hell, I would. I was running fast and far from anything to do with Dan and his minions. I was done. Instead of telling him that, though, I lied like the best of them. "Will do."

"I'll be in touch."

I ignored Dan's sign-off and just hung up. I fought the urge to throw my cell phone into the creek below. I was through with being a puppet while the powers that be held my strings and forced me to dance.

My jaw worked as I stared at the horizon. It was time to take back control of my life. Step one was getting out of this contract.

Once that was done, I'd have all the freedom in the world to explore how I wanted to make music.

The golden grasses of the field rippled in the wind. Maybe I'd buy property here. I'd always wanted to build a house somewhere with enough land to have a separate recording studio. A place where I could have total creative control. Land with room for horses and cattle. A home my parents would love to visit.

I chuckled remembering the first time my mom had come to my place in Malibu. "It's lovely," she'd said with a look of confused horror on her face. It was pretty modern. No real personality. Not *me*.

I needed to build a retreat. A true home. Tessa's face flashed in my mind. I wondered what she'd want in a house. An art studio for sure. Maybe space for her own horses? I shook my head. I was losing it. *It might help to have the girl agree to a date before you start building a house with her in mind.*

CHAPTER
Nineteen

Tessa

ALIGHTNESS HAD ENGULFED ME SINCE MY CONVERSATION with Jensen yesterday. I hadn't realized just how much I needed to release my burden. To tell someone my story. It wasn't like any of my problems had been solved. Garrett could still find me at any moment, but I felt freer than I had in almost a decade.

The simple power of feeling seen. Heard. Understood. *Believed.*

Jensen had reassured me that she wouldn't tell anyone what I'd shared with her, but she made me promise that I would think about going to Walker at some point. My muscles tensed at the thought. I couldn't. It was too risky. I wouldn't put it past Garrett to kidnap me and bring me back to DC where I had no one in my corner, no one who would believe my claims.

A chill skittered over my skin. That wasn't going to happen. I was safe.

The late-afternoon wind picked up, so strong it lifted my braid off my back. Phoenix whinnied against the air's force, the mare's mane flying wildly around. I set my sketchbook on the boulder, careful to weigh a corner down with my bag so it wouldn't fly away.

I hopped off the rock. "Come on, Phee. You need a good grooming before you get dreadlocks in your mane."

Phoenix seemed to give me the side-eye as though she knew what I was suggesting. It had taken months for her to allow me anywhere near her with a grooming kit. Now, she at least enjoyed a good brushing of her coat. But she still wasn't crazy about me tackling the knots in her mane.

"Come on now," I coaxed. "I'll give you a carrot if you stand still for me."

Phoenix's ears twitched. I swear the mare could understand everything I said and was negotiating. "Okay, fine. Two carrots."

Phoenix started trotting after me. I let out a laugh. "You're a smart little troublemaker." She huffed.

I led the way down the fence line to where I'd left my assortment of brushes. I bent to slide under the fence. Phoenix slowed her pace. "Come on, now. No use dragging your feet. The sooner we get started, the sooner you get your treat."

Phoenix edged closer. I scratched between her ears. "Good girl." I made quick work of using a curry comb to rid her coat of any dirt or mud. As the weather was getting warmer, the horses were losing more and more of their winter coats, which meant… horse hair everywhere. "Geez, you needed this big time."

Phoenix nibbled playfully at my shoulder. "You grooming me, too?"

My head snapped up at the sound of gravel crunching under tires. The movement made Phoenix paw the ground anxiously. Jensen wasn't supposed to pick me up for at least another hour. My stomach dropped to my toes. Dark Escalade. Tinted windows. Liam.

I ran my hand along Phoenix's neck. "Everything's fine." I'm not sure who I was reassuring, her or me.

Liam hopped down from the SUV. My heartbeat picked up its pace. He was dressed simply in dark jeans and a flannel. Like everything else about him, it was casually sexy, as if he weren't even trying and still looked like he could grace the perfectly-styled cover of a men's magazine. I swallowed, my throat suddenly dry.

Liam ducked between the rails of the fence. *Shit.* There was no avoiding this. I straightened my spine and headed in his direction. Liam deserved an explanation of why I'd run out on him. I couldn't give him that, but I could at least give him an apology.

We met at the boulder, my safe space. My hiding place. I wasn't sure how I felt about having Liam here.

He grinned, and my stomach flipped. "Hey, Tessa."

I fidgeted with the zipper on my fleece. "Hi."

"I hope you don't mind, Jensen said you were up here."

Traitor. I'd get her back for that. "No, it's fine."

Liam's gaze roamed over the pasture. "It's beautiful up here."

I followed his line of sight. "It is."

His eyes moved to something behind me. "Looks like you've got a protector."

I shifted to glance over my shoulder, but before I could, Phoenix moved beside me. I patted her neck, and she scooted closer, resting her head on my shoulder. "This is Phoenix."

Liam took a step closer. "Hey there, Phoenix." He slowly reached out a hand.

"I wouldn't—" My words were cut off when Phoenix gave his hand a sniff. My eyes widened. The mare usually avoided men like the plague. And if they insisted on invading her space, she'd let them know her displeasure with a nip or a swift kick.

Liam's gaze came to my face. "Is she a bit skittish?"

A small smile tipped my lips. "She normally bites men who hold out a hand to her. You're lucky you've still got fingers."

Liam's brow furrowed, and he slowly pulled his hand back. "Maybe I'll just wait till we know each other a little better."

I chuckled. "Not a bad idea."

Liam studied my face. "So, how are you feeling?"

I could feel color rising to my cheeks. "I'm fine. I'm really sorry about the other day—"

Liam held up a hand, silently cutting me off. "You don't have to explain, I just wanted to make sure you were all right."

I couldn't believe that he wasn't pressing for more information. I sure as hell would've wanted to know why someone freaked out and took off. It was my turn to study him. Liam knew I wasn't ready to share my secrets with him, and he wanted me to share with him freely, not because he'd coerced me into it. "Thank you." The words came out softly and were almost carried away on the breeze.

Liam's expression softened. "I'm just glad you're okay." His shoulders seemed to relax with that knowledge. "So, tell me what you do up here." Liam searched the wide-open space stretching around us.

"Well, I—" My words cut off as Liam's gaze settled on my sketchbook. The wind had blown it open, and a sketch of Phoenix was facing up.

Liam moved to the book, picking it up quickly. "You did these?"

My stomach twisted. "It's just something I do for fun. To relax." I stepped forward, trying to grab the book from his hands.

Liam twisted out of my reach as he flipped through the pages. "Tessa, these are incredible."

I froze. No one had ever told me my drawings were anything special. Garrett had always thought the hobby was cute but nothing worth pursuing. The churning in my stomach intensified. I snatched the sketchbook out of Liam's hands. "They're just for me."

"They shouldn't be. You should be sharing that gift with the world."

I stared at him, trying to figure out if he was pulling my leg or trying to manipulate me in some way. Liam's eyes seemed to dance with excitement. I hated that I questioned it. I mentally cursed Garrett for ruining my shot at something with Liam. For twisting my mind in a way that made me second-guess every male's actions.

I pushed down the bitter taste of resentment. "Thank you."

Liam took a step closer. "I want you to do the cover art for my next album." He chuckled. "Well, if I ever *make* another album."

My mouth had fallen open at the first statement, but it was the second that had me drawing closer to Liam. "You might not make another album?"

Liam ran a hand through his hair. "I have a bit of a case of writer's block. And being past deadline isn't exactly helping."

He said the words carelessly, but there was something in his eyes and the way he held his body, an underlying tension. I had the sudden urge to relieve his burden the way Jensen had eased mine yesterday. I edged a little bit closer. "I'm sorry. That has to be incredibly frustrating. I don't know much about music, but I would think it would be hard to write when there's a lot of pressure to produce and to do it quickly."

"It's pretty much a disaster." Liam looked out at the land around us. "My label is trying to force me to record music that isn't mine." He shoved his hands into his pockets. "I hadn't realized, but I was starting to lose my voice on the last album, giving in to changes the label wanted. Letting them cut songs I believed in." Liam turned his gaze to me, and it held me captive. "I don't want to give them the power to dull my voice anymore."

I knew what it was to have your voice taken from you. It was about the most intimate betrayal I could imagine. "You shouldn't let them." I spit out the words like bullets, surprising myself with the ferocity in my tone.

Liam's eyes widened. "Maybe I should let you at them instead of my lawyer."

I grinned. "Your lawyer might be better with the actual legal terminology." Liam returned my smile. "Do you think you'll be able to get out of the contract?"

Liam moved a touch closer. There were only inches between us now. I could feel the heat coming off his body, smell the faint scent of his cologne. I so badly wanted to lean in to him, to feel his strong arms wrapped around me.

Liam's gaze held mine. "My lawyer's a shark. He'll get me out." He broke the stare, looking out at the view again. "The question is, will I be able to write once I feel a little freer? That, I'm not sure about."

My heart squeezed. If he only knew what a gift his vulnerability was. Sharing his doubt, his fears, Liam was different from any man I knew. I wanted to laugh. I'd really only known one other man at that level. But I wasn't going to bring Garrett into this and ruin the moment.

It didn't matter anyway. Something told me that Liam was uniquely special. Masculine. Protective. But with the most tender heart at his core. One that cared deeply for others. A heart that yearned for authenticity and truth. Liam Fairchild was a potent mixture of hard lines and smooth edges. And I knew I was sunk.

My fingers itched to reach out, to give Liam some form of physical comfort, but I couldn't quite work up the nerve. Instead, I opted for simple truth-telling. "You'll find your voice again. And I can't wait to hear what you have to say."

CHAPTER
Twenty

Liam

HER WORDS CUT RIGHT TO MY CORE. HER FACE, SO FULL of light, of hope, of belief in me. In that moment, I felt like I could've written a hundred songs. And they would've all been about Tessa.

I forced a chuckle, needing to break the intensity of the moment. If I didn't, I worried I'd end up kissing the life out of her, and then I'd really freak her out. "So, your kitten is ready to be picked up."

Tessa's eyes danced in the sunlight, the rays making the purple in them stand out even more. "Really?" Her brows pulled together. "You paid for all his surgery. Don't you want to keep him?"

I fought the laugh that wanted to surface. "Uh, no. I'm not really a cat person." If I was going to get a pet, it'd be a dog. A big one. A Golden or a Lab.

Tessa stroked a hand down Phoenix's neck. "Not manly enough for you?" she asked, laughter in her voice.

I grunted. "Just not my personal choice."

Tessa looked at my SUV and then moved her gaze back to me. "Would you have time to take me to get him?" The uncertainty in her voice made me want to wrap her up in my arms. I resisted the urge.

"I'd be happy to take you." I'd been about to offer to take her, but the fact that she'd asked had me wanting to pound my chest with pride.

"We'll need to stop at a pet store first so I can get some supplies."

I inclined my head towards the SUV. "I've got you covered."

Tessa's brows rose. "You do?"

"All good to go." I looked around the pasture. "Do you need to do anything here before you leave?"

Tessa followed my gaze before giving Phoenix another pat. The mare nuzzled Tessa's neck. And now I was jealous of a fucking horse. Tessa scratched under Phoenix's chin. "You've been saved from a grooming for another day." The horse seemed to snort. "Yeah, yeah. I know you're thrilled."

Tessa turned back towards me. "I just need to put my grooming kit away and grab my bag."

I reached towards her large purse. "I can grab that."

"No!"

Her words halted me in my tracks.

Color rose to her cheeks. "Sorry. I mean, I'll get my bag. You can grab the kit over there if you want."

"Sure. No problem." My gaze traveled from Tessa to the bag and back again before I headed to pick up her grooming supplies. What was in that bag that she didn't want me to see? I wanted so badly for Tessa to truly let me in. But whatever had happened to her meant trust did not come easily. And I knew it had to be a gift freely given. Patience. I just needed to have patience.

I picked up the grooming kit and ducked between the rails in the fence. "Where should I put this?"

Tessa motioned to the open door of a small storage barn. "You can leave it in there."

I rested the box of grooming supplies on a bale of hay. "Good?"

She nodded, nibbling on her bottom lip. "Thanks."

"No problem. You ready?"

Tessa nodded again. "Just need to lock up." She slid the heavy door closed, flipping a padlock into place. Tessa was stronger than she looked in every sense of the word.

We headed for the SUV. Tessa glanced in my direction as we walked. "Do you have everything we need in the car?"

"Yup." I pulled open the back hatch of the vehicle.

Tessa's jaw dropped. She looked from the storage compartment to me and back before dissolving into laughter. Her laughter was quickly becoming my favorite sound. "Did you buy out the whole store?"

Heat crept up the back of my neck as I surveyed the back of my SUV. It was crammed full of everything a cat could want or need. A litter box, litter, toys, enough food to last six months, and a climbing tree that, even disassembled, took up almost the entire space. I shrugged. "The little guy deserves some perks after all he's been through."

Tessa placed a hand on my shoulder. I froze. "You have a kind heart, Liam."

Would I have preferred that she tell me I was ruggedly handsome and incredibly manly? Yes. Would I take *kind heart* and run with it? Yes, I would. "Just looking out for our new friend."

Tessa squeezed my shoulder lightly and then released her hold. "He's lucky to have you in his corner."

My eyes searched hers. "I'm in your corner, too."

Tessa's expression shuttered, and I wanted to curse. "Thanks," she said and spun to head to the passenger-side door.

I shut the back of the SUV with a little more force than was necessary. "So much for patience."

Tessa reached into the small carrier she held on her lap. "Everything's okay now. I'm taking you home with me." The kitten mewed and then dissolved into purrs so loud, I could hear them on the other side of the vehicle.

I turned the key over in the ignition. "The little guy sounds happy."

Tessa took her eyes off the furball in her lap and looked in my direction. "He does, doesn't he?" The kitten batted at her hand as if to say, "Hey, pay attention to me." Tessa giggled then returned her attention to him.

I reversed out of the parking spot and pulled out into traffic. "So, how about a late lunch?" It was after three, so…really late. But I would do just about anything to extend the time I got to spend with Tessa.

She toyed with the zipper on the cat carrier. "Aren't you worried someone will spot you and your cover will be blown?"

I slipped on my sunglasses. "We'll go somewhere in Sutter Lake. Everyone there has been great about keeping my secret. Plus, it's not exactly prime eating time."

Tessa's hand clenched around the zipper. I hated that something as simple as going out to eat with me caused such a struggle within her. I went with my gut and reached over to gently place my hand over hers. "We don't have to go. But if you want to try, we can have a secret sign. If you feel uncomfortable at any time, just give me that sign, and we'll leave. No questions asked."

Tessa stared down at the kitten in her lap. "Why do you put up with…?" She trailed off without finishing, as though she couldn't find the right words.

We stopped at a red light. I gave Tessa's hand a squeeze, and her gaze met mine. I didn't blink. I didn't look away. I needed to make sure she really heard. "Because I think you're worth knowing."

Tessa's hand spasmed in mine, and the beginnings of tears gathered in her eyes. "I want to know you, too…I'm scared."

The simple truth. It was a powerful blow. "We'll just take it one step at a time. If anything's too much, you just let me know."

She licked her lips, the action drawing my attention to her mouth. My jaw clenched. I wanted to taste that mouth. Feel her lips on mine. Tangle my tongue with hers. My pants grew tighter. *Shit.* I shook my head, trying to clear the image from my mind. "So, what do you say? Lunch?"

"Lunch."

I grinned. It was so wide, I probably looked like an idiot. I didn't give a shit. I was taking Tessa on our first date.

It didn't take long for us to make it back to Sutter Lake. I pulled into a parking spot in front of the bakery, which also housed a café that served simple but delicious fare. I glanced at Tessa. "You ready?"

Her hands fisted the strap on the cat carrier. "What about him?" she asked, glancing down.

I turned off the SUV. "Bring him."

Tessa's brows rose. "Really?"

"I'm sure they won't mind." I glanced through the large windows of the shop. "There's hardly anyone in there right now."

Tessa bit her lip but nodded. "Let's go."

I let out the breath I'd been holding. We exited the SUV, and Tessa held the carrier protectively in front of her. I reached the door to the bakery first, pulling it open for her. "After you."

Tessa stepped cautiously through, her gaze traveling all around as if she were waiting for someone to jump out and attack. I placed a hand on the small of her back, my body warming when she didn't jolt in surprise. I ushered her forward to the hostess stand.

Moments later, Nina, the owner of the bakery appeared. "Well, what do we have here?" She eyed the pet carrier skeptically.

I slipped my wallet out of my back pocket. "We just picked up this little fella from the vet. He's a rescue, and we don't want to leave him alone before he gets settled. Any chance you might pretend you don't see him." I opened my billfold, about to offer her a tip as incentive, but she waved a hand in front of her face.

"Put your money away, Hollywood. We don't take bribes here. You can keep him with you." Nina eyed me sternly. "But he stays in his carrier. The last thing I need is to be reported for a health code violation."

I grinned at her. "He'll stay put."

Nina let out an exasperated sigh. "You're too charming for your own good, you know that?"

My grin widened. "It's served me well."

Nina eyed Tessa. "I can see that. Treat this girl right, you hear me?"

Tessa blushed, but I chuckled. "I'll be on my best behavior."

Nina grabbed two menus and led us towards a back table. "You better." She glanced at Tessa. "How are things at the Kettle?"

Tessa gave Nina a small smile. "Good. I'm still working on expanding our menu, hoping to give you a run for your money."

Nina laughed. "One of these days, we need to get in the kitchen together, invent some new recipes."

Tessa's eyes seemed to light up at the idea. "I'd love that."

Nina placed the menus on the table as we sat. "We'll get it on the schedule." Tessa nodded. "You two browse the menu, I'll be back in a few to take your order."

Tessa carefully placed the carrier on the empty chair next to her, unzipping the flap just an inch to stick her finger inside to scratch the kitten's ear. He made a sound between a purr and a meow. "We need a name for him."

I studied Tessa's expression, so full of adoration. God, her heart was so good. "We do. Any ideas?"

Tessa looked up to meet my gaze. The kitten clearly didn't appreciate her change in focus because he stuck his little paw out of the bag and batted at Tessa's hand. She giggled. "How about Bubbles?"

I had just taken a sip of water and almost choked. "Bubbles?

For a male cat?"

"What's wrong with that? He's got a bubbly personality."

I rubbed a hand over my jaw. "It's not exactly masculine. He's already been through one trauma, you want to add another one to his plate by naming him Bubbles?"

Tessa wadded up a paper napkin from the holder between us and threw it at me. "Fine, mister expert on all things masculine and tough, what should his name be?"

I caught the napkin and placed it back on the table. "Hmmm. How about Killer?"

Tessa's face wrinkled in disgust. "No. Just, no."

I loved that more of her spark was showing, and I couldn't help but needle her just a bit. "Spike?"

Tessa's nose twitched as if she smelled something bad. "You're horrible at this."

I tapped the table. "I've got it. Lucifer."

Tessa's jaw fell open. "You didn't."

I grinned, but that smile soon morphed into a look of alarm. "Tessa, catch him!" The kitten had managed to unzip the bag and was about to make a break for it.

Tessa's eyes widened, but her reflexes were quick. She caught him just as he leapt onto the table, cast in tow. "You're going to get us in so much trouble." She hurriedly stashed him back into the bag.

I was laughing so hard my stomach hurt but still trying desperately to keep as silent as possible so as not to draw attention. Tessa looked at me with an exasperated sigh. I reached across the table and squeezed her hand. "I think he's named himself."

Tessa's lips twitched. "Oh, yeah, what?"

"Trouble."

She glanced down at the kitten trying to paw open the bag. "I think you're right."

The remainder of lunch passed uneventfully. We chatted

mostly about my music and her art. I learned that Tessa had never taken an art class beyond high school and was largely self-taught. I was careful with my questions, and she didn't balk at any of them. *Progress.* It might not have been her life story, but Tessa was slowly letting me in, and it was the most precious gift I'd ever received.

We called our goodbyes to Nina as we left and climbed back into my SUV. I snuck glances at her as we drove. Tessa's braid had fallen out, and her dark hair hung in loose waves, framing her face. Her creamy complexion and rosy cheeks just made her vibrant eyes stand out all the more. She was breathtaking.

I tore my gaze away from her, narrowly avoiding swerving into oncoming traffic. *Shit.* This woman was going to be the death of me.

I pulled to a stop behind The Tea Kettle, shutting off the car. "Can I help bring all the gear up to your apartment?"

Tessa stilled in the seat next to me. I knew this was asking a lot. No one else was here. Late in the day, the Kettle was dark and locked up tight. Allowing me into her space when no one else was around would be a huge show of trust on Tessa's part. She stared down at Trouble, nibbling on her bottom lip. I gave her time. Let her process whatever she needed to go through to make her decision.

Tessa twisted the carrier strap between her fingers. "That would be nice. Thank you."

I tried not to let my elation show too much, but really, I wanted to run circles around the car with my fists in the fucking air. "You're welcome. I'll grab the big stuff. Why don't you just take Trouble and unlock the doors."

Tessa nodded. She moved somewhat jerkily as if she weren't used to the movements required to exit the vehicle and unlock the door. But I knew the truth. She was terrified. My smile fell as my chest constricted in a vicious spasm. I hated whoever had done this to her, forced her to live in such tremendous fear. I wanted to end whoever it was. Make them suffer as Tessa suffered.

I stared down at the pavement, clenching and unclenching my fists, trying to get my body to relax. Tessa picked up on everything, and if she got one whiff of the fury running through me, she would run for the hills. I took a few deep breaths, willing my tense muscles to release. I pictured Tessa with Phoenix, Tessa throwing the napkin at me, Tessa cuddling Trouble. It worked. My heart rate slowed, my body relaxed, and my breathing evened out.

I took hold of the cat climbing tree in the back of my SUV. Maybe I had gone a little overboard. One piece of this thing had to weigh fifty pounds. I started up the stairs and piled the items one by one just inside the door to Tessa's studio apartment. When I brought the final items in, Tessa appeared from the kitchen.

Her hand shook as she gave me a glass of water. "I thought you might be thirsty."

I took the drink from her hand, careful not to get too close. I knew I needed to play this just right. No sudden movements. No going in for a kiss or even a hug. I moved so that she had an open line to the door, and I saw her shoulders relax slightly. *Fuck.* I didn't want this woman to be scared of me. Ever. I knew it was a reaction she couldn't control, something ingrained in her over time or through trauma or both. It didn't mean I had to like it. I fucking despised it.

I was careful to keep my expression neutral. "Thank you."

Tessa nodded. "Thank you for everything you did. For me. For Trouble." She glanced at the carrier sitting on her bed, then back to me. "Think I can let him out now?"

I grinned. "I think he'll find a way out if you don't."

A small smile teased her lips, and she headed towards the bed. Tessa slowly unzipped the carrier and carefully lifted Trouble out. "This is your new home." She nuzzled his tiny face.

"You're safe here."

Trouble sniffed the air. Tessa cautiously set him down. She looked up at me. "Do you think he'll be okay with his cast?"

I edged a step closer. "I think he'll figure it out."

Tessa released her hold on the kitten. Trouble wobbled at first, and Tessa braced to steady him if he needed it. Slowly, he found his footing and began to wander around the small apartment.

I finally took in Tessa's space as we watched Trouble wander. She had made small efforts to make the apartment homey: a pitcher of flowers on the small kitchen table, a worn quilt on the bed. But there was very little stuff. Not much she couldn't grab in a moment's notice if she needed to. The thought had my gut tightening.

I would do anything to get her to stay.

CHAPTER
Twenty-One

Tessa

M Y HEART HAMMERED IN MY CHEST. I WILLED IT TO
slow. It refused. Its reason was two-fold. One, this
was the first man I had ever allowed up here. Not
even Walker, Tuck, or Andrew had been inside since I started
living here. Anything that needed fixing, I did myself.

Two, it wasn't just any man in my apartment. It was *Liam*. I
bet he thought I was jittery because I was scared, but he wasn't
entirely right. Sure, my instinct was to be on guard at all times.
Always have an exit plan. But my gut told me that Liam would
do anything to prevent my pain. He wasn't a man who would ex-
ercise his frustrations in anger on another person. He was kind.
Gentle. Generous. And a million other things that I hadn't yet
learned.

But I wanted to. I wanted to know Liam in every way possible, with a soul-deep ferocity that terrified me. He also made
butterflies take flight in my stomach when he got close. Made my
skin tingle when he touched me.

I fisted my hands at my sides. My face heated. I hadn't been
with a man since Garrett. Up until recently, I'd thought the desire
to ever be close to someone in that way was dead and buried
along with my past. But slowly, over the past few weeks, my body
had come alive again.

My nerves had been deadened for so long. I'd had to turn off as much feeling as possible to survive—in my body and in my heart. The more I felt, the more I hurt. I hadn't realized just how much I'd been missing out on. The simple pleasures of enjoying delicious food, confiding in a friend, and maybe, just maybe, letting the embers of a crush catch fire.

I glanced in Liam's direction. My belly warmed as I took in his gorgeous face, those broad shoulders. *What would it feel like to drag my fingers through his hair? To tangle my mouth with his?*

He studied me carefully. "Want to tell me what's got those cheeks turning such a pretty shade of pink?"

I knew my blush deepened when Liam chuckled. "Ummm, no."

Liam scrubbed a hand over his cheek. "That's fair enough."

A crash sounded from the kitchen. We both dashed towards the noise. Rounding the corner, we took in Trouble, peeking out of one of the cabinets, having shoved a pan out and onto the floor. My mouth fell open. "That cabinet was closed. How did he get in there?"

Liam shook his head, laughing. "I have no idea. But I'd say his name definitely fits."

I bent to scoop up the kitten and the pan. "You can't be doing that," I cooed. "You're going to get hurt."

I set the pan on the counter and then stole a quick glance out the kitchen window. Habit. Two years of running had instilled in me a need to continually check my surroundings. My kitchen window looked out onto the back of the building. Behind Liam's SUV, another idled.

I sucked in a breath. The hand that held back the curtain started to shake. I didn't recognize the vehicle, and there was no reason for anyone to be back there. The Tea Kettle wasn't open. I felt heat at my back.

"What's wrong?" Liam's voice was alert with an edge of hardness.

"I don't...there's a car just idling." As soon as I uttered the words, the SUV pulled away, continuing out of the alley.

"They were probably just lost. Or texting. Better they pull over than cause an accident."

"Probably." I squeezed my eyes closed, trying to force my fears out of my brain. I would not let my paranoia ruin another day with Liam.

"Want me to hang out for a little bit? I can help you assemble the climbing tree thing. Let me tell you, that fucker is complicated. Probably need a masters in rocket science to put it together."

I turned to face Liam, Trouble still in my arms, purring contentedly. Liam's face was so damn hopeful. And I wanted him to stay. That idling SUV had freaked me out more than I wanted to admit, and I didn't want to be alone. But more than anything, I wanted to spend more time with Liam.

I gave him a smile. "It would be a bit of a challenge to do major construction and hold this little fella at the same time."

Liam grinned. "And you know if you put him down, he'll just destroy something."

I let out a light laugh. "So very true."

"Thank goodness, I'm here to assist."

I scratched under Trouble's chin. "Thank goodness."

Liam stepped back. "Point me in the direction of your tool box."

I inclined my head towards the sink. "It's under there."

Liam bent to retrieve it, and I couldn't help but notice that he had a ridiculously muscled ass. A paw smacked me in the face. "Ow."

Liam straightened. "You okay?"

I stifled a giggle. "Just Trouble causing trouble."

Liam shook his head. "Where do you think we should set this thing up?"

I glanced around my small apartment. "Maybe over there?" I pointed to a window a few feet from my bed. "So he can look outside?"

Liam surveyed the area. "I think that's perfect."

We carried the pieces needing assembly over to the window. Well, Liam carried. I moved a few odds and ends while trying to keep Trouble balanced in one arm.

Liam studied the pieces of the climbing tree and then the window. His eyes caught on the boards I'd placed vertically on the sides of the window to keep anyone from opening it from the outside. Liam glanced at me, his gaze probing, questioning.

I shrugged, trying to keep my tone light even as my heart rate sped up. "Can't be too careful."

Liam looked around my apartment. The few windows all had boards. My door had a new deadbolt and chain that I'd installed. My coin-filled can alarm system sat to the side of the door. I fought the blush that wanted to rise. I had nothing to be embarrassed about.

Liam's eyes bore into mine. "Do you feel safe here? I can talk to Jensen about having an alarm system installed."

I shook my head. "My system works fine."

Liam slowly nodded. "Okay. But let me know if you change your mind."

"I will." I wouldn't. If I wanted to ask for an alarm, I'd talk to Jensen myself, not go to Liam.

Liam shook his head. "You won't, but I'll pretend I believed your lie."

My mouth fell open. This man saw far too much.

CHAPTER
Twenty-Two

Liam

TESSA'S NEWLY RESTORED CAR BUMPED ALONG THE gravel road as I drove up to where she was taking care of the horses this afternoon. I drummed my fingers on the steering wheel in a staccato beat. I hoped I wasn't shooting myself in the foot by returning her car.

Over the past couple of weeks, we'd spent more and more time together. I'd offered to give Tessa rides home when she was done with her afternoon duties at the ranch so Jensen didn't have to go back into town. Tessa had taken me up on the offer without me having to convince her. I took that as a sign that we were moving in the right direction.

I'd taken to coming up early and bringing my guitar. I'd tool around, working on different songs while Tessa sketched. There was something about being with her, both in our own worlds to a degree but together at the same time. There was a rightness about it that I'd never felt before.

So, hopefully, I wasn't messing up a good thing by returning Tessa's car. I might give back her wheels, but I wasn't going anywhere. I was just going to keep showing up.

I pulled to a stop at the fence. Tessa glanced over her shoulder at the sound of my arrival. One look at her stole all the damn air right out of my lungs. Her hair was loose today, swirling around her as the breeze twisted it into flowing shapes. Her cheeks were a rosy pink from working outdoors, and her eyes seemed to glow in the sunlight.

I swallowed hard, willing my body under control before I did something stupid like maul her or propose. Or both. *Think about anything except how fucking gorgeous she looks. Getting my ass kicked at my friend Austin's MMA gym. Sweaty dudes. Gutting fish with my grandpa.*

That did the trick. Well, it did until I got out of the car and Tessa was right in front of me, close enough for me to see the violet in her eyes and smell the faint lavender scent of whatever perfume or lotion she wore. I was fucked. "Hi." It came out as a croak, like I was going through puberty. What the hell was wrong with me?

Tessa didn't seem to notice. She clasped her hands in front of her chest. "My car's fixed?"

She was fucking adorable. I patted the hood of the vehicle. "Good as new." It practically was a new car. It probably would have been cheaper to go that route. I'd pretty much rebuilt the entire engine, installed new brakes, tires, the works.

Tessa studied the vehicle and began to twist the hem of her shirt. "Thank you so much for doing this. How much do I owe you for everything?"

I rubbed a hand over my jaw. "We were lucky, the place I got most of the parts from was having a sale. I got everything for three-hundred dollars." It was a bald-faced lie. I really hoped she didn't know much about cars because if she did and took one look under the hood, she'd know I was full of it.

Tessa's brows rose. "Really?"

The tension in my shoulders eased a bit when she didn't immediately call me out. "Yup. And you can pay me whenever. There's no rush." I hated that she was paying me at all. I had such a strong urge to take care of Tessa, but I knew that was the last thing she wanted. Her pride and self-reliance were too strong.

Tessa shook her head. "I can give it to you tonight. I honestly thought it would be way worse than that. That car was on its last legs when I bought it."

I shuffled my feet. "You'd be surprised what you can do with a few spare parts."

Tessa grinned. "I'll take your word for it. I can fix a leaky sink or bake just about anything, but I know next to nothing about cars."

I breathed a sigh of relief. I was safe. "Well, I'm happy to help you out whenever you need."

Tessa laughed. "Be careful what you ask for."

I didn't think I'd ever wanted someone to ask me for help so badly in my life. Tessa could ask me to work on her car every day for the next fifty years, and I'd do it with a smile on my face. If my friends, Austin and Ford, back in LA, could see me now, they would laugh their asses off. I was a total goner for a girl I hadn't even kissed.

Tessa took a step closer to me. "Do you have time to hang out for a bit, or do you need to get back?"

I flexed my hand, wanting so badly to reach out and tuck a strand of Tessa's hair behind her ear. "I've got no plans and could use a little writing time."

Tessa beamed up at me. God, I could get lost in that smile, the way her eyes danced, and her nose crinkled. Yep, I was so totally gone for this girl. "Good, because I could use some drawing time, and your playing always gives me good inspiration."

I grinned down at my boots and turned to pull my guitar from the car. "Happy to keep an artist in her creative flow."

Tessa let out an adorable little snort. "I don't know about that, but I like the company."

I lifted my guitar case through the rails and then ducked between them myself, holding a hand out to Tessa. We settled into our usual spots on the boulder—Tessa with her sketchpad, me with my guitar. We lost ourselves in our tasks, in the beauty around us, in simply being with each other.

I set to work on what I'd secretly dubbed *Tessa's Song*. I had snatches of lyrics and sections of music, but I couldn't quite fit it all together. I let my mind wander as my hands shaped chords. Nonsensical musical creations that floated away on the wind. I took in the horses, the rolling hills, the forests below, but my gaze kept traveling back to Tessa.

A smile stretched across my face. Tessa was so damn cute. When she was really focused on her task, the end of her tongue peeked out from between her lips. My gaze zeroed in on Tessa's mouth. I wanted to taste her so badly I could almost convince myself I had. My playing slowed as my eyes focused more intently on those perfect bow lips.

Tessa looked up from her work. "What's wrong?"

I blinked a few times, attempting to clear the haze in my brain. "Did you know that when you concentrate really hard, you stick your tongue out just here?" I couldn't resist the pull, I swept my thumb across the corner of her mouth.

Tessa sucked in a breath but didn't pull away. "Um, no. I didn't."

The air seemed to still around us. I didn't dare move as she leaned in, didn't even breathe. Tessa needed to be the one to close the distance between us. Just as our lips were about to touch, a large creature shoved between us. Phoenix.

Tessa burst into laughter. "Phoenix, were you jealous you weren't the center of attention?" She scratched between the mare's ears.

I eyed the horse dubiously. Next time I got Tessa alone, it needed to be an animal-free zone. No horses. No tiny terror kittens. Hell, no zebras either. Nothing to keep me from my girl's lips.

CHAPTER
Twenty-Three

Tessa

I BIT MY LIP TO KEEP FROM LAUGHING AS LIAM STUDIED THE bakery case as though he were about to attempt to defuse a bomb. I tapped the top of the case from behind the counter. "You know this isn't a life or death decision."

Liam's eyes shot to mine. He straightened, pinning me with a very serious stare. "This is my afternoon dessert choice. The fate of the rest of my day hangs in the balance. If I get a sugar cookie but then realize I should have gone with the peanut butter and chocolate Rice Krispies treat, my entire afternoon will be ruined."

I couldn't hold in my giggle. "You could always get both."

Liam's eyes lit. "I like the way you think. Just give me one of everything sweet."

A snort of laughter escaped me. *Cute, Tessa. Real attractive.* "There are at least eight different desserts in there."

Liam shrugged a shoulder. "Better to have too many than to be riddled with what-might've-beens if I pick wrong." He leaned on the top of the case, his face so very close to mine. "We can take my selection up to the horses, I might share with you."

A flash exploded. My heart stopped. It was almost closing time, and Jensen had already left to pick up Noah from school. I hadn't even heard the bell on the door sound. Liam had that much of an effect on me. And now, someone had taken a photo of the two of us. Together. My heart rate tripled as my breathing picked up its pace, blood roaring in my ears.

A teenage girl I'd seen in here more than a few times dropped her phone from in front of her face, blushing. "Sorry, I couldn't help it. You guys are so freaking cute!"

I rounded the counter, movements jerky like a robot who hadn't been used in years. I reached out a hand. "Give me your phone."

The girl's face scrunched. "Why?"

"Because you don't take people's photos without their permission. Now, give it." When she hesitated, I plucked it from her hand.

"Hey!" she protested. From my peripheral vision, I saw Liam move to calm the girl down, and I think I heard him offer something about an autograph. I was too focused on the phone.

I tapped on the photo icon, my stomach churning as the photo of Liam and me appeared. He was looking at me with such adoration. I didn't have time to care. I hit delete and then double-checked to make sure there were no others. I handed the phone back to the girl. "If you want to be allowed back, you don't take photos of anyone in this café without their permission."

The girl stuffed the phone into her pocket and crossed her arms in front of her chest. "I'll just go to the bakery, you're crazy." And with that, she turned and left.

I let out a slow breath and realized that my entire body was trembling. That was so close. If she hadn't accidentally used a flash, I never would have known she took a photo. It could have been on the cover of a tabloid, and I wouldn't have known until Garrett was at my doorstep.

My breaths came even quicker, short pants that had my fingertips tingling. I knew I was moments away from a full-blown panic attack. I glanced at Liam. "You should go." My words came out half-choked.

Liam eyed me, concern filling his expression. "Tessa, everything's okay." He reached out a hand to rub it down my back, but I stepped out of his grasp. "What's this all about? I know it was rude of her but—"

I couldn't catch my breath. I needed to be alone. I needed to focus on my calming exercises. But I couldn't with Liam here. "Leave! Please—" My legs began to crumple as dark spots danced across my vision.

"Fuck!" Liam caught me just before my knees hit the floor. "Tessa! What's going on?"

"Can't breathe." My chest felt as though it were in a vise. No matter how hard I tried, I couldn't get a good breath.

Liam pulled out his cell. "I'm calling an ambulance."

I batted at his arm. "No!"

Liam's brows pulled together. "Why the hell not? I can't help you!"

I shook my head, hoping he'd listen. "Five. Things." The words were wheezed, but they came through. Liam looked even more confused. "Liam. Tile. Table. Chair. Window." The breaths I took between each word burned.

"Five things." I fisted Liam's shirt. "Shirt." I shakily planted a hand on the tile. "Floor." It took more effort to bring that hand back to my leg. "Jeans." I ran the hand down to my feet. "Boot." Then to the side of the shoe. "Zipper."

My heart was beginning to slow. My breaths didn't hurt as much. "Five things." I inhaled slowly. "Lemon." I knew from what we used to mop the floor. "Tea and honey." Another inhale. "Cinnamon." One more. I sucked air deep into my lungs. Crisp. Clean. Something totally unique. "Liam." The final word came out as a whisper.

My eyes flew open as a hand ghosted over my face. Liam cupped both of my cheeks in his hands. His eyes blazed with an unnamed emotion. "Please don't *ever* do that again." He pressed his forehead against mine. "You just took ten years off my life."

My breathing hitched, but for a whole other reason. I pushed at Liam's chest. "Let me go."

Liam pulled back, hurt filling his eyes. "What did I do?"

I couldn't let myself see the pain in his expression, couldn't allow myself to take it in. I needed him away. Gone. For good. I had been such an idiot to take these risks, thinking my past wouldn't catch up with me. "I can't be anywhere near you."

Liam pushed to his feet. "Why the fuck not?" Anger tinged his words, but I wasn't afraid.

I hugged my knees to my chest as I leaned back into the counter. "I can't tell you why. I just can't."

Liam ran a hand through his hair, pulling roughly on the ends. "We spend every day together for weeks, and you don't even have the courtesy to share why you're telling me to get the hell out of your life and not look back?"

I threw my arms wide, frustration getting the best of me. "Because if even one picture of the two of us gets out there, he'll kill me!"

The room went wired. We both froze.

Liam's jaw was so tight, it was a wonder he didn't crack a molar. "Who?" I'd never heard his voice sound like that. Ice-cold. Lethal. I never would have thought he had it in him. But he did.

I pressed my back harder against the counter, wanting distance between me and that cold rage.

Liam squeezed his eyes closed as if in pain. His hands flexed and clenched, over and over until he seemed to get himself under control. "I'm not mad at you, Tessa." His eyes flared open. "I want to gut whoever has made you live your life in a constant state of fear."

The tension between my shoulder blades released ever so slightly. "He's not worth it."

Liam shifted towards me, easing himself onto the floor. He sat next to me, not touching but close. "Who is he?"

I might as well go for broke now. "My ex-fiancé."

Liam's body locked. "Was he abusive?" He didn't look at me when he asked, just stared straight ahead as if sensing I wouldn't be able to take it if he looked me in the eye.

"Yes." The word came out as a whisper on an exhale.

Liam edged closer so that the side of his body pressed against mine. His jaw worked. "I'm so sorry, Tessa." He blew out a harsh breath. "I want to tear this place apart right now. Demand his name and fucking destroy him." He took a quick peek at me from the corner of his eye. "But I know that probably isn't what you need."

Liam slowly reached over and gently laced his fingers with mine. My skin tingled as though a mini explosion of fireworks were going off in my hand. He pulled our clasped hands to his lips and kissed the back of mine. Liam's mouth caused a riot of sensations. His lips, so incredibly soft, filled my body with warmth. But the stubble surrounding those lips sent delicious shivers up my arm.

Liam dropped our joined hands in his lap. "I don't want to say or do the wrong thing. The last thing in the world I want is to make anything harder for you. So, tell me what you need. If it's to leave you the hell alone, it might break something inside me, but I'll do it."

An invisible fist squeezed my heart. Tears pricked at my eyes. "I don't want you to leave me alone. But I can't see a way out of this mess. I tried everything I could think of, and the only thing that worked was to cease to exist."

Liam dropped my hand, reaching around to pull me to him. "You're not alone. Not anymore. You don't have to figure this out by yourself."

My heart so badly wanted to believe that, to fall into what it meant to belong to someone in a healthy way. To belong to a family of someones. To Jensen. Walker. Taylor. The whole extended Cole family. And to Liam most of all.

Liam squeezed my shoulder. "Tell me this. Did you report him?"

I ground my teeth together. "I tried once. He's got too many connections at every level of the system."

Liam's hand flexed. "Fuck. From near here?" I opened my mouth to protest, but Liam waved a hand. "You don't have to tell me where, just tell me if he lives near here."

I swallowed, my throat dry at the idea of sharing any details of my past. "No."

Liam trailed a hand up and down my arm. "If he's not from around here, and hell, even if he was, I think Walker is your best bet."

I stiffened. "No. If my ex finds out certain people are helping me, he'll do everything in his power to ruin them."

Liam squeezed my arm. "Walker's a great cop. He signed up for that job for a reason. To serve and protect. He's not gonna let some asswipe with connections run him off his job."

Liam didn't know what Garrett could do, just how powerful he was. I wouldn't put my friends at risk. "I can't." The words were a whisper.

Liam brushed his lips against my temple. "Okay. I won't press on that for now. Just think about it." I nodded into his shoulder, soaking up his warmth. "What are we going to do about us? I don't know what this is yet, but it's something. I don't want to lose it."

I shivered, and Liam pulled me tighter against him. "I don't either."

Liam cupped my cheek with his free hand. "Then we won't. Now that I know what you're concerned about, I'll be more careful. I won't flirt with you here or take you out to dinner at the saloon. We can spend time together where random passersby can't catch a glimpse."

My heart thudded against my ribs. "Really? You'd do that?"

Liam's thumb swept across my cheek. "I think I'd do just about anything for you."

It was me who closed the distance. I couldn't express what I wanted to any other way than my lips on his. The kiss was tentative at first, almost a little jerky. I was unsure if he might pull away. But the second his lips moved with mine, all of my hesitations vanished.

Liam tilted my head for better access as his tongue swept inside, dancing with mine. He groaned. The kiss went on forever and yet was over far too soon. Liam pulled back with a muttered curse. "I have to stop now. I mean, fuck, I don't want to stop, but I don't think this is the time or the place."

Sheer panic at someone seeing us and at us taking this any further had my mind racing. And that same anxiety had my next words tumbling out before I could stop them. "I don't know if I'm any good at sex."

Liam's eyes widened, and then he burst out laughing. "What are you talking about?"

I smacked him lightly on the chest. "It's not funny."

Liam grinned down at me. "It's a little funny. Why in the world would you say that?"

I looked down, toying with the edge of my shirt. "I just... I've never really had *good* sex. I've only been with one person." My cheeks heated. "And looking back, it was always about him. What he wanted. What he needed. It was all about power." I swallowed thickly, embarrassment filling me at the admission.

Liam placed a finger under my chin, gently lifting so that my gaze met his. "We are going to take this nice and slow. I'll learn what you like, and I'm pretty damn sure whatever you do to me will drive me out of my skin because I'm basically a walking hard-on whenever you're around."

My hand flew to my mouth as my eyes widened. "I wouldn't have known."

Liam shook his head. "I guess that means you're not looking at my crotch. I don't know if I should be flattered or insulted." I let out a snort of laughter. Liam squeezed me to him. "We'll find our way, Tessa. Just give us some time."

Time was one of the many things I wasn't sure was on our side.

CHAPTER
Twenty-Four

Liam

THE LIGHT WAS FADING AS TESSA AND I DROVE BACK through Sutter Lake after tending the horses. Tessa's anxiety seemed to have lessened. Time with the horses always seemed to bring her peace. It was amazing to watch the way they eased each other.

But an afternoon with Tessa in all the beauty that was the Cole Ranch had done nothing to dull the rage pumping through my veins. Not a damn thing. I clenched the steering wheel harder.

I would never understand the need to tear someone down to make yourself feel better, whether that be physically or emotionally. And I had no doubt now that Tessa had endured both.

I took a deep breath, forcing my hands to relax. Tessa did not need my rage right now. I glanced over at her. She stared out the window at the passing stores with a small smile on her lips—those gorgeously kissable lips. *Don't think about that, jackass.*

I cleared my throat. "Why don't I drop you off, and then I'll pick us up some dinner from the saloon? Burgers sound good?"

Tessa turned to meet my gaze. That smile directed at me was like a fist to the gut in the best way possible. "Burgers sound great."

I pulled to a stop at the back of the Kettle. Shutting off the SUV, I jumped down to make it to Tessa's door before she could open it. She grinned at me. "Such a gentleman."

I returned the tip of lips. "My mama did her best to raise me right."

A slight blush tinged Tessa's cheeks. "I'd say she did a pretty fantastic job."

I guided Tessa towards the door with a hand at the small of her back. "What about your parents? Do they know where you are?" I wanted to take the question back as soon as I asked it.

Pain filled Tessa's eyes. "I don't know where my dad is. My mom died in childbirth. I grew up in the foster care system."

My chest seized. This girl had been through far too much. In this moment, I knew I would do anything in my power to make her life easier, to let her know she had people now. She wasn't alone. I brushed my lips against her temple. "You're amazing, you know that? So fucking strong."

Tessa shuddered against me. "Some days, I don't feel very strong. Some days, I feel like a coward for running."

I squeezed her to me. "You did what you had to do, and it was so damn brave."

Tessa ducked her head as she fumbled for the keys in her bag. "Thank you."

I took them from her and unlocked the door. "I'll walk you up." It was going to be a battle for me to leave Tessa alone for even a second. I knew I'd have to at some point, but I could also take a few extra precautions.

Tessa tucked a strand of hair behind her ear. "You don't have to. I'm fine."

I edged closer, kissing her temple again. It was fast becoming an addiction. Just that brush of lips against innocent skin, that hint of lavender as I inhaled, it eased me somehow. "You're gonna have to put up with me being overprotective after what you told me today." Tessa stiffened in my arms. I gave her a squeeze. "Please, I'm trying to hold it together. Just give me this."

Tessa relaxed the slightest bit in my arms, her head falling to rest against my chest. "I'm sorry I burdened you with all this."

I tugged gently on Tessa's braid, tipping her face up so she met my gaze. "Never apologize for sharing yourself with me. Hard things you've been through, amazing things you've experienced...I want to know everything. I want it all. Every last piece of you."

Tessa stretched up on her toes, brushing her lips against mine. "I'll work on it."

A grin stretched across my face. "Let's start with the important stuff. What kind of cheese on your cheeseburger?"

The most gorgeous smile split her lips. "Sharp cheddar."

I let my head fall back. "Thank, God." Tessa giggled. I tipped my head back down. "French fries or onion rings?"

"French fries."

I shook my head. "You're losing me there..."

Tessa pushed at my chest. "I think you'll survive. But you've forgotten the most important question of all."

My eyebrow arched. "Oh, yeah? And what's that?"

She grinned. "Flavor of milkshake."

I stepped back, my hand clutching my chest as I let out a gasp. "How could I forget?"

"For a self-proclaimed dessert connoisseur, I'm pretty appalled."

I reached out for the edge of Tessa's shirt, pulling her to me. "Okay, Miss Milkshake, what's your flavor pick?"

Tessa looked up at me, her eyes dancing. "Oreo cookie malt, of course."

My mouth fell open. "That's my favorite, too."

She brushed her lips against mine. "I guess that means I can keep you around."

I pulled my ballcap down as I leaned against the bar, waiting for our food. My low profile had just become that much more important. I pulled my phone from my back pocket. I shot off a text to Austin and Ford in LA, asking how things were going for them.

I kept scrolling through various icons before pulling up one of my social media accounts. My label kept them active for me, but I did my best to respond to fans whenever I could. I looked through comments on a photo of one of my live shows last year, replying to every few messages.

My thumb froze over a comment. "Why don't you ever respond anymore? I guess I'm just going to have to come and find you." People were freaking crazy sometimes. I took in the user name. KSpeak. It had to be the same girl. Her motionless body on blood-soaked sheets flashed in my mind. Fuck.

I motioned to the bartender. "I gotta make a call. I'll be right back."

He jerked up his chin at me. "Sure thing."

I made my way through the restaurant and to the back alley, scrolling as I went. The username appeared again. And again. I exited the app and thumbed through my recent contacts. I hit the LA area code.

A gravelly voice answered. "Detective Ruiz."

My hand tightened around the phone. "Hi, Detective. It's Liam Fairchild."

"Hello, Mr. Fairchild. What can I do for you?"

I was probably making too much of this. My nerves were on edge after everything that Tessa had shared with me today. "I think I might be making too much of something."

A door snicking closed sounded across the line. "Always better to err on the side of caution. Why don't you tell me what's going on?"

I pulled a guitar pick out of my pocket and began flipping it back and forth between my fingers. "I got a slightly weird comment on a social media post, and I think it might be Kimberly Speakman."

"Can you text me a link to the post?"

"Sure. Hold on." I minimized the phone call, pulling up my social account and sending the link off to Detective Ruiz. I put the phone back to my ear just as a ding sounded.

"Give me a second."

"Of course." I paced the narrow width of the alley as I waited, listening only to the muffled sound of music from the restaurant, and Ruiz clicking his keyboard.

The sounds of typing stopped. "I think we might have a problem."

My gut tightened. "What?"

"The account does appear to belong to Ms. Speakman, and she's commented on your page eight hundred and sixty-two times in the past two days alone."

I swallowed. "She's obviously sick. I just don't want her to hurt herself again. Can't they bring her in for another hold?"

"I'll get in touch with her doctor and see what we can do. In the meantime, I want you to be cautious. You never know how people who become this singularly focused will react."

Ruiz had no idea how cautious I was going to be, but it wasn't because of some obsessed fan. "Trust me, I'm cautious. But I really don't think it's me you need to be worried about. It's this woman."

Detective Ruiz cleared his throat. "We'll be careful all the way around. How about that?"

I adjusted my ballcap. "That's fair."

"I'll keep you up-to-date with my progress."

I headed back towards the door. "Thank you. I appreciate that."

"Talk soon."

"Have a good night." I hit end on my screen and pulled open the door. This was the last thing I needed to deal with. I roughly shoved the phone into my pocket. I just needed to take precautions. No photos with fans. Avoid going out as much as possible. It wasn't forever. It was just for now.

I grabbed my food from the bartender with a muttered thanks and walked back to the Kettle. Tessa had let me borrow her keys, so I was able to let myself in through the back door. My boots stomped up the wooden stairs. I knocked on the door to Tessa's apartment, not wanting to let myself in.

"Just a second." The door swung open, and there stood Tessa in nothing but a towel.

My Adam's apple bobbed as my throat went dry. Long, lean legs peeked out from terrycloth that was too short and too long all at the same time. Her skin was creamy white, and my hands itched to see if it was as smooth as it looked. My gaze traveled up Tessa's body to where she held the top of the towel together at her breasts. Creamy swells. *Shit.* I blinked furiously, trying to break my gaze.

Tessa cleared her throat, and I finally focused on her face, her cheeks pink. "Sorry, I needed a quick shower. I smelled like horses."

I nodded, the movement jerky. What was I, fifteen again? "I got our food." I held up the bag in my hand.

"Thank you for doing that. I'm just going to get changed real quick."

I stayed rooted to my spot. "Of course."

Tessa turned and picked up a pile of clothes from her bed. The towel rode up higher on her thighs. I looked at the ceiling. "There are drinks in the fridge if you want to grab something," she called as she headed for the bathroom.

"Thanks." I closed and locked the door and then headed for the kitchen. "You've got to get a grip, man," I muttered to myself.

I pulled plates from the cabinets, distributing the burgers and fries on each one and placing them on the table. I set the milkshakes down next. Opening the fridge, I grabbed myself a Coke.

I felt pinpricks in my leg, and my gaze shot down to see a tiny, orange furball climbing up my jeans, cast and all. "Trouble. Why aren't I surprised?" I pulled the kitten off my pants and held him to my chest. He swatted at my face, apparently upset that I'd ruined his fun climbing game. "You have a whole climbing tree that cost about three hundred dollars. Why don't you use that?" Another swat.

The sound of the bathroom door opening reached my ears, and Tessa rounded the corner wearing a pair of yoga pants that hugged every curve and a tee that hung off one shoulder. Her hair was twisted up in a towel. She had no idea how gorgeous she was.

Tessa took in the Coke in one hand and the kitten in my other. "Sorry I don't have beer or anything." She reached out, taking Trouble from me. "Come here, baby," she cooed. Of course, the cat curled up in her arms and started purring, no clawed swats at all.

I shook my head and looked at the can I was holding. "This is perfect." The last thing I needed was alcohol. I needed all the restraint I could muster around this woman. "What can I get you?"

"I'll take one of those." Tessa inclined her head towards my Coke.

I reached into the fridge and pulled out another can.

Tessa took in the table. "Do we need anything else?"

I pulled out her chair. "I think we're good."

"Thanks so much for doing this," Tessa said as she sat, placing Trouble in her lap.

"No problem." As soon as I sat, worries began to swirl. I needed Ruiz to come through, to get Kimberly Speakman the help she needed. And I really needed the whole thing not to blow up in the media. Especially now.

Tessa carefully studied my face. "What's wrong?"

"What do you mean?"

Uncertainty filled Tessa's expression. "You're tense all of a sudden."

Of course, I was fucking tense. In the last five hours, I'd found out that Tessa was on the run from an abusive ex, had to talk to the police about a potential stalker, and seeing Tessa in a towel had me hard enough to split my zipper. So, yes, I was tense. I blew out a breath. "I just had to deal with some stuff back in LA."

Little worry lines appeared in Tessa's forehead. "Is everything okay?"

I rolled my shoulders back. "I'm not sure, honestly. It's a situation with a fan. The cops will figure it out."

The worry lines deepened. "Are you in danger?"

I waved a hand in front of my face. "No, nothing like that. They're just concerned about her mental health. But a doctor's involved now. I'm sure everything will be fine." I hoped that was the truth.

Tessa reached across the table and grabbed my hand. "Not everything is your responsibility, you know."

Damn, this girl could see right through me. Between the Speakman woman attempting suicide and not being able to stop Taylor's kidnapping, I was carrying around a healthy dose of guilt these days. "Some things aren't so easy to let go of."

Tessa gave my hand a squeeze. "I know."

She did know. Better than most. I flipped my palm over so that I could grasp her hand. "You're pretty wise, you know that?"

Tessa grinned. "Just call me the wise baker."

I chuckled, releasing her hand and picking up my burger. "The wise baker horse-whisperer."

"I certainly have a unique cluster of jobs, don't I?"

I took a pull from my Coke. "Life could get boring if you

didn't." I studied Tessa's face. "Have you ever thought about doing something with your art?"

Tessa's gaze dropped to her plate. "I have no real training." Her eyes lifted back to me, a new light in them that looked a lot like hope. "But maybe, one day, when I've improved my technique. It would be amazing to paint for a living."

"You know, true talent doesn't require formal skill. And you've got that. But, if you want, I'm sure you could find some classes around here that specialize in technique."

Tessa twirled a French fry in her hand. "I'd like that. But right now, I have other things to focus on."

My back teeth ground together. One day, I would make sure Tessa could have all the art classes she wanted. For now, I steered us away from art and back to safer topics like the horses and what recipes she was currently perfecting for the Kettle. Dinner passed way too quickly, and I found myself looking for excuses to stay.

A tiny meow came from under the table. I'd forgotten all about Trouble. His head poked up, and he attempted to snag a French fry. Tessa pulled him back. "No-no, baby. Those aren't good for you." She cuddled the kitten to her neck.

I'd never wanted to be a cat so badly in my fucking life. I cleared my throat. "I guess I should go."

Tessa looked up from the kitten. She toyed with Trouble's collar, suddenly looking unsure. "Maybe you could stay?" Her cheeks heated, but her voice strengthened. "I'd like it if you stayed. I'm not ready for..."

"I'd love to stay," I jumped in. Expressions flashed across Tessa's face that told me she was at war with herself. One part of her wanted me here, the other part was scared to death. "I could sleep on the couch." I eyed the worn sofa that looked as if it would barely hold me.

Tessa's shoulders relaxed. "That would be perfect."

"Tessa, all you ever have to do is ask." Our gazes locked, an unnamed emotion flitting across her eyes.

"Thank you." It came out as a whisper. Trouble batted her cheek, breaking the moment. A small smile curved her mouth. "I'm honestly exhausted. I could probably go to sleep right now."

My expression softened. "Then let's go to bed."

We made quick work of cleaning up the kitchen and, before long, Tessa was handing me a pillow and a blanket. "I'm just going to put on my pjs," Tessa said, a faint blush tinging her cheeks.

I bit the inside of my cheek to keep from laughing. She was so damn adorable. "Take your time."

Tessa pulled open a drawer and then dashed to the bathroom. I shucked my boots and clothes, leaving my boxers firmly in place, and then slipped beneath the blanket. A few minutes later, Tessa appeared from the bathroom with a kitten in her arms, wearing what looked like flannel unicorn pajamas.

I couldn't hold in my chuckle. "Are those unicorns on your pjs?"

Tessa looked down. "Yes…"

I laughed harder. "How old are you?"

She huffed. "Oh, shut it."

I grinned. "Come on, time for sleep."

Tessa shuffled towards the bed. "You gonna be nice and not make fun of my super awesome jammies?"

"Only if you never call them jammies again." There was something so refreshing about Tessa. Most girls in my world would have come to bed in their most revealing lingerie, and here Tessa was with flannel pajamas practically buttoned up to her neck. She sat on the bed, placing Trouble in the middle of the mattress.

I looked from the kitten to Tessa and back again. "You let him sleep with you?"

"Of course. He's so tiny, and he needs lots of cuddles after his rough start in life." Tessa pulled the covers up around her, and

Trouble curled into her side.

I bit back a laugh. "You're going to spoil him."

Her gaze met mine as she reached over to turn out the light. "He deserves to be spoiled." She clicked off the light, darkness engulfing the room. Silence filled the space. Nothing but the sound of Trouble's soft purrs. I thought she might have fallen asleep. "Thank you for everything you did today."

My words reached out in the darkness the way I couldn't yet with my body. "Always."

CHAPTER
Twenty-Five

Tessa

I AWOKE TO THE SOUND OF A MUTTERED CURSE. FOR THE briefest moment, I panicked, thinking I was back in DC. Back with *him*. When I heard a meow and a grumbled "Trouble," I released my death grip on the covers. *It's just Liam. I'm safe.* I took slow and steady breaths.

My muscles released, and a sense of calm washed over me. Usually, a trigger like that would have sent me into a full-blown panic attack, but yesterday aside, I was getting better at talking myself through these moments, at identifying something as a trigger and not a true threat. Hope filled my chest. Maybe I could do this with Liam. I knew without a shadow of a doubt that I wanted to try.

"Your cat is a terror," a voice griped from the other side of the room.

I pushed up in bed, trying to get a peek at what was going on. Liam lay on the couch, muscled chest bare. I swallowed hard. It took me a few seconds to tear my eyes away from those broad shoulders and notice that Trouble had perched himself on Liam's pillow and was batting at his face. I let out a snort of laughter. "You might want to stop that, Trouble. It sounds like Liam is a bit of a grump in the morning."

Liam grunted. "That cat is disturbing my beauty sleep."

"He wants to play with you."

Trouble popped Liam right on the nose, and Liam growled, swinging Trouble into his arms and sitting up. "I guess there's no more beauty sleep for me."

My lips pressed together as I resisted a smile. "I think you're plenty pretty enough already."

Liam pushed to his feet and prowled towards me. "Oh, really?" I nodded, my breath catching. Liam leaned forward, dropping Trouble on the mattress and nuzzling my neck. "You smell amazing."

I shuddered, a pleasant chill skittering over my skin. My lower belly clenched. My body was at war with itself. One part of me was dying for Liam to touch me everywhere, the other was terrified out of my mind.

He placed a gentle kiss on my neck. "We're not going there until you're one hundred percent sure."

I was surprised by the overwhelming flood of disappointment. Sure, there was a little relief since I was unsure if I was ready for sex with Liam. But there was so much more disappointment. "Okay." The word came out as a whisper.

He placed a gentle kiss to my temple. "We'll get there. Give us time."

My muscles relaxed. God, I hoped so. I wanted this little bit of living my life to the fullest. This tiny slice of normality. Meeting a guy, the butterflies of those first encounters, maybe even falling in love.

Liam straightened. "What time do you have to be at work?"

I stroked Trouble's fur. "It's actually my day off."

"Want to spend the day with me?"

A smile split my face. "I'd love that."

Liam reached out, taking my hand and pulling me out of bed. "Well, then, let's get moving, the day's a-wasting."

I let out a light laugh. "Suddenly a morning person?"

Liam bent, brushing his lips against mine. "I am when I get to spend the day with a beautiful woman."

My cheeks heated. "Don't kiss me. I haven't brushed my teeth."

Liam snuck in another quick kiss. "Don't give a fuck."

I shook my head. "You're incorrigible."

"And don't you forget it." Liam stood from the bed, and my eyes zeroed in on his boxer-clad form. My belly clenched again. He was gorgeous: broad shoulders, defined pecs, rippled ab muscles that had me leaning forward just a bit, and that dusting of dark brown hair that disappeared beneath the band of his boxers. "Mind if I grab a quick shower?"

Liam's voice brought me out of my daydream. I cleared my throat. "Oh, yeah, of course." Liam smirked. He totally knew I'd been checking him out. "I'll just make us some breakfast while you shower."

"That'd be great." Liam headed for the bathroom, and I watched his butt the whole way.

I'd just put the biscuits in the oven when Liam emerged from the bathroom. His hair was still damp and fell in artful waves. My fingers itched to run through it. "Find everything you need?"

Liam scowled. "I smell like a girl."

I placed the mixing bowl in the sink. "What do you mean?"

"You only had that girlie lavender body wash in your shower. I smell like flowers."

I chuckled. "Sorry about that."

Liam pulled me into his arms, kissing me soundly. My toes actually curled. Who knew that was a real thing? "I need to brush my teeth."

Liam released me. "Go, get ready. I'll pull whatever you just put in the oven out when the timer goes off."

"Perfect." I darted for the bathroom, Trouble on my heels. He'd become a master at doing all things with his cast in tow. I made quick work of brushing my teeth and washing my face. I even threw on a little mascara and lip gloss for good measure. I was spending the day with Liam. I had the urge to let out a girlie squeal but restrained myself.

By the time I exited the bathroom and made my way to the kitchen, I knew I was grinning like a fool. When my gaze met Liam's, I froze. He stood there, holding a gun. My gun. I swallowed hard.

Liam weighed the metal in his hand, his grip natural. "I was looking for a potholder. Imagine my surprise when I came across a 9mm instead."

I mentally cursed. How could I have forgotten to move that? I had two guns. One in my nightstand, and one hidden in a kitchen drawer. I'd gotten neither through exactly legal means.

Liam's eyes pinched closed. "Please tell me you know how to use this properly."

My spine stiffened. "I know enough." And I did. I knew basic gun safety. What I didn't know was if I could actually hit something if I tried.

Liam grimaced. "Okay. New plan for today." My brows rose in question. "You need to feel safe. I'm going to help with that."

"We don't need to—" I started, but Liam cut me off.

"I want to do this. Please, let me." The look in his eyes was pleading.

I crumbled under its weight. "Okay. What did you have in mind?"

Liam set the gun on the counter. "First, we're going to a gun range."

I stiffened. "We can't. Someone might see us and take a picture." Panic flared to life within me.

Liam pulled me to him. "Let me worry about that. No one will take our picture."

I closed my eyes, letting out a long breath. *Trust him.* Liam wouldn't put me at risk. "Okay."

Liam kissed each of my closed eyelids and then my temple. "Thank you."

My eyes opened. "Anything else you have in mind besides a shooting range?"

Liam grinned. "How about a little self-defense training?"

"You know how to teach me self-defense?" A healthy dose of skepticism filled my tone.

He shrugged. "You know one of my best friends is an MMA fighter and owns a gym in LA, right? I helped out there some. Took a lot of classes. Learned from Austin himself. I can teach you the basics."

I'd wanted to take a self-defense class for years, but I had always been too scared that I'd freak out the second someone got me in one of those holds. "I don't know if I can do that."

Liam's expression softened, and he brushed the hair away from my face. "We can go as slow as you want. You set the rules. You're in control."

My teeth tugged on my bottom lip. I could do this. "I want to learn."

Liam gave me a squeeze. "Good. Give me a few minutes to make some calls, and then we'll eat and go."

"Okay." I stared after him as he began dialing.

I rolled my shoulders back as Liam set a bag of sandwiches in my lap that he'd grabbed from a deli down the street from the shooting range. A shooting range that he'd somehow convinced the owner to close for two hours so that we could have the place to ourselves.

Liam turned the keys in the ignition. "How do you feel about everything?"

"Better." I hated to admit it, but I felt a hell of a lot more confident about my ability to handle the guns I owned. Before, I had hoped that just having them would be enough, that the threat of metal that could end a life would keep Garrett away from me. Now, I had the foundation to wield those weapons. Liam had worked with me on my stance, a slower pull of the trigger, and where to focus my gaze for the most accurate shot.

"I talked to the owner, and he said we could come back after hours whenever we want." Liam reached over and tugged my hand into his lap.

Warmth spread up my arm. I loved Liam's casual touches. A simple brush of his hand against my skin calmed my frazzled nerves. It brought comfort. Peace. "Thank you, for everything."

Liam shot me a grin. "The day's not over yet. We have a workout next."

My stomach dipped. My body was already simmering from Liam's lip touches and gentle caresses. I wasn't sure how I would handle full-body contact for an entire afternoon. "Where are we doing that?"

"We'll head back to my place. I set up a gym in the garage of the guest cabin. We can eat and then get to work."

So, we'd be all alone. It was crazy how much had shifted in a matter of weeks. I was no longer scared to be alone with Liam because of past fears, I was scared to be alone with him because I might be falling. And falling meant running would be that much harder if the time came when it was needed.

CHAPTER
Twenty-Six

Liam

TESSA WAS THINKING SO HARD, I COULD PRACTICALLY hear the gears turning in her head. I squeezed the hand I was holding. "We don't have to do this if you're not ready."

Tessa shook her head. "No. I want to."

I pulled to a stop outside the guest cabin, throwing the SUV in park. "Let's eat first." The last thing I wanted to do was push her too far, too soon. But I wanted her to be safe. I'd almost lost it when I found that gun in her kitchen drawer. If you were going to own a gun, you needed to know how to use it.

The shooting range had been about Tessa's safety, but self-defense was about her reclaiming her power. I'd seen so many women come through Austin's classes. Many of them had been mugged or worse. The transformation as weeks went by was always miraculous. Yes, they had new skills that would enable them to defend themselves, but it was about so much more than that. It gave them back their lives.

I wanted to give Tessa the same thing. I hit the clicker to the garage, exposing the space I'd transformed into a gym. It wasn't anything fancy, but it would do the trick. I glanced at Tessa as she surveyed the area with interest. "Want to eat down here? We can spread out on the mats and talk about the basics while we have lunch."

Tessa smiled. "A picnic."

I chuckled. "Sure. Let me just run up and grab us some drinks and paper towels."

"Sounds good."

I squeezed Tessa's hand, pulling her towards me and pressing my lips against hers. I couldn't seem to stop touching her, I always wanted some point of connection, to feel her skin brushing mine, smell that scent that was uniquely Tessa's. "Stay put. I'll come open your door."

She smiled against my mouth. "Okay."

I released her and circled the vehicle, opening her door. "There you go."

Tessa took my hand as she got down. "I love your gentlemanly ways."

I grinned. "My mama would be so happy to hear that." I wanted Tessa and my mom to meet. They'd love each other. And as soon as my mom heard that Tessa didn't have any family left, she'd bring her into the Fairchild fold and never let her go.

Warmth filled my chest. I wanted that to happen. And soon. "I'll be right back." I released Tessa's hand, leaving her in the gym, and jogged up the stairs to grab us drinks.

By the time I made it back down, Tessa had taken a couple of towels from a stack I kept next to the weight bench and spread them out like placemats on the workout mats, setting our sandwiches and chips on each. I chuckled. "So fancy."

Tessa looked up, eyes dancing. "Only the best for the famous rock star."

My chuckle deepened. "Champagne and caviar for me, please." I took a seat opposite her.

Tessa studied me thoughtfully. "You know, for a rock star, you really aren't that spoiled."

I arched a brow. "I'm not *that* spoiled? What am I spoiled about?"

Tessa laughed. "Well, you did close down an entire shooting range for us today."

I shrugged. "Fame does have some perks."

Tessa opened her bag of chips. "I'm sure it does." She popped a chip into her perfect mouth, and I fought the groan that wanted to surface. "So, what's been the best one?"

I blinked, attempting to clear my mind. "Best one what?"

"Best perk."

I unwrapped my sandwich, thinking about the most fun I'd had because of my fame. I grinned. Two things immediately popped into my mind. "Playing the Hollywood Bowl and getting to skip all the lines at Disneyland."

Tessa's mouth fell open. "They let you cut the lines?"

I chuckled. Of course, she'd be more impressed with amusement park perks than playing one of the most famous venues in the world. "They have these ambassadors that take you around and bring you to the front of every line. And you get to see some cool behind-the-scenes stuff, too."

Tessa's expression took on a longing quality I'd rarely seen, and my gut tightened. I was such a callous ass. "You've never been, have you?" I'd doubted one of her foster families would have had the money to take her, and I'd be shocked as shit if her ex had been a frequenter of the happiest place on Earth.

Tessa met my gaze as if forcing herself not to be embarrassed. "No. I've never been. It looks so fun, though."

"We're going." My words came out with finality.

Tessa's brows pulled together. "You want to go to Disneyland now?"

I leaned forward, cupping her face in my hands. "Not now. When we get all this stuff with your ex figured out, and we don't have to hide anymore, we're going. We are going to cut every line and eat so much food we feel sick. We'll bring all our friends from Sutter Lake and mine back in LA, and we'll make a whole day of it."

The smile that split Tessa's face would have brought me to my knees if I weren't already sitting. So pure. So full of joy. I didn't deserve her, but I was going to do my best to take care of the gift she was.

Tessa twisted her head to plant a quick kiss on my palm. "I'd love that."

I pulled her to me, brushing my lips against that spot on her temple—a spot that was all mine. "Good." I released my hold and settled back. "Now, ready to talk some self-defense?"

Tessa groaned. "I'd rather talk Disneyland."

"We can talk Disneyland after. How about that?"

"Deal." Tessa picked up her sandwich. "Instruct away."

I sobered. "We're going to have to talk through some scary scenarios. But we do that so that if those things happen, they aren't quite as frightening, and you know you're prepared."

Tessa took a sip of her Coke, uncertainty filling her expression. "Okay."

I thought through all the things Austin had covered in his basic self-defense class for women. I'd need to call him later and see if he had any specific ideas for Tessa. "The first thing is, do everything in your power to not be taken to a secondary location. Even if someone has a knife or gun. Run and scream first. Don't go willingly."

Tessa nodded, nibbling on a chip. I pushed on. "If you are taken, stay as alert as possible. Keep track of where you're headed if you can. Survey your surroundings. Almost anything can be used as a weapon."

I gestured around the garage turned gym. "Let's practice. Look around here. What could you use to defend yourself?"

Tessa had abandoned her food and now nibbled on her thumbnail as she searched the room. She pointed at a row of dumbbells. "I could use one of those if they weren't too heavy."

I nodded. "Good. What else?"

Tessa's eyes roamed the space, stopping on the weight bench itself. "If I took the weights off the end of that bar, I could use that."

"Great choice. That's one that if you surprised your attacker, wouldn't require you to get as close as the dumbbell."

A small smile tipped Tessa's lips. "What else?"

I walked her through everything else I could think of. How to break zip tie or duct tape restraints. Getting out of basic holds. Typical safety precautions she could take. While Tessa had been hesitant at first, she was eating it up now.

We lay sprawled on the mat after I'd taken her through a series of punches and kicks. My arm curved around Tessa as her head rested on my chest. She tilted her face towards mine so that we made eye contact. "I want to learn more. It's actually kind of fun."

I squeezed her side. "I'm glad you're enjoying it. I'll call Austin tonight and see if he can put together a training program I can take you through."

Tessa kissed the bottom of my chin. "That would be awesome. Thank you so much for doing this." Her expression turned pensive. "You're good about challenging me just the right amount." She let out a frustrated breath. "I know I'm cautious about a lot of things, scared even. It's smart for me to play some of those things that way, but I don't want to miss out on my life because I'm scared all the time."

My eyes bored into Tessa's. "You're not going to miss out on life. You're doing everything you can to make sure that doesn't happen. And I'm going to do everything in my power to help you."

Tears gathered in the corners of Tessa's eyes. "It's been so long since I've had someone in my corner."

I pushed back the hair that had fallen in her face. "I'm always in your corner."

I tapped Austin's contact in my phone as I pulled away from the Kettle after dropping Tessa off. It had taken everything in me not to ask to stay, but I could tell that she needed some space to process everything that was happening between us. And I needed to call Austin and get some suggestions for how to best help her.

The phone rang through my SUV's speakers. It wasn't long before Austin's gruff voice answered. "Please tell me you're calling to say you're coming back to LA. Ford is getting on my last nerve."

I heard another voice from the background. "I heard that, jackass!"

"I meant for you to!" Austin shouted back.

I chuckled. "No dice, man. What'd he do now?"

"He's flirting with my wife." Austin's words came out on a growl.

My chuckle grew into a laugh. "Oh, man, I miss you guys." And I did. I had amazing friends in LA. A close-knit bunch that had divided a bit when Taylor moved up to Sutter Lake and I followed. "You guys should come for a visit."

Austin grunted. "We will, but I'm leaving Ford here."

I grinned at the road. "Whatever you say."

The sound of a door opening and closing came over the line. "So, what's up?"

I gripped the steering wheel a bit tighter. "I need your professional expertise."

Austin chuckled. "You thinking about taking up mixed martial arts?"

I pulled onto the gravel road that led out of town. "No, I think I'll pass on being beaten to a bloody pulp for a living."

"That only happens if you lose. Just don't lose."

I shook my head. "I'm not taking up MMA. I need a self-defense training program for a friend."

Austin was silent for a few seconds. "A friend?"

I cleared my throat. "A girl."

"Oh, how the mighty have fallen." I could hear the smile in Austin's voice. "What does she need self-defense training for? Anything specific?"

My jaw clenched. I knew Tessa wouldn't want me to share details of her past with anyone, but I had to give Austin enough broad strokes so that he could help. "She had an abusive ex. I want her to get some of her power back. I walked her through the basics, and it clicked for her. I thought you might be able to put together some exercises I can take her through and stuff."

"Fuck, man. I'm sorry. Guys that pull that shit are the lowest of the low."

I forced my hands to release their death grip on the steering wheel as I pulled up to the guest cabin. "Yeah." I gritted out the word, not trusting myself to say more.

"I can come up with a plan for her tonight and have it to you by tomorrow. She safe now?"

I ran a hand through my hair and tugged roughly. "No. But I'm working to make her that way."

CHAPTER
Twenty-Seven

Tessa

J ENSEN GROANED AS SHE STOOD, STRETCHING HER ARMS over her head. "Thank God, that's done. You'd think inventory would get easier after a while, but it's always a bitch."

I closed the door to the pantry and gave her a sympathetic smile. "Well, on the bright side, we don't have to worry about that again for another month." It was past eight p.m., and we had been at this for hours, only breaking for dinner.

"True." We walked down the hall towards the office. "Thanks for always being such a trooper about it." Jensen set her laptop on the desk. "What have you got going on for the rest of the night?"

Heat rose to my cheeks. "I think Liam is going to stop by with ice cream."

Jensen arched a brow. "Ice cream, huh? Is that what the kids are calling it these days?"

My blush deepened. "No! Actual ice cream." Well, ice cream and maybe some of those toe-curling kisses.

Jensen chuckled. "Okay, just boring ol' dessert, then."

"Yes, just dessert." I eyed the computer on her desk. "J, could I borrow your laptop if you're not using it tonight?" I'd let my search for more information on Bethany fall by the wayside with everything that had been going on, but this flare of a beginning with Liam had me wanting more firepower in my arsenal against Garrett. I wanted to be truly free—once and for all.

"Of course. You can use it anytime you want. I usually just leave it in the office, so just help yourself."

I took the machine she handed me. "Thanks. I'll have it back by morning."

Jensen waved a hand in front of her face. "I don't even want to see that thing for another month."

I laughed as we headed to the back door. "You're free for a month."

"Hallelujah." She pulled open the back door just as Liam hopped out of his SUV.

"You ladies done slaving away?"

My stomach flipped at the grin he sent our way, and my heart rate picked up speed. His hair was a touch darker than normal, still damp from a recent shower most likely, and he wore a flannel shirt that brought out the green in his hazel eyes and hinted at the muscles I knew lay beneath. I swallowed. Hard.

Jensen returned his grin. "We are free from the hell of inventory. And this one"—she inclined her head towards me—"is all yours."

I had the instant urge to study my shoes.

Liam shut the door to his SUV and headed in our direction. "You're welcome to join us." He held up a bag. "I've got cookies and cream *and* cookie dough."

Jensen shook her head. "I've got to get home and relieve my babysitter." Her brow furrowed. "Aren't those basically the same flavor?"

Liam clutched his chest and let out a mock gasp. "That is sacrilege. These are two totally unique yet equally wonderful forms of ice cream."

Jensen rolled her eyes and turned to me. "I'll leave you to debate ice cream with the cookie monster over there." She pulled me into a gentle hug, and I didn't flinch. Jensen had been doing this more and more since our heart-to-heart. For the first time in more than two years, I felt like I had a real friend again.

I squeezed her back. "Tell Noah I said hi."

"Will do." Jensen headed for her own SUV and took off into the night.

Liam crossed to me, tugging on the hem of my shirt and drawing me to him. My body seemed to tingle at the contact, the pressure of being flush against him. "Hey." He brushed his lips against mine, and I sank into the kiss. His tongue slid between my lips, teasing, caressing, and then taking. His free hand slipped beneath the fall of my hair, and he tipped my head back, granting him better access.

Far too soon, he pulled back, gasping. "You pack one hell of a punch."

I scowled. "I'm not sure that I want my kisses to punch you."

Liam chuckled. "It's a good thing. Trust me." He kissed my temple. "Come on, let's get inside before this ice cream melts."

"Can't have that."

Liam held open the door for me. "No, we can't."

We locked the back door and headed up to my apartment. Just as we walked in, Liam's phone began to ring. He pulled it from his pocket and grimaced, tapping the screen. "Hey, Jim. Hold on a sec." Liam covered the bottom of his phone and looked at me. "It's my lawyer. I need to see what he wants."

I set Jensen's laptop on my bed and gave Trouble, who was curled up on my blanket, a scratch under his chin. "Of course. Want me to put the ice cream in the freezer?"

"Nope, I've got it." Liam gave me a quick kiss and headed for the kitchen, stowing the ice cream in the freezer. "I'm back. What's up?"

Liam and his lawyer started to get into some heavy legal issues from what I could tell from the side of the conversation I could hear, and it sounded like it might take a while. I sat down on my bed and opened the laptop.

Clicking on the internet browser, I started sifting through search results. There were hundreds, maybe thousands, and I soon lost myself in the other woman's story. Her triumphs and her heartbreaking end.

Tears pricked at the corners of my eyes as I read an interview with her parents. They begged for information. When the subject of Garrett Abrams came up, they were careful not to open themselves up to what might later be called slander, but they clearly weren't convinced that Garrett had nothing to do with their daughter's disappearance.

"What's the story with this girl? Who is she to you?"

I jumped at the sound of Liam's voice and slammed the laptop closed. I hadn't even heard him come up behind me. "It's nothing."

Liam's expression shuttered. "Don't lie to me."

"I'm not." I tucked the computer under my crossed legs.

"It makes it even worse to double down on the lie. I'm not an idiot. You're looking into this girl's disappearance for a reason. I thought we were past you lying to cover things up."

My spine straightened. "It's none of your business."

Liam ran a hand through his hair, tugging on the ends. "At least I know that's what you really think." He began to pace the small apartment space. "I keep thinking you've let me in, but you haven't. Only little pieces that you're either forced into sharing or things you think are safe enough to share. What is it going to take for you to trust me?"

The anger that had begun to bubble to the surface at Liam's accusation deflated. "You're right. It was a lie. I'm sorry. It's habit more than anything. I just... You don't know how hard this is for me." I met his gaze, pleading for him to understand. "I've trusted you with more than I ever thought I'd be able to. It's going to take time for me to get used to lowering my walls. I've worked so hard to reinforce them, making them as strong as possible so that no one could ever hurt me again. I'm going to have to get used to letting people past them. But you have to let me go at my own pace."

The tightness in Liam's frame seemed to ease, and he crossed to the bed, sitting and wrapping an arm around me. "You're right. I'm sorry." He kissed my temple. "I was already frustrated from talking to my lawyer, and I just want to make things easier for you, share your burdens. But you need to do that when you're comfortable, not because I badgered you into it."

I twisted around on the bed, framing Liam's face with my hands, his scruff tickling my fingers. "You do both of those things. You ease me. You give me hope for a future I thought might be lost to me."

Liam bent, brushing his lips across mine. "I'm glad."

I burrowed into Liam's chest, soaking up his warmth. I wanted to stay here forever. The yawn overtook me, and my mouth stretched against Liam's pec. He chuckled. "You've had a long day. Why don't we call it a night? We can do ice cream another night."

I straightened, my palms growing damp. "Want to stay? We could, um, cuddle." My face heated as I realized how totally dorky that sounded.

Liam cupped my cheek. "I'd love that. Are you sure?"

I bit my lip and nodded.

Liam gave me a mischievous grin. "Good, because I've been dying to see those unicorn pajamas again."

I awoke to heat everywhere. Liam's large frame curved around me in what felt like the world's coziest cocoon. I hadn't been sure I'd be able to fall asleep, but approximately thirty seconds after my head hit the pillow, I was out.

I stretched. Trouble meowed in protest and jumped off the

bed—he'd mastered that, cast and all.

Liam mumbled against my neck, the action sending a pleasant shiver down my spine. "Sleep well?"

"I slept great." I burrowed back against him, wanting more of his warmth. I came up against something long and hard. It pulsed against my backside. I froze.

Liam chuckled. "He's just saying good morning, don't be alarmed."

I bit my lip to stifle a giggle. "Does he, uh, always do that?"

"Pretty much." Liam's hand moved from my hip and slipped under my pajama top.

My breathing hitched. "Good to know."

"Tessa," Liam rumbled in my ear.

"Yes?"

He ran his nose up and down the shell of my ear. "Can I make you feel good?" My mouth opened and closed, words refusing to come. "Just with my fingers. Nothing else."

My lower belly clenched, and I felt dampness between my legs. "Yes."

Liam slipped his hand beneath the waistband of my pajamas and groaned. "You're already wet."

"Well, you've been pressed up against me and nuzzling my neck so..."

His finger eased between my folds. Teasing. Exploring. Lazy strokes that had more wetness gathering between my legs. "I love how responsive you are."

I hummed, having lost the ability to speak as a single long finger entered me. I let out a moan.

"Love hearing that." Liam worked his finger in and out of me in a slow but steady rhythm. My hips began to move against him of their own accord. I needed more friction, a quicker pace, something. "Need more?"

I nodded, still not quite able to find words. Liam added a

second finger. There was a stretch, a hint of pain—it had been so long—but it quickly melted into heat and sensation. My breath stuttered as his thumb circled that bundle of nerves I knew would be my end.

My entire body tightened as Liam drove me higher, sending sparks throughout my nerve endings. He curved the fingers inside me in a come-hither motion as he pressed down on my clit. Those sparks caught fire. Light danced behind my eyelids, and my walls clamped down on Liam's fingers.

I tried to steady my breathing as I came back to myself. Liam slipped his fingers from my body and brought them to his mouth. My breathing stopped altogether.

"You taste amazing." He nuzzled my neck. "Thank you for giving me that."

I let out a soft laugh. "I'm pretty sure I'm the one who should be thanking you."

Liam shook his head. "You gave me another piece of yourself, more trust. I'm never going to take that for granted."

I swallowed against the emotion gathering in my throat. "You're pretty amazing, you know that?"

Liam chuckled. "Oh, I know." I groaned. Liam rolled to his back, reaching for his phone on my nightstand. "Shit. I've got to get moving. I have to go to Pine Ridge to sign some papers my lawyer sent there, and I wanted to get in and out before a ton of people were around."

I shifted to my side. "But what about you? Don't you want—?" I wasn't really sure how to finish that question.

Liam leaned forward and brushed his lips against mine. "That was just for you."

I bit my lip and nodded. Lying back against the pillows, I watched as Liam quickly dressed. I was never going to miss the chance to enjoy his body on display. He toed on his boots and slipped his phone into his pocket. "I'll meet you at the pasture after your shift?"

"I'll be there."

He paused at the door. "Wish I could stay in bed with you all day."

A soft smile stretched my mouth. "Me, too."

"One of these days."

"One day." I had more hope than ever that we'd get that day. I'd make it so.

"Want to follow me down so you can lock up behind me?"

I shook myself out of the sexual haze I was apparently still in. I never forgot to lock up after people left. I pushed out of bed and slid on my slippers. Following Liam down the stairs, I gave him a quick kiss I wished could've been a hell of a lot longer and sent him on his way.

I checked the clock as I headed back up to my apartment. I didn't need to start my Kettle shift for an hour and a half. I picked up Jensen's laptop from my coffee table and powered it on. I opted for one of the social media sites I had fake accounts on, wanting to send a message with a few questions to one of Bethany's classmates.

I logged in and clicked on the envelope icon. I had three new messages, but the one that caught my eye had no photo, and the name read, *John Doe*. My stomach dipped. I clicked on it.

I've heard you're nosing into something that's none of your business. You're not who you really claim. I know who you really are. And you're about to join Bethany...

My blood turned to ice. I had to run. Now. I needed to destroy my phone, grab my go-bag, and get on the road as soon as possible. I pushed off the bed, striding towards the bathroom when my steps faltered.

My gaze caught on Trouble in his climbing tree. The one Liam had spent way too much money on. The climbing tree he had put together. I glanced back at the computer. Closing my eyes, I took a few steadying breaths. *Think before you do anything crazy.*

I walked back over to the computer and read the message again. If this person really knew who I was, wouldn't they have said so? It would've driven their threat home. And if it was Garrett behind the message, he'd already be at my doorstep, wouldn't he?

I was done with Garrett stealing all the joy from my life. I wasn't going to let the paranoia that he fueled destroy what I was building with Liam. I would simply delete the accounts and stop messaging people. I would find another way to nail Garrett for what he did. I just hoped I could do it without him finding me.

CHAPTER
Twenty-Eight

Liam

I LET OUT WHAT SOUNDED LIKE A CROSS BETWEEN A CURSE, A groan, and a yell. My frustration had reached new limits. After my tease of getting a little bit of my music back, it was all the more aggravating when I hit what felt like a brick wall. The song was at a stalemate.

I didn't know if it was dealing with all the lawyer stuff that I had made it come to a halt, or if I had simply lost my touch. The latter had me rubbing a spot on my sternum that had begun to burn. I glanced at my phone. Only an hour before I could head to meet Tessa.

She'd become my peace lately. The one place the music flowed without frustration. Something about being around her just... how had she put it last night? Eased me. Even when I wasn't able to weave all the threads of a song together, I didn't hit this kind of wall. I didn't doubt if I'd be able to make an album again, I just kept playing until I found another piece of the puzzle to put into place.

I stood from the couch, rolling my shoulders back, attempting to relieve some of the tension that had settled there. My phone buzzed. Swiping it off the table, I tapped the screen. "What's the word, Jim?"

Jim's no-nonsense tone cut across the line. "How bad do you want out of this contract?"

I began to pace. "Pretty fucking bad."

"They aren't going to make this easy."

Of course, they weren't going to make it easy. The last thing in the world my label wanted was their cash cow leaving. "Can you make it happen?"

Papers shuffled in the background. "I can. But it's going to cost."

I dragged a hand through my hair, tugging on the ends. "I knew that going in."

"All right. As long as you understand that *and* that this means you'll be burning a lot of bridges in the process."

I slid open the door to the back deck, inhaling the fresh, pine-scented air. "I'm done, Jim. I don't want that life anymore. I want to make music on my terms. No one else's."

"That's going to be a challenge with all the resources you're cutting off." He was silent for a moment. "But I know if anyone can do it, it's you."

"Thanks, man." I leaned against the deck's railing, staring out at the fields and forests before me. "I signed all the papers you sent over but let me know if you need anything else."

"Will do. I'll keep you updated."

"Thanks."

"Goodbye." With that, my lawyer ended the call.

It was official. I was leaving my label. Or trying to. I watched as a hawk dipped and rolled, keeping an eye out for an early dinner. I couldn't wait to be truly free.

I checked the time. Fuck it, who cared if I was early. I needed to hold Tessa in my arms, inhale her scent, feel my peace.

I hopped out of my SUV, my eyes on nothing but Tessa. She was breathtaking as she broke apart a bale of hay for the herd surrounding her. Her long braid swung as she worked. Her cheeks were pink from the wind. Her eyes—shit. Her eyes that usually held a sparkle around these creatures were dull. Worried.

I quickened my pace, ducking between rails in the fence. She tossed the last of the hay on the ground and turned to face me, forcing a smile. I took her face in my hand. "What's wrong?"

Tessa opened her mouth to speak, a denial most likely on her lips, and then shut it again. She let her head fall to my chest, her arms wrapping around my waist. My arms encircled her. Tessa sighed against my pec. "I need to tell you something."

I fought my muscles' urge to tense. "All right."

Tessa straightened. "Let's go sit on the boulder." I nodded, and we made our way over to the rock. Once settled, Tessa began toying with the fraying hem of her jeans. "The missing girl. The one you saw me looking up online. She's someone my ex used to date."

I said nothing, sensing that Tessa needed to do this at her own pace. She pushed on. "She went missing in college, not long after reporting my ex to the campus police for domestic abuse." My entire body locked.

Tessa stared out at the field in front of her. "Once I made it to Sutter Lake and settled in, I started searching, hunting for any information that might help me make a stand against him. I was hoping I might find an ex who'd be willing to go to the police with me. That if there was more than just me reporting it, they'd have to believe me."

Tessa glanced in my direction, and I did my best to keep the rage and fear off my face. "That day I ran into you outside the library in Pine Ridge, I'd just learned that she was missing. Presumed dead."

My teeth ground together, but I didn't speak. Tessa looked down at her boots. "Today, when I signed in to a fake social media account, I had a message. It said if I didn't stop asking questions, I'd end up like Bethany."

I couldn't stay silent anymore. "Tessa, we have to take this to Walker. He'll believe you."

Tessa shook her head, a look of deep sadness and almost exhaustion filling her eyes. "I know he would. But it's not that simple. Walker can't prosecute my ex. We're not in the same state. And my ex has an alibi for the weekend Bethany went missing."

I reached out, cupping the back of Tessa's neck. Her skin was so smooth, her hair so soft. "We have to try. He can get someone to look into that account."

She placed a palm on my chest. "Liam, there's nothing to find. No photo. The name was John Doe." Anger flickered in her expression. "My ex is a lot of things, but he isn't stupid. He wouldn't leave any trace. And trust me, if he knew it was me, if he knew where I was, I wouldn't be getting anonymous messages."

I pulled her to me, soaking up her warmth, her scent. "Nothing can happen to you."

"It won't."

I held her closer. "Promise me you'll stop looking into this. Or you'll let me hire someone to do it for you."

Tessa pushed off me, eyes wide. "You can't hire anyone." She pushed wisps of hair back from her face. "I thought of doing that myself, but it's too risky. My ex has too much power. He could get to anyone you might hire, flip them, get them to tell him information about you. About me."

"Okay, okay." I pulled her back to me. "I won't. But you can't keep looking into this on your own either. Promise me."

She sighed against my chest. "I promise. I just want this to be over. I want to be free of him forever."

I kissed the top of her head. "We'll figure something out. Together."

CHAPTER
Twenty-Nine

Tessa

MY HEART POUNDED AND CHEST HEAVED, SWEAT dripped down the side of my face. Next to being with the horses or getting lost in my art, this was the best feeling in the world. I pulled the boxing gloves from my hands and grinned up at Liam.

He tossed me a towel. "Your right hook is looking deadly."

My grin turned into a smile as I wiped off my brow. I'd been working on the plan that Liam's friend had put together for a few weeks now, and I was already feeling stronger in every sense of the word. There was something incredible about taking out all my frustrations on the heavy bag, about learning how to truly defend myself. I loved it. I was freaking addicted.

Liam tugged on the hem of my tank, pulling me flush against him. My body heated a bit more. "You're a total badass." He leaned in, taking my mouth in a slow kiss that ratcheted up the fire in my belly a few degrees. My breasts pressed into Liam's chest, and he groaned, pulling away.

We'd settled into a routine of sorts. Liam would help me with the horses each afternoon, we'd hang in the pasture—me sketching, him strumming his guitar. Then we'd run through a workout in his home gym before heading back to my apartment where I'd cook us dinner, and we'd play with Trouble.

Liam spent every night with me now, and the touches and

caresses had continued. He would stroke me to orgasm but refuse to let me return the favor. It was as though he sensed I wasn't quite ready to take things further. But lying close to Liam every night, feeling his body pressed up against mine, was driving me mad.

I deepened the kiss. My tongue dueling with Liam's. I felt him harden against me, and I wanted to moan.

Liam pulled back with a gasp. "You're going to kill me." His expression softened. "But it'd be a hell of a way to go."

I opened my mouth, ready to say the words that I knew Liam needed to hear, that I wanted more, that I was ready for all of him. Fear swept through me, stealing the things I so badly wanted to say. It wasn't that I was scared that Liam would hurt me, I was terrified that I wouldn't be any good at sex with an equal partner, with someone who wasn't trying to overpower me, someone who got off on my powerlessness.

I balled up my fists in frustration. Maybe I needed some more time with the punching bag. I let out a long breath.

Liam tucked a strand of hair behind my ear. "What's wrong?" He always knew when something was going on, his gaze unbelievably perceptive, taking in every micro-expression and movement.

"I want more. But something keeps holding me back from asking for it." My hands clenched tighter.

Liam wrapped his arms around me, and my own followed suit around him. "We have all the time in the world. You'll know when you're ready."

I let out an aggravated growl. "I want to be ready now. I feel like I'm about to combust." Liam chuckled, the sound sending vibrations through me. "That's not helping."

He only laughed harder. "I'm just glad I'm not the only one."

I sighed. "You're definitely not the only one." I tipped up my chin so that it rested on his sternum. We were both sweaty and gross, and there was nowhere I'd rather be. I stared into Liam's hazel eyes, trying to beam all the thoughts I wasn't quite ready to say out loud to him.

He brushed his lips against my temple, the spot that always sent delicious shivers down my spine, and then released me. "Come on, we need to grab showers if we don't want to be late for dinner at the Coles."

My stomach flipped. Liam and I were still keeping a low profile in public, but our friends had slowly begun to realize that something was going on between us. Jensen would waggle her eyebrows at me every time Liam came into the Kettle, but she hadn't outright said anything after the night that Liam had brought me ice cream. I knew that time was coming to an end.

Tonight, we were going to dinner at the Cole Ranch. We were arriving together, and Liam had already made it clear that he wasn't shy about showing his affections when no one would be able to snap a picture.

I picked up my boxing gloves that I'd let fall to the mat. "Are you sure about this?"

Liam studied my face. "What's got you nervous?"

I pressed my lips together before speaking. "I just want to make sure you're ready for everyone to know."

Liam wrapped me in another hug and whispered in my ear, "I wish the entire world could know that I have somehow conned the most beautiful, badass girl in the world to agree to be mine. But since that's impossible right now, I'll settle for telling our friends."

He kissed my temple again. "They'll understand that we're keeping a low profile in public because we don't want any press attention. They won't need another reason."

My muscles relaxed at his reassurance. I hadn't realized how nervous I was about everything until that moment. I stretched up on my tiptoes, brushing my lips against his stubbled cheek.

"You're pretty great, you know that?"

Liam chuckled. "Don't tell me that too often, I'm liable to get cocky."

I ducked under Liam's embrace and pulled his arm behind his back in one of the holds he'd shown me. "Can't have that now."

Liam groaned. "Should've never given you the tools to kick my ass."

I released his arm. "It really wasn't the wisest decision."

Liam moved with a speed I'd had no idea he possessed. In a matter of seconds, he'd swept my legs out from under me and taken me down to the mat with a gentle thud, his body covering mine. He kissed me, long and deep. His tongue slipped between my lips, stroking my own in a tempo that sent fire licking through my veins.

The kiss was over far too soon. And as Liam retreated, he nipped my bottom lip. "Gotta keep you on your toes." He winked and pulled me to my feet, but the daze he'd left me in remained until the cold water of my shower snapped me back to reality. This man was going to be the death of me.

We pulled to a stop outside the Cole family's ranch house. I fidgeted with the hem of my shirt. Liam pulled my hand up to his mouth, pressing his lips to my fingers. "Everything's going to be fine. And if it gets to be too much, just squeeze my hand three times, and I'll make an excuse for why we have to leave."

I nodded. "Okay."

Liam's gaze met mine. "Everyone in there loves you."

My heart warmed. He was right. The people in that house only wanted the best for me. This would be fine. "Let's go."

Liam gave me a quick kiss. "That's my girl." He exited the SUV, and by now I knew to stay put. The man got all scowly if I didn't let him open my door.

I took the hand Liam offered and slid from the vehicle. He linked his fingers with mine, and I soaked in their reassuring pressure. When we reached the bottom of the porch steps, the front door flew open, and Jensen stood there, a massive grin on her face. "I *knew* it!"

I couldn't help the smile that stretched my face. Liam kept hold of my hand and led me up the stairs. "Hello, to you, too, Jensen."

Jensen waved a hand in the air. "Yeah, yeah, nice to see you, Hollywood. Now, release my friend so I can take her to the kitchen and get every single detail about how this all came to be."

Liam looked down at me, checking to see if I needed him to run interference. I shook my head and reached up to brush my lips against his cheek. "I'll be fine."

He kissed my temple and let me go. "Take good care of my girl, Little J."

Jensen scowled at the use of the nickname. "You two are so cute I could puke."

Liam chuckled and headed for the huddle of men in the living room, while Jensen linked her arm with mine and led me to the kitchen. Sarah was bustling about, making last-minute preparations, while Irma and Taylor sat in their usual spots sipping wine.

Jensen cleared her throat before anyone could say anything. "Ladies, I need you all to know that Miss Tessa just arrived with a certain musician, and they were *holding hands.*" My cheeks began to heat as everyone turned to stare at me.

Irma raised her half-full glass. "What did I tell you? Are you finally going to believe I have a psychic gift now? I could use a little more respect around here."

Sarah shook her head and then looked at me. "You couldn't have picked someone else to date? We'll never hear the end of it now."

Irma huffed. "Zero respect, I tell you."

I laughed. "Well, I'm kind of partial to that one." I jerked a thumb in the direction of the living room.

Sarah hummed. "He is rather handsome."

Taylor patted the stool next to her. "Come, sit. I want to hear everything you're willing to share." Her nose scrunched. "Well, not the sexy stuff. That'd just be weird because Liam is like my brother."

Irma leaned forward on her stool. "Ignore her. I want *all* the dirty details."

"Mother," Sarah chided.

Irma shrugged. "I'm old, I'm not dead. And that man has an ass that doesn't quit."

My mouth fell open. There was a three-count of silence and then we all dissolved into laughter. Warmth spread through my body. I realized that this is what it was like to let yourself belong. To ease up on your guard enough to let people in. It was the best feeling in the world.

CHAPTER
Thirty

Liam

"YOU SEEM HAPPY."

I shifted my gaze from the view off my back deck and turned towards Taylor. "I am." I loved coming out here each day to watch the way the morning sun painted the fields. Loved working on music out here. Sutter Lake was good for me. Tessa was good for me.

Taylor grinned into her mug of coffee. "Don't overwhelm me with words."

I chuckled. "Tessa makes me happy."

Taylor's grin widened. "I'm so glad. For both of you."

I sobered slightly. "I don't know that I deserve her, but I'm going to do everything in my power to keep her."

My statement did nothing to dull Taylor's smile. "It's good you feel that way, it means you'll treat Tessa right."

I took a sip of my coffee. "I'll do my best."

Taylor studied me. "How does she feel about the fame factor?"

I stiffened. "Tessa doesn't need that kind of attention right now, so we're keeping things as low-key as possible in public."

Little lines of worry creased Taylor's face. "You know that can't last forever, right? She's going to have to deal with it at some point."

"Tessa doesn't have to deal with anything she doesn't want to." The words came out harsher than I would have liked. My instinct was to defend Tessa, even to one of my best friends. "I'm sorry. I didn't mean to snap at you. But you don't know the whole story."

The lines of worry in Taylor's brow deepened. "What do you mean?"

I studied the brown liquid swirling in my cup. "It's not my story to tell."

Taylor searched my face, deciding whether or not to push for more information. Whatever she saw there made her back off. "Okay. She's lucky to have you. I hope you two can work it out."

"We will." There was no other option, because this life I was building with Tessa, even one hidden in the shadows, was sweeter than anything I ever imagined. I switched gears to a safer topic. "How are things with you? Any luck on the job front?"

Taylor's expression brightened. "I have an interview at Sutter Lake Elementary next week."

I grinned. "T, that's great."

She settled back in her rocker. "I really hope I get it. I hadn't realized how much I missed teaching until I started tutoring Noah. I'm ready to get back to it."

I took another pull of coffee. "You have a great resume. They'd be a fool not to hire you."

Taylor laughed. "You sound like Walker."

"Well, he's right. How are things with you two?"

A starry-eyed softness settled on Taylor's face. "We're great."

I was about to make fun of my clearly head-over-heels friend when my phone buzzed in my pocket. I pulled it out and tapped the screen, hoping it was Tessa. Who was I kidding? If anyone was head over heels, it was me.

Dan – Label: *We have a situation. The press got word late last night about your fan attempting suicide. They're concocting all sorts of crazy stories about you two being romantically linked, and you dumping her before the attempt. They're bribing everyone and their brother, trying to figure out where you are. You need security.*

Tell me where you are so I can send them.

I felt the blood drain from my face. Before, I had just been a celebrity the paparazzi hadn't seen in a while. Now, they would be desperate for information. Rabid for photos. And if they found me here... Tessa. *Fuck.*

I jumped as a hand grasped my forearm. Taylor leaned forward. "What's wrong?"

My phone buzzed again.

Dan – Label: *Never mind. They know where you are. Stay inside and don't answer the door. And send me your goddamned address so I can get security to you now!*

I stood, sending my rocking chair flying back. "Fuck!"

Taylor rose. "Liam, tell me what's going on. You're scaring me."

Those words were like being dunked in ice water. After everything that Taylor had been through in the past year, the last thing she needed was me being an asshole and freaking her out. I pulled her into a quick hug and kissed the top of her head before releasing her. "Remember that fan I told you about?"

Taylor paled. "Is everything okay?"

"With the fan?" I shook my head. "As far as I know, she's fine. But the press just found out last night, and now they know I'm in Sutter Lake. There are probably paparazzi already here or at least on their way."

Confusion filled Taylor's expression. "That sucks that your hideout's been revealed, but just stay put, and they'll lose interest eventually."

She didn't get it. My stomach roiled with how careless I'd been. "Taylor, you can't tell anyone."

"Okay..."

I squeezed the bridge of my nose. "Tessa's hiding from an abusive ex. If one townsperson tells a member of the media that they've seen the two of us, it doesn't matter if I stay hidden.

They'll take photos of Tessa, and her ex will know exactly where she is."

Taylor's eyes widened. "Tessa knows why you're hiding out here, right? That there was a chance the press could descend in a feeding frenzy?"

I grimaced. "Not exactly."

"Liam. She deserves to know that. You need to warn her right now."

I tapped the screen on my phone again and hit Tessa's contact. It rang and rang before going to voicemail. "No answer."

Taylor grabbed her purse. "Come on, I'll drive. With any luck, the paps won't have made it here yet."

We jogged to Taylor's SUV and hopped in. Gravel spun as Taylor reversed. I stared out the windshield, willing the vehicle to go faster. "Please hurry."

Taylor gripped the wheel tighter. "I'm going as fast as is safe."

I caught her gaze in the rearview mirror. "I'll never forgive myself if something happens to Tessa because of me."

CHAPTER
Thirty-One

Tessa

I HUMMED ALONG TO THE TUNE ON THE RADIO AS I ROLLED out dough for a new sugar cookie recipe I was trying today. I didn't usually hum. My singing voice was more likely to call dogs than match the notes of whatever song was playing, but I didn't care. Because I was happy.

For the first time in a long time, I had hope for my future. Hope that I would eventually be able to extricate myself from the shadows of my past and that on the other side, there would be a beautiful life. I grinned down at the dough, thinking about how much fun I'd had at dinner last night. How I'd gossiped with the girls and laughed when the guys gave Liam a hard time.

It was so simple. But the gift of belonging was everything.

"Someone has that falling in love glow."

I turned at the sound of Jensen's voice. "I don't know about that." I did know, and I was pretty sure I'd already fallen.

Jensen grinned. "Whatever you say. I think the breakfast rush is finally over." She glanced out the kitchen door to the front windows. "But I've seen a lot more cars drive by than normal. There must be something going on I don't know about. You might want to double the recipe for whatever you're making next."

"Will do—"

My words were cut off by a voice on the radio saying a familiar name. "*Liam Fairchild is in the news again today. Rumors are circulating that a woman he was involved with attempted suicide in the singer's hotel room after he broke things off with her. Others are saying it was a fan who was stalking Liam. What we know for sure is that he was the one who found her."*

My stomach pitched. The man continued. *"Fairchild's team hasn't responded to our request for comment, but it turns out he's been hiding out in our neck of the woods. Sutter Lake. Can you believe that, folks? We have a reporter on the ground, and we're getting word that he's been seen cozying up to a local woman in recent months."*

Jensen unplugged the radio in a swift motion. "Are you okay?"

Oh, God. There had been so much more to this story than Liam had told me. He could be in real danger. My vision tunneled slightly as I could feel the wall of protection I'd built begin to crumble around me. *I* could be in real danger. "What am I going to do, J? What if someone tells them my name? Where I work? Garrett could find me."

Jensen stormed to the front of the store where only one customer lingered from earlier that morning. That guy Al, who seemed to be here every day now. "I'm sorry, sir, but we need to close unexpectedly. If you come back tomorrow, I'll get you breakfast on the house."

The man's brow furrowed as his eyes darted from Jensen to the kitchen. "I hope everything's okay."

Jensen ushered him out the front door. "It'll be fine. Thank you." She shut the door behind him, flipping the lock and switching the sign to *Closed*. Then she strode back to the kitchen and wrapped me in a tight hug. "It'll be okay. We'll figure this out."

I pulled back, shaking my head, hot tears filling my eyes. "I have to go. I have to pack as quickly as I can, get Trouble, and go."

Jensen gripped my shoulders tightly. "Don't do anything yet. It's not like there are pictures of you floating around. You just need to lie low for a few days. I can get Taylor to help out at the shop, and you can just stay in your apartment. I bet Liam's freaking out. You might want to call him."

A sharp pain pierced my heart. Liam had known this might happen. He'd mentioned the issue with a fan. Tip of the freaking iceberg. I'd had no idea it could blow up to something like this, but Liam must have known. I let myself sink to the floor and wrapped my arms around my legs. "I can't call him right now."

Jensen sank with me, placing an arm around my shoulders. "Do you want me to?"

Tears tracked down my cheeks. "No. He knew about the fan. Knew this might happen. Why didn't he warn me that this was a possibility, at least? He basically lied. Right to my face. Lied when he knows how hard it is for me to trust people."

Jensen winced. "Tessa, I don't think it was a lie exactly. He probably just didn't want to burden you when he knew you had so much going on yourself. And he probably thought no one would find him here even if the news did break."

My heart began to pound faster in my chest. I loved Jensen, but she was wrong about this. Liam had deliberately kept something from me. And if he'd kept this from me, then what else might be lurking beneath the surface? My breaths started coming quicker.

Pounding sounded on the back door. "Tessa, Jensen? It's Liam. Let me in."

My body tensed. I shook my head at Jensen, panic licking my veins. "I can't talk to him right now."

The banging continued. Jensen pushed to her feet. "Are you sure?" I shook my head vehemently, and she gave me a sympathetic look. "I'll get rid of him. Hide in the pantry in case he gets pushy."

I nodded, ducking into the small, dark space, a place that smelled of some of my most comforting scents. It didn't help.

I heard the sound of the back door unlatching before Jensen's voice. "Get in here before someone sees you."

"Where is she?"

The door shut and locked. "She doesn't want to see you right now."

I peeked through the crack in the door, just enough to see Liam. My heart clenched as his shoulders sagged.

"I just want to make sure she's safe."

Jensen squeezed Liam's shoulder. "She is safe. You just need to give her some time."

Liam straightened. "I can get her out of here. I'll have a private plane at the airstrip in a few hours, and we can go wherever she wants."

Jensen's voice softened even further. "Liam, anywhere with you puts her at risk. If you really want to help her, take that plane and go back to LA. The media will follow you and leave Tessa alone, thinking their tipsters got it wrong."

I bit down on my fingers to keep from crying out. It would be best if Liam left. It would keep me under the radar. My stomach roiled. Jensen was right. I wouldn't be safe anywhere in the world if Liam were with me. Wherever he went, curious eyes and shuttering cameras would follow. Maybe I had been kidding myself this whole time. There was no way for us to make this work. We were too different. So why did it feel like my heart was being torn in two?

CHAPTER
Thirty-Two

Liam

ICE CLINKED AGAINST MY GLASS AS TAYLOR REFILLED IT. SHE gave me a sympathetic smile. "In times of trouble, it's all about the Patron."

I took a sip of the tequila. It burned, but the blaze down my throat was a welcome distraction. I'd spent the day putting out as many fires as possible, approving a statement for my publicist to release, hoping that it would give the vultures something to feed on and maybe make them go back to LA.

I sure as hell wasn't going. I wasn't leaving Tessa. We had to work this out. I let my head fall back on the couch and groaned.

Walker rested his booted feet on the coffee table. "Are you two going to tell me what's going on? I know it's a shitstorm with these photographers crawling all over town, but I get the feeling that's not the whole story. And I'm thinking it has something to do with the fact that Tessa isn't here right now."

I rubbed a hand over my jaw. "I fucked up. I can't tell you why, but Tessa can't be photographed with me. I knew this whole thing with the fan might hit the papers and drum up the media's interest in me. I didn't tell Tessa that was a possibility."

Walker whistled. "Look, I know she's running from something." He eyed Taylor. "I know a little something about that. Don't let her use this as an excuse to bolt. Apologize—"

"Grovel," Taylor interrupted.

Walker grinned. "Beg if you have to. But keep steady pressure on those walls. Don't give her a chance to push you out."

I swirled the liquid in my glass, staring at the patterns it made around the ice. "I think I'm in love with her. And I might've just ruined the best thing that's happened to me by being a dumbass."

Taylor reached over and squeezed my hand. "Tessa knows you have a good heart." Taylor glanced at Walker, love filling her eyes. "We all make mistakes. If it's meant to be, you'll mend those cracks and come back stronger than you were before."

I sighed and took another pull from my drink. "I hope you're right."

I braced myself as I lifted my hand to knock on the Kettle's door. It was early. Way before opening, but I knew Tessa was back from taking care of the horses. Her car was here.

I rapped on the door. Silence. I knocked again. Still nothing. I pulled out my phone and sent a text.

Me: *I'm at the back door. Please talk to me. If you don't like what I have to say, I'll leave you alone after that.*

It was a total lie. I wouldn't leave Tessa alone for anything, but I could be patient if I needed to be, slow our pace even more. I would do anything for a little bit of Tessa in my days.

The door flew open. "What are you doing here?" Tessa's hair was wild, all loose waves flying around her face. Her violet eyes were blazing, and her cheeks were a rosy pink. She was breathtaking in her anger.

Tessa opened the door wider. "Get in here before someone sees you."

I didn't hesitate, quickly ducking inside and closing the door behind me. "Tessa, I'm so sorry—" I reached out a hand to draw her to me. It was instinct. I couldn't seem to be around Tessa without wanting to touch her in some way.

She ducked out of my grasp. "No. You don't get to do that. You kept this from me. Something that could put my life at risk. The lives of those I care about. God, Liam. What if Garrett found me? What if he hurt Jensen for giving me a job and a place to stay? Did you not believe me when I told you he was crazy?" By the end of her speech, Tessa was yelling.

My chest spasmed at the idea of anyone trying to hurt Tessa. "I'm so fucking sorry. I messed up. I thought if I stayed out of sight for a while, this thing wouldn't hit the media. And I didn't want to tell you about the risk because I didn't want to give you a reason to push me away."

Tessa crossed her arms. "So, you were just thinking about what you wanted."

I ran a hand through my hair, pulling on the ends. "It was selfish and wrong. You should have all the information you need to make whatever decisions you want about your life. All I can say is that I was an idiot because I was falling in love with you. I was selfish because I want more nights to hold you, more afternoons in the pasture to make music you inspire."

Tessa sucked in a sharp breath, but I pressed on. "I didn't think about the fact that I was taking away some of the power you've fought so hard to regain. You'll never know how fucking sorry I am. But please don't let my one fuck-up ruin this."

I took a step closer to Tessa, she didn't move out of my path. "I know we're just getting started, but this thing between us is the most real I've ever felt." Another step. "Don't squash it because it's your instinct to run."

I slowly reached up to cup Tessa's face, staring into eyes now brimming with tears. "I'm going to mess up. But I promise from now on I will always be honest with you, even if it's something I know you aren't going to like. I promise I will do my best to be the man you deserve, someone who empowers you and stands by your side while you fight whatever battles you need to fight."

The tears in Tessa's eyes spilled over, and I wiped them away with my thumbs. "I know we have a long way to go, but I want to take that journey with you. Please, let me."

Tessa's eyes searched mine, looking for something. I wasn't sure what. "I love you." The sentence came out as a hoarse whisper, but it was the most beautiful thing I had ever heard.

I pulled her face closer to mine. "Say it again."

Tessa licked her lips as she brought herself even closer. "I love you."

My mouth crashed down on hers, my lips and tongue tangling with hers. It was a kiss of pent-up frustration, of passion, of love. My hands fisted in Tessa's silky hair, needing purchase to bring her as close to me as possible. Her body pressed harder into mine. The feel of her curves against me had my dick jerking.

I pulled back with a gasp. Catching my breath, I brought my forehead down to hers. "I love you so fucking much."

Tessa started to laugh. I moved back so I could take in her expression. "It's hilarious that I love you?"

She only laughed harder. "It's not that. I mean, it's a little funny that you had to curse when telling me you loved me for the first time."

I grinned. "Curse words show important emphasis."

Tessa shook her head. "I'm laughing because I'm happy." My brow quirked. She pushed on, explaining. "I yelled at you when you first came in."

"Yeah…" I wasn't sure where she was going with this.

Tessa smiled as though she had just discovered the cure to cancer. "I haven't yelled at anyone in over six years."

My hands fisted at my sides. I couldn't imagine the state of fear she must have been living in for her to never raise her voice to even a single person.

Tessa cupped my face. "You don't understand. I yelled at you. That means I trust you. Even though you fucked up. And I know we both will in this. I trust you. I trust you not to hurt me. I trust that I can totally express myself. You are…safe to me."

Tessa was letting me in. And, God, it was so beautiful.

Tessa's violet eyes caught fire then, sparking with a heat that had my blood simmering. She brushed her lips against mine, hands running through my hair, tugging on the strands. "Take me to bed."

CHAPTER
Thirty-Three

Tessa

MY HEART HAMMERED AGAINST MY RIBS, BUT IT wasn't from fear or even nervousness, it was from anticipation. I wasn't sure why it took everything falling apart for my trust to slide into place, but I guess that's how things worked sometimes. It took my life breaking apart, the one I'd thought I wanted with Garrett, for me to start building the beautiful one I had now. It wasn't perfect, but it was real. And perfection was overrated anyway.

Liam's eyes widened. "Are you sure? A lot has happened in the past couple days—"

I cut him off with a deep kiss. "I'm sure."

Liam's arms tightened around me as he picked me off my feet. I wrapped my legs around him, laughing as he took the stairs two at a time as though I weighed nothing.

He pushed open my door, sending it flying into the wall, and making Trouble run for his kitty climbing tree cave. Liam closed the door behind him with a booted foot and carried me to the bed. He laid me down carefully—so gently it made my heart hurt.

I stared up at Liam. Strands of hair swept down on one side of his face, framing his hazel eyes. Irises that seemed to blaze just a bit brighter as he gazed down at me. I watched in fascination as his strong hands started to unbutton his shirt, hands that I was going to feel all over my body.

I shivered as Liam's shirt fell to the floor and he toed off his boots. My heart skipped a beat as my eyes traced his upper body. His skin, still sun-kissed from his time in California, seemed to glow in the early morning light.

I reached out a hand, needing to feel that flesh beneath my hands. Liam leaned over me, granting me access. My fingertips began to tingle just before they touched his chest as if they knew they were about to experience a feast for the senses.

I trailed my hands lightly over Liam's pecs. Soft skin with just a dusting of hair tickled the pads of my fingers. I kept exploring, circling Liam's nipples that seemed to grow harder under my touch, then lower to those abs that seemed to defy nature.

I met Liam's gaze. "You're beautiful."

He grinned down at me. "I prefer ruggedly handsome, but I'll take beautiful."

Liam swept his mouth across mine, just a soft brush, but the promise of what was to come sent heat flooding through my veins. He pulled back and traced my lips with his thumb. "These lips. So pink. So perfect. I've wanted them on my body since the first time I saw them."

I sucked in a breath, and my core tightened at the thought of all the places my lips might travel. Liam's eyes flared when my mouth parted on that inhale. His hands left my face and skimmed under my shirt, lifting as he went. The pads of his fingertips, roughened from all the time spent playing the guitar, created delicious sensations across my skin.

I lifted my hands over my head, helping Liam ease off my shirt. He let out a groan. "No bra?"

My cheeks heated. "You started pounding on my door when I had just gotten out of the shower, I didn't have a lot of time."

Liam's gaze shot to my yoga pants, his hands following. He ran his thumb lightly over the seam in my pants, and my hips bowed off the bed. "Fuck, you're bare here, too, aren't you?"

My teeth pressed into my bottom lip and I nodded. Liam cursed. "I need to see all of you. Can I?" His hands paused at the waistband of my yoga pants.

"Yes." The word came out as half whisper, half pant.

Liam slowly pulled the spandex down my legs until he was kneeling before me, gazing down the length of my body. "You are so fucking beautiful, it almost hurts to look at you."

My chest constricted. Liam looked at me with such reverence. He didn't touch for a long moment, just stared as though he were committing every detail of my body to memory.

I couldn't take it anymore. My skin was on fire, and I needed to feel him against me, inside me, everywhere he could be. "Touch me. Please."

It was all Liam needed. He unbuttoned his jeans, shucking them with a speed that was shocking, and then he covered my body with his own. His hands framed my face first. "I love you. And what you're giving me right now…trusting me with your body… It's the most precious fucking gift."

My eyes began to fill. "Don't make me cry."

Liam smiled and took my lips with his. The kiss was slow, and he spent all the time in the world exploring my mouth, infusing my taste with his own. It was sexy as hell. Liam rolled to his side so that he was pressed up against me, his erection digging into my hip in a way that made my thighs tingle with anticipation.

Liam raised himself up, resting his head on one arm so that he could watch while his other hand explored. He tucked a strand of hair behind my ear and then trailed his digits lower, the roughened fingertips leaving goosebumps in their wake.

He ran a single finger down the column of my throat and along my collarbone. It dipped into the valley of my chest before Liam changed directions and palmed a breast in his hand. He circled my nipple with his thumb, and I pressed my head back into the mattress, letting out a moan.

"Does that feel good?" Liam's voice was rough, just like the skin of his fingertips, sending shivers down my spine.

"So good." I let out another moan as he rolled my nipple between his thumb and forefinger.

Liam kept up the motion, sending zaps of sensation through my nerve endings. "I want to make you come just like this."

I let out a garbled sound of frustration. That would take too long. "More."

Liam chuckled. "Okay, I'll give you more." He slipped from the bed, and I wanted to cry out at the loss of his heat, of his body pressed against mine. He kneeled between my legs at the end of the bed, and with a single tug, pulled me to the edge of the mattress.

My instinct was to close my legs, but I couldn't, Liam's shoulders kept them apart. He grasped my thighs, staring so damn intently at my center. He softly stroked circles on my inner thighs. "Every inch of you is gorgeous."

I sucked in a breath. "I, um, I've never done this before." Liam's gaze shot to mine. "I mean, I've had sex, but, uh…not *this*."

Liam's eyes blazed with anger for a brief moment before softening. "I love that I'm the first man who gets to give you this." A wicked grin tipped his beautiful mouth. "You're going to love it."

My stomach dipped and tightened. Liam ran his lips up the inside of my thigh, a mixture of kissing, licking, sucking, and nipping. I could never predict the touch that would come next, and each one drove my body into a riot of sensations.

Liam stilled for a moment just before he reached where I wanted him most. His thumbs parted me. My heart picked up its pace, tripping over itself in its erratic rhythm. Liam inhaled deeply, and I stilled. "You smell so fucking good."

My cheeks heated, and my body shuddered, Liam's words sending a rush of wetness between my thighs. Liam's tongue began to explore, and as he got closer to that bundle of nerves, my breaths came quicker and quicker. He circled my clit, and I moaned.

The sound turned into a groan as a single finger entered me. Liam lazily stroked me as his tongue drew circles around my clit. Closer and closer. Without warning, his lips covered that bundle of nerves, sucking deeply.

I exploded. It was as though my body burst into a million particles and just floated through the air until I came back to myself.

Liam continued lazily stroking me, watching me with intensity. "The most beautiful thing I've ever seen, watching you come."

I squeezed my legs around him. "I didn't know something could feel that good."

Liam grinned. "We're just getting started."

My body shivered. "I want you inside me."

Liam's grin widened. "Your wish is my command." He stood, dragging me just a bit farther down the bed. He gripped my thighs, his tip bumping my entrance. "Fuck. I don't have a condom."

I bit my bottom lip. "I'm clean, and I have an IUD."

Liam leaned over me, brushing his lips against mine. "I'm clean, too." He pulled back, studying my face. "Are you sure?"

I latched my legs around his back. "I'm sure. I need you."

Liam's tip was at my opening again, just the tease of him felt like heaven. Slowly, so very slowly, he entered me. Stretching me. He was so big, the sensation almost to the point of pain but stopping just shy.

Liam let out a guttural groan as he bottomed out. "Better than anything I could imagine." He gazed down, cupping my face. "You okay?"

I nodded. "Just give me a second."

Liam bent over me, his mouth caressing mine, his tongue slipping between my lips. The heat of the kiss eased my muscles, lessening the stretch. Liam's hand palmed my breast, circling my nipple with a rough thumb. The inferno grew, sparking my nerve endings.

I deepened the kiss before retreating. "Move, please move."

Liam did as I asked. At first, the movements were slow. The ridges of his cock dragging against my inner walls, stoking the flames higher. Liam picked up his pace, each thrust sending me closer to the edge. My core tightened, and Liam cursed, his thrusts reaching a frenzied pace. He reached between our bodies and thumbed my clit.

That was all it took. I tipped over the edge in a cascade of sensations. My core gripped him so tightly, I had the fleeting thought that it must have been painful. Liam thrust deep, one more time, and released into me.

He collapsed on the bed, rolling so that I was on top of him. We lay there. Silent. Slick with sweat. Heat rolling off our bodies in waves. Liam pressed his lips to my temple.

I listened to the rapid drumming of Liam's heart. So strong. So fierce. "I didn't know it could be like that." Tears pricked at my eyes. "That I could feel that much."

Liam's arms wrapped tighter around me, his lips ghosting across my brow. "Tessa, I am going to make it my mission for you to feel that much as often as possible."

My body relaxed, soaking up Liam's warmth, his words. His love.

I sat cuddled between Liam's thighs, Trouble on my lap. We'd showered, eaten breakfast, and now were back in bed.

Liam kissed the top of my head. "We need to talk about what's next." I stiffened. Liam wrapped his arms more tightly around me. "We're going to figure this out, it'll be okay."

I took a deep breath. "I think I need to talk to Walker and see if I can file a restraining order." It scared me to death, the idea that Garrett would know where to find me. The knowledge that legal action would cause a rage in him that no one would be able to control. But if I wanted a shot at this beautiful life with Liam, I had to take a chance. I couldn't live in the shadows anymore.

Liam kissed my temple, and then his lips traveled down to my ear. "I'll be with you every step of the way. We can get security up here if you want. Whatever you need to feel safe."

I shuddered, knowing I'd never be able to trust a stranger tasked with my safety. And it would feel too much like the jail of my past, being constantly watched and studied. "I'd rather not have security. Just having you by my side makes me feel safe."

Liam smiled against the side of my face. "I'm going to be stuck to you like glue. You'll probably get sick of me."

I wiggled my butt against him. "I don't know, you have some handy uses."

Liam groaned in my ear. "Please don't make me hard before we go talk to Walker."

I laughed. "All right, I'll wait till we're home."

Liam nipped at my ear lobe. "I like the sound of that." He nuzzled my neck. "You want to go now?"

I pressed my lips together and nodded. "Yeah, I just need to let Jensen know what I'm doing. She said she was going to get Taylor to help out downstairs for a few days so I could lay low, but I don't want to hide anymore."

Liam squeezed me tighter. "You never have to hide again."

I kissed the bottom of Liam's jaw, and he released me. I pushed off the mattress, keeping Trouble cradled in one arm and then depositing him on his kitty climbing tree. I turned to face Liam, who was studying me as he put on his boots. "I just need to check one thing."

Liam's brow furrowed. "Okay."

I found my bag in its usual spot by the door, ready to be grabbed at a moment's notice. I wouldn't need that anymore, I was standing my ground. For the first time in a long time, I was fighting back. But I did need something from inside.

I stuck my hand in, feeling around until my fingers found the envelope I needed. I pulled it out, nausea sweeping over me at the idea of anyone seeing the photos. I clutched them to my chest, breathing deeply, waiting for the roiling in my stomach to pass.

A hand touched my shoulder, and I jumped. Liam's concerned eyes filled my gaze. "Are you sure you're ready for this? We can wait."

I straightened my shoulders. "Two years ago, my life was a broken mess. I've been slowly putting it back together piece by piece, but I haven't let myself have the things that truly make life worth living. I'm ready now."

Liam pressed his lips to my forehead. "Sometimes, it takes life breaking apart for it to get you where you're truly meant to be." His eyes bored into mine, emotion filling them.

"I wouldn't change any of it. It was hell on Earth while it was happening, but it made me who I am today. And I like that person. She's not perfect, but she's strong and kind and she's the woman you fell in love with. I wouldn't want to be anyone else."

Liam tugged me to him. "You're everything to me."

I tipped up my head so that my chin rested on his sternum. "Let's go reclaim my life."

CHAPTER
Thirty-Four

Liam

I LACED MY FINGERS WITH TESSA'S AS WE WALKED UP THE steps to the police station. I'd texted Walker, and he'd said that he'd be waiting. I glanced down at Tessa. I was so damn proud of her. Walker would help. I wasn't sure what the specific steps would be, but we would figure it out.

I pulled open the door to the department, placing a hand on Tessa's back and ushering her through. Walker was talking to the clerk at the front desk and turned at the sound of the door. "Hey there. Why don't we head back to my office?"

Tessa's fingers gripped mine in a tight hold. I began tracing circles on the back of her hand, trying to ease her in any way I could. "That sounds good. Thanks for making time for us, Walk."

Walker jerked up his chin and led us towards his office. "No problem." He pushed open a door and gestured towards the two chairs in front of his desk. "Have a seat."

I glanced around the space. It was simple, utilitarian. But it had a few personal touches. A photo of Walker's family, another of Taylor and Walker, and a mug that read *World's Best Uncle*. It was enough to put anyone who came into the office at ease that this was a real man who would understand their problems.

Walker settled behind his desk as Tessa and I took a seat. "So, you ready to tell me what's going on?"

I looked to Tessa, unsure if she wanted me to start or her.

Tessa released her hold on my hand. Her skin was paler than usual, but her jaw had a determined set to it. She took a deep breath. "My name isn't really Tessa."

It was more of a blow than I'd thought it would be, the fact that I'd been calling her a name that wasn't her own. It made logical sense that she wouldn't be using her birth name, but it still smarted.

Tessa pressed on. "Well, it's not my legal name." She looked at me, eyes pleading for understanding. "But it's the name I chose for myself when I started over."

The grip on my chest eased. I knew this woman, who she really was. And that woman had given herself the name Tessa. It didn't matter what was on her birth certificate.

Walker cleared his throat. "And what were you starting over from?"

Tessa's hand that wasn't holding the envelope fisted. "I was running away from an abusive fiancé."

Walker's jaw hardened. "I'm so sorry, Tessa."

Tessa straightened her shoulders. "I'm away from him now, and that's what matters."

Walker nodded. "Did you have a restraining order in place back home?"

Tessa shook her head. "I went to the police once." Her cheeks reddened, not with her usual adorable embarrassment but with anger. "My ex is very well connected in the political and legal fields. The police didn't believe me. In a matter of hours, my ex had them convinced I was having a breakdown and that he was going to get me medical help."

Walker cursed, and I gripped the arms of my chair so hard, I worried I might snap them off.

Tessa stared down at her hands and the envelope in her lap. "I didn't have anyone I could go to for help. He'd slowly cut me off from everyone in my life. The only person I had was my hairstylist." Tears filled her eyes, and I couldn't stop myself from reaching out to comfort her. I leaned over and kissed her temple, running a hand up and down her spine.

Tessa gave me a watery smile. "Her name is Gena. And she's amazing. She helped me escape." Tessa turned back to Walker. "I took trains and busses until I got to Sutter Lake."

Walker's brows pulled together. "Why here?"

A wistfulness filled Tessa's expression. "I grew up in the foster system. My mom died during childbirth. I only have a couple things of hers, but one was a postcard from Sutter Lake. When I was making a run for it, one of my options was Portland. I took it as a sign."

Walker pulled out a pen and a pad of paper. "Does your ex know where you are now?"

Tessa shook her head vehemently. "No. That's what's kept me safe for this long." She snuck a peek back at me. "But it's come to my attention that my life has been somewhat on hold. I don't want to hide anymore. I want to fight."

A gentle smile stretched Walker's face. "That's real good, Tessa. It takes a hell of a lot of guts to run, but even more to stand and fight. You know that my family and I will do everything we can to help." Walker tapped his pen against his notepad. "I'm going to ask you to walk me through an overview of your history." His face sobered. "But first, I need you to hear me."

Walker pinned Tessa with an intense stare. "I believe you."

Tessa was silent for a moment, and then her shoulders began to shake with silent sobs. I couldn't bear it. I scooped her up into my arms and deposited her on my lap, holding her to my chest. She tried valiantly to get her tears under control, but they just kept spilling over. "You don't know how much that means. Your belief."

Walker stood, rounding his desk and squatting in front of Tessa. He took her hand in his. "I do. Unfortunately, our system isn't perfect. For our best shot at nailing this bastard to the wall, we're going to need as much proof as we can get. Did anyone ever witness the abuse?"

Tessa stiffened in my arms. "I don't care about filing charges. I just want a restraining order or something that will make him leave me alone."

Walker straightened, leaning against his desk. "When was the last instance of abuse?"

Tessa thought for a moment. "It's been over two years now."

Walker's jaw hardened. "Has he made threats in that time?"

Tessa shook her head. "I don't know. I threw away my phone and haven't checked my email since the day I left. I've had no contact with anyone from my old life. I had an anonymous threat recently, but nothing actually tied to him."

Walker ground his back molars together, and I didn't get a good feeling. "To file a restraining order, there must be an instance of abuse or threat made in the last six months."

"That's bullshit." I couldn't hold the words in. Tessa flinched at my tone, and I tugged her tighter to me, kissing her hair. "Sorry, baby," I whispered. She burrowed deeper against me.

Walker clasped his hands in front of him. "In circumstances like this one, I completely agree. The good news is the statute of limitations on domestic violence is longer. Three years to the most recent incident." He met Tessa's gaze. "If you file charges against him and he makes any sort of threat or attempts to harass you, we can file the restraining order then. But, hopefully, his ass will be in jail."

Tessa straightened in my lap. "I want to file charges, then."

Walker nodded. "Good."

With a shaky hand, Tessa extended the envelope. "I don't have any witnesses, but I do have photos. Will that help?"

Walker took the envelope from Tessa's hand. "They will. Did you take these yourself?"

She shook her head. "No, my friend Gena did."

Walker held the packet gently in his hands. "That's helpful. She's also someone who can corroborate the timeline even if she didn't witness any of the incidents themselves. You okay with me looking at these?"

I could feel a slight tremor run through Tessa's body, but she nodded. "Go ahead."

I held my breath and continued running a hand up and down Tessa's spine as Walker opened the envelope. He sucked in an audible inhale, rage flaring to life in his eyes. When he finished with the first Polaroid, he placed it on the desk, moving to the next in the stack.

I froze. Someone might as well have jammed a hot poker through my chest. There, in slightly faded color, was my Tessa. In the photo, she faced away from the camera, wearing nothing but a simple bra and underwear. Her back and thighs were riddled with long lines of dark purple bruises. I looked more closely and saw gashes running through the center of each injury.

My brain short-circuited. *Who could do this to another human being?* "Baby, no." The words were guttural, torn from somewhere deep inside. I hugged Tessa tighter to me as if I could erase what had happened to her.

Walker snapped to attention. "Has he not seen these?"

His voice sounded far away as I continued staring at the image, unable to tear my gaze away from the carnage.

I could feel Tessa's head shake. "No."

Walker snapped up the picture on his desk. "I'm sorry."

Tessa turned in my lap, framing my face with her hands. "I'm okay. I'm all right now. I'm right here, and I'm fine."

I buried my face in her neck. There was wetness there. I belatedly realized it was from my own eyes. My beautiful girl, someone had broken her body. The despair morphed into rage on a dime, thick and swirling in my gut. I brought my head up and met Walker's gaze. "You get this fucker. You get him, or I will."

Tessa fisted my shirt. "No! You stay the hell away from Garrett." She shook her fists, keeping hold of my button-down. "I will kick you out of this room and finish this interview alone if I have to. I didn't want to keep anything from you, but I need to know you won't go off half-cocked and do something crazy."

Tessa's fire brought me back to myself, her strength and her fierce protectiveness. "Half-cocked?" A small smile tipped my lips at a time when I would have thought it would be impossible.

Her shoulders sagged in relief, and then she blushed. "You know what I mean."

I took her face in my hands, kissing her lips and then her temple. I spoke quietly. "This isn't easy for me to hear. But I'll do my best to keep it reined in."

Uncertainty filled Tessa's gaze. "You don't have to stay, you can wait outside if you want."

Fuck, I was the world's biggest bastard. Tessa had lived through this nightmare, the least I could do was support her when she told her story. "I'm with you. Always."

We walked down the steps of the police station, and I fought the urge to punch something, maybe kick the shit out of the trash can on the corner. My gaze caught on a familiar figure across the street. Bridgette. She glared in my and Tessa's direction.

I ignored her and pulled Tessa closer to me, wrapping an arm around her shoulders. The last thing we needed was a Bridgette encounter. We'd spent the past three hours in Walker's office. Three hours of Tessa recounting mental and physical abuse that made me sick. Three hours of trying to come up with a plan of attack.

Walker was filing a report with the Washington DC police now, and we would go from there. I'd texted my lawyer and gotten the name of the best attorney he knew who handled these types of cases. I wanted Tessa protected in every way possible. And after I had seen those photos, I was rethinking having my security team up here.

I paused at the passenger door of my SUV, tilting my head down to study Tessa's face. She was so fucking strong. So strong, but very much at risk right now. "I want you to move into the guest cabin with me. At least until we know what's what with the filed charges."

Tessa nibbled her bottom lip.

I tucked a strand of hair behind her ear. "You can stay in the other room if you want. I just want you safe." I would completely understand if sex was off the table for a good long while after what she'd had to relive today.

Tessa stiffened, and her voice shook when she spoke. "I get it if you don't want me after you heard what I put up with for so long, but I don't want to stay with anyone out of pity."

"Baby, no." I pulled her to me in a fierce hug. "None of what happened is your fault. You are so strong. I'm in awe of you. I just didn't want you to feel pressured if you needed a little space after everything you had to talk about today. I want you with me always, as close as you'll let me be. You hear me?"

Tessa nodded against my chest. "Your touch erases his. It's more healing than you'll ever know."

Warmth flooded my chest. A pride that I had never felt from millions of records sold or winning my first Grammy. Being a part of this woman's healing—no matter how small—would forever be the thing I held most precious. "I love you." I kissed her temple.

A camera flashed. "Liam, who's your girlfriend?"

"Shit." I quickly pulled open the passenger door and helped Tessa in. Rounding the SUV, I ignored the questions the reporter peppered me with. Slamming my own door, I turned to Tessa, thankful for the darkly tinted windows. "I guess we're outed."

She let out a shuddered breath but gave me a small smile. "Worth it."

CHAPTER
Thirty-Five

Tessa

T ROUBLE'S PURRS VIBRATED MY LEGS AS HE SOAKED UP the pets and attention I was lavishing on him. I let my fingers sift through his fur, his contentment bringing me peace. We were settling in. I glanced out the windows at the back of the cabin, taking in the fields dotted with horses and cattle, the forests that met mountains still topped with snow. It was breathtakingly beautiful, so settling in wasn't a hardship.

I smiled as my gaze caught on the massive cat climbing tree set up by the back windows. Trouble was in heaven, able to survey what he considered his domain from his perch. I scratched his ears, and Trouble's purrs deepened.

I loved it here. But I was also ready to get back to some semblance of normality. Walker had been doing all he could to make it so I could file charges without having to return to DC. In the meantime, pictures of Liam and me had surfaced on gossip sites everywhere. Jensen had forced me to take a couple of days off to deal with everything that had gone down and to settle into the cabin with Liam.

It was kind of her, but I needed to be doing something. Anything that would make me feel productive and distract me from the thoughts running through my mind on a never-ending loop. *Did Garrett see the pictures? Does he know where I am? Is he on his way?* My stomach churned.

Liam sat down on the couch, curling me into his side. "What are you thinking about so hard over there?"

I burrowed deeper into his warmth. "I'm ready to get back to normal."

Liam chuckled. "I think that might take a minute. But I did just get a text from Taylor inviting us to dinner at the ranch house. Want to go?"

I tipped my head back so that I could see his face. "That sounds perfect."

Liam brushed his lips against mine. I tried to deepen the embrace, but he retreated. "I'll let them know we'll be there." Liam had been so careful with me since we'd left the police station two days ago. Too careful. Both nights, he'd held me but nothing else. I was about ready to come out of my skin.

I straightened, pushing away from Liam. "I'm going back to work tomorrow."

Liam stiffened. "I don't know if that's a good idea. We have no idea if Garrett knows where you are. Not to mention, the press is still salivating for more photos."

I stroked Trouble's fur. "I can't just stay in this cabin forever. I went to Walker and reported everything so that I wouldn't have to hide anymore. But here I am, *hiding*."

Liam sighed, reaching up to toy with a piece of my hair. "I just want you safe."

Something in me melted at the look in his eyes. His gaze was so filled with worry. I set Trouble down on the couch cushion and curled back into Liam, kissing his jaw. "I'll stay in the kitchen at the Kettle as much as possible. Jensen has already put a sign on the door warning away photographers. I'll be fine."

Liam pressed a kiss to my temple. "Will you promise me you won't go anywhere alone?"

I soaked in the feel of his lips on my skin. "I promise." I checked my watch. "I need to shower and get ready if we're going to dinner." I drummed my fingers on his chest. "Actually, do you mind if I take a bath?" The master bathroom had the tub of my dreams, and a little soak sounded heavenly.

"Of course. Use whatever you want. You don't have to ask."

"Thank you." I pushed up to standing and then bent over to give Liam a quick kiss. His eyes zeroed in on the opening in my shirt and the bra he could see peeking out. I grinned. Maybe Liam just needed a little encouragement. "Well, I'll just be in the bath. Naked. And wet."

Liam groaned. "You don't play fair."

I laughed as I headed for the bedroom suite. I started the water for a bath. The Cole family had even stocked the cabinets with all sorts of bubble bath and bath salts. I opted for bubbles after sniffing something that smelled amazing. I poured it into the water.

I piled my hair on top of my head and then stripped off my clothes and tossed them in the hamper. Stepping into the foamy water, I moaned. This was heaven. I submerged myself up to my neck. Perfection. I wanted to live in this tub forever.

I rested my head against the edge of the porcelain and let my mind go blank. I didn't allow myself to dwell on Garrett or photographers or even if Liam would ever touch me again. I just let it all go. My body didn't want to let go, though. I was wound so tight. The stress of the past week, the fact that I'd been sleeping next to Liam without really touching him had me in knots.

I needed release, and Liam hadn't taken my hint to follow me into the bathroom. I fisted the water in frustration and squeezed my thighs together. The action sent little sparks through my core. I closed my eyes, imagined what it had felt like when Liam touched me.

I trailed my hands up my inner thighs, remembering Liam kissing, sucking, biting that skin. Heat swept through me. I ran a finger over my core, lazily exploring, trying to find the spots that Liam had. It wasn't as good, but at least it was something. I dipped a single finger inside and let out a little moan.

"What are you picturing right now?"

My eyes flew open at the sound of Liam's rough voice. I bit my bottom lip, refusing to be embarrassed for giving myself what I needed. "I was remembering you. The way you touched me."

Liam dropped to the side of the tub. "I could reenact that for you."

Heat pooled low in my belly. "So now you can touch me?"

Liam's eyes flared. "You've just been through so much—"

I put a finger to his lips. "I told you. Your touch erases all the bad."

Liam closed his eyes as if in pain. "I've been fucking this up at every turn."

I gripped Liam's neck, and his eyes opened. "No, you haven't, but we need to talk to each other. And listen. I miss feeling close to you."

Heat filled Liam's gaze. "I think you deserve an apology." A wicked grin spread over his face, and his hands dipped below the bubbles, cupping my breasts.

My nipples beaded under his touch. "Now this is an apology I can get behind."

Liam chuckled. "Just you wait. You're going to want me to fuck up all the time." He rolled my nipples, giving them a little pinch. I sucked in a harsh breath. "Good?"

I nodded, having suddenly lost my ability for words. One of Liam's hands stayed on my breast, carrying out a delicious assault on my nipple, while the other trailed lower, down my stomach and through my small triangle of curls. He paused to pull on them. "I love this," he whispered in my ear. "So damn sexy." Another tug, sending a jolt deep inside.

A single finger circled my clit. I gasped. The pad of Liam's finger with its roughened skin wreaked havoc on my nerve endings.

Liam's finger kept trailing down. It slipped inside, and I pushed my hips against him, needing more. He added another finger, creating a delicious stretch, pumping in and out of me. He slowly picked up his pace until I was panting.

All at once, he pressed his palm down on my clit and twisted my nipple. My back arched, and I broke apart in a million spasms of sparking nerves.

Breathing heavily, I slowly opened my eyes. Liam stared down at me. "My favorite sight in the world, watching you come apart at the seams."

I smiled a grin that was lazy and sated. I reached over the tub, going for the waistband on Liam's jeans. "My turn."

Liam stilled my hand and took my mouth in a slow kiss. "That was just for you. My amends."

My smile grew. "You have my permission to screw up anytime you want."

Liam chuckled and pulled me to my feet. "Time to get ready." His eyes traveled the length of my body, catching on the cluster of bubbles on my breasts and at the juncture of my thighs. The muscle in his cheek ticked.

I leaned forward and touched my mouth to his, whispering against his lips, "Tonight."

I wiped my hands down the legs of my jeans as I got out of Liam's SUV. He claimed one of my hands as soon as I finished. I looked up at him, my stomach twisting. "Walker told everyone what's happening, right?" I wanted the extended Cole family to know what was going on so they could be aware, but I had no desire to recount the events myself.

Liam squeezed my hand. "He gave them the very broad basics and showed them a picture of Garrett so that they could all keep an eye out. He showed the picture to all the ranch hands, too."

I slowed my steps, pulling Liam to a stop next to me. "I don't want them to look at me any differently. I don't want them to pity me."

Liam brushed a strand of hair behind my ear and pressed his lips to my temple. "They aren't going to look at you differently. But they love you, so they're going to hurt because you were hurt. That's just the way love is."

My tightly wound muscles loosened just a bit. "You're right."

Liam wrapped an arm around me and led me up the steps. Before we reached the door, it swung open, and Walker stepped out. "Hey, you two. How is everything going?"

I glanced up at Liam and smiled before turning back to Walker. "Life is good, all things considered."

Walker grinned in a way that said he was happy that the two of us were finding our way. "I wanted to update you on things before you descended into the madness of another Cole family dinner."

We stepped to the side of the door, and Liam wrapped both his arms around me. "Thanks, man."

Walker scrubbed a hand over his stubbled jaw. "Don't thank me yet." My stomach dropped. "The DC police haven't been able to reach Garrett. I found a guy, a friend of a friend from the academy, who's on the force there. I trust him. He knows Garrett's connected, but he's pushing this through."

I hated the idea that even bringing charges against Garrett was putting people at risk. I burrowed deeper into Liam's hold.

Walker pushed on. "This guy couldn't reach Garrett at home or on his cell, so he finally went by the law firm. Garrett took a sabbatical from work, supposedly to look for his missing fiancée. No one has spoken to him in weeks."

Liam had become granite behind me. "Fuck. Do we know where he is?"

Walker shook his head. "Not a clue. The cop in DC is working some sources he has and hoping he'll come up with something there. In the meantime, everyone here is on alert. All my officers have his photo, and we're putting the word out to people we trust at hotels and vacation rental companies. If he shows up here, we'll know."

A shudder ran through me, but I steeled my spine. I would not let Garrett terrorize me anymore. "Thank you for everything you're doing for me, Walker. It means so much." I ducked out of Liam's hold and wrapped Walker in a hug. When I stepped back, I saw surprise in Walker's eyes. I wanted to laugh. I realized it was probably the first time I'd ever touched him.

Walker cleared his throat. "Anything I can do to help."

The front door opened again, and Sarah popped her head out. "Walker Cole, you do not keep guests outside without even offering them something to drink. I taught you better than that."

Walker chuckled. "Sorry, Ma."

Sarah shook her head. "Come on in, you two. Walker can stay out here if he likes it so much."

We made our way to Sarah and the front entrance of the house. When we stepped inside, Sarah immediately wrapped me in a hug. "I'm so sorry for all you've been through. I want you to know I'm here for whatever you need. And I also want you to know that I'm so proud of you for fighting back."

Tears stung the backs of my eyes. "Thank you, Sarah. And I'm sorry I wasn't always honest with you, about who I was or—"

Sarah cut me off with a wave of her hand. "Nonsense. You did what you had to do. No apologies needed for that."

I took a deep breath. "There's actually one other thing." Sarah waited. "I think you knew my mother." Her eyes widened. "You mentioned that I looked like your friend, Anne." My heart hammered against my ribs. "Was her full name Anne Tessa Fitzpatrick?"

Sarah inhaled sharply. "That's her. You're her daughter?" I

nodded. "Where is—?" Sarah's words cut off as she remembered what I'm sure Jensen had shared with her, that I had grown up in the foster system. Grief filled her expression. "What happened to her?"

"I don't know everything, just that my grandparents disowned her when she got pregnant." My heart clenched. "And that she died giving birth to me."

Sarah wrapped her arms around me again, hugging me tightly. "I'm so sorry. She was such a sweet soul. I hate that she went through that alone." Sarah pulled back slightly so she could meet my gaze. "How did you find out about Sutter Lake?"

I reached into my back pocket, pulling out the postcard. "I didn't have much of my mom's, but this was one of the things. I knew she didn't grow up here, but that this place must have been special to her somehow."

Sarah sighed. "She loved it here." Her gaze shot up from the postcard. "I have photos of the two of us, would you like to see them?"

My heart stutter-stepped. "I'd love to." The words came out as a hoarse whisper.

Sarah took my hand and led me into the living room, ignoring everyone around us. She held onto me the whole time, as though I might vanish if she let go. Sarah pulled two photo albums off the bookshelf and then guided me to the couch. "I think these are the right ones."

I held my breath as Sarah flipped through pages, and my heart seemed to catch in my throat when she finally stopped on one. I knew it was my mom the moment I saw her. The same violet eyes I saw in the mirror stared back at me. They were dancing with laughter as her arm was thrown around a much younger Sarah. "She was so beautiful."

Sarah's eyes filled with tears, and I knew mine were doing the same. "Inside and out, baby girl. Inside and out."

I held back a sob. "Will you tell me about her?"

Sarah's tears spilled over, tracking down her cheeks. "There's nothing I would rather do."

Andrew sat down next to his wife, brushing the tears away. "Now what's got these waterworks going?"

Sarah beamed up at him. "Just long-lost family finally coming home."

Andrew's expression turned puzzled. He looked from Sarah to the album. When his eyes zeroed in on the photo we were looking at, they widened and shot to me. "Are you Anne's?"

I nodded, not quite able to speak. The couch depressed next to me, and a strong arm encircled my shoulders. I inhaled Liam's scent. "She is," he answered for me.

Andrew's smile was soft. "Welcome home, Tessa."

This is what it felt like to belong, to have a family. To be truly loved and accepted. I sent a silent message of thanks to my mother, thanking her for bringing these people into my life in the roundabout way she had. For loving me enough to keep me even though she was probably terrified. For all the gifts she had given me.

I looked at Sarah. "I can't wait to get to know her through you."

Sarah reached out, wiping away one of my tears. "I can't wait to introduce you."

CHAPTER
Thirty-six

Liam

I TOOK A LONG PULL OF COFFEE FROM MY TRAVEL MUG AS Tessa and I drove into town. A five-a.m. wake-up call to take care of the horses had come far too early that morning. We'd stayed late at the Coles' last night, and Sarah had told Tessa story after story about her mother. They'd cried a little, but mostly, they'd laughed. And then they'd laughed so hard they cried.

I was so glad that Tessa had a piece of her history now, that she had family in the truest sense of the word. Someone who knew her roots. I yawned as I set the cup in the center console. I just wished our night hadn't meant only five hours of sleep.

Tessa reached over and rubbed the back of my neck. "You didn't have to come with me. The shop is locked up tight, and Jensen will be there in an hour or so."

I scowled at the road. "I don't want you alone. Ever." I glanced at Tessa. "You promised, remember?" If she thought I would be okay with her wandering off by herself, she was crazy. Especially since we had no idea where that fucker, Garrett, was.

Tessa threw up her hands. "Okay, okay. I just wanted you to get some rest." She grinned at me. "You're grumpy when you don't get your beauty sleep."

My scowl deepened, but I couldn't hold it in, I started to chuckle. "It takes a lot to look this good." I sent a wicked grin in Tessa's direction. "Maybe you can take a nap with me this afternoon. Help me catch up on my sleep."

Tessa leaned over and ran her tongue over the shell of my ear. "That sounds like a real restful plan."

My jeans tightened. "You're going to make me get in a wreck."

Tessa laughed but settled back in her seat. "I trust your control."

I shook my head as I pulled up to the back of the Kettle. "You shouldn't. I have none when it comes to you."

Tessa grinned at me as I slid out of the SUV and rounded the front of the vehicle. When I opened her door, she jumped into my arms, wrapping her legs around me. "I love you."

A smile stretched across my face as I gripped her pert little ass with my hands. "What was that for?"

Tessa ran her hands through my hair. "I'm happy. There may be a whole bunch of shit we can't control, but I don't care. I'm happy."

My chest got tight, and I took her mouth in a slow, deep kiss. "I'm so glad you're happy."

Tessa studied my face. "Thanks for helping to make me this way." She dug her heels into my ass. "Now, take me to work," she said with a laugh.

I shook my head but carried her to the back door. When Tessa slid down my body, I groaned. "Woman, why do you always have to make me hard?"

Tessa giggled and unlocked the door. "I need to grab a couple things from my apartment to take back to your place."

"Okay, I'll come up with you."

Tessa led the way up the stairs. "Sounds good. You can do the heavy lifting."

"As long as it's lighter than that damn cat tree."

Tessa looked back at me over her shoulder. "You're the one who bought the thing."

I chuckled. "I was trying to impress you through the freaking cat."

"Well, it worked. Trouble loves it—" Tessa's words cut off, and she came to a stop so abruptly, I ran into her.

I grasped her shoulders, my grip tight as I scanned the hallway. "What's wrong?"

Tessa reached out a shaking finger. There, on her door, was a blown-up photo of us after we had left the police station. I was cupping Tessa's face and gazing into her eyes. The picture itself would have been sweet if it weren't for the large red letters scrawled across it. *Whore.*

My chest seized. I gripped Tessa's hand and started pulling her back towards the stairs. "Come on." I hustled us down the staircase and over to the SUV. Depositing Tessa in the passenger seat, I rounded the vehicle myself, hitting the locks as soon as I was inside. I pulled out my cell and hit Walker's contact.

He answered on the second ring. "What's wrong?"

A six-thirty a.m. call didn't usually herald good things, I guessed. "There's a threatening note on Tessa's apartment door."

"Fuck. I'm on my way. You guys somewhere safe?"

I looked around the back parking area, totally empty. "We're in my SUV behind the Kettle."

"I'll be there in less than ten. Keep your doors locked."

"Thanks, man. I will." I hit end on the screen and looked at Tessa.

She stared out the windshield at the back door of the Kettle. "How did he get into the building so easily? The door was locked, and there was no sign of a break-in. Does he know how to pick locks now?" Tessa's words picked up speed as she spoke. "I have to leave. What was I thinking? I can't bring that kind of maniac into these people's lives."

I grasped the back of Tessa's neck, turning her head so she met my gaze. "Don't let Garrett win. What he wants is to get you alone. Away from all the support and protection you have here. Don't fall into his trap." My blood boiled at the thought, and I knew that's what the asshole wanted. To get Tessa alone in as helpless a situation as possible.

Tessa's eyes widened at the realization. "He's trying to scare me into leaving."

I gave her neck a gentle squeeze. "But you're smarter than he is, and you're not going to play into his hand."

Tessa let out a shuddering breath. "You're right. I'm not." She let her head fall back against the seat. "God! Why can't he just leave me alone?"

I massaged her nape. "We're going to deal with him." My words were a vow. I was going to get this fucker out of her life once and for all.

In way less than ten minutes, Walker's truck pulled into the parking lot, followed by a cop car. We jumped out of the SUV to meet him. He strode towards us, his jaw ticking. "Want to show me what we've got?"

I turned to Tessa. "Do you want to wait down here?"

Her eyes flashed. "No. I want to hear whatever Walker has to say."

God, I loved her spine of steel. "Let's go." We took Walker to the door, and he let out a curse.

"Did you touch anything?"

I stared at the image, my blood heating. "No, nothing."

Walker rubbed a hand over his jaw. "Good. I'm going to get a crime tech out here to see if we can get any prints. It'll take at least a few days to get that processed, but in the meantime, I want to pull someone else in on this."

I raised my brows in question. "Who?"

Walker pulled his cell out of his pocket. "Tuck and I have a friend from college. His name's Cain. He runs a crazy successful tech company, but he has a hobby that comes in handy every now and then."

I waited for Walker to continue but quickly got impatient. "What?"

Walker met my gaze. "He's a ridiculously talented hacker."

"Isn't that illegal?" I asked as I eyed the badge hanging from Walker's belt.

Walker looked over my shoulder to make sure the other cop hadn't followed us in. "It's questionable. If I don't know how Cain comes across the intel, then everything's on the up and up on my end." Walker grinned. "So, Cain never tells me how he gets the info."

I glanced at Tessa whose arms were wrapped around herself so tightly she must have been cutting off her own circulation. I turned back to Walker. "Call him. I'll pay whatever his price is."

Walker shook his head. "Cain doesn't need the money. Trust me." He eyed Tessa. "And he has a thing about guys who hurt women. He'll dismantle Garrett's life in a few keystrokes."

"Do it." I pulled Tessa into my arms as Walker headed down the hall to make his calls. I swept my lips across the skin at her temple. "We're going to fix this." I just hoped like hell it would happen before things got worse.

CHAPTER
Thirty-Seven

Tessa

WHEN WE ARRIVED AT THE KETTLE THE NEXT morning, Walker was there, installing new locks. He looked up as Liam and I climbed out of the SUV. "Just taking a few extra precautions."

Liam grunted. He was grumpy, had been since yesterday when I refused to go back to the guest cabin after the photo incident. But I wasn't going to let Garrett hijack my life anymore. And what would I do if I went back to the cabin? Twiddle my thumbs and worry? No, thank you.

I made my way to the back door where Walker was working. "Thank you for doing this. I'm sorry about all the extra trouble."

He gave me a soft smile. "It's no trouble. We're gonna keep you safe, Tessa."

Liam wrapped an arm around me. "Thanks, Walk. Let me know if you need any help with this stuff."

Walker jerked up his chin. "I'm almost done. Jensen's already inside getting set up for the day."

Liam and I headed through the back door, making our way into the kitchen and then the front of the shop. Jensen turned from wiping down tables at the sound of our footsteps. She grinned. "Look, it's the tea house's number one fan."

Liam scowled. When I refused to return to the cabin after yesterday's incident, he'd taken up residency at the Kettle. Jensen had teased him the entire day. Therefore, this morning, we had Liam the grump.

The only bright spot yesterday was that a major cheating scandal with some Hollywood movie star had come to light, and almost all the photographers had left town. I felt bad about being grateful for someone else's heartache, but we needed a break.

I rubbed my thumb in circles on Liam's brow, attempting to ease his scowl. "You know, being at the Kettle means free treats all day, starting with your favorite ham and cheddar scones."

Liam's frown eased a bit. "You gonna make chocolate potato chip cookies today?"

I grinned. "If it means you'll be less of a grumpy butt, yes."

The scowl was back. "I'm not grumpy."

Jensen cackled. "You're pouting worse than my eight-year-old when I tell him he has to eat all his broccoli if he wants dessert." Liam's eyes narrowed at her. Jensen crossed to him and thumped him on the back. "I know you'd like to lock Tessa away until we find this asswipe, but she'll go crazy. If she's here, she's surrounded by people looking out for her, and you can keep an eye on things all day long while eating us out of house and home."

Liam let out a reluctant chuckle. "You have a point." He looked at me, worry filling his eyes. "I just want you safe."

I wrapped my arms around Liam and brushed my lips over his jaw. "I am safe here."

Liam nuzzled my neck. "Okay. I'll quit being a grump."

"Thank you," I whispered.

Liam tapped me on the butt. "Now, get in that kitchen and fix me some scones. I'm a growing boy, and I need my sustenance."

I pulled back, laughing. "Just for that, I'm giving you the burned ones."

Liam's expression was crestfallen. "I take it back. Please, oh goddess of baked goods, would you honor me with one of your delicious concoctions?"

I shook my head, backing away to the kitchen. "That's a little better."

I got to work on the dough for scones and the early morning rush passed quickly with no photographer sightings or ominous messages. Things almost felt normal. Well, other than the rock star who had planted himself at the only table that had a view of the kitchen.

I grinned down at the marionberry muffins I had cooling. It was a recipe of Sarah's, and I knew Liam loved them. I popped one on a plate and headed out to my guard dog.

I was stopped on my way by our new regular, Al. "Good morning, Miss Tessa. How are you today?"

"I'm good, thank you. And you?" There was just something about this guy that didn't sit right with me, but I couldn't put my finger on why.

Al gave me a kind smile, and I instantly felt guilty for thinking poorly of him. I guess it would just take a while for my paranoia to ease. "I'm doing just great. I'm liking Sutter Lake so much, I decided to extend my trip."

I returned his smile. "That's great. I hope you enjoy the rest of your vacation." Liam eyed me and the muffin in my hand. "If you'll excuse me, I need to deliver this."

Al stepped aside. "Of course. You have a good day."

I nodded, and Al's gaze tracked me all the way to Liam's table. I could have sworn there was a look of concern on Al's face when I swept my lips against Liam's. I had to be reading that wrong.

I shook off those thoughts and focused on Liam. "Sarah's marionberry muffins, hot out of the oven."

Liam grinned and rubbed his hands together like a little kid. "You know the way to my heart." He broke off a piece and popped it into his mouth. "This is amazing." He eyed Al over my shoulder. "Who is that guy?"

I shrugged. "Just a new regular. He's been vacationing here for a few weeks, said he liked it so much he extended his trip." Liam nodded, suspicion filling his gaze. I ran a hand through his hair. "I'm fine. You're here. Jensen's here. Nothing's going to happen to me."

Liam took hold of one of my apron straps and pulled me towards him. "Damn straight." He took my mouth in a slow kiss, one that bordered on indecent for my workplace but I didn't give a flip.

The bell on the door sounded in the background. "You have got to be kidding me." I snapped up to find Bridgette with a look of disgust on her face. She looked from me to Liam. "This is who you shack up with? Really? A plain Jane with those freaky eyes?"

Liam started to rise, and I could feel the anger rolling off him in waves. But I held up a hand to still whatever he was about to say. I looked at Bridgette. Taking her in, I realized that all her anger and bitterness made her ugly. It didn't matter how perfectly styled her hair was, or how expensive her designer outfit was, that soul-deep ugliness had a way of seeping out.

I almost pitied her. *Almost.* But I was done taking her shit. "Can I help you?"

Bridgette's eyes widened, clearly not expecting my retort. "Yes, you can take your gross make-out session somewhere I'm not planning to eat. I'm not sure how you conned Liam into what I'm sure was a pity date or two, but he'll see the error of his ways soon enough."

I started to laugh, couldn't help it. I could barely get my words out, I was laughing so hard. "And what? He'll come begging to take you out?"

Bridgette flushed. "I'm not interested in a washed-up rock star. I need someone who actually has a respectable job. A *real* man."

Jensen appeared at my side. "Suuuuuure, Bridgette." Bridgette's face got even redder. "Can you taste the BS coming out of your mouth? I bet it's bitter. Because that's what you are, bitter that the guys you're so eager to sink your claws into, see right through to your ugly core."

Bridgette's mouth fell open, no words coming out. Jensen pressed on. "You know one of the best things about owning your own business?" Bridgette said nothing. "No, you wouldn't because you haven't worked a day in your life. One of the best things is that I have the right to refuse service to anyone I dang well please. Well, congrats, Bridge. You're banned."

Bridgette sucked in a sharp breath. "You wouldn't."

Jensen's hands came to her hips. "I just did. Now, get out."

Bridgette huffed, turned on her heel, and stomped out. The entire shop erupted in applause.

Jensen threw her arms around me, and we dissolved into laughter so strong, we had to hold each other up. When we finally calmed down enough to catch our breaths, I glanced up to see Liam with a smirk on his face. He shook his head. "You two are dangerous."

Jensen straightened. "Damn straight. Ugh, I can't stand that girl. I should've banned her a long time ago."

I wrapped an arm around her. "But then we would've missed out on this spectacular show."

Jensen chuckled. "Fair point. And our customers would have missed out on their small-town entertainment for the week."

I grinned. "So true."

Jensen sobered. "You know she picks on you because she's jealous, right?" My eyes widened. "You're everything she's not and wishes she could be. Beautiful in this breathtakingly natural way. Kind to everyone. Giving. She has to try and break you down to make herself feel better."

Jensen pulled me into a tight hug. "Don't dim your light for anyone. Never again."

CHAPTER
Thirty-Eight

Liam

I PULLED THE PASSENGER-SIDE DOOR OPEN AND HELPED Tessa out of the SUV, breathing a sigh of relief that we were now on the Coles' gated property. Hours on alert at The Tea Kettle while Tessa worked, not to mention the scene with Bridgette, had my nerves on edge.

Then Tessa had wanted to spend time with the horses and stop in to see Sarah, who of course decided she needed to feed us. It was so kind of Sarah, but all I wanted was Tessa home with me where I knew she was safe. Worry gnawed at my gut. I felt like I was constantly waiting for the other shoe to drop.

Tessa reached up on her tiptoes and pressed her lips to my jaw. "How about I draw us a nice relaxing bath. That tub's more than big enough for two."

My eyes widened, and I grinned. "You gonna put that flowery shit in the water and make me smell like a girl?"

Tessa grinned back at me. "Probably."

I brushed my lips against hers. "Worth it."

We headed up the front steps, and I unlocked the door. We made our way down the hall and into the open-concept living area and kitchen. I pulled open the fridge. "I'm going to grab a beer. You want anything?"

Tessa shook her head. "No, I'm good. I'm just trying to find my phone." She pawed through the massive bag she called a purse.

I chuckled. "It's a wonder you can find anything in there, that purse is the size of my gym bag."

Tessa stuck her tongue out at me. "Fine. I'll clean it out." She upended the bag, and the contents fell out over the kitchen counter.

I popped the cap on my beer and took a swig. "What the hell is all this stuff?"

Tessa grinned. "It used to be my go-bag, but since I'm no longer a flight risk, it's just become a collection of random crap."

I held up a small, cylindrical object. "Taser?"

Tessa nodded. "Yup." She continued to sort through the spread, throwing some things away, putting others in piles. She picked up a small, white, circular dot, no bigger than a quarter. Her brows pulled together. "What's this?" Tessa studied it for a second and then moved to throw it in the trash.

I caught her hand in a flash. "Don't."

Tessa's eyes flared in surprise. "Why?"

I cursed under my breath, taking a closer look at the thing. "I've seen these before. My security team warned me about them. Sometimes, extra sleazy paparazzi will plant them in your car if they can. I'm pretty sure this is a tracker."

Tessa dropped the dot as if she'd been burned. "What?"

I resisted the urge to pick it up off the counter, wondering if we might be able to get fingerprints off this thing. "When's the last time you cleaned out your bag?"

Tessa's brow creased, and she eyed the pile of stuff on the counter. "It's been a while."

My jaw worked. "So, we have no idea when someone could've planted it." I pulled out my phone. "I'm calling Walker."

Tessa rubbed her hands up and down her arms as if she were suddenly freezing. I pulled her into my body with my free hand just as Walker answered his phone. "What's up?"

I gritted my teeth. "I'm pretty sure I just found a tracker in

Tessa's bag. One of those circle tracker pads."

Walker cursed. "I'm on my way. You at the cabin?"

I rubbed a hand up and down Tessa's back. "Yup. Thanks, man."

"Of course. See you in a few."

I hit end on the screen and shoved my phone back into my pocket. Tessa was still burrowed into me. I lifted her chin. "You okay?"

Tessa nodded. "So, he knows where I am now, right?"

My gut tightened, and I clenched my teeth. "Most likely. But he can't get to you. There's a gate to the property, an alarm system on the house, and you're not ever going to be alone. You're safe."

Tessa shuddered just as a meow sounded from her feet. "I just want them to find him."

I grunted. "Me, too." I just hoped I got a little one-on-one time with him first. Tessa bent to pick up Trouble, but apparently, he had already had enough of being ignored and began to climb up my jeans-clad leg. "Fuck, Trouble! Your nails are sharp." I lifted him off my leg before he drew blood.

Tessa giggled. "He loves you."

I gave her a playful scowl. "More like he loves causing me pain."

Tessa's lips pressed together in a look of disapproval. "No, he doesn't." She nuzzled Trouble's head, and he began to purr loudly. "You love Liam, don't you?" she cooed. "I get it. He's very loveable."

"And don't you forget it." Gravel crunching under tires sounded from the front of the house, and I handed the cat to Tessa. "I think it's Walker, but let me check." I headed to the front of the house, Tessa trailing behind me, and peeked out the window to the side of the front door. I recognized the truck and breathed a sigh of relief.

Walker hopped out of his rig and jogged up the stairs. I pulled open the door. "Thanks for coming."

He gave me a tight smile which gentled when he met Tessa's gaze, and then he gave the kitten a little scratch on the head. "How are you holding up?"

Tessa gave Walker a somewhat-forced smile. "I'm not gonna lie, this freaks me out more than the picture and note for some reason. I guess because it means he got close to me somehow."

My blood turned to ice. I hadn't thought about that. Up until recently, Tessa was never more than ten or so feet from that bag. It had been her life preserver of sorts. My gaze jerked to Walker. "Do you think he has someone working for him?"

Walker's jaw worked. "It's possible, or he's using a disguise of some sort." He motioned us towards the main area of the house. "Why don't you show me what you've got."

I nodded. "It's in the kitchen." When we reached the counter, I pointed at the white disc.

Walker pulled a pair of gloves and an evidence bag from his back pocket. "Did either of you touch it?"

Tessa stepped forward. "I did. I was cleaning out my purse." She blushed as she gestured to the mess. "As you can probably tell, it's been a while. I had no idea what it was and was about to throw it away, but Liam stopped me."

Walker nodded and picked up the disc with his glove-covered fingers. "Good catch, Liam. This looks like a tracker to me. I'll bring it to the station first thing in the morning and see what the techs can find out, either from fingerprints or who it might be registered to."

Tessa sagged into my side. "Thank you. I really appreciate all you're doing, Walker."

Walker placed the tracker in the evidence bag and then squeezed her shoulder. "Of course. Do you mind if I go through the rest of this stuff just to make sure there's nothing else?"

"Of course, not. Do you need me here for that? I'd like to take a bath and go to bed early."

Walker gave a jerk of his head. "You go on. I can handle this."

I cupped Tessa's cheek. "Do you want me to come with you?"

She shook her head. "No. You stay and keep Walker company. I'm sorry I'm bailing, I just feel like I hit a brick wall."

I pressed my lips to her temple. "Go take a nice, hot bath and crawl into bed. I'll be in there in a bit." Tessa kissed my jaw and headed for the bedroom.

Walker and I watched her go. He gave my shoulder a squeeze. "You're good for her, man."

I blew out a harsh breath. "I'm not so sure about that. Because of me, this asshole knew where to find her."

"Liam, she had to face this eventually. If not, she would've been hiding forever. And what if she got sick? She wouldn't have gone to a doctor because she doesn't have health insurance or a real ID. This charade wasn't going to hold up indefinitely."

I picked up my beer from the counter and took a swig. "I guess you're right."

Walker grinned. "I'm always right."

I chuckled. "Taylor agree with that?"

Walker's grin fell away comically fast. "Don't tell her I said that."

I held up both hands. "I'd never. Bro code."

"Thank God."

I inclined my head towards the pile of Tessa's belongings on the counter. "What else are you looking for?"

Walker focused on the items and began combing through them all. "I just want to make sure there's not another tracker anywhere, and I want to check Tessa's phone for a bug."

My knuckles bleached white as I gripped the beer bottle tighter. "I want to end this fucker."

Walker kept sifting through the pile on the counter. "Don't say that in front of a cop. If Garrett winds up dead, I'll have to interrogate you, and that'll just be awkward."

He was trying to keep it light, but I knew Walker got it—better than most. He'd been the one to pull the trigger on the man trying to take Taylor from him. "Do you have any guilt?"

Walker straightened and met my gaze. "Not a single bit."

I nodded. "I need a gun. I have a concealed carry permit, but my firearms are either in LA or back at my parents' in Georgia."

Walker was silent for a minute, studying me. "I'll loan you something. Officially, I have to run a background check, but I'll do that tonight and drop it off tomorrow morning. If I were you, I'd want to be carrying, too."

I grunted. I would do anything to keep Tessa safe. *Anything.* "Did your man, Cain, have any luck tracking the asshole?" I didn't even want to use his name, it was an insult to Garretts everywhere to let him carry the moniker.

Walker examined Tessa's phone, popping off the cover. "Nothing good, unfortunately. Garrett has dropped off the map. He withdrew a large amount of cash from his bank account three weeks ago and has been under the radar since. No record of him on any flight manifests or any other travel systems Cain could get into."

I scrubbed a hand over my head. "Fuck."

Walker snapped the phone back in its case. "Cain's still working. He discovered a few well-hidden accounts, and he thinks there might be more. That could give us something."

I tossed my empty beer bottle in the recycling bin. "We need that something *now.*"

Walker set down the phone and met my gaze. "I know the last thing in the world you want to hear is to be patient."

"So don't fucking say it."

Walker held up a hand. "I wasn't going to. I was just going to tell you not to do anything stupid in the meantime." Walker snapped off his gloves. "I'm not sure what this guy's plan is, but he might try to approach you. Talk shit until you take a swing at him. Then he gets to press charges, and I have to put you in jail. And what does that mean?"

I cursed. "Tessa's unprotected." I hated that Walker was right. I would've totally fallen for that play.

"This guy might not be smart enough to realize he should try to get you out of the way. Or he might be too cocky. Let's hope that's the case. I just want you to be prepared if it's not." Walker tossed his gloves in the trash. "There's nothing else here. I'm going to take this with me and let you go and take care of your woman. Call me if you need *anything*. I mean it." He met my eyes in an intense stare.

"I will." I grabbed his hand in a manly shake and a slap on the back. "And I won't do anything stupid."

"Good."

I led Walker to the front door and stood on the porch as he got into his truck and drove off. I kept standing there, searching the land all around the house, wondering if that fucker was out there watching right now.

CHAPTER
Thirty-nine

Tessa

I WOKE TO THE SOUND OF VERY LOUD AND CONTENTED purring. I was curled into a ball, my head and knees pressed against Liam's chest. I always slept in weird positions like this. Luckily, Liam seemed to adapt.

I slowly uncurled, careful not to wake Liam. It was still early, and it wasn't my day to feed the horses so we had time before we needed to be up. I stretched, taking in Liam's sleeping form and had to stifle my laughter with my hand. Atop Liam's head, practically smothering his face, was Trouble.

A soft smile stretched my face. It was one of the cutest things I'd ever seen. Carefully, I reached over to the nightstand and grabbed my phone. Opening the camera, I snapped a photo. Liam's eyes flew open. He scowled. "Did you just take a picture of me?" His voice was raspy from sleep, ragged in a way that sent pleasant shivers down my spine.

Liam's eyes squinted as if trying to put pieces of a puzzle together. "What the hell is on my head?"

I started to laugh, couldn't help it. They were just so adorable. "Trouble."

Liam grimaced and reached up to grab the kitten, setting him at the foot of the bed. Trouble swatted at his hand. "That cat. We should have named him Docile, maybe he would've lived up to that name."

I set my phone on the nightstand and lay back on the pillows. "He loves you. He wants to be close to you and your scent."

Liam grunted. "More like he's trying to assert his dominance over me." I chuckled. Liam raised the covers. "Come over here, you're too far away."

My body hummed, and I didn't hesitate. I scooted right over and was instantly enveloped by Liam's warmth. He flipped me around so that my back was to his front, and he seemed to cover me. It had to be one of the best feelings in the world. Safe. Warm. Loved.

I kissed his forearm that was wrapped around me. "Good morning."

"Morning, beautiful." Liam's raspy voice tickled my ear. "You sleep well?"

I nodded. I'd passed out as soon as I hit the sheets last night and didn't even remember Liam climbing into bed. "Sorry I was dead to the world when you got done with Walker."

Liam swept his lips across my temple. "You don't have to apologize. You needed your rest."

I wiggled against him, trying to get even closer. "I missed you, though." Something long and hard pressed up against my backside. My core clenched.

"You have me now." Liam's hand slipped under my tank, drawing little circles on my stomach, slowly trailing the pattern up.

My heart rate picked up. "I'm glad."

Liam palmed one of my breasts, kneading and massaging. It was the slowest of builds, he took all the time in the world as he worked his way closer to my nipple. He sucked the lobe of my ear into his mouth, and I arched back into him.

Liam's fingers closed around the hard points at the tips of my breasts. "I have a thing for these. An obsession, really. I could play with your tits all damn day." I felt him grin against my neck.

"Actually, that sounds like a great plan. Call in sick to work, and we can stay in bed all day."

I laughed, but it turned into a groan as Liam gave one of my nipples a pull. Two could play this game, though. I reached my hand behind me and slipped my fingers beneath the waistband of his boxers. I gripped Liam's cock, and he let out a curse.

I grinned. His skin was so soft, such a juxtaposition to the hardness beneath. I let my hand explore every curve, dip, and ridge, the dusting of hair at his base, the tip that leaked at my touch. I left no stone unturned.

Liam worked one hand under the band of my pajama pants, his breathing heavy. "You're going to undo me."

I turned my head so that my lips could meet his. "That's the plan."

Liam's finger slipped between my folds. My blood seemed to simmer in anticipation. He dipped a digit into my opening, taking the wetness and spreading it to my clit. I tugged my bottom lip between my teeth as Liam drew lazy circles around that bundle of nerves.

Each sweep of his finger drove me a little bit higher, twisted that cord inside me a little bit tighter. I let out a moan. Liam pulled my pajamas lower. "Let me come inside."

I pushed back against him, instinctively seeking what I needed most in that moment. "Yes." It came out as a hoarse whisper.

Liam pulled his boxers down, and then he was entering me, the stretching sensation delicious. It was still almost too much—in the perfect way. Liam gave me a moment to adjust, for the hint of pain to turn to molten heat.

I arched back against Liam, my sign for him to move. And he did. Slowly at first, entering and retreating. Then a little bit faster, deeper. And then he hit a spot I didn't think existed.

"Liam," I breathed his name as though I weren't sure if he was real, if this feeling was real. My legs began to tremble, and my body started to clench.

Liam drove even deeper, hitting that sweet spot over and over. As I arched back into him, Liam pressed down on my clit. He gave one more thrust, the deepest yet, and released inside me. Light flashed behind my eyes, and I came apart, fracturing into a million little pieces, each piece dancing and sparking until they came back together, and I came down to Earth.

We were both breathing heavily. Liam, still inside me, twitched. I groaned. "That was..." I let my words trail off, unsure of what would do that experience justice.

Liam kissed my temple, the spot that always sent a pleasant shiver down my spine. "That was everything." He held me even closer to him. "I love you, Tessa. *You* are everything to me."

My heart fisted and relaxed. "I never thought I'd have this. I'd resigned myself to being alone." Liam gave me a squeeze. I shook my head. "I was okay with it because better alone than always hurting, right?"

Liam froze behind me, his body going rigid. I pushed on. "But then I met you. When I'm with you...I don't know how to describe it. It's like the colors of the world seem brighter. I see things I would've missed before."

I turned my head so that I could meet his gaze. "You make this life so much more beautiful."

Liam took my mouth in a hard kiss. When he pulled away, his eyes were blazing. "I'm pretty sure you should be the one writing love songs."

I giggled, and Liam groaned. He grew hard inside me again. My eyes widened. "Really? So soon?"

Liam grinned. "I'm pretty much insatiable around you."

The morning rush at the Kettle was insane. Summer was officially upon us. The tourists had descended, and we were a popular stop on their way into town. Jensen had even put Liam to work grabbing orders of baked goods and passing them out to customers.

It was hilarious to see their double-takes as Liam served them. One middle-aged woman even stopped him, saying, "Has anyone ever told you, you're the spitting image of Liam Fairchild?"

Liam had shrugged. "I get that a lot."

Jensen and I had dissolved into laughter. As busy as we were, as heavy as the threat was that lay in wait, I loved this day. Working alongside two of my favorite people in the world, the energy of tourists who were excited to experience the beauty that was Sutter Lake, it invaded my system and gave my blood a happy buzz.

"What the hell are you doing here?" Jensen's voice boomed from the front of the shop.

I stuck my head out of the kitchen to see Bridgette hovering in front of the bakery case. She straightened invisible wrinkles in her skirt. "Come on, you weren't really serious about banning me, were you? You make the best chai latte in town."

Jensen's hands went to her hips. "You should have thought of that before you were such a raving you know what."

I fought my giggle at Jensen's attempt to keep it clean around a shop full of families. Bridgette's eyes narrowed on me. "This is your fault. I bet you've been crying to Jensen, trying to get her to ban me for months."

I straightened, taking a step forward. "Actually, I find you rather amusing. If you weren't so disruptive to our customers, I'd ask you to stay."

The red on Bridgette's cheeks deepened. "You're the one who's amusing. This whole town laughs at you behind your back. At how weird you are. Like a mangy, skittish cat."

I didn't want the jab about my weirdness to hit home. I tried to deflect it, but it was still a glancing blow. I knew people occasionally thought I was odd. I'd always decided that strange was better than letting someone close enough to hurt me. That wasn't who I was anymore, but I still had love for the girl who'd had to keep her distance from others to protect herself, to keep her shields up while she took the time to heal—until she was strong enough to let people in again.

I took a deep breath. "Bridgette, you use words like weapons. One of these days, all those vicious arrows you've slung are going to come back to you ten-fold. I hope you're prepared for that." I believed it. Karma was a powerful thing, and I was sure Bridgette would get hers.

Bridgette sneered. "You're the one who should be careful about what's coming for you. Just you wait." And with that, she turned on her heel and left. I sighed. Clearly, Bridgette was not done bringing me into her drama.

Liam turned to Jensen and me. "What is wrong with that girl?"

Jensen shook her head. "Not enough cuddles as a child? Daddy didn't buy her the pony she wanted for her eighth birthday?"

Liam chuckled and crossed to give me a kiss. "I was really tempted to throw a muffin at her head, but it seemed like you had it handled. You okay?"

I grinned at the mental image of Bridgette being pelted with a marionberry muffin. "Thanks for not stepping in."

I knew it was hard for Liam. It was in his nature to come between me and anything that might cause me pain. So, it meant even more that he supported me while I fought my battles but didn't try to fight them for me. Liam knew that I had spent years under someone's thumb, every last second of my life seemingly under that person's control. Liam empowered me to be stronger so that I could stand on my own, knowing that he'd always be there whenever I called.

I pressed my mouth to his and whispered against his lips, "I love you."

Jensen cleared her throat. "Okay, lovebirds, this is cute and all, but I could really use some help over here."

I looked up to see a long line of customers waiting to be served. My cheeks heated. "Sorry about that. What can I do?"

Jensen grinned at me. "We're running low on just about everything. Will you grab napkins, to-go cups, and the other essentials from the pantry?"

"No problem. I'll be back in a few." I started for the back of the shop.

Jensen handed a customer her change. "Come on, lover boy. Start plating some treats."

Liam grumbled something about expecting to be paid in baked goods at the end of the day. I laughed to myself as I rounded the corner and headed down the hall towards the back pantry. Pulling open the door, I hit the light and went in search of napkins, cups, and stirrers.

I was going to make Liam's favorite chocolate potato chip cookies this afternoon. He'd earned some of his favorite treats. A whoosh of air lifted the hair at the back of my neck. I turned to see where it was coming from and was met with blinding pain at my temple. Agony, and then nothing at all.

CHAPTER
Forty

Liam

T HE CUSTOMER I WAS HANDING A PLATE TO EYED ME with confusion, likely trying to reconcile a famous musician behind the counter of a small-town tea shop. The woman shook her head, deciding that I must just *look* like Liam Fairchild, and joined her family. I could get used to this weird dose of normality. It was kind of fun.

Jensen tapped my arm with her elbow while she counted out change to hand to a customer. "Will you go see if Tessa found napkins? We're all out up here."

"Sure." I ducked back into the kitchen, calling her name. "Tessa?" The kitchen was empty, so I headed for the back hall. The whole shop sort of formed one big circle and wasn't much bigger than a two-bedroom apartment.

As I hit the back hall, my heart stopped. Beats skipped. My blood turned to ice. The back door was wide-open. Panic jolted me into action. My hand went for the gun holstered at my back hip. "Tessa!" No answer.

My blood roared in my ears. *Where was she?* I checked the back parking area. Nothing. I jogged back inside and made my way down the hall. The pantry door was open, the light inside still on. The roaring in my ears intensified. She was gone.

My gaze traveled over every inch of the brightly lit space and stopped at a spot on the floor. *What was that?* I crouched down to get a better look, wanting to touch but resisting the urge. My stomach roiled. Drops of blood.

I shot straight up, pulling my cell from my back pocket and running outside. I hit Walker's contact. He answered on the second ring. "Hey, Liam. Everything okay?"

Everything was not fucking okay. My chest constricted as I searched for any movement in the parking lot and alley. Nothing. "Tessa's been taken."

"Where are you?" Walker was all efficient business now.

"At The Tea Kettle. She was getting something from the pantry and then she was just gone." I squeezed my eyes closed against the pain, at the knowledge that I had failed Tessa. My voice got quiet, hoarse. "There are drops of blood in the pantry."

I could hear Walker shouting something to what I assumed was another officer in the background. "I'm on my way. Tell Jensen not to let anyone leave."

I nodded and then realized that Walker couldn't see me. "Got it." I tapped end on the screen and strode back inside. I didn't touch the door, even to close it, hoping maybe they would find something there that could help.

Jensen was laughing with a customer when I reached the front room. She turned to say something to me, but taking in my expression, she froze. The color drained from Jensen's face. "What happened?"

I fisted my hands so tightly it was a miracle I didn't break a knuckle. "Tessa's gone. I called Walker. He's on his way. He said not to let anyone leave." My voice was even, devoid of any emotion. It was the only way I could say what I had to.

Tears filled Jensen's eyes, but she clenched her jaw and forced them back. She raised her voice above the din of the shop. "Excuse me, everyone. We have a missing woman. The police are on their way, but I need you all to stay put so they can ask you some questions."

The café erupted in conversation. Jensen lifted her voice above them again. "We will have complimentary snacks and beverages while you wait."

Time seemed to pass in a blur yet move as slowly as molasses at the same time. I wanted to get in my SUV, tear out of there, and go look for Tessa. I had some weird notion that my heart would lead me to her. It was ridiculous. We had no clues yet. No idea where Garrett was or where he might be headed.

I needed out of the shop. Too many people. Too much noise. I strode down the hall, forcing myself not to look at the pantry, the place where Tessa's blood possibly lay on the floor. I reached the back alley and tried to slow my breathing. I couldn't. Rage flowed through my veins.

Tessa. My beautiful girl was in the hands of a monster. I'd promised her that she was safe. That I'd be with her every moment. I'd failed. My breaths came faster, the rage hotter. I turned and slammed my fist into the dumpster. Pain bloomed, radiating up my arm.

I welcomed it. Anything that would distract me from the agony shredding my chest. I slammed my fist into the dumpster again. And again. And again. Someone roughly grabbed my shoulder, and I spun, ready to turn my rage on them, but Walker knew what was likely coming and blocked my shot.

Twisting my arm, Walker held it firmly behind my back. "Get it together, man. Breaking your fucking hand isn't going to help you find your girl."

I heaved, trying to catch my breath. As I relaxed, Walker loosened his hold. I turned to face him. "I'm sorry."

Walker slapped me on the shoulder. "You needed to let it out somehow. You ready to walk me through this? I've got officers interviewing everyone inside."

My throat was suddenly dry as a desert. "Yeah." The word came out scratchy. We headed towards the door. "This was open when I came back here."

Walker crouched to study the lock. "You guys were keeping this locked, right?"

"Religiously."

Walker's eyes narrowed. "There's no sign of forced entry, so either someone had a key, or the door was unlocked from the inside."

I gritted my teeth. I knew the how was important, but not nearly as important as the where. "How do we figure out *where* she was taken?"

Walker straightened from his crouch. "I've called Cain, he's working on things from his end, tracking a new bank account. And Tuck is on his way, too. It's going to take him a bit because he was working a ways away, but he'll get here as fast as he can."

My shoulders relaxed just a bit. Tuck was one of the best trackers in the state, maybe the country. He had been the one to help Walker find Taylor when she was abducted. If Tessa had been taken somewhere in the surrounding forest, Tuck just might be able to bring her home. "Thank you."

Walker jerked his head for me to follow him inside. "Honestly, our best bet is information from the Kettle's customers today. They may have seen something and not even realized it."

Crime scene techs were already at work in the pantry. Walker gripped my shoulder as we passed the open door. "We're doing everything we can."

"I know." I just prayed it was enough.

The last few hours had passed in an impatient blur. Jensen and I had talked Walker through everything that had happened, every customer we could remember who had come through. Officers had gone to interview those whose names we knew, hoping to catch a break. So far, nothing.

My mind flashed to another gathering of police when Taylor was taken. Yet again, I was powerless. Yet again, I had failed to protect someone I loved.

The bell over the door jangled as Tuck strode through, a look of pissed-off determination on his face. "Do we know anything new?"

Our whole group stood, but it was Walker who spoke. "One witness who was taking a smoke break in the back a few shops down reported seeing a dark SUV idling in the alley. She didn't get a look at the plates, though."

Tuck swiped a hand through his hair. "Fuck. Any idea where he might have taken her?"

Walker's jaw tightened. "We're working on that." Walker turned to talk to one of his officers who was finishing up with one of the few remaining customers in the tea shop.

Tuck's gaze traveled to Jensen. She was hiding her distress well, but I knew she was struggling. I'm sure it was bringing back all sorts of memories of when Taylor was taken, of when Jensen's ex had almost killed her. Tuck pulled her into his side. "You hanging in there, Little J?"

Jensen scowled at the nickname, shaking off his arm. "Don't call me that."

We were all on edge. Impatient. I began to pace. There had to be something we could do. Sitting around here wasn't getting us anywhere. I palmed the keys to my SUV and turned to tell Tuck I was going to drive around and see what I could find, but I stopped as my gaze caught on something out the window. Some*one*.

Kimberly Speakman. The fan whose obsession had twisted her mind. My stomach dropped. *What is she doing here? God, no. Please, no.* What if none of this had to do with Garrett? What if it was I who had brought a monster into Tessa's life?

CHAPTER
Forty-one

Tessa

P

AIN WOKE ME, WAVES OF IT CRASHING OVER ME IN A relentless storm. I blinked, trying to alleviate the pressure in my head. There was a ringing sound that felt deafening. I needed to find the source and make it stop.

I blinked my eyes again. My vision was blurry at first, but it slowly began to clear. *What happened?* I tried to pull my hand up to my head, but there was pain there, too.

I looked down. My wrists were bound together with plastic twine. A zip tie, my brain slowly processed. That sent a jolt of adrenaline coursing through me, clearing my mind a little bit more.

My gaze shot around the space. *Where am I? Am I alone?* I prayed the answer to the second question was yes. The room was small. Old. Bare. A worn, wooden floor, and wallpaper that had yellowed with age. The only furniture was the twin bed I lay on, and a chair with a sagging seat in the corner.

I let out a shuddering breath. I was alone. For now. My body tensed at that thought, sending another flash of blinding pain through my skull. I slowly reached my hands up to prod at my face. I winced as they touched the right side of my head.

I eased my exploration, ghosting my fingers as carefully as possible over my skin. That side of my face was definitely swollen. My fingertips touched a large bump, and I bit down on my lip to keep from crying out in pain.

I pulled my hands away from my head and found dried blood. *Shit.* I focused on keeping my breathing even. The last thing I needed was to have a panic attack and pass out. I counted my inhales and exhales. I needed to try and sit up.

I rested an elbow on the bed and tried to push myself up. The zip tie dug into my already raw wrists. I whimpered. I hated the sound of weakness as soon as it escaped my lips. I wasn't the girl who cowered in the corner anymore.

I clasped my hands together in an attempt to prevent the zip ties from cutting into me any more. I gritted my teeth and pushed as hard as I could on my elbow, swinging my feet over the side of the bed at the same time.

The room swam as I sat up. I squeezed my eyes closed as waves of nausea hit me hard. *Do not puke. Do not puke.* Gradually, it subsided, and I opened my eyes again. The world wobbled for a moment and then straightened. Moving slowly would be key.

I carefully turned my head to take in the space again. It looked like an old cabin. I prayed that meant I was still in Oregon, maybe still in Sutter Lake. *What is the last thing I remember?* My mind sifted through memories. The Kettle. Working with Jensen and Liam. Going to the pantry. Blinding pain.

Someone had knocked me unconscious. There was only one person it could be. My stomach pitched, vomit crawling up my throat. Garrett. I inhaled through my nose, trying to still my belly. I had to come up with a plan.

I surveyed the room with different eyes now. I had to find an escape. No windows. There was light, but no lamp. I tilted my head back, ignoring the pain that shot down my spine. A skylight. A skylight that was way too high for me to reach even if I stood on the bed.

There was a door, but I knew who must be on the other side of that panel of wood, and I had no desire to meet him any earlier than necessary.

I needed to see if I could stand. I had to see what else I could find. Most of all, I needed a way out. I shifted my weight forward and extended my clasped hands to help me rise. My body screamed in protest. I felt like someone had thrown me down a rocky hillside.

After two failed attempts, I finally rose. My legs wavered, and I grasped hold of the bed frame. The *metal* bed frame. Excitement licked at my veins. If I could take apart the bed, maybe I could use one of the rungs to defend myself. I heard Liam's voice in my head. "*Almost anything can be used as a weapon.*"

Hearing that sweet sound, even just as a memory, almost brought me to my knees, but at the same time, it gave me a wave of strength that steeled my spine. I had to get back to Liam. I had worked too hard to build this new life. And I'd only just gotten my first real taste of living. I would not let Garrett steal it from me.

I looked down at my hands. My wrists were raw and red, the skin broken on one. The zip ties had to come off. I thought back to how Liam had shown me to break them apart. I hesitated. I had to play weak until the time was right. Until I had a plan. If Garrett came in and I was free of my restraints, he would know that I was stronger than he remembered. I needed him to believe I was a weak girl he could push around.

I kept the zip ties in place. Hooking my thumbs so the restraints wouldn't pull at my skin, I ran my hands over the frame of the bed. I looked for any joint I could unscrew or any fusion of metal that was weak. I found nothing. Silently cursing, I moved on to the wall. Maybe I could find a stray nail, something sharp, *anything* that could cause some damage.

My fingertips ran across the peeling wallpaper. Something in the cabin creaked. I froze. My breaths came quicker as my heart picked up its pace. Footsteps sounded on what I thought might be stairs. This was it. I was about to face my nightmare. And I wasn't the least bit prepared.

CHAPTER
Forty-Two

Liam

I PACED BACK AND FORTH IN THE BREAK ROOM OF THE Sutter Lake police station. Anger. Disgust. Self-hatred. They all mixed together in an ugly stew in my gut.

"Liam." Jensen's voice paused my pacing. She looked at me from her seat at one of the tables. "You don't know that this girl had anything to do with Tessa going missing."

My jaw worked. *But what if she did?*

Walker strode in, and I was instantly on alert. "We've got her in an interrogation room. She hasn't asked for a lawyer, so I'm going to question her now."

I stepped forward. "Let me talk to her."

Walker held up a hand to stop me. "I think that would do more harm than good. Let me take a crack at her first. If she doesn't open up, then I'll think about letting you in there."

I took another step, pitching my voice low. "I need to be in there. I need to hear what she has to say."

A muscle in Walker's cheek ticked. "I'll let you in the viewing area. I shouldn't even do that—"

I cut him off. "Thank you."

Jensen stood. "I'm coming, too."

Walker let out an exasperated breath. "Sure, let's just make it a party."

Walker led Jensen and me down the hall and pushed open a

door. Tuck was already inside, along with another officer I didn't recognize. Walker jerked his chin at Tuck. "Make sure they stay put." Tuck lifted his chin in response.

Where the hell did they think I would go? I wanted to know everything the girl had to say. Maybe they were worried I would charge into the interrogation room and attack Kimberly Speakman. I never thought myself capable of harming a woman, but if it got Tessa back safely, I'd do it.

I studied the woman in the chair. Kimberly faced the two-way mirror but kept her head down, staring at a spot on the table I couldn't make out. Her light brown hair was matted and dull, and she twisted a strand around her finger.

I barely recognized her. It was as if life had put her through the wringer, and she had come out battered and bruised. Had her obsession with me done that?

Walker opened the door. He took a seat in front of her but just to the side so we still had a good view of Kimberly's reactions. "Hello, Ms. Speakman. I'm Deputy Chief Cole."

Kimberly met his eyes. "Do you know where Liam is? I need to let him know I'm okay. He's probably worried."

My stomach twisted. *How had Kimberly's doctors released her if she was this far gone?*

Tuck let out a low curse. "She's totally delusional."

Walker placed his hands on the table. "I can let Liam know you're okay as soon as you answer a few questions for me." Kimberly looked doubtful. "Liam actually asked for your help with this."

Kimberly's face brightened. "He did?"

"Yes, he did."

Kimberly nodded enthusiastically. "Yes! What can I do? I'd do anything for Liam. Anything."

Walker pulled a small notebook and pen from his pocket. "When did you arrive in Sutter Lake?"

Kimberly seemed to bounce up and down in her chair. "Yesterday. It took me a while to find Liam, but I found him today. I'll always find him."

Walker scribbled in his notebook. "Do you remember what time it was when you first saw Liam today?"

Kimberly squinted her eyes as if trying to remember. "No, I don't know. Morning sometime."

Walker studied the woman carefully. "Where were you when you saw Liam today?"

Kimberly's expression took on a dreamy quality. "First, I was on the main street, and I saw him through the window. He was helping in the shop." Kimberly twirled the lock of hair around her finger more tightly. "I wanted to get a closer look, maybe tell him that I was here, so I went around the back."

My heart seemed to trip over itself in its rhythm. *Please don't let Kimberly have hurt Tessa. Please.* I said the words over and over in my mind. Begging God, the Universe, anyone who might have the power to hear my call.

"Then what happened?" Walker prodded.

Kimberly scrunched up her face. "There was too much going on back there, people in my way. So, I waited." A huge smile stretched her mouth. "Then Liam came out." The smile fell. "But he was really angry. He started punching the dumpster. And then you were there." Kimberly looked at Walker with a soft smile. "You stopped him from hurting himself. Thank you. I don't know what I'd do if something happened to my Liam."

Walker turned his head to shoot a look in our direction. If Kimberly had seen me losing my shit on the dumpster, there was no way she could've taken Tessa. Relief and terror flooded me at the same time. Relief that Kimberly hadn't seen Tessa as a threat and killed her, and terror that Garrett must have Tessa. I squeezed my eyes closed, pinching the bridge of my nose.

Tuck clapped me on the shoulder and squeezed. "We'll find

her. We're getting more information. And SWAT is on alert whenever we do."

I let out a breath and nodded, turning my attention back to the interrogation room.

Walker was refocused on his questioning. "Kimberly, this is really important. What did you see in the back alley before Liam came out?"

Kimberly cocked her head to the side. "Why?"

Walker kept his voice even, but I could read the undertones of frustration. "Liam needs to know. It's important."

Kimberly pushed hair away from her face. "Okay. There was a car in the alley when I came around. It was still running, and the hatch was open."

Walker jotted notes. "Do you know what kind of car?"

Kimberly's hands made the shape of a box. "It was big. Like Liam's."

"An SUV?"

"Yes. And then this guy came out of the back door. He was carrying someone over his shoulder. He put her in the trunk and drove away."

My chest was so tight, I could barely suck in air. My beautiful girl, thrown in the back of a vehicle like she was trash when she was the most precious thing on this Earth.

Tuck gripped my shoulder again. "Keep it together. If you lose it, Walker will have to send you home."

I clenched my teeth so hard, I thought they might crack. I didn't give a fuck.

A soft hand took mine. "We're going to get her back." The hand might've been soft, but Jensen's voice was hard as steel.

A knock sounded on the door to the interrogation room. An officer popped her head in. "Deputy Chief, there's someone here you need to talk to right now."

I straightened. Jensen dropped my hand, and we all headed

for the door. Piling into the hall, we followed Walker, who was already striding towards the lobby.

A man stood there. He was vaguely familiar, but it took me a second to place him. He was the regular from the tea shop who had stopped Tessa to talk to her the other day. My blood started to heat. *What does this fucker know?*

The man had a sober look on his face, and when he saw me, Jensen, and Tuck, he winced. He reached out a hand to shake Walker's. "I'm Al Burke. I'm a private investigator."

Walker studied the man. "Walker Cole, Deputy Chief of Police. What do you have for me? I'm in the middle of trying to find a missing woman, and I don't have time to fuck around."

Al pulled at the collar of his shirt as if it were too tight. "I have a business out of DC." My muscles tensed. "I do everything on the up and up. I'm not one of those shady assholes." Walker nodded and made a motion for Al to continue. "A man approached me to help him find his missing fiancée."

I made a move to surge forward, but Tuck expected it. With Jensen's help, he jerked me back into place. Al's uneasy gaze flicked to me and then back to Walker. "I checked it out. Everything was on the level. Talked to cops on the case, and they said Garrett Abrams was a stand-up guy."

I couldn't hold it in anymore. "Yeah, a stand-up guy who beat his fiancée so badly she could barely walk at times."

Al's voice shook. "I didn't know. I swear. I did my research, and no one said one word about possible abuse. Mr. Abrams said that his fiancée was mentally unstable. Said that she'd had episodes in the past. I informed him when I located Valerie—or Tessa as you know her. He got on the first plane out here."

Al looked around the room. "But that was weeks ago. When he got here, things started to seem…off to me. So I stuck around."

"You didn't think to, oh, I don't know, report this to the police?" Walker's voice was brimming with fury.

Al's eyes darted all around. "I didn't have anything to report. But I went by The Tea Kettle this afternoon, and it was closed. Someone told me what happened. It has to be Abrams who took her."

"Where is he?" I growled the words.

Al shook his head. "I don't know. I swear, I don't. I've tried his cell, and he's not answering. It goes straight to voicemail."

Walker extended a hand. "Give me your phone." Al swallowed hard but did as instructed. "Did you unlock the back door of the Kettle for Garrett to get in?"

A look of puzzled confusion filled Al's expression. "No."

Walker leaned in. "You steal a key for him?"

Al held up his hands. "No. No way."

Walker studied Al closely. "Have you seen Garrett with anyone else since he's been here?"

"Just once. A woman."

Walker straightened. "You know her name?"

Al shook his head. "No."

Walker handed Al's cell phone to the officer who had come to get him and pulled out his notebook and pen. "Describe her."

Al's Adam's apple bobbed. "She was, uh, tall. Bleach-blonde hair. Real, uh, curvy. And she was dressed fancy. It stuck out in my mind because it didn't really seem to fit with the feel of Sutter Lake. I've seen her around a few times, and she's always dressed the same."

Our entire group froze. Froze because we knew exactly who he described.

CHAPTER
Forty-Three

Tessa

I HURRIED TO THE BED, DOING MY BEST TO IGNORE THE WAY my vision swam, and my stomach churned. I collapsed against the mattress. Pain radiated through my skull, and I bit my lip to hold back my whimper. I curled into a ball. I needed to appear as weak and feeble as possible.

A key sounded in the lock. I squeezed my eyes closed. God, I wasn't ready to face this. Face *him*. My heartbeat seemed to echo all the way to my toes. The creak of an old door opening sounded. I held my breath.

The bed dipped, and the familiar scent of a too-fragrant cologne filled my nostrils. I had to fight a gag and the bile that wanted to surface. What I wouldn't give for the crisp, clean, uniquely-Liam scent right now. I held onto that smell in my mind.

A finger ran down the side of my face. "Time to wake up, Valerie."

I wanted to shudder. I didn't. I also didn't open my eyes. Maybe if I didn't react, Garrett would leave.

He leaned over me, shaking the mattress around my head. "Wake up!" He screamed the words, sending blinding pain through my head.

I blinked against the light, spots dancing in my vision. They did nothing to disguise the monster right in front of me.

"There she is. I was worried for a minute that I might have caused permanent damage." Garrett's eyes gleamed as if the prospect thrilled him.

I said nothing. I knew whatever I said would only end up causing me more pain.

The look in Garrett's eyes hardened. "Thought you could run away from me, did you? Do you have any idea how *foolish* you made me look?" Spittle flew from his mouth, hitting my cheek. I cringed. "I had to pretend you'd been kidnapped to save face in front of my colleagues."

Garrett pushed to his feet and began to pace. "Thankfully, they believed me hook, line, and sinker." A small grin appeared on his lips. "I actually think they felt so bad, it helped me get a promotion." The grin fell away. "But I wasn't going to just let you go. You belong to *me*."

I bit the inside of my cheek. *Belong.* The way Garrett meant it, was a dirty word. I thought of how it felt to belong to the extended Cole clan, to belong to Liam. That was beauty, light, and love. Garrett had twisted something pure and made it into something evil.

Garrett stalked closer, grabbing me roughly by the face. I couldn't hold in my cry of pain. His eyes flared, clearly enjoying the sound. "And then you had to turn into a whore. Spreading your legs for that filthy musician. You'll pay for that."

Garrett released his hold with an angry thrust, snapping my head back, and forcing me to let out a gasp. He took up his pacing again. "Now we can't go back to DC. My colleagues have seen the photos. They know you ran away. I'll never be respected there again."

I closed my eyes and inhaled slowly through my nose, trying desperately to ease the waves of agony coursing through my body.

"Look at me when I'm talking!"

My eyes snapped open at Garrett's bellow. "I'm sorry."

"She's *sorry*," he sneered. "You're not sorry now, but you will be."

I swallowed against my dry throat. *How long have I been without anything to drink?* I pushed the thought from my mind. "Where are we going?"

A slow smile stretched across Garrett's face. It was pure evil. "Well, *sweetheart*—" I cringed at the nickname he always used when he was furious with me. "We are going somewhere far, far away. A country where there are no extradition treaties. A place where no one will have the power to do anything about the bruises on your face."

Nausea swept through me. If Garrett got me on a plane, I was as good as dead. Worse, I'd wish I was.

He stalked closer to me. "I'd like to fuck some sense into you right now, but you know I can't stand to touch you when your face is messed up." He gritted his teeth. "Why do you always have to make me so mad? Why do you force me to hurt you? There must be something twisted in you that likes it."

Rage, hot and thick, swam through my veins. There was a dark time in my life where I would've believed Garrett's words. Thought that I had done something to deserve his slap of my face or the whip of his belt across my back. There was a time I would have believed that there was something broken in me that called out for that kind of attention.

But now I knew the truth. Garrett was the sick one, the twisted mind.

Garrett straightened, pulling a phone from his pocket. "This is my pilot. I need to take it." The words were so normal, as if he were simply telling me it was the office and he needed to answer. I blinked rapidly but said nothing. Garrett's eyes narrowed. "The pilot has been paid handsomely, he'll be of no help to you."

The thought hadn't even crossed my mind. I didn't want

anyone else getting hurt or worse because they tried to come between Garrett and his attempt to escape with me in tow.

Garrett strode towards the door. "I'll be back to collect you soon."

It was a promise and a threat. The door closed behind him, and a lock flipped into place. I sucked in a shaking breath. There was only one person who could get me out of this nightmare. Me.

CHAPTER
Forty-Four

Liam

I WAS BACK TO PACING IN THE POLICE STATION BREAK ROOM. Waiting. It felt like all I was doing was fucking *waiting*. Two officers had gone to pick Bridgette up while Walker wrapped things up with Kimberly Speakman.

Jensen was hissing and spitting while Tuck tried in vain to calm her. "That *bitch*! She's always been jealous of Tessa, but I never thought she'd stoop this low. What's wrong with her?"

Tuck handed Jensen a bottle of water. "They've got her in custody and are bringing her in. We'll get answers."

Jensen gripped the bottle so tightly, her knuckles turned white. "Let me at her. I'll get us some answers."

Tuck let out a low chuckle. "Slow your roll, tiger."

Jensen's head snapped in his direction. "None of this is funny. Why the hell are you laughing?"

The grin fell from Tuck's face. "J." He edged closer to her. "I'm sorry. You know I go for levity in stressful situations."

Tears began to pool in Jensen's eyes. "Not *this* situation."

"Shit." Tuck pulled Jensen into a hug, resting his chin atop her head. She seemed to sag into his hold.

I had to look away. I wanted to pull Tessa into my arms so badly I could almost feel her body against mine. I gripped the back of my neck and continued to pace.

Walker appeared in the doorway. "We have medics taking

Kimberly Speakman to the closest hospital with a psych ward." He looked at me. "I talked to the LAPD detective you said handled her case, and he's getting in touch with her family and doctor." Walker sighed. "She had no part in this, but she's clearly sick and needs help."

I ran a hand through my hair. "What do we know about Bridgette?" I felt bad for Kimberly, I did, but my focus was on one thing and one thing only: Tessa.

Walker rested his hands on his gun belt. "Just heard from my officers. They're two minutes out. You guys can watch from the viewing room again if you want."

Of course, I wanted. I wanted to be in the room with them. I wanted to demand to know how one woman could do this to another. I let out a harsh breath. "Thank you."

I headed straight for the viewing area. I didn't trust myself or what I'd do if I happened to come face-to-face with that conniving bitch. Tuck and Jensen followed me into the room.

I pulled my phone out of my pocket and tapped the photos icon. I pulled up one of my favorites. It was of Tessa sitting on the boulder, nuzzling Phoenix. Her eyes were closed, her forehead pressed to the mare's as the breeze made her hair swirl around her.

The photo encompassed so much of who Tessa was. Kind. Caring. With such a deep connection to the land and creatures around her. My throat burned. She had to be okay.

The door to the interrogation room opened, and I shoved my phone into my pocket. Walker led a pale and wide-eyed Bridgette into the room. He gestured to the chair that faced the two-way mirror. "Have a seat."

As Bridgette sat, I could see her hands tremble. *Good.* I hoped she was scared out of her fucking mind. She put on a false air of bravado. "Walker, what am I doing here? Should I call my father and have him send the family lawyer?"

Walker remained stone-faced. "If you'd like a lawyer here, you're welcome to call one. Do you *need* a lawyer, Bridgette? Have you done something wrong?"

Little dots of color appeared on her cheeks. "No, of course, not."

"Good." Walker pulled out his notepad and pen. "Then you won't mind helping us with an investigation."

Bridgette's throat bobbed as she swallowed. "Sure."

Walker clicked his pen. "Are you familiar with someone by the name of Garrett Abrams?"

Bridgette's gaze darted all around the room. "H-h-he's my boyfriend."

Walker's eyebrows raised. "Were you aware that he was stalking Tessa?"

Bridgette's eyes narrowed. "He was not."

Walker flipped open his notebook. "Garrett Abrams is now wanted for criminal stalking, assault and battery, and kidnapping. He took Tessa from The Tea Kettle late this morning. Not long after *you* left. So, I have to ask you, Bridgette, did you unlock the back door for him?"

All color drained from Bridgette's face. "Y-y-you have to be mistaken. Garrett is a very well-respected lawyer from DC. He would never do those things."

"Answer the question."

Bridgette's eyes jumped from Walker to the mirror and back again. "He told me he just needed to talk with her. That she's been trying to take him to the cleaners in their divorce. Tessa scammed him. Got him to marry her just out of college and then spent all his money and cheated on him. I just unlocked the door so he could talk to her. I tried calling him earlier, but he's not picking up his phone."

Walker set his pen down. "Bridgette, Garrett and Tessa were never married." Her mouth fell open. "They were engaged. He was incredibly abusive. She ran away to escape." Walker's eyes narrowed on Bridgette. "You've helped put an innocent woman in the hands of a monster."

My hands fisted, the pain of those words tearing at every nerve ending in my body.

Bridgette fumbled her words. "I-I-I didn't know, I swear."

Walker shook his head in disgust. "You're going to tell an officer everything, but right now, all I need from you is his location. Where is Garrett?"

Bridgette held up her hands. "I have no idea where he is. I haven't spent any time with him wherever he's staying, we always went to my place."

Walker extended a hand. "Give me your phone." Bridgette handed it over without a word of protest. "You better pray we find Tessa without a hair harmed on her head. Because if we don't, you're an accessory to whatever crime was committed."

Bridgette started to sob. Walker said nothing. A phone rang. Hope filled my chest that it might be Garrett calling Bridgette, but Walker ignored the phone in his hand and pulled another from his pocket. He tapped the screen. "Cain. Tell me you have something."

The hope was back. And like an addict jonesing for my next fix, I gripped that hope with everything I had. Walker left the interrogation room, slamming the door in his wake. Tuck, Jensen, and I followed.

Walker stood in the hallway, gripping the phone tightly. "That's great. Will you text me the exact location?" Pause. "I owe you big on this one. Come on out to the ranch one of these days, and I'll pay up." Another pause. "Okay. Talk soon."

Walker hit end on his phone. "We think we found him." My chest seized. "Cabin property twenty miles outside of town. He rented under an alias. The same one that has a plane scheduled to take off from a private airstrip tonight with a flight plan to

South America."

My whole body seemed to lock. The bastard was trying to take Tessa out of the country. "We have to get her, *now*."

Walker's gaze shot to mine. "I'm assembling the SWAT team now. But you have to stay here. Tuck and I will bring Tessa home safe."

I got right up in Walker's face. "I'm going with you."

Walker's expression grew hard. "No civilians."

Tuck placed a hand on my shoulder but locked gazes with Walker. "He can wait in the truck at the assembly point."

"It's a bad idea." Walker let out a muttered curse. "Fine. But if you even look like you're thinking of getting out of that vehicle, I'll cuff you to the armrest."

I shook off Tuck's hand. "Fine. Let's go."

Jensen pushed her way into our huddle. "I want to go, too."

Walker shook his head. "No way, Little J. You're staying here."

The determined expression on her face melted into worry. Her gaze jumped from her brother to Tuck and lingered there, fear filling her eyes. "Please be careful."

Tuck held her gaze for a moment before giving her a cocky grin that didn't quite reach his eyes. "No need to worry about us. We could do this in our sleep."

I felt for Jensen's worry, I did. But right then, Tessa took precedence over everything and everyone. "We need to get moving. Now."

Walker's jaw worked. "We don't head into the middle of an unknown situation without a plan. We have to look at maps of the area, pick our point of attack, divide into teams. It takes time."

My hands clenched at my sides. It took everything I had not to punch something or someone. "While you're taking the time to come up with the perfect plan, what is that monster doing to Tessa?"

CHAPTER
Forty-Five

Tessa

I PUSHED MYSELF INTO A SEATED POSITION. MY VISION STILL wavered, but not quite as badly as before. The pain in my head had only worsened. Garrett shaking me like a rag doll hadn't helped on that front.

I raised my bound hands to my head, trying desperately to get my mind to focus. I blinked a few times, clearing my vision and then lowered my hands. I'd only have one shot at this.

Slowly, I stood. My legs trembled slightly, but not too badly. I thought back to the day Liam had taught me how to break out of restraints. Just seeing him in my mind strengthened my resolve. I could do this. It was going to hurt like a bitch, but I could do it.

I extended my arms out in front of me, my wrists together. Liam had shown me one swift downward movement with as much force and speed as possible, right to your middle. Ideally, the plastic bracket holding the zip ties together would pop right off.

I took a deep breath, summoning all my strength, and slammed my hands towards my stomach. All the air whooshed out of my lungs. My wrists felt as if they had been lit on fire. I fell back onto the bed, and black dots danced across my vision. I tried to lift a hand. My wrists were still fastened together.

A sob gathered at the back of my throat. My whole body burned and throbbed. The temptation to give up, to surrender to my fate was so strong. *No.* That wasn't who I was anymore.

I forced myself up, ignoring the blood dripping from my wrists. I replayed Garrett's threats in my mind. I would not let myself stay at his mercy. I thought of all the beatings. How he berated me. The taunts. I reached my hands out.

Never again.

I slammed my bound wrists into my middle. This time, there was a pop, and then blessed relief. My hands were free. Tears spilled over my eyelids and down my cheeks.

My gaze traveled in fits and starts around the room. I needed a weapon. That was the only thing that would even the playing field between Garrett and me. He hadn't had a gun or knife when he entered the room earlier. He clearly thought he had beaten me. He hadn't.

My eyes caught on the chair. It was so old. If I tried to hit Garrett over the head with it when he came back into the room, it would probably dissolve into pieces without doing any real damage. An idea flashed in my mind.

I looked from the chair to the door and back again. Then my gaze traveled to the bed behind me. I pulled the old, wool blanket off the mattress and moved towards the chair. Laying it on the floor, I tipped the chair over onto the fabric so it was lying on its back.

I took an edge of the blanket and wrapped it around one of the chair's legs. Carefully, I placed one foot on the chair's back while my other remained firmly planted on the ground. My body protested each movement in a pattern of sharp pains and dull aches. I ignored it.

I gripped the chair leg as tightly as possible through the fabric and pulled. The wood cracked with a satisfying sound. Splinters fell to the ground. And just as I had hoped, I was left with a jagged piece of wood in my hands.

I stilled, listening to see if Garrett had heard any of my

activities and was coming to check on me. I heard nothing but a single muffled voice from below. He was still distracted by his phone call. I let out a sigh of relief.

I lifted the piece of the chair to my face to inspect it more closely. I could work with this. But I could also make it better. I eased myself to the floor, opening my mouth in a silent scream as my muscles cried out in pain.

I inhaled slowly through my nose and out through my mouth, giving my body a chance to calm. But I couldn't take long, time was running out. I leaned against the wall and brought the chair leg to my side. It had broken off in a jagged point, but I needed to make the point sharper, stronger.

I began filing the piece of wood against the floor. The planks beneath me were rough and worked almost like a nail file. When my palms began to bleed, I tugged the wool blanket closer, wrapped the end of my stake with it, and resumed filing.

I wasn't sure how much time had passed as I worked. I kept my eyes focused on the task at hand and my ears strained for any sound of approaching footsteps. I lifted up the chair leg, studying it. It looked sharp. I tested the point against the palm of my hand and winced. The key would be surprise and enough force.

I braced myself against the wall and pushed myself up. Surveying the room, I decided the best place for me was to the side of the door. Hopefully, Garrett would step into the room before he realized that anything was amiss, and I would have my opening.

I would have one shot, and one only. If I missed, if Garrett fought off my attack…I was as good as dead. I wouldn't miss. I couldn't.

I positioned myself beside the door, my back to the wall, and waited. Time seemed to drag on forever. My back screamed. My skull pulsed in a vicious throb. I wanted so badly to give in to the call of sleep. Each time it beckoned, I replayed Garrett's words in my head. His fists.

Loud footsteps sounded, and I straightened, tightening my grip on the wood in my hands. The whole world slowed as I heard a key in the lock. Blood pounded in my ears. The knob turned.

The door swung open. Garrett stepped through.

I didn't hesitate. I thrust the stake in an upward motion, catching Garrett in the back, right below his ribs. I used every ounce of strength I possessed, forcing the spike higher. I thought of my mother and everything she had done to fight for me. I thought of the Coles and all they had done to try and protect me. I thought of Liam and the beautiful life I wanted with him. I fought for all of them. But most of all, I fought for myself.

Garrett howled in pain, whirling on me and causing me to lose my grip on my weapon. "You bitch!"

He tackled me to the floor, grasping me by the throat and squeezing. "You. Are. Going. To. Pay. For. That." Each word was punctuated by a wet wheeze.

I kicked as hard as I could, tried desperately to work my hands under Garrett's arms so I could break his hold on my neck. The adrenaline helped, but not enough. I was fading. Dark spots danced in front of my eyes.

Garrett began to cough, and blood sprayed from his mouth, splattering on my face. His hold loosened. With a sputter, he collapsed on top of me. Too late. The darkness was claiming me. And there was only one word on my lips. *Liam.*

CHAPTER
Forty-six

Liam

I HAD NEVER FELT SO POWERLESS IN MY LIFE. SITTING IN Walker's truck, watching as the SWAT team divided into three groups and began their approach to the cabin. I couldn't see the house from where the cars and command station were located. I just prayed that Tessa was there and that she was unharmed. That I would have her in my arms in a matter of minutes.

I watched as an older man studied the map laid out on a folding table the team had assembled. He listened to a radio I couldn't hear from the truck, even with the window open. My ears strained to pick up any stray word, but all I got was the squawk of static when the radio clicked in and out.

I trained my eyes to the woods that stood between the house and the truck. Between Tessa and me. The SWAT teams had disappeared. I had to move. I couldn't sit here a minute longer, I felt like I was going to crawl out of my skin.

I pushed open the truck's door, and the SWAT team leader's gaze shot to me. "Get back in the vehicle."

I wanted to pop him one, but I kept my tone even. "I need to stretch my legs. I'm going crazy in there. I promise I won't bother you."

The man, whose name I didn't even know, shook his head and returned his focus to the map and the radio. I edged closer to his setup—slowly, so he hopefully wouldn't notice. Still, I couldn't hear much. The whole operation was much quieter than I'd thought it would be. I thought there would be yelling, maybe even a flashbang. But there was nothing, only the occasional location update.

I fisted and flexed my hands, trying to use the motion to release some of the tension rolling through my body. It didn't help. Images of the Polaroids Tessa had given to Walker flashed through my mind. My imagination took those memories and ran with them—Tessa's body broken and crumpled on the floor, Tessa no longer breathing.

I scrubbed a hand roughly over my face, trying to clear images I could never un-see. The radio squawked, and my head jerked in its direction. The team leader spoke in low, rapid tones. My heart seemed to speed up and sink to my stomach at the same time. *Tessa.*

The man looked in my direction, taking my measure. He spoke into the radio. "I'll bring him up."

I strode quickly towards him. "Is Tessa all right? What happened?"

The team leader jerked his head for me to follow him up the long, gravel drive that led to the cabin. "We don't know. The perp is dead, though."

All sorts of scenarios flashed through my mind. *Is she still missing? Injured? Dying?* I couldn't even feel relief at Garrett being dead because all I could think about was Tessa. I ignored the unhelpful man next to me and picked up my pace to a run. I needed to get to her.

"Slow down, would ya?" The team leader grunted and gave up. "Fucking civilians."

I ran faster, pushing my muscles until they burned. An old cabin that looked on the verge of falling apart appeared around a bend in the road. At least a dozen SWAT team members milled around out front. I spotted Tuck heading towards me. I slowed my run, trying to catch my breath. "Where is she?"

Tuck directed me towards the house, guiding me inside and up the stairs. "Walk is with her. But I need you to be quiet and make no sudden movements."

"What the fuck is going on?" I spit the words at him on a whispered growl.

We reached the landing at the top of the stairs, and I froze. Tessa. Covered in blood. She cowered against a back wall, holding out some sort of stake. Her arm trembled.

Tuck gripped my shoulder. "She's in shock. She killed Abrams." My heart spasmed in a mixture of pride and grief. Pride that my girl was so fucking strong, and grief that her tender heart would have to carry that burden. Tuck pressed on. "She won't let anyone near her. Doesn't recognize me or Walk. With all Tessa's been through, we don't want to have to restrain and incapacitate her."

My body locked. "No. Let me talk to her."

Tuck nodded. "Slow, okay? No sudden moves."

"Got it." We headed towards the open door. I spared the body on the floor only a quick glance, then my gaze stayed fixed on Tessa.

As I reached the doorway, her head snapped in my direction. "Don't. Stay away." Tessa's eyes were wild as she shook the crude weapon at me.

I held out a hand in a placating gesture. "Tessa, it's Liam." She blinked rapidly. "You know me."

Tessa shook her head. "Stay back."

Fuck. I surveyed the room. Tessa huddled on the floor, three large men looming over her. I looked at Walker and Tuck. "You need to leave. Let me talk to her alone. She's terrified."

Walker shook his head. "No way. We're already breaking just about every regulation known to man having you in here."

I gritted my teeth. "Stand just outside. You'll be able to hear everything. But right now, she's outnumbered and scared to death."

Walker let out a frustrated breath, his gaze went from me to Tessa and back again. "Fine. But we hear anything going south, we're back again. I have an ambulance on the way, coming in quiet."

"Thank you." I waited while Walker and Tuck slowly left. Tessa's eyes followed the action in jerky movements, her head and gaze jumping from me to the two men leaving and back again. She kept the stake pointed in my direction.

Slowly, I eased myself to the floor, wanting to be on her level. Then I began to talk. "Do you remember the first time we met?" I didn't wait for her answer. "I didn't make a very good first impression, nearly knocking you over, trying to get away from Bridgette." Rage heated my blood at just Bridgette's name on my tongue, but I pushed it down.

I studied Tessa as I kept talking. "But you forgave me for my rudeness. Eventually." I drew patterns on the wood floor with my fingertips. "You let me help you take Trouble to the vet. I think seeing how much you cared for that little, defenseless kitten was when I first started to fall in love with you."

Tessa's head quirked to the side slightly as if she were searching for a memory just out of reach. I pushed on. "And when I saw you with Phoenix. That bond, so deep and rare, I loved you a little more."

Tessa blinked rapidly. I slid just a bit closer. "Watching your talent bring images to life on the pages of a notebook...another piece of my heart. Gone." Tears stung the backs of my eyes. "But most of all, you saw me. Who I really am beneath the façade the rest of the world sees. Fuck-ups and all. And you loved me in return."

Tears filled Tessa's eyes. I pushed myself even closer to her, trying to pinpoint any injuries. There was blood everywhere, but

I had no idea if any of it was hers. "You are so kind. And strong. And beautiful. I've never loved anyone as deeply as I do you."

Tessa's arm began to shake violently, and I froze. "L-l-liam?"

Relief rushed through me in a wave. "Yes, Tessa. It's me. Can I come closer?"

Tessa dropped the stake and launched herself at me in a half-jump, half-collapse. When I caught her, she cried out in pain. I froze. "Baby, where are you hurt?"

Tessa's voice was weak and incredibly hoarse when she answered. "Head. Don't know."

I cradled her in my lap, brushing her hair away from her face. As I did, I saw that one side of her face near her temple was swollen and turning a deep purple. My gaze shot to the body on the other side of the room. I wished I could bring that monster back to life so I could have the honor of killing him again.

I looked back at Tessa, her eyes drooping. "No, Tessa, stay awake. Stay with me. I need to bring some people in here to help you, okay?" Tessa started to nod and then winced. "Don't move." I looked at the doorway. "Walker, get those EMTs up here."

Walker stepped into view. "Tuck's bringing them up. She okay?" His eyes looked pained.

My heart seemed to rattle in my ribs. "I'm not sure. He hit her over the head with something." I examined as much of Tessa's form as I could without moving her. Red finger-sized marks stood out on her throat amidst the blood. I cursed. "And he strangled her at some point." Walker let out a curse.

EMTs charged into the room, and Tessa jolted against me. "No!" She waved her hand as if to ward them off.

I held Tessa to me as I shot daggers at the idiot EMTs for their blundering approach. "It's okay. These people are here to help."

Tessa clung tighter to me. "Don't leave me."

"I'm not going anywhere." I rocked her back and forth.

A female EMT approached slowly. "Tessa, we're going to

give you something that's going to help you relax and ease your pain. But your—" She paused, not knowing how to refer to me. I mouthed *Liam* to her. "But Liam can stay with you, okay?"

Tessa looked at me, her eyes wide. I brushed the uninjured side of her face, cupping her cheek. "It's okay. I'll be with you the whole time."

The EMT gently took hold of Tessa's arm, carefully sliding a needle into her vein and starting an IV. The male EMT stood off to the side, holding a bag of saline and injecting something else into the line. Within a matter of minutes, Tessa's eyes were fluttering, and her body sagged.

The female EMT gave me a gentle smile. "We need to move her now. Get her to the hospital so she can be examined."

I nodded but couldn't seem to release my hold. I'd just gotten Tessa back, how could I let her go?

The EMT touched my shoulder. "We'll take good care of her. I promise. And you can ride with us."

I nodded again, slowly releasing my hold of Tessa and allowing them to roll her onto a backboard. I watched it all, but it was like trying to see through a haze. Everything was too slow and yet too fast at the same time.

I followed the medical team as they navigated the staircase and moved out into the yard. Walker clapped me on the back. "We'll be right behind you."

I jumped into the back of the ambulance with the female EMT and took hold of Tessa's hand. She needed to know that I was here. She wasn't alone. Never again.

I paced back and forth in front of the trauma room door. When the doctor had told me that I had to leave while they worked on Tessa, the only thing that had come between him and a fist to the face was Walker and Tuck. I'd told Tessa that I wouldn't leave her alone, but there she was, in a room full of strangers. I hoped against hope that she wouldn't wake up and find me gone. Then I really would deck that doctor.

"This is the right thing. They need to assess her injuries. Take x-rays. Run other tests." Walker leaned against the wall, worry lining his face.

"She shouldn't be alone," I growled.

Tuck toyed with the water bottle in his hands. "She's not. Tessa's surrounded by people taking care of her."

My gaze snapped to him. "People she doesn't know." The door to the trauma room opened, and the asshole doctor strode out. "How is Tessa? Is she going to be okay?"

The physician held up a hand. "She's going to be fine." My body sagged in relief. "Ms. Fitzpatrick does have a rather severe concussion along with some other contusions and scrapes. She'll have to remain in the hospital for now, but I predict we'll be able to release her in the next couple of days."

I could barely get my next words out. "Do you know, was she raped?" There was a tearing sensation in my chest at even having to ask.

The doctor's expression gentled slightly. "There were no signs of sexual assault."

I let out a shuddered breath. "Can I go in now?"

The doctor nodded. "The nurses are preparing her for transport, and we'll take her up to a room."

"Thank you." I pushed open the door, and my heart faltered. They had changed Tessa into a hospital gown, but there was still dried blood caked on her face and arms. I couldn't let her wake up to that. I looked at one of the nurses. "Can you get me a washcloth and a basin of warm water?"

The nurse gave me a gentle smile. "Of course. We were planning to clean Ms. Fitzpatrick up as soon as we got her upstairs, but you can do it yourself if you'd prefer."

I swallowed hard. "I'd like to." I needed to do *something*. I'd failed Tessa in so many ways, but I'd be with her every step of the way now.

The nurse nodded. "They have her room ready, so let's take her upstairs first. That'll give you more privacy."

An orderly unlocked the bed and rolled her towards the door. Walker and Tuck took Tessa in as we passed, rage lighting both of their gazes. Walker's jaw worked. "I'm going to head out to the waiting room and let everyone know Tessa's going to be just fine."

I locked eyes with him and Tuck. "Thank you. For everything."

Walker jerked his chin in a nod. "Of course."

I stayed in step with Tessa's bed until we reached a room. It was a private one, thankfully. It had a window that looked out at the mountains. She'd like that. The orderly locked the bed in place and turned to leave.

Tessa was so pale. So very still. I fucking hated it. I took the hand that wasn't connected to an IV and placed it in mine. "You're safe now. No one is ever going to hurt you again."

A soft knock sounded on the open door, and I turned. The same nurse was there, but now she wielded a cart with towels and a basin of water. "This should do the trick. Just be careful around her head and the IV line."

"I will." I looked from the nurse to Tessa and back again. "Any idea when she might wake up?"

The nurse settled the cart next to the hospital bed. "It's a waiting game now. She's been through an incredible trauma, both mentally and physically." My gut clenched, hating that I hadn't been there. "We'll be back to try and rouse her in an hour or so."

I took a washcloth from the cart. "Thank you."

The nurse gave me a kind smile. "Just hit the call button if you need anything at all."

"I will."

The woman left, pulling the door closed behind her.

I dipped the cloth into the warm water, squeezing out the excess liquid. "Let's get you cleaned up." Carefully, I began to wipe the fabric against Tessa's unmarred cheek. As the terrycloth turned pink, an invisible fist gripped my heart. I felt wetness on my face, but it took me a moment to realize it was my tears.

I could've lost her. It was fucking close. I didn't know how I'd ever let her out of my sight again. I couldn't process everything I was feeling. Instead, I poured all my emotion into the task at hand: cleaning every sign of what that bastard had done to Tessa from her skin. I couldn't erase the bruises, but I could eradicate the blood.

I worked methodically and as gently as possible until there was not even one dot of dried blood left. Then, as lightly as possible, I brushed my lips against Tessa's bruised temple. "I've got you. Come back to me."

CHAPTER
Forty-seven

Tessa

THERE WAS A FAMILIAR VOICE CALLING TO ME. TENDRILS of music swirled around me. I wanted to crawl into the warm, rich sound and never leave. The last notes of a song, familiar somehow, floated away. I needed to hear it again.

"Come on, Tessa. Time to show me those pretty eyes."

My lids fluttered. The light made my head pound.

"There you go."

The room, blurry, came into focus in degrees. "Hurts."

"Can you turn that light down?" the voice asked.

"Of course," another voice answered. The lights dimmed, and the pain subsided along with it.

"Hey there." Liam's face filled my vision. "What hurts?"

I took a mental inventory of my body. "My head. My throat." My voice had a rasp to it that was usually reserved for Liam's crooning. Things came back in flashes. The room. Garrett. Blood. My body jolted, and I cried out at the sharp pain in my skull.

Liam cupped my cheek, his face ravaged. "It's okay. You're safe now."

My breaths came in quick pants, stinging my throat. "Garrett. Is he?"

Liam's expression turned to stone. "He's gone. You saved yourself." Liam bent closer. "I'm so fucking proud of you."

Hot tears stung my eyes. "I killed him?"

Liam closed his eyes as if pained. When he opened them, the sage green in them seemed to be full of fire. "You did what you had to do. But I'm so sorry you had to do it. I'm sorry I wasn't there to protect you."

There was so much pain in those eyes. So much guilt. I hated it. "No."

Liam pulled back, his brows drawing together. "No?"

My voice shook, but I had to tell him. "I'm alive because you showed me what to do. Garrett, he zip-tied my hands, but I got out of them like you showed me." The fire in Liam's gaze blazed hotter. I rushed on. "And then I thought about what you told me about how almost anything can be a weapon. So, I broke off a leg of the chair…" I let my words trail off. I didn't need to tell him what I'd done with that.

Liam bent and brushed his lips against my temple on the side of my head that wasn't throbbing. "You're so strong."

I soaked up the warmth of his touch. "I'm so glad you're here."

"Always," he whispered against my skin.

I tried to remember what exactly had happened after my fight with Garrett, but I couldn't seem to grasp it. "What happened?"

Liam straightened, studying my face. "What do you mean?"

I swallowed, fisting the blanket. "After…I don't remember."

Liam lifted a cup with a straw to my lips. "Here, have a little of this. It's apple juice." I took a small sip, it tasted like heaven. "The doctor said it's normal if you don't remember for a while. You were in shock when the police found you. You wouldn't let anyone get close."

I hated the blank space in my mind, loathed the thought that anything could have happened in that time and I wouldn't know it, as if my memory, my brain, were betraying me. "Will you tell me what happened?"

Liam brushed the hair out of my face. "Are you sure you want to talk about all of this right now?"

I clutched the blanket tighter. "I need to know."

Liam's expression shuttered slightly. "You didn't recognize Walker or Tuck, so they called me in to see if you would let me get close." Tears gathered in Liam's eyes. "Tessa, when I got there, you were covered in blood. We had no idea how badly you'd been hurt. I've never been so terrified in my life."

I reached out, touching Liam's stubbled cheek. He pressed his face into my palm. "I made everyone leave. I just kept talking to you. Telling you all the times I fell more and more in love with you. Eventually, you came back to me."

Tears stung my eyes. "Thank you for bringing me back." My gaze caught on a guitar leaning against the bed. "Were you singing to me?"

Liam turned his head so that he could kiss my palm and then placed my hand on his chest. His heartbeat was steady and strong, just like Liam himself. "You were unconscious longer than the doctor expected. He said talking to you, playing music, might help. Taylor picked up my guitar, and I've just been playing nonstop since she brought it." His gaze met mine and held. "I finished your song."

"You wrote me a song?"

Liam squeezed my hand. "It turns out, you were the key to finding my voice again."

My chest warmed. "I can't wait to hear it."

He eyed the door to the hospital room. "That might have to wait for a bit."

My forehead wrinkled. "What do you mean?"

Liam chuckled. "There's a whole lot of people who are anxiously waiting to see you."

My chest warmed. "Really?"

"Of course. The entire Cole family, Taylor, Tuck."

A smile stretched my face. "I have a family."

Liam brushed his mouth against mine. "Now and forever."

THREE WEEKS LATER

"Thank you for continuing to come out to the ranch and working with me here," I said to the gray-haired woman in her sixties at my side.

Susan stroked Phoenix's neck. "It's my pleasure. Working alongside these mustangs is a true gift."

I smiled at my therapist. Susan was the gift. Sarah had brought her over to the guest cabin one afternoon not long after I had been released from the hospital. Susan was a friend of Sarah's, a therapist who specialized in equine therapy. I'd never known that therapy involving horses was a thing.

Susan was kind, incredibly gentle, and had an air about her that resonated with me. She had offered to come and spend time with the mustangs and me whenever I wanted. I took her up on the offer immediately.

I wasn't in denial. I knew I had a hell of a lot of things I needed to process. Trauma that had begun long before I took Garrett's life. I'd met with Susan every day for that first week, and then every other the next. Now, we were settling into a twice a week schedule that we'd keep for the foreseeable future. She'd also connected me with a support group I'd attended for the first time the night before.

My bruises were almost faded, but my mind, my soul, they'd take a little longer to heal. There had been what felt like unending questions from police officers, and while Walker had tried to shield me as much as possible, there was only so much he could do. The police in DC had been able to put more of the puzzle pieces together, including finding evidence that led them to the place where Bethany had been buried. I hoped finding her had given her parents a measure of peace.

I shuddered against the breeze. I just needed time. Time and the people I loved. Thankfully, I had both, and everyone in my life was incredibly patient and supportive. I'd even reconnected with Gena. We'd spent an entire two-hour phone call alternating between crying and laughing, and she was already planning a trip to come and see me. I couldn't wait.

Susan inclined her head to the side. "Looks like your young man is ready for you."

I turned to see Liam sitting on our boulder about fifty yards away, the most patient person of all. He was just like that rock, a steady source of strength that I could always lean on. He held me at night when the nightmares gripped me, stayed up with me if I couldn't sleep, always listened, and never pushed. I smiled in his direction.

Susan chuckled. "He's a handsome devil, that's for sure."

I laughed. "Don't tell him that, it'll go to his head."

Susan stepped away from Phoenix. "I'll try to refrain. See you on Friday?"

"Same time, same place." I scratched between Phoenix's ears as Susan headed up the hill with a wave to Liam. I bent my forehead to Phee's. "Thanks, girl." Phoenix had been alarmed the first time she saw me after I got out of the hospital. It was as though she'd known I'd been hurt. She'd circled me and wouldn't let Liam or Jensen near me for a good hour. But, eventually, she'd calmed, trusting that I was okay. Safe. Working with Susan was healing us both.

I kissed the mare's muzzle. "I'll be back tomorrow." Phoenix whinnied and followed me as I walked towards Liam. The fading sun picked up the lighter tones in his hair. God, he was handsome. My body warmed with comfort and the first licks of desire. "Hey," I called as I approached.

"Hey." He patted the spot next to him on the rock, and I sat. "Good session?"

I burrowed into Liam's side, and he wrapped an arm around me. "Really good."

He brushed his lips over my temple in that spot that was only his. "I'm glad." We sat in silence for a while, just watching the sun sink lower in the sky. "I wanted to ask you something."

"Ask away."

Liam toyed with a strand of my hair. "You can say no if it's too soon."

I straightened so that I could get a better look at his face. Liam sounded...nervous. "What is it?"

"Will you move in with me?"

My eyes widened a bit. I'd been staying with Liam at the guest cabin since my kidnapping, but the majority of my belongings were still at my apartment at the Kettle. I bit my lip. "Can I ask you one thing before I answer?"

Liam tucked a strand of hair behind my ear. "Anything."

I took a deep breath. "Why are you asking?"

Surprise lit Liam's eyes. "Because I love you. And I know you're just about physically healed." He looked out at the view in front of us. "I don't want you to go back to the apartment." He looked back at me and smiled. "Or, if you do, take me with you."

I grinned, and my heart flip-flopped in my chest. God, I loved this man. "Then, yes, I'd love to move in with you."

Liam looked at the sky. "Thank fuck." Then he took my mouth in a searing kiss. I moaned into his mouth, and Liam pulled back on a groan. "Not here." I giggled. His gaze traveled over my face in the most tender of caresses. "Why did you want to know why I was asking?"

I threaded my fingers through his. "I only want to move in with you if it's because you truly want me there and want to take that step in our relationship, not because you're scared that something's going to happen to me."

I studied Liam's face carefully. This was an area we were still finding our way in. Everything that had happened had been traumatic for Liam in its own way. It was incredibly hard for him to let me out of his sight for more than a few minutes. He'd eventually had a session with Susan to talk about how much he was struggling, but it was a long conversation with Walker that had really seemed to help.

The two men shared a bond, their woman had been harmed, and they had to deal with the guilt they'd placed firmly on their own shoulders. It didn't matter how many times I told Liam it wasn't his fault, he would always carry a piece of misplaced responsibility inside himself. I pressed my lips to his and then whispered against them, "I love you."

Liam framed my face in his hands. "I'll always worry about you." I stiffened slightly in his hold. Liam kissed me quickly to silence any protest. "I'll always worry because you're the most precious thing on this Earth to me." My muscles eased. "I lived an entire day thinking I might lose you."

Tears stung the corners of my eyes. Liam caught one on his thumb. "It taught me not to waste a single moment of this life with you. I want you with me. Always and forever. And I'm ready for forever to start right now."

I swept my lips across his, not caring a bit that tears were streaming down my cheeks. "Not soon enough."

Epilogue

Tessa

ONE YEAR LATER

"WHAT ARE YOU UP TO?" I asked from the passenger seat of Liam's SUV. He had that smirking grin on his face that said he was up to *something*.

Liam adjusted the radio dial and kept his eyes on the gravel road in front of us. "What? A man can't take his girl on a picnic lunch when he feels like it? I thought I was being romantic."

I leaned across the console and pressed my lips to his cheek. I'd never get tired of the way his stubble sent pleasant shivers down my spine. "You're so romantic. And I'm very grateful."

Liam eyed me from under his lashes. "You can show me your gratitude later."

I chuckled and settled myself back in the passenger seat. "So, where are we going on this picnic?" We were headed away from the lake and the Cole Ranch, our usual spots.

Liam put on his blinker. "I found this spot the other day, I think you're going to love it."

I frowned as we pulled off the main road and moved through what looked like a gate to some private property. "Uh, Liam?"

"Yeah?" he asked absently.

"I think this is someone's property."

Liam navigated the SUV around a dip in the road. "It is, but I got permission, don't worry."

My gaze traveled and took in the land around us. There wasn't a house for as far as I could see, only rolling hills and forests. It was beautiful. "How did you find this place anyway?"

Liam turned the vehicle to head up a hillside. "I'll tell you when we get there."

I let out an exasperated sigh. "Stop being so cryptic."

Liam grinned even wider and looked out the window. "Stop being so impatient."

I was just about to snark back at him when we crested the hill. I sucked in a breath. The view was absolutely incredible. Just like at the Cole Ranch, you could see the mountains, the town, and the lake. There wasn't one direction that didn't have something beautiful to look at. "Liam," I whispered.

He picked up my hand and brushed his lips against my knuckles. "Beautiful, right?"

"Breathtaking," I answered, not looking away.

Liam squeezed my hand and released it. "Here." He reached into the back and handed me a wool blanket. "Pick us out a spot, and I'll grab our lunch."

"Okay." I took the blanket from Liam and slid out of the SUV. The summer breeze swirled my sundress around my legs as I headed towards a vista that gave us a view of everything we could ever want to see.

By the time I had the blanket spread out, Liam was walking over with the basket I knew Sarah had put together under one arm, and some sort of tube in his other hand. My forehead wrinkled. "What's that?" I asked, inclining my head towards the tube.

Liam set the picnic basket on the blanket. "So full of questions today."

I toyed with the fringe of the blanket. "Just curious." That wasn't a total lie, I was curious. But I was asking so many questions because I was afraid I might spill my own news at the wrong time.

Liam settled himself next to me on the blanket. "What do you think?"

"Of our picnic spot?" I looked out at the view again. "It's gorgeous."

Liam pressed his lips to my temple. "What would you think about building a home here?"

My body jerked, and I sat up straight. "Here? Really?" Liam had been searching for the perfect piece of property to build a house on for what felt like forever. His fancy lawyer had been able to get him out of his record contract, and he'd released the album he always wanted to make. But now he was more focused on producing and he needed a place where he could record. Right now, we had to travel back and forth to LA every month or so. It wasn't ideal.

Liam popped off the end of the cardboard tube. "Right here." He spread out what looked like blueprints on the blanket. "These are just some preliminary sketches the architect put together for our options."

His finger dusted over the plans. "The whole back of the house would be windows so we could take advantage of the view. My recording studio could go there." Liam tapped the paper. "And over here, your art studio."

My heart squeezed. Liam had never stopped championing my art. He had, in fact, put a drawing of mine on the cover of his album, a charcoal sketch of Phoenix, and it had led to quite a bit of attention. I'd had a few showings in galleries over the past year, and had enough private clients to make art my full-time job.

Tears pricked at my eyes. "It's perfect." I looked up, meeting his gaze. There was so much emotion in those eyes.

Liam cupped my cheek. "Let's build a home here."

"I can't imagine anything better." I pulled myself over to Liam so that I straddled his lap. "Well, maybe one thing could make it better." I began pulling his shirt up and over his head. I paused for a brief second. "No one's coming up here, right?"

Liam ripped off his shirt the rest of the way. "I'd shoot them if they tried."

My hands made quick work of the button on Liam's shorts. My need for him fueled my movements, as if I would die if he weren't inside me soon. "Need you."

"You have me." Liam kicked off his shoes and bucked his hips to shuck his shorts and boxers. The movement ground his hardening cock against my center. I moaned. Liam cursed.

Liam lowered the straps of my sundress so that my breasts fell free. His lips closed around one nipple, and he sucked. Hard. I cried out. He released the bud from his mouth. "Too much?"

I took his mouth in a swift kiss. "They're just sensitive today."

Liam's hands massaged my breasts with a soft pressure that had wetness pooling between my legs. "I'll be gentle."

I ran my hands through his hair, tugging. "Don't be too gentle."

One of Liam's hands dipped beneath my dress and froze. "No panties?"

I smiled devilishly. "I had high hopes for this picnic."

Liam groaned as his fingers began to explore. "One of these days, you're going to kill me."

I laughed and bent to suck his ear lobe between my teeth so I could nibble. "Need you inside me, Liam. Now."

His fingers were gone, and then his tip was pushing in. I arched back as he entered me fully. The delicious stretch that turned to heat was my favorite feeling in the world. I began to rock, finding that slow and steady rhythm that built and built.

I picked up my pace, Liam guiding my hips as my hair, now blonde again, fell in a cascade around us. "So close." I moaned out the words.

Liam thrust his hips, hitting that deep spot that always caused me to shatter. But this time was so intense, my entire body shook. I collapsed on Liam's chest, breathing heavily. His lips pressed against my temple. "Love you, Tessa."

"Love you more." I burrowed into his neck. We stayed like that for a long time until Liam had to pull out. I whimpered at the loss. Quickly dressing, he pulled a towel from the picnic basket and cleaned me with such tenderness, tears filled my eyes.

Liam brushed the drops away with his thumbs. "Hey now, what's this about?"

I straightened my dress. "Sorry, I'm just emotional." Liam gave me a puzzled smile. I took a deep breath. "What do you think the chances are we could get this house built in the next six months?"

Liam sat back down next to me, trailing a hand up and down my spine. "I think it would be a challenge, but we might be able to do it. Why?"

I looked into his eyes, so full of love and acceptance, and I hoped like hell this news made him happy. "Because I thought it would be nice to be settled before the baby comes."

Liam shot up straight. "Baby? Are you? How?"

I nodded, nibbling on my bottom lip. "My IUD got out of place somehow. And, well, I guess you have some determined sperm."

Worry passed over Liam's face as his hands came to my stomach. "With everything with the IUD, are you and the baby okay?"

Tears tracked down my cheeks. "We're fine. Are you okay with this? I know we didn't plan—" I couldn't finish my sentence because Liam was suddenly kissing me.

When he pulled back, I saw that his eyes were a little misty. "Nothing would make me happier than starting a family with you. I was going to ask you to marry me our first night in this house, but I don't want to wait. Marry me, Tessa."

I was smiling so widely, my cheeks hurt. "That doesn't sound like a question."

"Fuck, no." Liam framed my face with his hands. "It's a promise. To love you. To honor you. To protect you. To help you fly. And to give you the most beautiful life possible. Marry me."

Love. A family. Roots of my own. I couldn't imagine anything else I'd ever need. "Always."

THE END

ENJOY THIS BOOK?

You can make a huge difference in *Beautifully Broken Life*'s book life!

Reviews encourage other readers to try out a book. They are critically important to getting the word out about a novel and mean the world to every author.

I'd love your help in sharing *Beautifully Broken Life* with the world. If you could take a quick moment to leave a review on your favorite book site, I would be forever grateful. It can be as short as you like. You can do that on your preferred retailer, Goodreads, or BookBub. Even better? All three! Just copy and paste that baby!

Email me a link to your review at catherine@catherinecowles. com so I can be sure to thank you. You're the best!

BONUS SCENE

Want to find out what happens when Tessa and Liam finally get that epic trip to Disneyland? By signing up for my newsletter, you'll get this bonus scene. Plus, you'll be the first to see cover reveals, excerpts from upcoming releases, exclusive news, and have access to giveaways found nowhere else. Sign up by going to the link below.

www.subscribepage.com/BBLbonus

ACKNOWLEDGMENTS

As a reader, acknowledgments are one of my very favorite parts of every book. I love getting a behind-the-scenes glimpse into an author's journey on a specific novel. Who helped shaped things for them, who encouraged them when things got tough. What can I say? I'm nosy. But if you're still flipping pages, maybe you are, too!

Beautifully Broken Life was my toughest book to write so far. I wanted so desperately to do justice to Tessa's and Liam's story, but especially to Tessa's journey. But I battled a lot of self-doubt along the way. So many people helped make this book a reality and held my hand through the process so I didn't end up rocking in a corner somewhere.

The first thank you always has to go to my mom. She gave me my insatiable love of books and is my biggest supporter. Thank you for everything, Mom!

The indie romance community is just simply magical. I'm so incredibly grateful for the women who have been supportive in every possible way; from answering a million questions to sharing my books to giving desperately needed pep talks. Alessandra, Julia, Devney, Meghan, Emma (wormhole forever!), Grahame, and the ladies of KB 101…thank you from the bottom of my heart.

To my fearless beta readers: Angela, Emily, and Ryan, thank you for reading this book in its roughest form and helping me to make it the best it could possibly be!

So many people helped make this book soar. Susan and Chelle, thank you for your editing wisdom and helping to guide my path. Julie, for catching all my errors, big and small. Hang, thank you for creating the most magical cover for this story. Stacey, for making my paperbacks sparkle. And Becca, for creating trailers that give me chills.

To all the bloggers who have taken a chance on my words… THANK YOU! Your championing of my stories means more than I can say. And to my ARC team, thank you for your kindness, support, and sharing my books with the world.

Ladies of Catherine Cowles Reader Group and Addicted To Love Stories, you're my favorite place to hang out on the internet! Thank you for your support, encouragement, and willingness to always dish about your latest book boyfriends. You're the freaking best! Extra special shoutout to Lissanne for helping me come up with Cain's name. And Monica, not only for helping me on the kitten name front, but also for being such an incredible help, supporter, hype squad member, buddy reader, and all the other good things! So thankful for you!

To my own personal cheering squad: Gena, Jessie, the Lex Vegas ladies, Lyle, Nikki, Paige, and Trisha, thank you for endless encouraging conversations and lots of laughs. So grateful to have you in my corner. Special thanks to Gena for answering my hundreds of questions about the music industry and being an awesome sounding board in the early stages of this story.

Lastly, thank YOU! Yes, YOU. I'm so grateful you're reading this book and making my author dreams come true. I love you for that. A whole lot!

ALSO AVAILABLE FROM
CATHERINE COWLES

Further To Fall

Beautifully Broken Pieces

ABOUT
CATHERINE COWLES

Writer of words. Drinker of Diet Cokes. Lover of all things cute and furry, especially her dog. Catherine has had her nose in a book since the time she could read and finally decided to write down some of her own stories. When she's not writing, she can be found exploring her home state of Oregon, listening to true crime podcasts, or searching for her next book boyfriend.

STAY CONNECTED

You can find Catherine in all the usual bookish places...

Website: catherinecowles.com

Facebook: facebook.com/catherinecowlesauthor

Catherine Cowles Facebook Reader Group: bit.ly/ccReaderGroup

Instagram: instagram.com/catherinecowlesauthor

Goodreads: goodreads.com/catherinecowlesauthor

BookBub: bookbub.com/profile/catherine-cowles

Amazon: www.amazon.com/author/catherinecowles

Twitter: twitter.com/catherinecowles

Pinterest: pinterest.com/catherinecowlesauthor

Facebook Group: bit.ly/AddictedToLoveStories

Made in the USA
Middletown, DE
17 May 2024

54499358R00191